NO ONE LEFT TO CLAP!

Alan Greenhalgh

Alan Greenhalgh

"NO ONE LEFT TO CLAP!"

Published by

Interior Book Design and Layout by Alan Greenhalgh

Apart from the obvious exceptions of world leaders whose names I have used freely because they have acted heroically within this work of fiction, all other characters in this story are purely fictional and any resemblance to any persons living or dead is purely coincidental.

ISBN 978-0-9775844-3-7

DEDICATION

I dedicate this book to all the courageous individuals who have faced the wrath, disenfranchisement and humiliation of their peers in their quest to save our ailing planet. You are many but alas, still too few. You are unsung heroes. Thank you for trying.

To the brave men of the Royal Australian Navy Clearance Diving Team 3 and the veterans of the Battle of Long Tan, I salute your courage and integrity and beg your forgiveness for creating fictitious villains in your midst to suit this story's purpose.

Alan Greenhalgh

FOREWORD

At the outset let me say I hope you will enjoy this novel whether or not you agree with the science of climate change. If you hold a contrary view please just treat the story as you would any work of fiction. Go with the flow and accept the hypothesis of an Australian citizenry who have become so concerned about the effects of climate change on their lives that they have elected a government that has promised to set an example for the rest of the world on this most crucial issue by respecting and changing the biosphere for the better so that future generations may enjoy a safer, sustainable way of life.

For those readers interested in facts behind the science of climate change I have included the fruits of my extensive research at the rear of the novel should you wish to know more. I have done this because I am conscious of the need to prevent technical data destroying the pace and flow of the story.

CHAPTER ONE

AUSTRALIA'S SADDEST DAY

Bespectacled, with iron-grey, straight hair hanging limply over youthful, bookish features, the politician's baby-blue eyes stared roundly into the camera lens. Connor Bowker didn't like close-up shots. He'd once overheard a political opponent say that when magnified by the Coke-bottle lenses of his glasses his almost colourless eyes resembled raw oysters.

Bowker cleared his throat nervously. His well-manicured hands gripped either side of the podium. The conservative nature of his well-cut grey suit was contradicted by the pillar-box red tie that betrayed his ambitious nature. "Power-dressing", his critics said, but Bowker had more pressing issues on his mind than the jealousy of his enemies and political opponents.

Before the prime minister's lectern, Greenpeace, Get Up and a plethora of lesser known environmental groups had coalesced, rallying in support of his new government's proposed environmental initiatives. Mostly sceptical and afraid Labor's election promises would be watered down now they were in office, the growing eclectic band of citizens feared the increasingly-likely spectre of catastrophic climatic change and were eager to demonstrate solidarity for Bowker's environmental reforms.

Foreseeing the heavy impact of alternative energy sources on the profits of fossil-fuel based corporations, powerful industry groups and unions had wasted no time in lobbying Connor Bowker and his cohorts, expressing their anger through thinly veiled threats to engineer Labor's downfall.

Bowker began his speech hesitantly at first, to buy thinking time. Fortunately, Bowker's election-weary fans were prepared to tolerate his dreary style of "poly-speak" which journalists loved to refer to as "Bowkerism."

That would no doubt change if he looked like reneging on his promises.

'It is heartening to see so many of you here in support of my government. Firstly, let me say the previous liberal-coalition under Brian Caldwell refused to accept the hard reality of climate change, burying their heads in the sand like global-warming wombats. In fact, Caldwell demonstrated shocking ignorance and criminal stupidity by disregarding the overwhelming evidence and referring to climate change as crap.

'They have wasted fifteen years or more of valuable time when they could, and should, have acted to address what has become the most pressing issue facing mankind.

'The previous government's intransigence means we now must expend greater efforts and dip more heavily into the public purse to mitigate the effects of climate change. Instead of working to sway world opinion Mr Caldwell chose to take the easy option rather than incur the displeasure of big business. His short-sightedness and the short-sightedness of other world leaders will result in unnecessary deaths, suffering and hardship.

'Make no mistake, we are here for the long haul and we will make the tough decisions necessary. We know there are many who oppose us but Australia must lead the way in the hope that the rest of the world will come to its senses and follow our example. Although we are only a small nation and our contribution to carbon emissions is less than two percent of the total greenhouse gas emitted by all countries, per capita we are the world's heaviest polluter!

'How can we say to America, China and India, "clean up your act," unless we sort out the mess in our own backyard?'

Bowker paused, looking intently through the forest of placards and banners proffered by the pro-green crowd assembled in Sydney's famous Martin Place. The ever-present drone of traffic and the rumble of a low-flying Qantas jet went unnoticed, overwhelmed instead by the palpable emotion of what was to become a truly historical occasion

Unfortunately history would record the occasion for all the wrong reasons.

Bowker's peripheral vision detected a faint movement near the faux-sandstone pillars lining the entrance of a nearby office building. Alarm bells sounded briefly in his head.

Why was someone lurking in the recesses of a shadow-darkened doorway? Why weren't they amongst the enthusiastic and vociferous crowd craning their necks to getter a better look at the face of their country's newest leader on this clear, bright autumn Tuesday morning?

Dismissing the sudden movement as unimportant, his voice grew stronger and his manner more resolute.

'Those opposed to our intention to lead the world in

the development of environmentally sustainable technologies must accept that we have a mandate from the people of Australia to create a cleaner, healthier and safer world.

'We cannot continue plundering this planet's natural resources at a speed far greater than Mother Nature can replenish them. Can they not see that, at the rate we are consuming natural resources; within twenty years we will need two planets to sustain our existence? Unfortunately, we cannot shift half our peoples to another world. We must sort out the problems on this one.

'Common sense dictates that we must rein in our greed and plan for the future of our children.

'We cannot continue belching greenhouse gases into the atmosphere from our factories, coal-fired power stations and diesel powered trucks and road trains .....Aaah!'

Bowker gasped as an invisible, astonishingly violent force doubled him over and thrust him backward across the stage. It was as if he had been punched in the stomach by a massive invisible steel fist. He lurched, knees collapsing, face contorted in agony, sprawling like a broken marionette across the laps of dignitaries seated on the podium behind him. The front of his expensively-cut suit changed rapidly from light grey to crimson.

Slack-jawed and grey-faced, those on the platform took several seconds to comprehend what had just happened. There had been no gunshot, merely a muffled "pop" from somewhere behind the massed humanity.

Momentarily, a stunned silence fell across the

crowded square. Heads began swivelling in all directions, unsuccessfully seeking the origin of the unprecedented political violence that most Australians prayed would never reach their shores.

The only ones to act immediately were Bowker's bodyguards. Spaced at strategic intervals around the raised platform, six plain clothes members of the Australian Federal Police Close Personal Protection Unit almost simultaneously drew their fully-automatic Glock pistols, pointing the muzzles skyward.

Seemingly emotionless and with poker-faced intensity they began scanning the crowd, trying to pinpoint the unseen shooter's location. At the same time, two other expensively-suited officers leapt onto the stage, clutching at shoulder holsters concealed beneath their jackets, preparing to return fire in defence of the VIPs.

Their attention never leaving the crowd, one took control and began ushering the bewildered politicians and guests to the safety of the nearby chauffeured government limousines while simultaneously shouting a SITREP and plea for support into his lapel microphone. The second federal agent knelt over the spreadeagled, still twitching body of the prime minister, fingers searching in vain for the victim's carotid pulse. White-faced and screaming incoherently, Bowker's plump, matronly wife scurried on hands and knees across the stage toward her husband. "Connor! Connor! Oh my god!"

The AFP officer began CPR. He didn't need to be a doctor to know Bowker's injuries were fatal but he'd be in hot water later if he didn't try his damndest.

Pandemonium erupted.

Like an invisible wave, panicked insanity swept the street. Shrill screams emanated from the confused, terrified melee. Pushing and shouting angrily, concerned only for their individual safety, young and old scattered. Some unfortunate souls found themselves knocked to the ground and trampled, as in the background, sirens wailed. Becoming rapidly louder and more intense, the electronic cacophony heralded the rush of paramedics and police reinforcements to one of Sydney's most famous streets.

Although mere seconds had passed since the country's first political assassination, there was no trace of the killer. It was almost as if the perpetrator had vanished within a millisecond of the muffled shot. Because all eyes had been on the prime minister, no one in the crowd knew the killer's gender or whether he or she had fled, or was simply blending into the chaos.

Within minutes, the crowd of over ten thousand had dissolved into the city's adjacent labyrinth of streets and alleyways, leaving a mere hundred or so inquisitive souls to gawp at the overturned seating and the Christmas tree-like spectacle of red and blue flashing lights rebounding off surrounding buildings. Making their way to Sydney's nearby underground railway stations, most could not believe the bloody carnage they had witnessed.

Among the departing throng, a stooped, bearded figure limped along muttering angrily, a filthy bedroll slung over one shoulder and dirty sandshoes scuffing faintly against George Street's time-worn, chewing gum-stained bitumen. With a small marijuana-leaf earring in one ear, dark sunglasses and faded, dirty blue jeans, the man's age could have been anywhere between thirty and fifty.

It was unlikely that anyone would remember this seventies-looking hippy figure later, and if they did, they would no doubt give a generic description, redolent of Sydney's ever-growing army of homeless souls. It is a strange quirk of human nature that the anonymity and invisibility of the homeless is almost guaranteed. Although psychologists might argue over human motives behind the apparent blindness to the plight of one's fellow, few people relish becoming the target of abuse, or want to risk the obnoxious experience of being in proximity to one with such a dirty, smelly and unkempt appearance. Similarly, who among us wants to deal with anti-social and unpredictable behaviour, or fend off the ranting of some poor, deluded or possibly psychotic societal outcast? Most, therefore, averted their eyes and gave the limping vagrant a wide birth.

This was just what he wanted.

Nearing the steps to Wynyard Station, the hippy stepped sideways into a narrow laneway. He hurried a hundred metres along the garbage-bin-lined path until enveloped by the shadows of the looming skyscrapers. There he grinned smugly at his successful escape and then glanced behind him to make sure no one had followed him into the filthy, urine-smelling throughway. Satisfied, he leant against the graffiti strewn brickwork. Pulling a half-smoked, hand-rolled, fag end from behind one hair-covered ear, he stuck the dog-end into the thin slash of lips concealed beneath nicotine-stained whiskers.

After drawing deeply on the pungent tobacco, he surveyed his surroundings, carefully filtering the sounds of the city until sure he had the alley to himself. He shrugged off the bedroll, then drew out the disassembled components of a high-powered and easily collapsible rifle. He walked rapidly along the dim alley, stuffing each part beneath rubbish-filled skip bins and an assortment of refuse containers until he had disposed of the assassination weapon.

Having invested many hours in assembling and disassembling the rifle and sighting it in, he had perfected the art of concealing it within seconds of hitting his chosen target. He therefore felt a strange regret for discarding such a magnificent tool that his profession demanded. Mentally shrugging off his sentimentality, he took comfort from the knowledge that he would be recompensed well by his employers.

The man's limp vanished as he bustled among the back alley detritus of the city's shops and restaurants, peeling away his dishevelled beard and the filthy, matted wig to reveal a youthful, almost babyish face and short, neatly groomed blond hair.

Reaching behind one of the graffiti-daubed bins, the assassin withdrew a concealed pilot's bag from which he removed a clean, neatly folded grey business suit, shirt, conservative tie and polished black lace-up shoes. He stripped off his rags quickly before throwing the final elements of his disguise into yet another rubbish receptacle.

Like a chameleon, he was ready to blend into a new background as a now-young, blond-haired yuppie, indistinguishable from the thousands of office workers who scurried between the glass phallic-like symbols of Sydney's office towers. Striding confidently from the alleyway swinging the pilot's bag, he hurried down a set of concrete steps into the subway. Blending into the bustling throng of the city's workers he vanished among the city's three million residents.

Federal Police Commissioner, Harold "Stormy" Knight answered the encrypted telephone on his desk and reeled back in his leather recliner chair. His squarish, smooth-shaven features paled and he ran his fingers through his greying buzz-cut. Stunned, he at first thought the caller was playing some cruel prank.

'Shit!'

The expletive was unusual for the veteran policeman. He rarely swore but under the circumstances, a little profanity was understandable.

'I knew there would be hell to pay if this new government pushed ahead with that bloody Zero Carbon Energy Bill. They're bloody babes in the woods when it comes to the forces that are at play here but I never thought some bastard would dare to assassinate the country's leader!'

Struggling to grasp the dreadful news, Stormy gasped into the phone's mouthpiece, 'Colin, have you rolled out the relevant contingency plans?' Somewhere in his brain Knight registered the white bow wave of a distant Jet Ski slashing across the placid waters of Lake Burley Griffin. From the busy street below, a crow cawed as it scattered takeaway food scraps from a council litter bin onto the kerbside. Stormy immediately regretted asking the question as the volume level of his subordinate's retort forced him to hold the handset at arm's length.

'We've discussed this eventuality many times. You know better than to ask me that!' Chief Superintendent Colin Burrows, the commander of Sydney's FEDPOL operation, admonished his boss. 'The entire CBD is now a major crime scene. We've got the best forensic officers from Canberra and the state police going over every square millimetre. We've issued nationwide appeals for anyone with information to come forward and the acting PM has authorised a $5,000,000 reward. That should overcome any reluctance for involvement, wouldn't you say?'

Stormy could picture the other man counting off the points on his fingers.

'ASIO is compiling a short list of possible suspects and checking on their whereabouts and movements at the time Bowker was shot. We've stepped up round-the-clock surveillance on major crime figures and set up telephone intercepts of any likely suspects. Every agent and operative within all law enforcement agencies, both state and federal, has been asked to tap their informants for even the slightest hint of who's behind this.

'We've asked Interpol, the FBI and MI5 for input and help in tracking down likely terrorists or international criminal syndicates with a motive for killing Bowker.

'The Defence Signals Directorate is filtering all telephone and internet communications for likely keywords in case there's any traffic linked to the killing.

'We've heightened the national level of alert and beefed up protection for all members of Bowker's cabinet, as well as the leader of the opposition, just in case it's not a party-specific killing.

'All the usual loony-tunes and ratbags have already started to come out of the woodwork to claim responsibility. These dickheads are wasting valuable time and resources,' Burrows lamented. 'We have to check every nutter that rings in just in case. It will only get worse. False confessions from nutcases looking for notoriety will go off the Richter scale, as will the calls from bloody so-called psychics claiming they know who's responsible.

'We're establishing a joint task force with the New South Wales, Victorian and Queensland police, who've all offered their best detectives. The South Australian and WA coppers have been alerted to watch airports, shipping, and traffic across the Nullarbor for anyone remotely suspicious, but it's like looking for one particular worm after a spaghetti throwing competition until we get some sort of lead.

'Nevertheless, nothing is being spared to solve this one. I think I've covered all bases at this point, given this happened less than thirty minutes ago.'

'Okay, Col. I am sorry. It's just that I'm absolutely stunned. I opened my mouth before putting the grey matter in gear. I know you're as on top of things as anyone could be,' the Commissioner apologised. 'I'll give the deputy, or should I now say, acting PM, a call. He'll want to convene an emergency meeting of SAC-PAV[1] and we'll want you on security encrypted phone

---

[1] Standing Advisory Committee for Commonwealth/State Protection Against Violence; Australia's Federal and State Government Body for combating terrorism.

hook-up to update them on your investigation.

'Let me know if anything or anyone is getting in your way, or, if I can do anything to help. I'll be on the first available flight to Sydney as the media will expect to see me fully involved, even though I've got the utmost confidence in you and your team.'

'A few hundred more coppers to track down all the bloody tree huggers and do-gooders who attended the rally would help, but we know that's not going to happen,' Burrows replied sardonically. 'Fortunately, for once the state plods have put aside their petty rivalries, although they'd obviously love to be the ones to yank Bugsy out of the proverbial hat by his long fuzzy ears.'

Stormy Knight drew a deep breath. 'Colin, I don't care who succeeds, or who gets the kudos. We have to bring these bastards to justice and quickly. This nation has been changed forever by what is clearly a politically motivated murder. We can no longer boast about being one of the most stable democracies in the world if we don't sort this out a.s.a.p.

'On that subject Col, do you have any ideas at all who might be behind this?'

'I'm just stabbing in the dark, but I reckon there's some pretty fired-up union heavies who think Bowker's betrayed them and their members. Some of the bastards can get pretty bloody feral. Remember the Painters and Dockers fiasco?'

'Takes a pretty psychotic type to go to these lengths, and one individual acting alone would be unlikely to go undetected for long. Whoever did this planned ahead and must have had considerable resources,' Stormy observed. 'The fact the offender got away points to it being an organised and well thought-out hit.

'Anyway, we need to examine what we have; when we work out what that is, rather than jump to conclusions. We both know better than trying to make the evidence fit a theory and I should know not to ask you such a stupid question so early in the case, it's just that I am still reeling from the implications.'

Stormy paused and drew a deep breath before continuing. 'I'm wasting your time, mate. I'll let you get on with it. Keep me posted twenty-four-seven. Use my private mobile number if I am not in the office.'

Commissioner Knight dropped the receiver into its cradle. After a brief pause he reached for the handset of the oddly shaped device which sat somewhat incongruously on a small table to one side of his enormous but tidy mahogany desk. His index finger stabbed the speed-dialled number connecting him to the deputy prime minister's office. He was immediately engaged in an animated conversation with Australia's newest and highest political executive.

++++++++++++++

Chapter Two

'So who is this McCarthy character? Where did he come from and how did he get to be so prominent in the Labor movement?' Keith Sutton glared at his fellow union delegates as he plucked at the bright red, gravity-defying braces that prevented his baggy trousers from slipping any lower on the pregnant bulge of his torso.

Looking like a bad caricature of a 30's gangster, the balding union heavyweight chewed agitatedly on the stub of an ever-present cigar in blatant defiance of the smoking ban in force in the union's headquarters. Although Sutton rudely filled the room with dense smoke, nobody was sufficiently brave or foolhardy to risk his wrath and contempt by reminding him of the ban.

Before anyone at the hastily convened meeting of the Mining Sector Workers Union could respond, the union boss slammed the long boardroom table with a pudgy fist. 'Bowker's death should have put an end to all this global warming bullshit. Now you're telling me this McCarthy character, this Johnny-come-lately-bloody-job-destroying-know-it-all is gunna step into Bowker's shoes? Shit, the world's gone fucking mad and they've put the inmates in charge of the asylum!

'You'd think they'd have come to their senses and given the job to Knox. While I don't think sheilas should run anything but a bloody washing machine, at least she seems to have a few clues,' he ranted.

Helen Knox, Bowker's power-hungry deputy, was tipped by the pundits as the deceased PM's successor and most folk assumed that she would automatically step into the country's top job.

A politically savvy, forty-something spinster, Helen Knox was intelligent, articulate, popular and physically attractive. In the weirdly-crazy, new world of political correctness, the rumours of latent lesbian tendencies only served to brighten her political plumage. Although many a journalist had tried unsuccessfully to unearth current liaisons or past sexual impropriety, Knox had so far succeeded in keeping a tight lid on her private life.

In keeping with Australian love of irreverence, she had been dubbed, "Miss Locked-box Knox" or, LBK for short.

Seated across the table from Sutton, Alistair McIntosh, the MSWU Secretary cleared his throat theatrically, halting any further outburst from his boss.

An educated, erudite and mildly spoken unionist, McIntosh was the real brains behind the MSWU's power and political influence. Sutton represented the union's muscle.

McIntosh understood that the loud-mouthed union thug did not subscribe to the wisdom of the old adage, "know thine enemy," for unlike McIntosh, Sutton had not followed McCarthy's rise to stardom, holding in disdain anyone with views contrary to his. He took a hasty sip from his water glass and declared, 'I've been keeping tabs on McCarthy since the party first nominated him for pre-selection. But before I give you his profile, I need to explain how the current political situation came about.

'McCarthy's outspoken views as a climatologist and CSIRO (Commonwealth Department of Scientific and Industrial Research Organisation) environmental scientist has often placed him in conflict with the previous government and his own peers and with his former employer. His interest in climate change began in 1992. He was one of two thousand signatories, many of whom were Nobel Prize Winners, to a petition imploring world leaders to address the global warming. McCarthy and his scientific colleagues were amazed at the lack of interest or resolve to deal with what they saw as a potentially life-threatening issue. Even worse, for them was the deliberate muddying of waters by vested interest groups, big business and the world's most powerful nations, including Australia, who commissioned scientific mercenaries to bring into disrepute the 1992 conference findings.

'For what it's worth and I know you won't like hearing it Keith but what the majority of scientists are saying about the threat of climate change is probably understated, in my humble opinion. It's just that I disagree with Labor's drastic rush to re-structure the entire energy and mining industry because it will hurt our members so badly.

'Anyway, let me continue, in the absence of a sense of government urgency and the truth being too unpalatable, our consumer-mad world continued to allow itself to be deceived and those who dared to speak out were castigated and ostracised.

McIntosh ignored his boss's clenched jaw and the outburst he knew would come when he finished his lecture. 'Rather than be labelled "doomsday prophets" and even "whackos" the scientific world largely retreated into its shell.

'

'Anyway, getting back to McCarthy, the final straw for him came when his beloved CSIRO demanded that he tone down his prognosis on climatic impact on the world because they feared it would spark widespread panic.

'Disgusted that so many of his peers were prepared to prostitute their scientific credentials for monetary gain, or cave in to political pressure, McCarthy created a virtual scandal in the conservative and insular world of the CSIRO by going on talk-back radio to answer Joe Public's questions about the likely impacts of climate change but he really pissed off the Establishment when he told the public they were being lied to by governments and big business!' McIntosh concluded.

'Are you saying the CSIRO administration was complicit in a cover-up?' The question came from one of the union delegates who had so far listened incredulously to the secretary.

'Let's just say, senior public servants know on what side their bread is buttered,' McIntosh replied dryly.

Sutton interjected. 'I still say it's all bullshit and he should have been discredited for the bloody loony tune he is! I can't believe you would swallow all that "world-is-coming-to-an-end" crap Alistair.'

The union secretary paused, wondering if his boss was really as dense as the statement suggested. In his opinion, McCarthy was far from being a "loony tune" but there was obviously no point saying so.

A man convinced against his will is of the same opinion still.

McIntosh paused to compose himself before

responding, 'Ah, well, the thing was, he had a number of aces up his sleeve. Knowing they would try that tactic, he produced copies of the gag orders from his bosses. It created a hell of a stink and they threatened to charge him with everything they could think of, including breaching confidentiality and anything under the Crimes Act that looked like it might fit the bill, but the cat was out of the bag and legal action against him would only have made the then Liberal government look even worse.

'They dropped their threats and hoped the storm would blow over. But of course, it hasn't.

'As you know, it was McCarthy who managed to convince Channel Ten to run the graphic "Your World" documentary series he authored, showing environmental destruction, ocean pollution, glacier loss, melting polar ice caps and species extinction.'

McIntosh held up a hand to halt the expected counter arguments Sutton was eager and ready to parrot.

'Keith, I know you still don't agree that climate change is the big deal scientists would have us believe, but these days it's on everybody's lips and public opinion is pretty much in favour of Labor setting an example to the rest of the world by tackling the issue. If it hadn't been, they wouldn't have been elected.'

Sutton stammered in protest, stabbing the air with his cigar. 'Bet the bloody public won't be so keen when they find their jobs going down the gurgler along with the Australian economy!'

'That may well be the case,' McIntosh countered, 'But "Your World" was so carefully orchestrated that it had the public hooked on the entertainment value before it hit them with the nasty and unpalatable truth, a bit like the sugar coating on a pill. It was actually TV's top rated documentary. Even bigger than Jacque Cousteau's famous series featuring the Calypso back in the seventies. "Your World" even screened overseas in God knows how many countries.

'It was a pretty significant achievement to get people to switch from watching soapies. Unlike Al Gore's Inconvenient Truth which was quickly forgotten, "Your World" has had a huge impact because it was ongoing and in-your-face for weeks. In fact, Channel Ten's now re-running it and McCarthy's website gets nearly as many hits as Green Peace does.

'Thanks to his good looks, adventurous spirit and a certain charisma, McCarthy became almost a cult figure. After the scandal at the CSIRO, he was instrumental in the coalescence of Green Peace, Get Up and half a dozen smaller environmental activist groups. In fact, he's managed to pull off a major coup by uniting the green lobby and scaring the Labor Party into developing their current strategy for combating global warming.

'All in all, it's a pretty impressive performance by one man, but McCarthy maintains the popularity of the show will count for nothing unless the world listens and acts. His catchcry, "There will be no one left to clap mankind's achievements if we all become extinct" has become the most popular saying of the day.

'The Labor Party knew they were on to a winner if they could get him onside. They understood that they would capture more votes by recruiting him than fighting him. For his part, McCarthy knew his best chance for the introduction of major environmental and economic reform needed to fight climate change would come from being inside one of the two major political parties and the Libs certainly weren't going to cosy-up to him.

'If he wasn't so eminently qualified, it might have been possible to discredit him, or brand him a doomsday prophet, but these days, as climate experts become more vocal and rebellious, he's won one heck of a lot of support from the scientific community including such renowned figures as Sir James Lovelock, Al Gore, David Suzuki, Sir Richard Attenborough, Tim Flannery, Ross Garneau, and even the renowned economist, Sir Nicholas Stern.'

Sutton couldn't take any more and exploded, 'Oh, for fuck's sake, it sounds like you're his biggest fan!' The veins in his forehead pulsated and spittle flew from his thin lips. 'Didn't Lovelock and Flannery publicly admit recently that they'd been too alarmist in their predictions about global warming and climate change? Shit, McIntosh, I'm beginning to wonder where your loyalties lie.'

'You know better than that,' the union secretary responded quietly, although he seethed inside. 'It's true that Lovelock and Flannery admitted that their early reports were too alarmist, but they and their IPCC colleagues still maintain that climate change remains a very real threat requiring immediate and concerted attention.

'As to McCarthy, I admit I respect him. He's an extremely well educated man who is also a worthy adversary.'

McIntosh continued unabashed, 'These days,

McCarthy can best be described as a reluctant politician. He's someone with unconcealed disdain for people with big egos and self-serving political figures.'

And those with narrow minds, he almost added.

'This makes him unique and endears him to the public who are fed up with the lies and broken promises of the political masters of old. He also nurses a healthy cynicism and distrust for most individuals in public office. However, it remains to be seen whether he will survive in the knife-in-the-back-world of politics because he's a straight-shooter, with no time for deception or political manoeuvring.'

'But won't the Labor Party be committing political suicide by putting a maverick like that in charge?' someone observed.

'Yeah,' Sutton concurred morosely. 'They've lost our members' votes and they'll get no financial backing now from the car industry, the transport union, the wharfies, the miners and the big business end of town. Doesn't that put them up Shit Creek at the next election?'

'Not necessarily,' McIntosh replied quietly. 'As you know, part of their election strategy was to increase the political term to five years. They argued that the previous three-year term of office was insufficient to introduce and finalise the major reforms and infrastructure projects they promised during their campaign. They had the numbers and got the bill through both houses and unless there is a double dissolution, we've got them for the next five years.

'During that time through a raft of measures outlined in their Zero Carbon Energy Bill they'll revolutionise the entire transport, mining and power generation industries.' 'And undoubtedly our way of life,' Alistair McIntosh added.

'While most countries have been throwing billions into keeping current technologies going in the hope of averting a global economic disaster, the Labor government proposes to stave off job losses by investing in new green industries and infrastructure projects. They consider these have long term benefits and will enable the nation to meet the challenge of water and food shortages and the need to relocate populations from areas that will become uninhabitable as temperatures continue to rise.'

Sutton interrupted. 'Well, surely when those other Labor bastards saw what happened to Bowker they will be so scared they'll meet the same fate they will change their minds? Besides, they've got to get these madcap schemes through the Senate.'

'In answer to your first statement, if they're putting Matthew McCarthy in charge, they're not put off. They obviously mean to push on with their reforms.

'In the short term, that's going to seriously piss off a lot of our members but when the changes come about it's going to seriously undermine our power base. Although most people hate change, they'll recognise they're destined to become dinosaurs unless they retrain and embrace McCarthy's brave new world.

'On the matter of getting their bills through the Senate, our research shows the Greens will side with them, ensuring they have sufficient numbers. And there are a few Liberals who might even cross the floor.'

'We'll have to make sure those Labor wankers

change their minds then,' Keith Sutton thundered. 'Christ, if Bowker's elimination didn't do it, then it's up to us to give 'em something else to think about!'

++++++++++++

Chapter Three

'God damn it Charlie. What's so blasted important that you've got to interrupt us at this point?' demanded Clement Arthur Turnbull II as he swivelled his luxuriously-soft Italian leather seat to face his unfortunate presidential aid.

Known to his enemies and friends alike as "The Panther" because of his Afro-American complexion and sleek, athletic body, the United States President was arguably the world's most consummate politician.

'I am sorry Mr President,' stammered his slim, baby-faced bespectacled aide, smiling apologetically at the half dozen presidential advisers seated around Air Force One's conference table. 'I would not intrude unless I thought you needed to hear this straight away.'

Nearly twelve kilometres above the Atlantic, the presidential jet was en route to London where leaders of European nations were scheduled to discuss tactics to deal with an unprecedented global financial crisis which threatened to plunge the world into a catastrophic recession not seen since the Great Depression of the 1930s.

'Okay, give it here,' the president sighed taking the telephone handset. Cupping his hand over the mouthpiece he grinned at the young aid. 'I apologise, Charles. I guess I'm a little sleep deprived but that's no excuse for snapping your head off.'

As the president pressed the handset to his ear, listening intently to the caller, the small group of financial experts cast uneasy glances at one another. Unsure whether they should leave the president to take the call in private, they stood slowly, taking their cue from the aid who jerked his head slightly, beckoning toward the cabin door as he retreated.

Outside the jet's conference room, the aid hurried down the aisle to his post at the communications console, a wave of relief and sympathy for the president washing over him. He muttered to the four men and two women following him, 'I wouldn't have his bitchin' job for the entire world. Less than a hundred days in office and already he's got two major wars and another Great Depression looming. Then there's global warming threatening to wipe us all out, terrorists about to take over Pakistan and its nuclear weapons, North Korea and Iran are rattling their cages like demented monkeys, Al Qaeda's running amok, and now this! No wonder he's friggin' edgy!'

'What's going on then?' One of the advisers asked the question on all their minds.

'There's been a political assassination down under. The Ozzie PM's been shot.'

'What? When?' They all stared open-mouthed. Australia was considered a peaceful hick backwater.

'Within the last half an hour,' Charlie replied, shaking his head. 'That was the Australian Deputy Prime Minister on the phone. As you can imagine, Canberra's in turmoil.'

Reaching the jet's media communications room, the aid flicked one of several flat screen televisions to a news channel. 'I don't know any more details but we'll see if CNN can enlighten us further.'

As the screen came to life the deep, well-modulated voice of the CNN anchor filled the confined space.

'...and to repeat news just breaking from Australia, the Australian Prime Minister, Connor Bowker, was shot dead today in what was that country's first political assassination.

'Our sources in Canberra and Sydney report that it is too early to speculate as to who's behind the killing but Mr. Bowker turned the Australian political scene on its head recently when he departed from the Labor Government's traditionally conservative stance on environmental issues, effectively hijacking the Green Movement's platform on fighting climate change.'

The television camera switched from the CNN anchor's urbane features to a portly, academic type.

'In the studio we have our political expert Doctor Ian Dinwoodie, who I'll ask to outline the current political scene in Australia. Doctor Dinwoodie, would you quickly sketch for our viewers a picture of what's happening down under?'

'I'd be happy to,' Dinwoodie responded in what could best be described as a plum-in-the-mouth English accent. 'Traditionally, the Australian political scene has been dominated by just two major parties, the Liberals, who when elected, usually form a coalition government with the lesser known National Party, and the Labor Party, which began as a socialist movement early in the twentieth century.

'In the past, the union-backed Labor Party received considerable financial support from major unions in exchange for pushing through industrial reforms and furthering the rights of workers.

'On the other hand, the Liberals are pro-business and the rights of the workers are secondary to company profits. Over recent years the ideologies and policies of the two parties have become very similar, although they would both deny the fact.

'Whereas Labor was once fairly representative of the working class, nowadays its ranks are little different from the Liberals who are comprised of lawyers, former bankers, accountants, doctors and other professionals. In fact, you won't find too many blue collar people in Labor's ranks these days!

'Despite global warming becoming a major concern, both political parties have been hamstrung in their ability to introduce environmental reform because the big players in mining and the manufacturing industries and the unions threaten to withdraw crucial financial support if they don't toe the line.

'In recent years, the Green vote in Australia has continued growing as more and more of the country's citizens become disenchanted with the two-party system which most see as self-serving, deceitful and incapable of delivering on promises to fix the ailing health system, effectively manage the country's economy and deal with the challenges of potentially catastrophic climate change.

'On this last point, one has to remember Australia has suffered under a nation-wide, and long running drought which has decimated the agricultural industry and forced the country to close down its food bowl in the Murray River irrigation area. In fact, the country's greatest river system is in danger of drying up. Its cities have been living with major water restrictions and escalating utility costs.

'Many blame an Australia-wide crisis in health care,

and the declining quality of life on political short-sightedness and government ineptitude. To put it bluntly, Australians have become terrified that prolonged droughts and the increased ferocity and occurrence of bushfires are going to get much worse and they want their leaders to do something about it.

'Following a long-running and popular television series in Australia called "Your World," there was a major shift in public opinion. "Your World" succeeded by stealth in educating viewers about the biosphere because it was spectacularly entertaining for people of all ages and educational levels.

'The show also screened extensively throughout America and Europe and swelled the popularity of Green parties, until vested interest groups used less than ethical scientists happy to reap huge bonuses for stating opposing views to launch so-called public education campaigns to discredit the programme as just apocalyptic sensationalism.

'Public admissions by the world renowned climate scientist, Sir James Lovelock that he and people such as Al Gore had been too alarmist with their early predictions didn't help the situation. Countries that don't enjoy freedom of speech banned the show.

'In Australia, the government had previously tried a similar strategy of discrediting scientists but it blew up in their faces, just as it did in the United States.

'The majority of IPCC climate scientists countered by admitting that while Lovelock had miscalculated as to the speed with which catastrophic events would occur; the threat was no less real and needed to be dealt with while the window of opportunity remained open.

'Knowing they would lose the balance of power to the Greens unless they abandoned their own "business as usual" stance on global warming and climate change, Connor Bowker and his Labor colleagues took a major political gamble, recruiting the charismatic environmental scientist Matthew McCarthy to their ranks. In an about face, they promised to heed the scientific warnings and set an example to other nations by reducing Australia's environmental footprint.

'Thanks to McCarthy, Labor so far has managed to convince the majority of Australians of the necessity to switch to renewable energy and re-vamp Australia's economy by moving away from globalisation to a more isolationist and self-reliant mentality that encourages sustainable living, reduces waste and discourages the consumerism gripping the rest of the planet.

'When business leaders cry foul and try to sway public opinion with the threats of job losses, McCarthy simply replies, "There won't be any jobs on a dead planet," or responds with, "There'll be no one left to clap mankind's achievements unless we change our way of living."

'It's difficult to counter such a powerful and simple truism.

'As you can imagine there have been major rumblings among the directors and shareholders in the big and powerful end of town. Many major corporations are threatening to pull out of Australia and the country's trading partners have made noises about banning imports from Australia if it continues with its plans.

'Despite the widespread concern as to the financial future of many companies under a Labor government, we must ask the question; who has felt sufficiently threatened by the proposed changes that they would resort to murdering the country's leader?'

+++++++++++

Chapter Four

In his plush penthouse apartment atop the fifteen-storey tower block at Milsons Point on Sydney's North Shore, Senator Philip Bacon, or "The Boar" as his enemies called him, leant his Italian leather recliner back to its full extent and smiled as he received news of the assassination. Replacing the telephone handset gently in its cradle, he downed the last dregs of his Grand Marnier and refilled the expensive crystal goblet. Reaching for the telephone again, he stabbed a number that was too dangerous to have in the phone's speed dial list into the keypad with a stubby, pale and hairy finger.

'It's time we had another meeting,' he growled. 'It seems Bowker's elimination has not changed their minds. We need to re-think our strategy.'

'I am guessing you want me to come there.' James "Flipper" Fleming, smarted at the Boar's arrogance.

Who does he think he is, talking to the head of ASIO like I'm some sort of low-paid office boy?

Fleming glanced at the bedside clock, noting the time: 12.30am. 'When do you want to meet?' he inquired, mentally cursing his nemesis.

The senator had him eating out of his hand, and for the moment there was nothing he could do about it.

'Of course I want you to come here,' the Boar snarled. 'I didn't choose to live on top of a commercial building for the view, you stupid bugger. I chose it for its privacy and security. Just make sure no one ever knows about our meetings here. I'll expect you in twenty.'

Dropping the handset back in its cradle, Philip

35

Bacon automatically erased the phone's memory, a reflexive act of self-preservation cultivated many years previously.

Fleming slid from his bed, careful not to disturb his wife who had apparently not heard the muted trill of the bedside phone.

Even if she had heard the telephone Cynthia Fleming would have merely rolled over and gone back to sleep. Twenty-five years of marriage to the Australian Security Intelligence Organisation's Director General had conditioned her to virtually ignore these clandestine and cryptic conversations which often took place at the most unusual hour.

Fleming pulled on dark trousers, black joggers, and a navy bomber jacket over his navy T-shirt, then hid his distinctive iron-grey hair beneath a charcoal deerstalker cap. Glancing in the dressing table mirror, he turned up his collar and donned a pair of heavy-rimmed spectacles.

There was nothing wrong with his eyesight. The glasses just helped complete the disguise.

Although few people outside the organisation's circle were familiar with the ASIO chief's features, he did not want to run the risk of being identified as a late night caller at the prominent and controversial senator's high-rise residence. For that reason, he did not drive his late model Lexus, choosing instead to use the ubiquitous ten-year-old Holden Commodore he kept in a rented garage two streets from his stately Wahroonga bungalow.

Although officially based at ASIO's Canberra headquarters, Fleming chose to spend the majority of his time in the Sydney office, reasoning he was closer to the front line and most of the action. Apart from that, he could reach Australia's capital city in little more than an hour by air and video conferencing and the other marvels of technology enabled him to keep in touch without being too accessible to the Attorney General under whose control ASIO sat.

Checking to ensure the street outside was deserted, he noticed with relief that his neighbours' homes were in darkness. The residents of the upmarket suburb had long since retired for the night. In any case, they would be unlikely to see him, as the shrubbery of their spacious gardens obscured any view of the dimly lit street.

On reaching the tower block, Flipper swiped his key-card across the reader outside the under-croft parking area and waited for the heavy security gate to creak along its track. Although CCTV cameras had been installed to alert the building's sole security guard if anyone attempted to bypass the access control measures by tailgating him, he stopped inside, checked his mirror, and waited until the gate had closed before parking his car close to the lifts.

At this time of the night, the car park was deserted because every one of the buildings fifteen floors, except for the Boar's penthouse, was leased to an eclectic collection of professional businesses that operated during daylight hours.

Fleming knew that being the building's sole tenant suited the senator because it eliminated the problem of nosey neighbours, unwanted visitors or the likelihood of a physical attack by his many enemies. He also knew such incidents were rare these days, because those who incurred the Boar's wrath, or threatened him, never escaped unscathed. They invariably met with an unfortunate "accident" conveniently orchestrated by the senator's underworld connections.

The ASIO chief rode the lift to the penthouse. Knowing the senator would be observing him closely via the lift's surveillance camera he resisted a childish impulse to proffer the universally recognised one finger salute to the camera, instead spending the time to reflect ruefully on events that had led to his first encounter with the man he so despised.

One day, he promised himself silently, I'll get this overfed pig off my back!

Bacon and Fleming's unfortunate association had all begun in late January 1965, when as an innocent, fresh-faced eighteen-year-old, Fleming's mother had asked him to check the letterbox outside the family's modest brick bungalow in the middle-class Sydney suburb of Jannali.

At first he'd thought the brown manila envelope with the OHMS stamp was meant for his parents. Why would Mum and Dad get a letter from the Defence Department? he wondered. Suddenly, the hair went up on the back of his neck as he looked more closely, realising sickeningly that the letter was addressed to him; James Arthur Fleming.

His stomach churned as he fumbled to tear open the thick paper envelope.

Everyone in Australia knew about the government's unpopular and recently instituted random ballot system. Designed to boost troop numbers for the Vietnam War, the lottery in human misery instilled fear into the hearts of parents and those who could see little point in offering their lives in the defence of what most in 1960s considered an irrelevant and far off land populated by peoples with whom Australia had little affinity.

The selection process was a little like a lucky dip where the unfortunate losers were chosen merely because they fell within an ever-changing range of birth dates.

'Don't tell me I've been called up,' Fleming groaned, horrified.

His fears were confirmed as he read the bald announcement demanding that he present himself for medical assessment at the nearest army recruiting centre at a specified time and date. In short, if he passed the medical examination he would undoubtedly join thousands of other young Australians in the savage fighting to prevent a largely corrupt democratic regime being overtaken by an equally corrupt band of communist idealists.

At that time, Fleming barely knew where Vietnam was. Like most Australians his history lessons had been confined to the pink sections of the world atlas which signified the ever-declining British Empire.

Appalled, he trudged back to the house, wondering why he should become cannon-fodder in some far-flung conflict just because paranoid bloody yanks kept seeing Reds under every bed and behind every bush. It was so unfair!

For most Australians attending school during the 1950s and 60s, learning either German or French was mandatory. It had been no different for Fleming.

However, while most boys and girls complained bitterly about learning a skill they were unlikely to use and consequently made little effort, Fleming discovered a penchant for foreign languages. Soon he could converse fluently in French, becoming dux of his school in that subject. Having graduated from high school, he had mapped out a Public Service career in his mind, acquiring a junior clerical position in the Department of Foreign Affairs. From there he had intended to work his way up the diplomatic promotional ladder so he could travel and put his linguistic skills and superior intellect to good use.

The letter turned all his plans upside down.

A born pragmatist, the young Fleming realised he could not fight the system. In fact, he demonstrated foresight well beyond his years and concluded that military service could actually enhance his career prospects as long as he survived.

And so, gritting his teeth and mentally stiffening his backbone he knuckled down to basic military training. The Spartan and fiercely homophobic training regime of the 5th Battalion Royal Australian Regiment (5RAR) Holsworthy army base, brought out a latent inner toughness and a resolve that surprised both Fleming and his trainers.

Although a loner by nature and not keen on contact sports, James Fleming quickly realised he would not survive army life unless he underwent both a physical and psychological metamorphosis. This would enable him to carve his place in the Alpha male environment. He did not relish the prospect of being bullied as he had been at the suburban all-boys high school, where his studious, introverted nature and the mollycoddling home life of an only child made him a target. So, with the attitude, that if you can't beat the system, you're better off joining it, he threw himself into all aspects of his training without complaint. He exhibited a chameleon-like talent for avoiding conflict, controversy, or attracting the unwelcome and often sadistic attention of his army instructors.

Knowing he would soon be in an unfamiliar and hostile environment where things would be tough enough without a language barrier, the young recruit set himself the additional task of learning everything he could about Vietnam, its people, culture and long and troubled history. That the small, divided and war-torn country had been under French rule for many years came as a pleasant surprise and he guessed correctly that many Vietnamese would have at least, a basic knowledge of the French language. However, Fleming understood he would still be at a disadvantage, unless he did his utmost to learn Vietnamese by the time he was forced to face the Viet Cong and fight alongside South Vietnamese forces.

In those days, finding someone to teach him the language in Australia's predominantly Anglo-Saxon population should have been extremely difficult, if not impossible. Few Australians had ever been beyond their island nation's shores. The difficulty of learning a foreign language would have been further exacerbated by the constraints of his rigorous army training had not the ever resourceful Fleming remembered Jimmy Ng.

Recruited from his native homeland to enhance Australia's ability to deal with its South East Asian neighbours, the diminutive Vietnamese also worked in Foreign Affairs as a diplomatic adviser and government interpreter. When Fleming approached Ng and intimated his desire to learn Vietnamese Jimmy Ng was delighted. Finding someone in the strange, unfriendly land of big-nosed, round-eyed, brash people sufficiently interested in his former home country to learn the language was a welcome change from the often hostile attitudes he encountered on a daily basis.

Ng agreed to give Fleming a crash course in Vietnamese, even managing to convince Fleming's superiors that it would be to the army's advantage to have a young soldier in their ranks with a working knowledge of the language. Although he didn't know it then, this decision would be pivotal in determining James Fleming's life and future career.

Despite his success as a soldier-to-be, Fleming found his considerable acting skills and fertile imagination taxed to the limit by many aspects of army life. Unlike the majority of his fellow soldiers, he was sexually naive and not in the least promiscuous. He had no desire to participate in his fellow recruits drunken excursions to Sydney's Kings Cross red light district and was at first confused as to why he did not share the same obvious heterosexual lust exhibited by his army companions. In fact, he was mystified by their ribald encounters with the women of the streets and couldn't understand why he was actually repulsed by their exploits.

Because homosexuality was considered unnatural and sexual acts between those of the same sex were listed as criminal offences, it took some time for

Fleming to accept the mortifying truth. For a time he even contemplated suicide because he realised it was just a matter of time before he was ostracised and labelled "a queer," or worse still, "a bloody arse bandit."

Knowing his life would become hell unless he dealt with the problem he "borrowed" a second cousin as his imaginary childhood sweetheart and displayed her photograph on his bedside locker. Whenever the others embarked on their weekly forays to the brothels and seedy basement nightclubs James Fleming trotted out the excuse that he much preferred to visit the love of his life.

Little did they know he actually occupied his time practising Vietnamese with Jimmy Ng.

Although a tide of powerful sexual urges and confused emotions eventually struggled to the surface as the young homosexual recruit matured physically, he fought hard to suppress them. At night his dreams were increasingly filled with vivid, lecherous male-dominated encounters and various sexual acts. The torment did not lessen as each day dawned. He often caught himself drooling over the young, muscular physiques of his fellow soldiers and imagined performing sexual acts with them.

Unfulfilled sexual fantasies hijacked his thoughts at the worst possible time but he dared not reveal the slightest hint to his fiercely homophobic barrack room companions. The fear of the horrendous consequences if his homosexuality were discovered forced him to become a consummate actor. He perfected the art of swallowing his revulsion and pretended to listen enthusiastically as other men boasted in explicit detail about real or fictitious sexual conquests. As part of an elaborate charade, he even adorned the back of his locker door with his own nude centrefolds and pretended to leer with the others when glossy photos of well-endowed young woman in provocative or blatantly pornographic poses were passed from bunk to bunk.

Somehow, Fleming hid his secret and survived what could just as easily have become a nightmare. When the time came to graduate he felt enormous pride, not because he was among the top ten of his fellow national service recruits but because he'd managed to conceal his sexual proclivity and survive the system.

Although most barely needed to shave, the system that had unexpectedly plucked them from their normal everyday lives now decreed that they were ready to fight and die for their country.

And so, one sunny autumn day in April 1966, having completed his basic training, Trooper James Fleming and his fellow soldiers from 5RAR strapped themselves into the webbing benches lining the unlovely bowels of an RAAF Hercules for the uncomfortable and seemingly interminable flight to Saigon.

Apart from a drawn out refuelling stop in Darwin, where they milled around in the tropical heat until ushered into the shade of an empty hangar, there was no relief from the boredom, until, in true Aussie style, someone organised an impromptu two-up game to pass the time until they could re-board their plane.

Eventually landing in Saigon's noisy, sweating hell of military confusion, a cynical James Fleming and his companions agreed they were involuntary fodder for the cannons of Asia's bloody little war. Surprisingly, however, there wasn't the customary 'hurry up and wait" that was part of the army life they had become used to. Instead, for once, the military hierarchy seemed to have planned well. The Australian troops had no sooner disembarked from the aircraft than a convoy of army vehicles appeared to transport them to Nui Dat where one hundred and eight young men from Brisbane's 6RAR already waited for them.

Occupying an elevated, well sand-bagged clearing surrounded by rubber plantations, Nui Dat comprised the usual assortment of APCs, trucks, Land Rovers, artillery weapons, tents and transportable buildings of a well provisioned army base. It would become their home and that of other young Australian soldiers who were to be known as the First Australian Task Force (1ATF) Vietnam.

Fleming did not expect a picnic. He knew it was likely to be the roughest and most dangerous experience of his lifetime, requiring him to live on his wits, but he hoped to just get through it all and eventually reclaim his former life and pursue his chosen career.

What he did not count on was his assignment to Delta Company under Lieutenant Philip Bacon.

At twenty-five, five-foot-seven and already fighting corpulent tendencies, Bacon's porcine features, squinty pink-rimmed eyes, poor personal hygiene and arrogant nature had earned him the unflattering nickname he would carry for the remainder of his life.

Fleming's instant dislike for his obnoxious Platoon Commander was further exacerbated when the Boar chose the young trooper to be his unofficial personal "gofer," ensuring Fleming was never far from his influence and control.

There was nothing the young trooper could do. The Boar had the power to make his life extremely miserable unless he complied with the conniving lieutenant's wishes. With an uncanny bloodhound-like ability to sense another's frailties, the Boar somehow sensed the Achilles heel of Fleming's sexuality. Ever ready to exploit a situation to his advantage, he was prepared to "groom" the young soldier to further his own nefarious goals.

Verdant corruption ensured Vietnam represented a jungle in more ways than one. While the evil spectre of illicit drugs was as yet virtually unknown in Australia, its supposed closest ally, the United States, was on the cusp of exploiting its vulnerability for huge financial gain. It mattered not to the scheming, malevolent and faceless individuals of the CIA that their officially sanctioned trade would ruin countless lives and become modern man's single biggest blight for decades to come.

Having formed an alliance with American and Asian drug lords, the ambitious, cunning and conscienceless Phillip Bacon was up to his ears in the sale of filthy, illicit substances to gullible, naive and fad-crazy baby boomers. In fact, he would stoop to anything, even things unthinkable to the most ruthless of the criminal underclass that thrived in the cesspit of war-fed corruption.

Exempt from Australian Customs checks, U.S. military flights shuttling the coffined remains of America's youth to their home continent flew regularly into Australian RAAF bases to refuel. Ever the opportunist, the Boar quickly devised a diabolical method of interweaving the heroin trade's pernicious tentacles into the very fabric of his own naive young nation while simultaneously building his drug empire. Who else would sink to the despicable practice of concealing heroin in the mutilated carcases of America's war dead?

Lonely, virginal, completely out of his depth in the moral and actual jungle that was South East Asia and still as morally pliable as plasticine, Fleming did not stand a chance amongst this seething human melting pot. Perhaps, given time and a different set of circumstances, he may have won his omnipresent struggle to suppress his latent proclivity toward paedophilia.

Unfortunately, he never stood a chance, for just as cancer cells invade and eventually dominate their host; evil also spreads and subjugates the unwary. It was therefore inevitable that someone like the Boar would recognise Fleming's vulnerability and contrive to ensnare the young man his sticky iniquitous web.

In dirt-poor South Vietnam, many young males were willing to sell themselves for a few dollars. Bacon knew a little carefully administered heroin would free Fleming's canary of inhibition from its cage of convention, allowing it to fly freely through the lush jungles of sexual perversion which were carefully contrived to cater for every taste. He knew once the fresh-faced soldier had crossed the line and tasted the forbidden fruits of paedophilia, he would be irrevocably corrupted and open to blackmail. It was all too easy.

Fleming had not understood why his lieutenant insisted on his presence during a sojourn to Phuoc Tuy on 15th August 1966. His tentative attempts to inquire why he was needed were met with a gruff, "It's a bloody order son. You should know by now, you do not question orders!"

On reaching their destination the Boar hurried away for a mysterious liaison with his cronies from the US Marines, leaving Fleming to wait around with half a dozen of his fellow soldiers. He was tempted to explore, however as a lowly "grunt" he was not prepared to risk his platoon commander's wrath any further so he contented himself by watching the ever-changing and fascinating world of a country under military occupation.

It was an incongruous sight. The rubbish-strewn streets teemed with humanity with an almost palpable urgency to fill a million different agendas at just as many mysterious destinations. Rickshaws, bicycles, naked urchins and skinny peasants stooped under strange burdens intermingled with an assortment of camouflaged machines of war. Scrawny chickens and mangy dogs dodged through the muddy streets and the cacophony of honking horns, bicycle bells and squalling street vendors. Perpetually cloudy skies made the oppressive humidity unbearable, trapping the stench of diesel fumes, rotting garbage and sweating humanity in a cloying miasma to which he would never become accustomed.

"What a shithole," he muttered to himself. "How the hell did I end up here?"

It was early evening by the time his platoon commander returned, amazing the young sapper by decreeing that Fleming and he should "hit the suds," as

Bacon called it.

To refuse meant weeks of being hounded, ridiculed and menial chores of mind-numbing drudgery, so the young soldier agreed. In any case, the tropical heat had left him and his fellow soldiers dehydrated.

Like a sheepdog cutting a ewe from the main flock, Bacon ushered Fleming away from the other soldiers and embarked on a pub crawl of the province's seedy bars, the older man seemingly putting rank aside for once and befriending him. Looking back afterward, Fleming was to wonder many times how he could have been so unsuspectingly stupid.

They shoved their way through throngs of drunken, noisy U.S. service personnel occupying the several ramshackle bars lining the squalid streets. After downing a variety of intoxicating elixirs forced on him by the Boar, Fleming's head was swimming in an alcoholic fug. By the time they arrived at the fifth establishment, the surreptitious spiking of Fleming's Coca Cola presented no problem for the Boar. He'd been through the same routine on many previous occasions.

And so it was that the semi-stupefied trooper found himself flattered by the advances of a young, good-looking male prostitute, whom he did not even suspect was in the Boar's employ. The Vietnamese youth's honeyed toned and flawless skin, pretty features and the flash of pearl-white teeth when he smiled alluringly at Fleming easily broached any last vestige of the young Australian soldier's inhibitions.

Fleming's later recollection of events was hazy to say the least. Sometime during the laughter-filled evening the room had spun uncontrollably. Lights and images of naked bodies swirled through his befuddled brain and he'd found himself returning soft kisses and erotic caresses in a darkened room heady with the miasma of extraordinarily fragrant tropical flowers.

Awakened on the morning of 16 August 1966 by Bacon shaking him roughly by the shoulder, he was mortified to discover the slim, naked boy of about thirteen beside him on a grubby mattress.

'Have a good time?' the Boar smirked. 'You better get your strides on, pretty boy. It's time to return to Nui Dat.'

Fumbling with his khaki trousers and shirt, Fleming knew with horror that his life had changed forever. Nothing he said could return the previous status quo. His stomach sank as he realised he'd been set up. 'You evil bastard!' he cried.

'It's not me who's the turd-burglar, son!' Bacon smirked. "But don't worry Jimmy boy. Your secret's safe with me. As long as you behave yourself that is,' the Boar added, grinning maliciously.

Fleming felt physically sick. He knew he was now the Boar's man. The platoon commander could lead him around using the nose-ring of threatened disgrace and humiliation, forcing him deeper and deeper into the iniquitous swamp of drugs, violence and depravity.

That he might also trap himself at the same time failed to register in the conniving Lieutenant's distorted brain.

Reunited with the remainder of their party, the return trip to the Australian base at Nui Dat had been one Fleming would rather forget. While the other

Australians had joked about their night of debauchery with the prostitutes, Fleming was nursing the mother of all headaches and the knowledge that he'd lost the battle with his sexual demons.

They reached Nui Dat through blinding sheets of monsoonal rain, cloying mud and deep water-filled potholes. The downpour was relentless, halting all but the most essential of activities.

Watching the steel-grey deluge from the entrance to the dormitory tent, Fleming could barely make out the blurred shapes of the howitzers and APCs which appeared to be sinking slowly into a sea of dung-like mud. Rain drumming on the overhead canvas made conversation impossible. Condensation dripped on stretchers and kitbags, pooled on mess tables and dripped into food. Everything smelt musty and the men joked that the Viet Cong didn't need to fire a shot to drive out opposing forces, but just wait until fungus and mildew did the job for them. 'Or die of the clap after last night,' one wag commented dryly.

That night the base came under enemy attack.

A barrage of mortar shells whistled overhead. Then, to the thud and crash of explosions, spouts of muddy water flew skyward. In the dark and confusion, they could not tell where the enemy were or how great their numbers. As each mortar shell found its mark, sandbagged gun emplacements crumbled. The cries of the wounded resounded through the confusion as Australian Medics grabbed stretchers, rushing shattered bodies to the hospital tents, hoping there, they could escape the carnage.

In shattered disarray, tents lay torn apart in the mud

like so much dirty laundry. Land Rovers, ambulances, APCs and trucks all suffered direct hits as the invisible barrage of recoilless rifle fire peppered their defences from the surrounding rubber plantations.

Scrambling to return fire, the Australians squinted through saturated blackness of the night attempting to locate muzzle flashes as the enemy shot at them from the almost impenetrable dripping foliage. It seemed the unseen force pitted against them was undefeatable.

Word filtered through their lines that the Viet Cong were amassing huge numbers to announce their political dominance of the Phuoc Tuy Province from which the Australians had driven them.

'We'll send out a platoon when daylight comes and try and run the bastards off,' Major Harry Smith, D Company's commander, announced.

Possessing an unquestionable courage and determination to triumph over the enemy, the Australians knew their foe's numbers were overwhelming. However, inexplicably, the Viet Cong vanished before daylight like ghosts into the thick vegetation. Few doubted they would return in even greater numbers.

Morning arrived with its usual tropical suddenness allowing the Aussies time to take stock and assess the night's action. Although there had been no fatalities, twenty-four Australians had been injured in the overnight attack.

Throughout the day on 17th August, platoons from 5 & 6RAR reconnoitred the surrounding countryside searching for the elusive enemy. In an unconventional war, it was impossible to distinguish between friend and foe, for their enemy often did not wear a uniform and resorted to the strategies of hiding among ordinary villagers and burrowing into their extensive subterranean networks of tunnels.

In sweltering humidity Aussie patrols pushed through dense, dripping foliage, expecting at any moment to be cut down by sniper fire, or hear the spine chilling chatter of machine guns as an accompaniment to a scything torrent of white-hot lead. Fearing booby traps and mines, they trod wearily, adrenaline and respect for the Viet Cong's mercilessness and cunning keeping exhaustion at bay.

Searching the rubber plantations, paddy fields and the banks of the Suoi Da Bang River throughout the day, they returned to the Nui Dat base, knowing the enemy the Americans had dubbed "Charlie" was playing a game of cat and mouse. Although at this stage they had failed to locate their attackers, the Australians did not doubt the Viet Cong presence or the enemy's resolve to destroy them.

When darkness fell, the shelling resumed, although this time the Diggers were better prepared and apart from sleep deprivation and frayed nerves, they survived the night of 17th without further casualties.

'Private Fleming, you've been deployed to make up numbers in Delta Company,' the Boar told James the next morning. 'You're going out with 2Lt Gordon Sharp's 11 Platoon. Just like yesterday, the mission is simply to locate enemy forces and drive them off.'

Introduced to men of 11 Platoon, Fleming shook hands with his fellow soldiers. Like him, most were barely old enough to shave. Untested in battle, their youthful faces belied the tremendous courage they would soon be called on to demonstrate.

Surprisingly 2Lt Harold Sharp also shook his hand. 'Christ, you've got a handshake like a dolphin's flipper,' the second lieutenant commented, unintentionally tagging Fleming with the nickname 'Flipper' forever.

By choosing him to replace an injured trooper in Sharp's platoon, Fleming knew Bacon was demonstrating the power he held over him. Nonetheless, he welcomed the chance to be free from the Boar's smirking influence and collect his thoughts so he willingly took his place with Sharp's 11 Platoon.

Major Harry Smith instructed Sharp's team to take the lead in beating through the rubber trees in a bid to oust the enemy. They pushed forward, examining the ground minutely for traces of their wily and troublesome enemy. By mid-afternoon, fatigued and frustrated, they had painstakingly searched every thicket and swamp of the five kilometres they had covered since leaving Nui Dat.

Fleming hoped they'd soon take a break from the relentless heat and humidity. Glancing at his watch he could not know that the time; 3.15pm; would be recorded in the annals of history.

The Vietnamese attack was swift, short and unexpected. Bullets whizzed like angry hornets, ripping bark and leaves from the rubber trees and steaming undergrowth.

Flinging themselves behind any cover they could find, Fleming and the men from 11 Platoon returned fire, successfully driving off the small group of North

Vietnamese soldiers they had obviously surprised.

'I think we stumbled on a small advance party. Watch yourselves because there's sure to be plenty more the little slit-eyed bastards waiting for us,' their platoon commander growled.

Moving cautiously forward to where the spectre of the Viet Cong had been but a few moments before, the Aussies discovered the bullet-riddled corpse of an emaciated enemy soldier.

'Shit, they were in such a hurry to get away, they left the poor bastard behind,' Fleming muttered. Rolling him over, they all stared down at the boyish features of the corpse around which the flies were already beginning to gather.

'Jesus,' someone blasphemed in astonished low undertones. 'He's just a kid. What's he doing running around trying to kill people?'

'You probably don't think so, but *we're* all just little more than kids. What are *we* doing killing people?' Fleming responded.

'Stop bloody navel-gazing and get moving,' their platoon commander ordered. 'Or you'll be lying in the mud with some little yellow bastard staring down at *you*!'

After radioing the result of their encounter, 11 Platoon resumed patrolling. Eyes flicking left, right, centre, up and down, they endeavoured to see as far ahead as the jungle permitted while at the same time filtering every detail of the surrounding terrain looking for anything that did not fit. With senses heightened to their maximum they searched, knowing the slightest oversight or mistake could spell instant disaster.

Maintaining complete silence and communicating by hand signals, or a nod, or shake of the head, they continued probing for the next thirty or so minutes.

The cursed tropical rain returned once more as a great, white, blinding curtain hampering their vision and battering the fronds of the surrounding palms and the dense tropical foliage so it bowed in submission.

At 4.15pm the gates of hell opened.

Viet Cong rifles spat a deadly tirade from the surrounding undergrowth. A split second later, the Diggers heard the unmistakeable and spine-chilling retort of semi-automatic weapons. Then grenades and mortar rounds began exploding around them.

All about, the ground erupted as grenades and mortar fire blew the mud up into the tightly packed canopy, raining filthy ooze on the beleaguered Aussie soldiers. The ugly, gut-churning clatter of enemy machine guns punctuated the relentless volley of automatic rifle fire as the Viet Cong slashed at them from all sides.

Under the merciless hail of molten metal, the Aussies dived for cover once more, firing blindly back at the barrage from the Viet Cong's 275 Regiment.

Fleming was surprised by the clarity of his thoughts. Although he had often wondered how he would react in battle, he realised he and his companions were too busy fighting for survival to contemplate the sheer terror of stumbling upon vastly superior enemy forces whose sole aim was to wipe them out.

Meanwhile, platoons from Major Harry Smith's D Company arrived. Joining the shattered 11 Company, they unloaded a courageously withering counter attack.

'Tell Nui Dat we need immediate back up and air support,' Major Harry Smith ordered. 'If we don't get help we're buggered! There must be at least a couple of thousand of the bastards.'

But through the crackling, hissing static of the radio operator's headphones the bleak response they dreaded came back. 'We've got ten tenths cloud cover over the base. We can't get anything off the ground until the weather lifts.'

Although it was no consolation, the Australians understood. Atrocious weather conditions and impossible visibility were weapons that Charlie often exploited to his advantage. The Vietnamese commander of 275 Regiment knew full well when he launched the attacks that almost zero visibility would negate any threat of retaliation from the air.

There was to be no support from American and Australian bombers and fighter aircraft. They were on their own.

Well, almost.

Desperate situations call for desperate measures. With the Viet Cong virtually overrunning the tiny Australian contingent Harry Smith knew they would not survive unless he made the possibly suicidal decision of calling on their Kiwi counterparts to shell the Australians' own lines with the New Zealand howitzers.

Would it work?

Pinned down, Smith's men battled to stay alive under the onslaught. In the pouring rain and confusion it was impossible to tell how many died in the first few seconds. Only now did James Fleming feel a sickening, cold terror as the dreadfulness of their predicament became apparent.

The bloodied and mutilated corpses of fellow soldiers lay about him in the mud. Pain-racked screams of the wounded and dying would echo in his head for years to come. The horrible images of the carnage would be indelibly imprinted in his psyche to haunt his dreams forever. However, for the moment, he concentrated on sighting his rifle on the flashes from the enemy's weapons. Emptying magazine after magazine, he was occasionally rewarded by a scream of pain, or the glimpse of a slumping body.

With the Grim Reaper seemingly mocking them from the jungle, the barrel of Fleming's L1A1 self-loading rifle sizzled hotly in the unrelenting monsoonal deluge and he prayed their ammunition would not run out.

Suddenly, above the hellish cacophony of battle, a new sound filtered through Fleming's shell-shocked consciousness; artillery shells.

Mercifully, the ANZAC's base at Nui Dat had commenced pummelling the Viet Cong with incredibly accurate retaliatory fire.

The New Zealand howitzers hammered away as fast as they could be reloaded. Round after round pounded the muddy battlefield until the cannon barrels glowed red hot.

By 5.00pm D Company's ammunition supply was dangerously low. Praying that Nui Dat had helicopters on hand to fly in supplies now that the cloud cover had lessened, the Aussie Major radioed his base.

As luck would have it, earlier that day, two Iroquois helicopters had flown a concert party to the base to entertain the ANZAC troops. Hastily loaded with much-needed ammunition, they were soon en route to the battle scene. However, with darkness fast approaching and hopelessly beleaguered by superior enemy numbers, a massive and bloody defeat of the 1st Australian Task Force seemed inevitable. With enemy forces amounting to between two-thousand-five-hundred and three-thousand determinedly hostile soldiers, the Australians were outnumbered nearly ten to one.

How could they survive the night as the North Vietnamese continued amassing yet more troops?

Filled with soldiers from 6RAR, armoured personnel carriers from the 1st APC squadron rushed across the rain-soaked terrain from Nui Dat determined to prop up their colleagues at Long Tan. Forcing their way through muddy, flooded waterways, they neared the battle scene, encountering heavy opposing fire from the Viet Cong.

Halted momentarily from their advance, 6RAR troops spilled from their vehicles. Ducking from cover to cover, they pushed forward on foot. Blasting back at the overwhelming numbers in a heroic but effectively-accurate counter attack, they pushed the enemy back into the jungle thus saving the day.

As the last light retreated from the leaden skies, Fleming looked aghast at the scene around him. Few of his companions from 11 Platoon had survived the vicious onslaught.

Shot through his lower right leg, Flipper Fleming was unable to walk. Afraid to move lest he give away his position to enemy snipers still lurking in the undergrowth, the young national serviceman was one of twenty-four wounded Australians who would have to wait until daylight for rescue.

And wait they did, for they were too close to enemy lines to risk further casualties. Until the Viet Cong decided to leave the area they had no alternative but to lie in the mud. Lest their moans were rewarded with a bullet to the head, they grimaced in pain and bit down on anything at hand as they strove to suppress involuntary gasps of pain.

Although the enemy had been driven back for the time being, the Australian soldiers hurried to consolidate their defences before nightfall. They weren't to know it yet, but they had succeeded in humiliating the might of the Viet Cong army and by 6.55pm the Battle of Long Tan was effectively over.

However, it was still a deadly place.

Throughout the night, Australian army helicopters flew in and out of the battlefield. Guided in the coal-black night by the lights from APCs, chopper crews risked their lives to rescue those still alive and recover the bodies of the slain, ferrying them back to Nui Dat's triage unit.

Meanwhile, delirious from blood loss and shock, Fleming watched wraith-like shapes moving about the darkness of the battlefield. Once, thinking he was about to be rescued, he almost called out. Fortunately before he could moisten his cracked, bloodied lips to yell, one of the figures called softly to a colleague in Vietnamese, 'The Australians fought very bravely but it will not stop me killing any of the round eyes I find still alive.'

'Yes, they might have won this time, but they and their Yankee friends will be driven out in the end.

'Long live Ho Chi Min!"

Chilling fear turning his skin to goose bumps, his bowels threatening to turn to water, Fleming stifled his cry and tried to flatten himself further into the mud as the enemy scoured the surrounding vegetation intent on rescuing their wounded and removing the corpses of their comrades.

It was to be the longest night of James Fleming's life.

Finally, as the sky began to lighten, the last of the Viet Cong 275 Regiment fled, allowing the Australians to safely retrieve the last remnants of their dead and wounded, including James "Flipper" Fleming.

History would record that the North Vietnamese Army had underestimated the courage and superior battlefield tactics of the Australians. Their serious miscalculation had cost them at least two hundred and seventy five dead, while eighteen Aussie soldiers had been killed and twenty-four wounded.

Although the war became increasingly unpopular the Australian government's failure for nearly fifty years to recognise the bravery of those who fought in Vietnam would prove a national disgrace that embittered the war veterans and their families and created a new nation-wide cynicism toward such future conflicts.

After his repatriation, the army put Fleming's language skills to good use, shifting him to their military intelligence unit at his request. Unfortunately, his sighs of relief at escaping the Boar's clutches soon died on Fleming's lips.

Recognising the army intelligence unit offered far more opportunities than ever to build his empire; Phillip

Bacon had also manoeuvred himself into the same intelligence unit. Now, Bacon's finger would be on the pulse of one of Australia's largest government organisations.

There seemed to be no escaping the evil man's clutches and even the horror of the terror-ridden days between 16th and 18th August 1966 did not overshadow the hell-filled years of drugs, crime and depravity into which Fleming was led by Lieutenant Phillip "the Boar" Bacon. In fact, those three eventful days merely hastened his moral demise. While others had turned to drink or drugs to forget the brutality of war, Fleming had sought solace from the recurring nightmares of the Battle of Long Tan by increasing his visits to the male prostitutes of Saigon and elsewhere in the war-stricken and divided country.

Bacon watched his every move, smirking inwardly at the power he wielded over the clever, bi-lingual soldier building a new career for himself.

Finally the war ended with the United States Marines' ignominious last minute withdrawal from Saigon. Fleming's usefulness as an expert on all things Vietnamese became all but redundant. However, his intelligence gathering skills and ability to work covertly had become legendary and ASIO almost leapt at the chance to add such verdant talent to its ranks.

As a war hero, Fleming's jet-propelled rise through its ranks was virtually assured.

Bacon, on the other hand, now chose politics where the enormous illicit, drug fuelled wealth, immense power and the influence he'd accumulated bought him a safe government seat in Australia's senate. He had also invested heavily in the pharmaceutical giant, Shriver, and now held a majority of its shares, extending his drug empire to both sides of the legal divide.

Although the two men trod different paths, the Boar dogged Fleming's life, calling upon him for numerous favours under threat of exposing Fleming's unsavoury proclivities.

It was a classic Mexican stand-off. While Fleming could also bring about the Boar's demise by telling all he knew, he could not do so without wrecking everything he had grown to love; money, power, prestige and the illusion of respectability. But what Fleming dreaded more was the ruthless savagery the Boar and his henchman would unleash upon Fleming's aging parents whom he held in high regard.

Fleming had tried to forget events in Vietnam, even marrying as part of an elaborate ploy to provide an outward appearance of respectability. Ever the skilful actor, and sufficiently bi-sexual to not find heterosexuality too abhorrent, he had successfully concealed his double life from friends and family throughout his ASIO career.

Now, years later, dressed in an expensive and well cut olive-green sports jacket and taupe trousers, Bacon ushered the ASIO chief into his mahogany-panelled study. The softly lit room was redolent with the smoke from Cuban cigars and expensive liquor. The gentle, soothing strains of classical music which Fleming identified as a composition by Brahms belied the solemnity of the occasion and he thought it strange how someone so evil and conniving could appreciate such beauty. But then, was he any different?

'Drink?' Bacon asked, waving a bottle of Grand Marnier at Fleming.

'If it's Scotch," Fleming replied. The Boar always offered him brandy knowing very well he despised the spirit. Both men knew it was the Boar's way of getting under Fleming's skin but Fleming would never give the Boar the satisfaction of knowing just how much the reminder of his undoing in Vietnam fed his inner hatred.

With liquor in hand, they sank into the white leather lounge chairs and stared hard at each other. Fleming was determined not to speak first and kept his features impassive as he waited for the aging but nonetheless powerful politician to break the silence.

'So Jim, what are we going to do about this situation?' the Boar asked, swirling the brandy in his oversize goblet.

'What situation?' Fleming asked. He smiled inwardly in satisfaction as the senator erupted.

'Don't fuck about, James. You don't think I called you here in the middle of the night just to waste my best single malt scotch do you? I want to know what plans you've got to stop Matthew bloody McCarthy from wrecking everything I've spent my entire life building.'

'Tell me again how McCarthy's environmental policies would ruin you.'

'Don't be so bloody dense. You know I don't give a fuck about his views on climate change and saving the frigging planet. Personally, I think it's all a load of baloney. What I do care about is his declaration that drugs are a threat to national security. His plan to accord all police forces with sweeping, nation-wide powers and the formation of a joint drug intelligence taskforce is receiving unanimous support from state premiers and their police commissioners. For once, it looks as if the state coppers will cooperate with each other instead of squabbling over territories and trying to score points over each other.

'It could decimate my supply network. I cannot allow it to happen.'

Fleming couldn't resist further provoking his nemesis. 'I have to admit, it was a pretty cunning move on your part to not only hook people on illegal drugs but to control the legal drugs such as methadone that are used to treat addicts.

'It doesn't matter to you whether addicts are on heroin, speed or dependent on prescription substitutes handed out by clinics; you even supply the bikie gangs with the ingredients for their methamphetamine labs.

'However, I suppose it keeps the armed holdups on pharmacies down,' Flipper added sarcastically. 'You've got it all sewn up haven't you?'

'Don't you look down your frigging, toffy nose at me, you've done your share to help further my operation over the years and profited nicely in the process, I might add.' The Boar glared. 'I still want to know what you're going to do to stop McCarthy.'

'Maybe we should just sit back, senator. Let things take their course, eh? Just because Bowker's removal didn't change the Labor government's mind doesn't necessarily mean we have to do anything.'

'What the hell is that supposed to mean?'

'It means Bowker's death will have caused such tremendous instability within Labor's ranks that they could now begin to self-destruct. There was plenty of disquiet on the back benches before the assassination and the pressure from the unions on those holding marginal seats could bring about a Labor mutiny.'

The Boar grunted impatiently. 'Unless you can guarantee that happening within the next few weeks, I cannot afford to take chances. I want you to arrange a deliberate intervention.'

Bacon's tone softened. 'James, can you guarantee Matthew McCarthy's government will stop their insane plans to wreck our entire manufacturing industry, decimate mining interests and virtually isolate Australia from its established world markets? Or can you at least ensure the Commonwealth Anti-Illegal Drug Bill can be stopped?

'As you know, I am not one to sit on my arse and wait for things to happen. There's too much at stake!'

James Fleming drew a deep breath. He knew what was coming. 'No, of course I can't. However, before you say what I know you're going to say next, I want you to understand this. Things are going to get a whole lot uglier than they are now if you want to move to the next stage. And, if it all goes to shit and I go down, I'll make sure I take you with me.'

'Don't threaten me, you fucking arse-bandit. You know who you have to thank for your palatial North Shore mansion with all its trimmings and the power you hold. I also make it possible for you to satisfy your perverted sexual appetite.

'I put you where you are and it comes with a price. It's time for you to pay your dues. So, do not ever forget who you're talking to and who really holds the reins. Now, keep your end of the bargain and get on with eliminating the problem once and for all!'

++++++++++++

Chapter Five

'Oh God Matt, what are we getting into?' Catherine McCarthy cried, shaking her long, blonde hair in despair. 'I am terrified you're going to be killed next. Do you have to take on the top job? I thought you were just going to help steer the government's policies on climate change?'

Australia's newest prime minister studied his wife's tear-stained features. Although they'd been married for over twenty years, he could not get over how gorgeous she looked. He thought himself a very fortunate man to have married a woman so intelligent and supportive and although he could understand her concern, he believed desperately in the need to take the nation's political reins at this time.

With Connor Bowker dead, the likelihood of anyone else pushing ahead with the reforms necessary to combat climate change was zero. Am I being arrogant and conceited to think I have what it takes to run the country and steer it through such radical reforms? he wondered.

'Cathy, I understand how you feel. I really do and I think perhaps we need to think about measures to protect you and the kids because I know we're all targets now.

'I don't want to appear melodramatic or conceited but you know how important this is. There's simply no one who's going to stand up to the unions and the captains of industry now Connor Bowker's gone. The rest of them will just fall in a spineless, vacillating heap like they always have. This problem the world faces is bigger than our individual needs.'

'You know I've always backed you, Matthew. I'm just scared for the children, that's all. How can we protect them? We don't even know who we're dealing with.'

McCarthy crossed the room and sat next to his wife. Putting an arm around her shoulders, he hugged her. 'Sweetheart, I'm sure if I talk to Stormy Knight he'll have some suggestions as to where you and the kids can go where your safety can be assured.'

'I'm not leaving you.' Catherine McCarthy smiled weakly. 'We've never spent more than a night or two apart in twenty years and I'm not going to start now. What makes you think we'll be any safer out of the country? Until we know who's behind this, it's better we stay here.

'I guess it's the price the kids and I pay for being stuck with someone so bloody popular and clever. Commissioner Knight will just have to do his best to protect us at the Lodge, although I don't relish being under virtual house arrest.'

'You know that I didn't ever want the rotten, bloody job or to get into politics, but I'm scared for the future of our kids. If you really want me to decline the prime ministership I will.

'Maybe, I'm just being egotistical to think I can make any difference. Perhaps the forces of greed and self-interest are just too great.'

'Matthew McCarthy, I would never ask you to compromise your beliefs. I wouldn't respect you if you did, and even if you did, you couldn't live with yourself.

Whether you meant it to or not, resentment at the lost opportunity to do something meaningful would drive a huge wedge between us if you walked away when you're needed. I'm sorry I am so upset. The world would be a hell of a better place if there were more people like you.'

'I don't know about that my darling but I do know I am so glad I have you,' Matthew said warmly. He kissed his wife and then added, 'Oh, while we're talking about security, did you know Stormy's found a federal copper who's a scuba diver to be my personal bodyguard?'

'That's a bonus. I'm pleased for you. You'll need your diving to let off steam.'

Shortly after his son's appointment to the prime ministership following Bowker's assassination, John McCarthy, had shaken his head in frustration on the opposite side of the country. 'Doc, I am not taking any more bloody pills. I've been trying to tell you for years, you're just treating the symptoms, not the cause. I want to stop taking all this bloody rubbish. It doesn't work anymore. All the medication's done is turn me into a drug addict.'

'But John, you need something for pain,' Doctor Wiltshire, his family doctor reasoned. 'Besides, you're depressed.'

John McCarthy's frustration flared. 'Of course I'm depressed! You try living with chronic pain every day for fifteen years and see if you're not depressed. The best cure for my depression is for you to find the cause of the pain and eradicate it. I guarantee the depression would vanish overnight.'

Wiltshire sighed. His blue eyes seemed to bore holes in his sixty-three-year-old patient's skull as he struggled to contain his exasperation. 'John, we can't find a single cause for your pain. Your body has been subjected to the ravages of chemicals from the work you did and you've been through so many different physical and emotional traumas in your life that your system has simply rebelled, sending you pain from all over your body when there's nothing physically wrong. It's called chronic fatigue and fibromyalgia or CFME.'

'Well, I'm not taking pills any more. I'm going to wean myself off them.'

'No problem. If you want to do that, you'll have to do it very slowly. Methadone is a very potent drug and it takes a long time to quit. I suggest that for the first week, you choose one day where you take half a dose. The next week, choose another day where'll you take half the dosage. The third week, choose a third day and so on until you're taking half the dose every day, then begin cutting the dose down by half again and so on.

'The other medications, particularly Avanza, which you need for depression, can be reduced by the same method. But do it slowly, John,' Wiltshire cautioned. 'Come back and see me in a couple of weeks and let me know how you're going.

'Oh, and by the way, pass on my congratulations to your son. He's got a hell of a battle on his hands but if he's as tough as his old man, he'll make a great prime minister.'

John McCarthy left his doctor's surgery fiercely determined to eradicate his drug dependency. For the previous fifteen years he'd shuffled between doctors and read everything he could find on the mysterious debilitating illness that had ruined his life and threatened his marriage. It didn't help that the so-called experts had finally given a label to the dreadful pains and overwhelming fatigue that racked his entire body daily.

Unconvinced as to the accuracy of the diagnosis, he'd nevertheless gone along with the tag ascribed to his affliction, even allowing a pain specialist to hospitalise and sedate him with the horse tranquilliser Ketamine in what had proved a futile attempt to reset his central nervous system. When that didn't work, the pain specialist had prescribed a cocktail of methadone, anti-depressants and medications normally used to treat epilepsy in an attempt to dull the pain. That his patient would become addicted was secondary to the specialist's personal desperation at his inability to relieve the strange affliction.

Now, the receptors in McCarthy's brain had become so used to the drugs, they no longer worked but he faced a quandary. If he didn't take the medication, the withdrawal symptoms were even worse than the symptoms they were supposed to alleviate.

As a former policeman, John McCarthy hated illegal drugs. Worse still, he despised drug addicts, believing they were spineless and that drug pushers were worse than sewage scum. Having absolutely no sympathy for anyone who willingly ingested or injected addictive, mind-altering substances, he believed any addiction could be overcome with willpower.

He was about to discover that his own courage and

determination would be tested to the very limit.

Upon returning to his suburban home, McCarthy decided he'd use the time while his wife was at work to expand his knowledge of methadone and its effects. Surfing the internet, he discovered site after site outlining the terrible toll the drug has upon the human body and the almost impossible hurdle faced by those who wish to overcome their reliance upon the mind-altering chemical substitute for heroin.

Entering the name Shriver Pharmaceuticals, McCarthy typed Septaphycine, Shriver's brand name for the methadone-based tablets he'd been prescribed into the web page's search box and clicked "search." Shriver Pharmaceuticals' colourful home page soon filled the screen.

Scanning through the usual anti-litigious warnings on the drug's possible side-effects, John was shocked by the chemical giant's revelation that cessation of Septaphycine could result in death of the patient.

'Bullshit!' he snorted. 'I don't accept that.'

The former policeman continued surfing. Finally, he stumbled upon a blog from an American doctor offering a ray of hope.

Although the article was a hastily typed strategy for withdrawing from methadone, John McCarthy realised that the information originated from someone with firsthand experience. Clearly, the author was not only a doctor who had helped many addicts, but a man who had beaten his personal demons.

"....*although others may tell you, you will die if you stop taking methadone, you will not! That is a lie perpetuated by drug companies who make enormous profits from people who believe their deception. However, make no mistake, you will certainly feel as if you are going to die!*

"Methadone is a potent drug with twice the half-life of heroin and is harder to kick than the heroin addiction for which it is so often prescribed.

"You will need emotional, medical and physical support and it is strongly advised that you seek assistance from an in-house program for drug addicts. Those who try to stop invariably fail if they try to do it alone.

"Do not believe medicos who tell you it is possible to wean yourself off the drug gradually. In my experience you cannot. At some stage, the addict must go through the dreadful phase that follows when the chemical receptors in the brain are deprived of the drug. Whether that happens from total and immediate withdrawal or later after gradually diminishing the dosage will make little difference.

"To be successful, any program for treating methadone withdrawal must be based upon good nutrition and unfortunately few doctors fully understand the body's nutritional needs, nutrition being a subject merely skimmed over during medical training.

"The body and mind of the methadone addict can be likened to a house damaged by a severe storm. Methadone will have taken its toll on your body's cells and even your brain, inflicting major damage. And just as a house wrecked by a storm must be re-built using lumber, shingles, nails, cement and other materials, your body requires certain chemicals, vitamins and nutrition so it can repair itself."

The article went on to list numerous natural substances and prescription medications necessary to help patients through the lengthy rehabilitation phase. Taking copious notes, John McCarthy soaked up every word.

Although the author offered hope, John realised he was in for a horrible time over the six weeks it would take until his system could repair the damage and his brain's receptors no longer bedevilled him with their need for satisfaction.

'I'll book myself into a drug treatment program if that's what it takes,' he told himself.

Unfortunately, he could find no suitable facility in his home state of Western Australia. Existing treatment programs were designed purely for those addicted to heroin, cocaine, methamphetamines or other illegal street drugs. Treatments appeared to consist of a strategy of substitution, advocating methadone as a safe replacement. In other words, released from the wicked clutches of faceless drug barons, only to be forever ensnared by the tentacles of some profit-motivated pharmaceutical giant, addicts just swapped the evil monkey of illicit drugs that clung to their backs and made life hell, for the illusion of a legal and more socially acceptable primate which was nonetheless physically and mentally demanding.

"Bugger that!" McCarthy determined.

Although John McCarthy knew he had only to pick up the telephone and call his son in Canberra for Matthew to foot the massive fees charged by overseas and interstate drug treatment clinics, he knew such a course of action could unleash a virtual Pandora's Box of problems. As the country's new leader, his son had enough to contend with, without the media frenzy having a father in drug rehab would create. It would matter not that the addiction resulted from legally prescribed medication which had not been over-used, the tabloids and his son's political opponents would relish the chance to throw mud and score points.

'In other words,' he muttered despairingly, 'I'll just have to do it alone! If I use a Western Australian based clinic I'll never become drug-free, just a lifelong prisoner of pharmaceutical companies who literally have a captive clientele.'

Hoping the internet article was inaccurate on the subject of gradual withdrawal, McCarthy senior decided to take his doctor's advice and gradually reduce his dosage. On the first day, he noticed little difference. However, the second day he began feeling decidedly unwell. Despite the fact that he'd shaved only a small amount from the tiny white pill, his brain knew immediately. Nevertheless, he persisted.

After the first week, he realised the internet doctor had been correct. Shaving the tablets down a little more each day to slowly reduce the dosage only prolonged the agony.

As a policeman, he'd often witnessed addicts suffering withdrawal symptoms in the cells following their arrest. The cold sweats, terrible tremors, skin-crawling itch, aching muscles, hallucinations, nightmares and insomnia they described became his tormented reality. At night, drained of energy but unable to sleep, he tossed and turned upon the lounge room floor, seeking a position acceptable to his shaking, fever-ridden body.

Nothing helped. Often he'd simply crawl into the foetal position, grit his teeth and hug himself tightly, praying for sleep and even death.

Each minute seemed like an hour of pain-racked hell and every hour was a lifetime.

After a week of endless, lonely, horror-filled nights, he was ready to concede defeat. Going to the pantry cupboard he reached for the Septaphycine packet. Picking it up John stared at the label, his hand shaking violently. Disgusted with himself, he muttered angrily, 'No, I am not going back now. I'm stronger than that!'

After savagely ripping open the foil sachets he flushed all the tablets down the sink.

'There's no going back now that's done,' he muttered to himself, throwing his body exhaustedly into a chair to wait for daylight.

'John, you can't keep going like this,' his wife Mary declared from the doorway.

Hearing him thrashing about she had come from their bedroom to check that he was okay. The dark shadows beneath her normally bright blue eyes, told him she had been awake worrying about him all night.

'You've got to get help,' she announced, running her fingers through her blonde curls. Although the years were beginning to show in the lines around her mouth and eyes, to him she was still a beautiful woman with the kindest heart he'd ever known.

'There's no one who can really help me. I've just got to get through it. Don't worry darling. I won't die,' he told her grimly. 'I've got as many of the natural pills and potions that the internet site recommended that I can find. If I could just get some sleep, it would make a hell of a difference. I'll go and see the doctor tomorrow for some sleeping pills just to tide me over.'

It took nearly six full weeks for his symptoms to ease; six weeks that had tested his resolve, his body and his sanity to breaking point. Then, just when he thought he'd won, the addiction gargoyle reared up to kick him anew as if it had merely been toying with him until this point.

I'm not going back now. I've been through too much to waste all that pain and suffering.

Seven weeks after throwing the medications away, the nightmare finally stopped. However, having existed on less than two hours' broken sleep each night for the past fifty days, he was physically, emotionally and mentally exhausted. He wanted nothing more than the blessed release of uninterrupted sleep, but his tormented brain would not shut down. He now had to retrain it to cope without medication.

That took another year.

Although Mary had done her best to support John throughout the ordeal, nobody but another reformed addict could possibly appreciate the enormity of the hurdle he had overcome.

Paradoxically, he now had less sympathy for drug addicts. But his hatred for those who perpetuated what is undoubtedly the biggest blight of modern times multiplied exponentially, even embracing doctors who too-readily prescribed addictive medications and extending to pharmaceutical companies who profited from the desperate millions trapped in a pervasive web of legalised drug addiction.

'I don't quite know how to go about it, Mary, but this nightmare has made me determined to help fight the evil of not only illicit drugs but legally sanctioned substances, such as Septaphycine.

'I know I'm not a copper any more but having been through the hardest battle of my life, I really appreciate the suffering others go through. No one should have to endure what I have experienced over the past seven weeks.'

'What do you have in mind?'

'I am not sure but maybe Matt will have some ideas. It would be good to get some purpose and direction back into my life and it might help distract me from the pain.'

+++++++++++++

Chapter Six

When Turnbull had been elected to the presidency, he aspired to address climate change as a matter of top priority. Knowing the crisis the world faced, he, like his Australian counterpart Bowker, resolved to tackle the issue head on. What he had not fully understood was the mammoth scale of his country's economic woes. That these could largely be attributed to the ineptitude of his grandstanding predecessor did not lessen the anger he felt at the mess he now had to clean up.

In Turnbull's opinion and that of many Americans, the previous administration had not only ruined the country's economy with its failure to deal with the financial excesses of greedy Wall Street financiers, it had tarnished America's international standing and its credibility through flawed foreign policies. Additionally, few would argue that the Iraq War had been a disaster, needlessly costing the lives of thousands of the nation's finest young men. Although many would still argue that the ends justified the means and an unorthodox war could not be won using orthodox methods, America could no longer hold its head high. Crossing the line of decency and humanity and justice with the so-called interdiction of suspected terrorists, the U.S. was, in the Panther's opinion, no better than the inhumane monsters it faced in the never-ending "war on terror".

In addition, his predecessor had deliberately chosen not to address the looming threat of climate change, choosing self-interest, greed, personal power and immediate gratification over the future of the world's children.

If the contents of documents outlining the previous administration's cavalier attitude to environmental problems now in President Turnbull's possession were ever revealed, they had the potential to shock the nation to its core.

Like the tentacles of some evil octopus, the web of corruption, deceit and lies encircled the globe, linking most world leaders and their governments to a conspiracy to impose a new world order that would continue to increase the divide between rich and poor.

Somehow the Panther had to unravel the mess and although he was said to be the world's most powerful man, his friends grew fewer while his often faceless enemies proliferated.

For that reason he had looked forward to Connor Bowker's presence at the financial conference. Now, with Bowker gone, the president understood his successor, McCarthy, could ill-afford to leave the country to the treachery of boardroom zealots and ruthless political opportunists.

Filled with an eclectic buzz as hundreds of people conversed in a dozen languages, the Great Hall of the Danish Parliament was akin to a massive wasps' nest. A warning bell brought an end to the cacophony of confusion, warning delegates, translators, hangers-on, reporters and carefully screened spectators to take their places.

The international conference convened to discuss the global financial catastrophe sweeping the world was about to begin.

It was all carefully orchestrated to avoid showing

favouritism. Each day over the course of the week-long talkfest, delegates and their entourages filtered through the many doors around the perimeter of the ornately decorated and historic building. They made their way to prearranged tiers of temporary seating that had been erected around the parquetry floor of the enormous oval amphitheatre and took their seats, gabbling noisily.

As the debate commenced, all eyes turned expectantly toward the chairman, a rotund, balding man with pince-nez spectacles balanced precariously on the end of his whisky-veined nose. As chairman of the World Bank, Salvatore Fiorini was one of the world's most influential men. He relished his power and enjoyed being on the world stage, addressing the conference with prolonged and pompous opening harangues.

To spare themselves the tedium of introductory debate and Fiorini's political posturing, many of the Third World's tin pot despots and leaders from the more powerful and wealthy First World nations avoided the conference until the final day. No different than most who find themselves in positions of power and influence, they hoped to grab kudos while avoiding the sweat and toil of discussion, negotiation and the laborious assembly of any workable compromise.

It was unfortunate that the new American president chose to listen to his political advisers' counsel that his attendance would have a more positive impact if left to the last minute.

It was to prove the event's downfall. The eleventh hour arrival of the world's most powerful figures displayed monumental contempt for humanities' second greatest crisis ever.

'The little bastard's a pain in the arse. I wish he'd get on with it.' The Panther leant over and whispered in the ear of Harvey Ledbetter, his personal adviser. Although such comments could be extremely damaging politically, the President and Ledbetter had been friends since schooldays and trusted each other implicitly.

Ledbetter hid his answering grin, pretending to cough into his fist. 'Anyone less than five-feet-six should never hold a position of authority. Small man syndrome,' he explained unnecessarily.

With the global financial crisis threatening the very stability of governments, the Panther knew he stood little chance of convincing world leaders of the need to keep their eyes on the ball regarding climate change. The rapidly overheating planet was destined to come a poor second to self-interest and the universal desire to keep one's snout in the constituent-funded troughs of wealth, privilege and status.

Nevertheless, when it was his turn to speak, the American president did his utmost. He decided to speak from the heart, decrying the carefully prepared speech from his advisors as too much of the same wishy washy drivel espoused by other delegates.

The Panther spoke at great length on the reasons for the world's mammoth financial woes. Accepting America's negligence in not reeling in the excesses of its corporate giants and its failure to implement the necessary checks and balances to prevent irresponsible lending by financial institutions had played a huge part in the GFC. He urged participating nations to treat the crisis as an unprecedented opportunity to restructure their financial systems and pull together to ensure an equitable division of wealth and living standards for Third World countries. While delegates listened attentively to this aspect of the president's speech his arguments for sustainable living and proposals to spend heavily on the development of *green* infrastructure projects and phase out fossil fuel use were met by stunned silence. No one had expected Turnbull to even mention climate change, let alone link it to the world's fiscal dilemma.

As the president resumed his seat, the Chinese delegate and that country's finance minister, Xian Yang Bao, jumped to his feet. Clearly agitated, the diminutive although portly Chinese began speaking in faultless, unaccented English deriding the United States and placing the blame for both the financial crisis and climate change on America's doorstep. Clearly China was unprepared to compromise on its rampant growth and aspirations for its people to enjoy higher living standards.

In the ensuring hubbub, delegates from other nations echoed China's rejection. While New Zealand and other small Pacific nations supported the US president's proposals, as the debate wore on, it soon became apparent there would be no consensus.

Although the Panther had guessed this would be the outcome, he had at least sparked a conflagration of international discussion; a major coup in itself. While there would be no real progress on fighting climate change, he had left the world in no doubt as to his personal position.

The conference concluded after barely two days of discussion with delegates agreeing to inject vast sums into their country's financial systems to further stimulate consumer spending.

As the cornerstone of commerce, banks were the big winners despite also being to blame in part for the world's monetary woes. Although some nations planned to inject capital into roads and other infrastructure, few planned to make anything more than a token gesture toward developing alternative energy sources or restructuring their heavily polluting transport systems.

Generally speaking, it was to be business as usual.

The only exception was Australia.

Clement Arthur Turnbull returned to America where memory of his controversial announcement quickly faded in the face of yet another crisis.

Amid freezing temperatures and snow flurries the US President left Air Force One and hurried across the tarmac to the enormous bulk of the waiting military helicopter. The great machine's drooping rotors began turning as soon as its doors closed. It rose into the murky, grey clouds that hung pall-like over the airport.

An escort of four F15 fighter jets immediately took up position around the massive Chinook helicopter to ensure there was no violation of the safety buffer around the President's aircraft and Washington airspace. With so many hostile nations baying for American blood lunatic elements loose throughout the United States, an attack on the world's most powerful man could never be ruled out.

The atmosphere in the White House Situation Room in the West Wing was electric.

A five-thousand-square-foot facility operating twenty-four hours a day, the "Sit Room" is in fact comprised of multiple rooms adjoining a central conference room. Equipped with the latest in high-tech wizardry, the facility has been in continual use since the Bay of Pigs to deal with every crisis affecting national security. Now, with the nation's top military and political figures all present, the sheer quantity of ribbons, braid and medals festooning dress uniforms was almost bedazzling.

As the President entered, the generals rose as one in deference to their commander-in-chief. The Panther waved a hand in acknowledgment. Eager to begin the briefing he addressed the group.

'Okay, I understand from the briefing I received on Air Force One that that North Korean madman Kim Jon Il has now ordered the mobilisation of his country's entire military. South Korean President Park is worried about the imminent invasion of South Korea and Japan has threatened retaliation if North Korea fires any more test missiles into the Sea of Japan. What else have we got?'

A burly, middle-aged four star general cleared his throat and waved for an aid to illuminate one of six giant plasma television screens dominating the room. Satellite images immediately filled the screen.

'Mr President, these pictures were taken within the last hour from the new generation of high resolution cameras on board the recently-launched Genesis satellite. We detected unprecedented activity in a mountainous area of the country's north-east inland from Chongjin which we have long suspected as hiding some sort of underground facility.

'As you know, we've been worried that since the

North Koreans retreated on promises not to develop nuclear warheads and enrich their plutonium they've been throwing everything into enriching uranium for their nuclear warheads.

'The recent upgrading of a narrow dirt track so that it is now a sealed highway leading only to a small peasant village obviously set alarm bells ringing. We've concentrated surveillance on the area and it is apparent from the type of equipment and heavy machinery now using the road, the North Koreans have established an extensive underground facility.

'Is there any chance it could just be a mine?' the President interrupted.

'No sir,' General Bayliss replied. 'We know it's not a mine because they never bring anything out the entrance to the complex except dirt and rocks which they've been using as road base for the highway upgrade. In addition, they've heavily fortified approaches to the area.

'As you can see on the screen, those are military vehicles moving along the highway. What's under the canopies remains a secret but we suspect they've been ferrying in missile components.

'Now let me show you the next set of images.'

The screen flickered briefly and General Bayliss used a laser pointer to indicate a dark circular shape almost hidden by surrounding undergrowth. All eyes in the room locked on close-up photographs of something which was clearly out of place on the snow-clad Korean hillside.

'What you're seeing here is undoubtedly the lid of an underground missile bunker. The North Koreans have done a pretty good job of concealment. They've even planted vegetation on the lid and if it hadn't been for the new generation cameras on the Genesis satellite we wouldn't have picked it up.

'Now, here's an actual shot taken at night with infrared cameras showing the same lid open. We suspect they were testing it under cover of darkness and didn't anticipate or didn't really care about our "eye in the sky."

'The dimensions of the shaft are inconsistent with those of the Taepodong rockets they've been testing recently. This shaft suggests a much larger missile. Although we know existing North Korean rockets have the ability to reach Hawaii, we do not know if they have secretly developed something capable of reaching the United States mainland.'

Turning to his CIA chief, Director Jerome "Jerry" Robson, President Turnbull enquired, 'What's your spin on this Jerry?'

Robson's tanned, cannon-ball head reflected the overhead lighting and he fingered his bushy moustache thoughtfully.

'Mr President, we've been listening to a hell of a lot of chatter through frequencies used by the North Koreans and it seems that the North Korean Mining and Development Corporation, aka KOMID, has been communicating regularly with some very real bad guys from the former USSR. By that I mean former KGB Colonel turned arms dealer, Yuri Divlenko, and some lesser players.

'As you know, KOMID is just North Korea's front for arms dealing and the DPRK has previously sold weapons to Syria and Iran and imported nuclear capability from Pakistan.

'Our sources in the Ukraine where Divlenko now operates have monitored covert meetings with key figures from Kim Jon Il's regime and KOMID. Divlenko has the wherewithal to access sophisticated nuclear weapons from the former Soviet empire's arsenal and he even has the capability to get disassembled weaponry into North Korea using any one of a number of decommissioned but still operable former USSR submarines.'

The President looked suitably shocked. 'So, I guess you're telling me we have to assume North Korea now has a new generation of nuclear weapons which their scientists may even have adapted to hit any target anywhere in the world?'

'That has to be our assumption until we prove otherwise,' Director Robson replied quietly. 'What is even more worrying; we now know they have also been supplying the Taliban.'

'What!' Turnbull exclaimed, shocked. Turning to his phalanx of generals, he said grimly, 'Nobody's mentioned biological weapons yet. Even if Kim Jon Il does not have long-range nuclear capability, we have to assume he has some nasty surprises that he can lob on the West. It seems there is no end to the lengths he'll go to knowing we'll ultimately just pay him off rather than risk bloodshed.

'It's bad enough that they sponsor illegal drug operations and try flooding us with counterfeit dollars but now they've gone too far. We've resisted bombing their military installations up until now because we did not want to risk having them hit Japan with Rodong missiles provoking an unholy war.

'Generals, I trust you've already taken the appropriate defensive action at this point?'

The Generals nodded in unison. General Bayliss broke the momentary silence brought on by the President's scenario of biological warfare. 'We have indeed, Mr President. As we speak, three of our military satellites have been positioned to watch North Korean military installations and unmanned drones are flying along the border between South and North Korea airspace. We're ready to encroach upon that space immediately there is any sign of hostility.

'More importantly perhaps, we have the nuclear submarine *Ulysses* on standby in the Sea of Japan off Chongjin ready to shoot down anything launched from North Korea.'

Addressing the United Secretary of State next, the Panther directed, 'Colin, we had better speak to the Chinese and see if they will intercede before that lunatic Kim finally oversteps and unleashes a holocaust upon the world. We also need to request the UN to convene immediately. Sanctions don't seem to be very effective against North Korea but we've got to let them know we will not tolerate this latest fiasco. We need to know China's position if we have to strike strategic DPRNK targets.

'In the meantime, we cannot just leave it to the *Ulysses* to knock out missiles; we must create an impenetrable shield. I'll leave it to the navy to decide how best to do this but increasing our anti-missile capability as soon as possible is absolutely crucial.

'If those mad bastards pull the trigger do not hesitate to hit them hard and fast.

'Let me know what you decide and when it will be in place.

'Now, let's move on to other matters. Update me on the latest with the situation in Afghanistan and Pakistan. I don't want to discuss Iraq. They've got to sort out their own problems now we no longer have military involvement. There's no way we're going to get mixed up in that mess again even if my predecessor did create it!'

By anyone's standards, the Iraqi situation looked exceedingly grim, but because America's fingers had been burnt by the previous US administration's invasion on the thinly disguised pretence of fighting terrorism, the new American President refused to return troops to the region, choosing instead to supply Iraq's military in the hope the largely corrupt government would not crumble.

It was a dangerous game of Russian roulette.

Meanwhile, in Afghanistan, Taliban resurgence continued. With Pakistani forces unable to crush the lunatic Islamic fundamentalist group, the Taliban were growing increasingly bold and powerful. The added threat brought about by North Korea's support added an entirely new dimension to an already dire situation.

All attention was now on the president's foreign advisor. He began his summation hesitatingly. 'Mr President, unrest is worsening in Kabul. The Mustafa regime seems powerless to stop suicide bombings and rocket attacks by Taliban insurgents.

'General Mustafa's postponement of the promised

general election and his recent declaration of martial law appeared to be a step in the right direction and we thought for a time he could control his military commanders and push the Taliban out. Unfortunately, it seems that there are too many Taliban sympathisers within the Pakistani army and its air force. Entire divisions have mutinied, taking their weapons with them as they shift allegiance to side with the Islamic fundamentalists.

'Mustafa is still refusing to give permission for America and its allies to enter his country and eliminate Taliban strongholds, insisting Pakistan will triumph, but it is my view and the view of most in this room that the Pakistani government will soon fall.

'India will not countenance the prospect of Pakistan's nuclear arsenal falling into the hands of the Taliban. We all know they are the most repressive bloodthirsty maniacs since Attila the Hun. Its military is poised to invade and they have made no bones about the fact that they will use their full might, including nuclear weapons, to destroy the Taliban if they seize control of Pakistan.'

The US President paced the room, hands clasped behind his back, head bowed and deep in thought, he swore, 'Shit! Is there any good news?'

It was a rhetorical question. The Panther and everyone in the Situation Room understood that not since the Cuban missile crisis of the Kennedy era had the world been so close to a nuclear apocalypse.

With so many unscrupulous lunatics controlling nations it seemed just a matter of time before one of them unleashed events resulting in catastrophic worldwide nuclear war.

++++++++++++

Chapter Seven

Just to the north of Australia lies the world's most populous Islamic nation; Indonesia. The politically unstable nation is an archipelago of hundreds of islands, many of whose two hundred and twenty million or so people live in abject poverty. Paradoxically, there is also great wealth but that wealth is controlled by a small but powerful minority.

As with many struggling nations, disaffection flourishes wherever individuals have little hope, creating an ideal recruiting ground for religious fundamentalists and political reactionaries. People of their ilk understand only too well how easy it is to manipulate the minds of the desperate with promises of a better life if they join the cause.

Understanding the huge threat it faces from such massive numbers should the Indonesian government fall into the hands of Islamic fundamentalists; Australia has done its utmost to shore up the political stability of its closest neighbour. Despite having less than one tenth of Indonesia's population, every year Australia sends millions of dollars in aid, trains Indonesia's military and educates many of its citizens at Australian universities.

Cynics might say Australia is simply paying protection money.

However, despite Australia being a good neighbour and generous benefactor, millions of Indonesians hate Australians with a focussed and vicious intensity. And no one group hates Australia more than Jemaah Islamiyah.

Accredited with the murder of hundreds of

Westerners through suicide bombings and with links to Al Qaeda, the terrorist group is ruthless and bloodthirsty. In a country where corruption is almost an art form, attempts by the Indonesian government to outlaw the organisation and gaol its terrorist membership have somehow always failed.

In a nondescript apartment building in one of Jakarta's back streets, a small group of six young Indonesian men sat cross-legged on prayer mats, listening with rapt attention to their spiritual mentor. The gangly, white-bearded fanatic and hater of all things Western grinned at them with his large, yellow, horse-like teeth. His lined, seventy-year-old features resembled cracked yellow parchment and his brown eyes flared with manic zeal.

'With their prime minister dead, this is the ideal time to bring the Great Satan's puppet to its knees. We will strike the Australian infidels now while they are most vulnerable.

'Since the execution of our heroic brothers for their courageous sacrifices in Bali they may think they are safe. They fail to understand that Allah has rewarded our brothers with eternal life in his heavenly kingdom where they are each served by fifty beautiful virgins.

'Their memory and the beauty of the sacrifice they made will not be forgotten and now it is your turn to earn the same reward.

'You have each been chosen as the very special servants of Allah because you speak the language of the infidel dog and you have the intelligence to act out your part.

'This will be a great thing you do in the name of

Allah and for the people of Islam who will soon drive out all infidels and claim the world as their rightful inheritance.

'Arrangements are in place. When you each leave here you will separate. You will not contact each other again. You will not discuss what you are about to do. You will not mention the holy name of Jemaah Islamiyah for there are many who would rejoice in your failure. You will wait and carry on your lives as normal until a messenger comes with your instructions and details of what you must do when you reach Australia.

'Do you understand?'

'We do,' they nodded as one, faces alight with zealous intensity.

'Allahu Akbar!' yelled the cleric stridently.

'Allahu Akbar!' the young men cried in unison as they bowed and kissed the floor in supplication.

Over the space of the following week, the Indonesian cleric's messenger delivered sealed packages to each of the six would-be jihadists. The packages contained return airline tickets to Canberra, Sydney, Melbourne, Brisbane, Adelaide and Sydney along with details of hotel bookings and wads of Australian currency. The jihadists were also provided with Western style business suits, credit cards, the normal trappings associated with their purported occupations and Indonesian passports.

The passports were fakes. The airline tickets were intended for one-way use.

Upon reaching their respective Australian destinations, they were to each book into preselected hotels and await further instructions. Each man understood that if questioned as to the reason for his visit, he was to reply that he was looking for real estate opportunities on behalf of Indonesian investors.

The prevailing easterly wind carried dust from the great heart of the Australian continent, blowing thousands of kilometres to the drought-stricken eucalypts of Perth's Darling Scarp. It had been the hottest, driest summer since European settlement of Australia's most isolated city. With temperatures hovering above forty-two degrees Celsius for the preceding five days, the tinder-dry bush crackled in protest as the die-back-stunted gums bent in submission to the gusty furnace-hot winds.

In the hillside suburbs of Mundaring, Parkerville, Glen Forrest and further south in Kalamunda and Lesmurdie, residents sweltered in the face of the state government's ban on air conditioner use. Gardens had long since died under necessarily Draconian sprinkler bans. With the state's dams and underground aquifers severely depleted, authorities could ill afford to waste precious water and the ailing electricity network was unable to cope with the enormous and ever-growing demand for energy.

Assisted by the easterly wind at their backs, the three teenagers rocketed along the dusty track beside the disused rail path, their mountain bikes raising puffs of dust in their wake. Suddenly, the leading boy's hands clamped down on his brake levers, locking the heavily studded tyres of his bicycle. Throwing the machine in an exaggerated broadside, he skidded to a stop surrounded on all sides by bristling, thorny scrub.

'Hey, watch this!'

The lanky, pimply-faced youth dropped his bicycle beside the track and knelt down amid the undergrowth. Flicking the wheel of a plastic disposable cigarette lighter, he set light to the prickly acacia pulchella fringing the gravelly track.

'Okay, let's get outta here,' he yelled to his mates. 'We'll light up half a dozen more fires along the way and then we can watch the fun.'

'Yeah!' his companions bellowed joyfully. Giving each other high fives, they pedalled frantically away from the rapidly spreading conflagration.

'Yahoo. The sky will soon be full of water bombers and choppers. There'll be fire engines and sirens like you've never seen before,' pimply-face bellowed.

Lacking any concept of the tragedy they had unleashed, the juvenile arsonists belted along the pathway flicking lighted matches into the scrub at random before emerging from the bush some ten kilometres from the first fire. Already, the air was heavy with the acrid stench of burning. The sun appeared through the dense yellow-brown smoke as an ominously red ball as the scream of distant fire engines could be heard as volunteer bush fire groups rallied their pathetically inadequate resources.

Faces now ashen at the realisation of what they'd unleashed, the three teenagers sat astride their bicycles as a giant yellow helicopter raced eastward to the blaze. Already, six separately-lit fires had coalesced into one enormous blaze that thundered through the thickly forested hill suburbs.

Despite annual warnings to clear gutters of leaves

and remove trees that fire prevention experts considered too close to houses, most residents had not listened. Many homes in Perth Hills were consequently firetraps.

John and Mary McCarthy were just sitting down to lunch when they first smelled smoke. Going outside onto the veranda of their brick, colonial-style Darlington home, John was shocked to see burning embers raining from the smoke-filled sky. Although he could not yet see the flames a distant roar carried across the valley from the east.

'Jesus, it sounds like a bloody Jumbo jet!' he exclaimed.

'What is it darling?' One glance at her husband's terrified expression was enough for her to know the event most hills residents feared had finally arrived; a huge fire engulfing the entire Darling Scarp.

'We gotta get out of her now,' John told her grimly. 'That fire's going to be on us in a few minutes and we won't stand a chance.'

The McCarthys had discussed such an eventuality as this many times. Unlike many, they viewed the hills lifestyle as a gamble against inexorable disaster and had an emergency evacuation kit always at the ready. The kit contained their irreplaceable personal papers and insurance policies along with a few basic items needed to get through the first few days should they lose everything. Their cars were always parked facing outward and ignition keys were close at hand.

They grabbed the vital kit bag, and wasted no time getting into John's diesel-powered Nissan Patrol. As they negotiated their gravel driveway leading to the bitumen road outside their home, burning cinders pinged onto the car's paintwork. Small spot fires flared up all around them as the roaring flames seemed to take on a life of their own. The noise became deafening. Visibility was down to a few yards and John steered the vehicle through the smoke relying on his memory. Like enormous Roman candles, trees hundreds of metres away from the fire's front suddenly burst into flames. It was as if a giant hand was bombarding the forest with flaming missiles.

Every home they passed was ablaze. Had the occupants been trapped and burnt alive, they wondered, staring aghast at the blackened hulks of burning vehicles occupying garages and carports.

Knowing there was nothing they could do to save others; John McCarthy drove as fast as he dared. Reaching the highway, they turned westward passing several fire engines hurtling in the opposite direction. 'They haven't got a snowball's chance in hell of stopping it,' McCarthy called to his wife. 'I just hope the poor bastards don't get themselves trapped back there.'

Burning branches began crashing onto the highway around them as the forest on both sides of the Great Eastern Highway was engulfed. Through the car's windows the heat was intense. The Nissan's paint was already beginning to blister and the stench of burning rubber assailed their nostrils.

Mary was coughing and gasping now. Holding a towel over her nose and mouth against the smoke which somehow had penetrated the car's interior, she screamed hoarsely, 'I don't think we're going to make it.'

'We'll make it my girl,' John told her with a

confidence he didn't feel. 'We've been through too much to let a little old fire beat us.'

'Just in case we don't; I love you John McCarthy.'

'Shit!' John yelled suddenly, swerving the Nissan to avoid a blazing mass that appeared unexpectedly. The Nissan lurched onto its two right side wheels. Something struck the left side with a huge bang. For a terrifying second they were sure the vehicle would roll over into the leaping inferno along the roadside. With a bone-shuddering thump, they landed back on four wheels, their heads striking the hood lining as John brought the big four-wheel drive under control.

'Did ya see that Mary?'

'What on Earth was it?'

'It was a road-train. The whole bloody thing was ablaze.' John McCarthy did not add that he'd glimpsed the blackened almost unrecognisable shape of its driver still trapped in the burning cab. Hell's bells, he thought, his stomach suddenly churning. He felt his bowels loosen with a terror he'd never experienced throughout the many often life-threatening situations of a long police career. *Perhaps we won't make it if that bloke couldn't.*

Abruptly, the Nissan's engine died. The big RV ground to a halt. McCarthy turned the ignition key frantically. The engine did not respond. They were stuck. There was no escape. The roaring inferno surrounded them. They were about to fry.

Horrified, they wrapped their arms around each other. 'I'm sorry love,' John whispered in Mary's ear. Stinging-hot tears rolled down his cheeks as he tried to protect her with his own body.

Turning her face toward his, Mary kissed him tenderly. 'Good bye my beautiful husband,' she said, convinced they would be her final words.

All at once a deluge engulfed their vehicle. As the steam and spray cleared, the McCarthys turned in surprise to find they were sitting amid a cool clear oasis amid the wildfire.

'It was a water bomber Mary! A water bomber just dropped its load on us. We've been spared.'

With the hot metal of the car's blackened carcase sizzling, John turned the key again. The diesel motor growled, coughed and then burst into life with a throaty roar. As they made their way into the impenetrable blackness of the firestorm again, the welcoming site of large, red metropolitan fire tender appeared. The hulking, soot-stained monster stopped, looming over them, its lights flashing. A fire fighter beckoned that they should follow and the engine executed a U-turn. As they drew behind their savour, a curtain of fine spray began playing from nozzles connected to its onboard water tank, providing a life-saving, enveloping mist as the firemen guided them to safety.

Reaching the edge of the low hills providing a backdrop to the heavier population of the coastal plain, they discovered Perth submerged beneath a thick, filthy-yellow smoke blanket. Columns of denser black smoke rose through the murk from burning buildings on the flatlands below.

Now, not even the city dwellers were safe. The unrelenting easterly still howled, carrying embers from the ever-growing fire front across the city, igniting vast areas in a tragedy of unbelievable proportions.

'Oh, my God, it's as if somebody's taken a giant blow torch to Perth. Nobody ever foresaw a bushfire spreading so far,' John McCarthy groaned as they stared over the catastrophic spectacle from the relative safety of their vantage point.

Around them, fire trucks gathered, impotent in the face of nature's fury. Fire fighters blackened with soot and exhausted from their own hasty retreat from Dante's inferno mingled in small groups. They too were shocked beyond belief.

A tall fireman clad in his ash-stained protective suit approached. 'You two are so lucky to be alive. It was a miracle that water bomber pilot spotted your vehicle when he did. After dumping his load on top of you, he radioed for us to go and help you out.' The fire chief waved a yellow-suited arm toward the leaping wall of flames that stretched along the Darling Range as far as they could see. 'At that stage, we were convinced nobody could be alive in there.'

'We passed a fire crew heading in as we were coming out,' John told him. 'What about them? Are they okay?'

The fireman looked even grimmer. 'We had about six crews still in there when the fire just exploded unexpectedly in all directions. It's like a nuclear war zone. Everything's gone. Entire suburbs, shopping centres, everything. I don't think any of our boys and girls will be coming out of there now.'

'I am so sorry,' John replied, feeling stupid at the inadequacy of his words.

'At least we got the little bastards that started it!' The fireman gestured toward several police vehicles lined up beside the emergency disaster command post. McCarthy peered in the direction indicated. Three teenage boys, their heads in their hands, sobbed inconsolably in the rear of a patrol car.

'They just learnt that they killed their own families,' the fireman announced grimly. 'When these bloody kids start fires, they just don't understand the consequences. Where a fire of this intensity may have occurred once in a hundred years, it's likely to happen any time now. We're powerless to stop ones moving with such speed and ferocity. We just have to wait for them to burn themselves out.'

'Is there any way we could have been better prepared?'

'Not really. This fire just made a mockery of firebreaks and even roof mounted sprinkler systems. When you get an ember attack, howling winds throwing the fire across the tree tops and the heat is so great that it simply melts steel, nothing stands a chance. With successive summers getting hotter and longer we've now reached the stage where people will have to re-think their ideas of living amidst the trees and governments need to legislate against it. It's simply too dangerous.'

Mary squeezed John's hand. 'What are we going to do now?'

'You heard the man. There's nothing left. All the houses have gone. Our friends and neighbours have probably all perished and the trees have all been burnt. There's nothing left but ash and ruins.

'We've escaped with our lives and should consider ourselves fortunate. I don't know about you Mary, but I never want to go through that experience again. I think it's time to join Matt and Catherine in Canberra.'

It was a week before the fire finally ran out of fuel and fire fighters announced that they had the blaze under control. By that stage it was too late for hastily flown-in Californian and Canadian reinforcements to do anything but assist in the grim search for bodies. Meanwhile, Western Australia had not been the only area to experience colossal devastation. Similar fires had broken out in the Australian Capital Territory, New South Wales, Victoria and South Australia, making it impossible for interstate assistance to be sent to Perth.

Then, in a bitterly-cruel paradoxical twist of a nation reeling from the fires, cyclone Anika lashed the tropical coast of Queensland. destroying entire towns, flattening sugar cane plantations and flooding vast areas from Cairns to Brisbane. Across the simultaneously drought-stricken and flood-ravaged continent, the death toll numbered over eight hundred, far surpassing that of any previous catastrophe.

+++++++++++

Chapter Eight

Amid the turmoil of so many challenges in his first few days of office, Matthew McCarthy understood that no single individual could handle the enormous burden associated with overseeing the correct response to so many natural disasters. Therefore, like Churchill, he blessed the art of delegation which he was rapidly learning to master. Knowing there were far more knowledgeable, able and experienced generals than he could ever be in such important matters, he nevertheless maintained a guiding hand on the helm of the ship of state, steering it advisedly. While administering sympathy and promises of government aid to the victims and their families, he wondered if these calamitous events would persuade Australians to embrace measures essential for their very survival, or would their implementation be seen as too Draconian? Would he, like the US President, be forced to abandon the fight against climate change by the need to tackle the ever-growing forces of world-wide tyranny?

We simply cannot afford to be distracted by anything, he decided. No matter how dire other issues might be, they must not come between us and the need to avert a global apocalypse!

'Darling,' Catherine told him one night. 'You cannot keep pushing yourself so hard without some respite. You've been working almost nonstop the past two weeks. I know there is so much happening but you'll be no use to us, the nation, or yourself if you crack up from overwork and stress. Why don't you take that scuba diving bodyguard that Stormy Knight found for you and go diving somewhere nice?'

'It won't look too good if the media learn I'm off enjoying myself while the nation's grieving and the world's on the brink of a nuclear war,' McCarthy observed, stripping off the rumpled suit he'd worn for the previous sixteen, gruelling appointment-filled hours.

Catherine sighed in exasperation. 'Now you're starting to think like a politician instead of looking at what really matters. Since when did you start worrying about the critics? Let your PR people handle them.'

'Can't please all of the people all of the time and all that stuff, eh?' McCarthy laughed. 'As usual you're right my gorgeous wife,' he said thinking how beautiful she was lying there in her nightie as she waited for him to come to bed. 'Do you know, suddenly I don't feel quite so tired?' he said, staring pointedly at her still youthful breasts.

'Oh, you dirty old man,' she exclaimed, laughing as she followed the direction of his gaze. 'Is that behaviour befitting a prime minister?'

'Even prime ministers get horny you know. Let me take a quick shower and I'll show Australia's newest first lady some *very* un-prime-minister-like behaviour.'

After a torrid and magnificently exhausting love-making session, Matthew and Catherine McCarthy lay in each other's arms waiting for sleep to overtake them.

'Cath,' Matthew murmured, 'I've been worrying about my parents. They must be traumatised after the tragedy of the bushfire and losing their home and friends. It's great that they have chosen to come to

Canberra to be with us while they get back on their feet but they'll need a lot of emotional support and I simply can't hold their hands. I've been thinking the best therapy would for them to both be busy and active. What do you think of the idea of Dad becoming my personal security adviser? Mum will probably find plenty to keep her busy setting up a new home and spending time with Daniel and Sienna.'

Catherine propped herself up one elbow. It would be good for Daniel and Sienna to have their grandparents close by. Her long, curly locks tickled his nose. He sniffed her Opium perfume and began to feel aroused once more. 'Mmm,' she intoned thoughtfully, 'I thought that was Stormy's job, among other things.'

'Well, that's true. It is. But having Dad's ability to think outside the square and offer an alternative point of view would be a real advantage.'

'Is this your idea or his, Matt?'

'You're not just a pretty face, are you? He did ask me if there was some way he could get back into the workforce. His exact words were, "can you think of a role for a worn-out, old has-been cop to help a prime minister?"'

'I love your father very much but I would hate to think of him being put in danger as well as us.'

'When the old man learns just what a big job protecting us is, you won't be able to keep him out of it. Besides, the old bugger's always been able to look after himself. There'll be the ugly allegation of nepotism if I give him a job but if necessary, I'll pay him out of my own pocket.'

'He won't want payment. In fact, knowing John, he

wouldn't take it if he knew it was going to compromise you politically. Let him help as a semi-official unpaid adviser, Matthew. It's really what he needs after all he and Mary have been through.'

'Okay, and tomorrow I'll find time to talk to Dicky and see what sort of a dive buddy he's going to make. He should be good. Stormy tells me he used to be a navy clearance diver. He won some sort of bravery award in the first Gulf War.'

At first, AFP sergeant and former Royal Australian Navy Chief Petty Officer, Richard "Dicky" Nolan hadn't been able to believe his luck when he'd received a personal telephone call from Commissioner Knight asking him if he'd be interested in being the PM's personal minder. His colleagues in FEDPOL's close personal protection unit considered it a cushy number with a certain amount of personal prestige. The fact that it would allow him to also indulge his love of recreational diving at no expense was simply fantastic.

That morning however, things had begun to come unstuck when, he'd found the cheap "pay as you go" phone in his mailbox. With the phone was a typed cryptic unsigned note instructing him simply, "Keep this phone with you at all times until you hear from me!"

Richard Nolan's first thought was that this had something to do with the event in the Persian Gulf that had changed his life and defined him forever during the first Gulf War. Although he'd carved a new career since his navy days, guilt had continued to eat away at his soul like a malevolent cancer and in his heart he'd always wondered if his dreadful mistake would eventually come back to haunt him. All day he had felt sick with worry.

Oh God, it's been seventeen years! Surely it's all dead and buried by now.

Then, finally, the phone rang its shrill tone, startling him. He fumbled for it and pressed the button. 'Who's that?'

'Dickie boy, it's time you paid for your mistakes,' the vaguely familiar and slightly effeminate voice responded with false cheerfulness.

'What do you mean? Who are you?' he stammered, hoping it was all just some sort of practical joke concocted by one of his FEDPOL cohorts.

The voice dispelled any remaining doubts. 'Let's just say, I'm privy to something you did, or perhaps I should say, failed to do a long time ago. I know about the Persian Gulf and what really happened on 20th October 1992.

'The navy might not want the facts known because it will create a lot of adverse publicity for them that they can ill afford after all the scandal over sexism that's been going on in their ranks, but I've got no such qualms. Just think how the Sunday papers would love the real story about Chief Petty Officer Richard Nolan, Gulf War hero? Would that mess up your new career Dickie, or what?'

Nolan's stomach churned sickeningly. 'I should just tell you to go and fuck yourself. It's a long time ago. No one's interested now. Besides, I don't do blackmail.'

'Don't kid yourself. The tabloids love a good scandal. Don't forget the Voyager disaster,' the voice reminded him.

The RAN's greatest peacetime tragedy had been brought about when the Voyager's inebriated skipper had steered the destroyer into the path of the aircraft carrier HMAS Sydney. Most of the Voyager's crew had died when the vessel was cut in two and sank.

'That was nearly fifty years ago,' the too-cultured voice intoned. 'But the metaphorical skeletons still keep floating to the surface. So, you could tell me to fuck off, as you put it but Dickie boy, what would it do to your dear old mum's heart condition when she finds out her darling only son is a coward? You just about broke your staunchly Catholic parent's hearts when you converted to Islam, so this would no doubt be the final straw for them.'

Nolan's face flushed angrily. 'Keep my religious beliefs out of this!'

'I can't do that Dickie. You might have had the purest motives in the world but exploiting most Aussies' xenophobia is a handy tool I often use in my role as the chief of ASIO. The other thing you need to consider is what your lovely wife and children would make of the fact that their precious, heroic husband and father caused the death of five of his colleagues. Now you and I know that you're not going to suddenly develop the backbone needed to risk all that don't we?'

'What do you want me to do?' Nolan's hands shook. He knew he was taking an irreversible step by asking the question. He just hoped that whatever the blackmailer's price was, it would not be too high.

'Don't worry old chap. You'll be paid handsomely to perform a little service for your country. When you've done what I ask the slate will be wiped clean.'

111

'Oh sure,' Nolan responded sarcastically. 'How can I be sure of that? When or if you think of something else, you'll be on my case again.'

'Oh dear, Dickie, you are such a cynic. I guess I can't cure your cynicism and you'll just have to believe me. And don't think about reporting this conversation because no one will believe you ahead of the Director General of ASIO.'

'I repeat, what do I have to do?'

'Arrange a little accident. You're pretty expert at that.'

'What sort of accident?'

'Your new diving buddy has to have an unfortunate accident. One a little bit along the lines of Harold Holt, if you catch my drift,' Fleming replied, alluding to former Prime Minister Harold Holt's disappearance while scuba diving. It was one of Australia's greatest unsolved mysteries.

Nolan was too stunned to answer and the voice continued, 'How you arrange it doesn't matter. Just make sure it happens sooner rather than later. Destroy this phone when you hang up Dickie. I won't need to contact you again if you do the right thing, but make sure it's soon!'

Nolan's 'phone went dead as the ASIO chief cut him off. He stared at the mobile before gently placing it on the bedside cabinet. His guts suddenly churned agonisingly, his bowels turned to water and he barely managed to reach the toilet before he threw up.

After splashing cold water of his face, Nolan stared at his reflection, barely recognising the man who stared back. His somewhat hawkish features appeared pale.

His blue eyes were red rimmed. His straight light brown hair with the first signs of greying at the temples was tousled and worry lines seemed to have suddenly corrugated his forehead. Shit, he thought. I'm only thirty-nine but I suddenly look fifty.

That night, he could not sleep. Trying hard not to disturb his sleeping wife Jennifer, he lay awake staring at the dim red glow of the bedside clock, watching the inexorable count of its digital readout. What can I do? he wondered.

The idea of suicide crossed his mind. How easy it would be to don his scuba gear and just keep swimming down into the deep waters off the Continental Shelf until nitrogen narcosis overtook his brain and he lapsed into unconsciousness. They said it was a painless way to go but what if they were wrong? After all, nobody had ever come back from the dead to confirm the theory. What if, in the final few seconds when the regulator fell from his mouth, he suddenly recovered long enough to experience the horrible burning sensation of his lungs filling with water? What if he suddenly experienced the sheer terror of knowing he really did not want to die but could not swim back to the surface?

Lying in the darkness, his wife beside him and with his children whom he loved more than anything in the world just the thickness of a wall away, he had never felt so alone.

Why would Fleming want the prime minister assassinated? It's just too incredible for words. I've got to find out what this is all about and get some hard evidence to protect myself because he's right when he says no one will believe me. If I go down for this, he's coming with me.

Finally, he slept. Haunting images of the murky oil-slicked, mine-filled waters off the Iranian coast and the forbidding grey of HMAS Sydney's familiar hull tumbled chaotically in his mind. The silent screams of his fellow divers and best mates seemed to fill the turbid, oil-slicked waters as he abandoned them to a dreadful fate.

He awoke sweating and choking back a scream in his throat. As the memories flooded back, he asked himself for the umpteenth time if he would have the courage to behave differently if the same circumstances arose again, but in truth, he simply did not know.

It had begun after Saddam Hussein's forces invaded Kuwait on 2nd February 1990. As part of the coalition's contribution to the First Gulf War, the Royal Australian Navy's elite Clearance Diving Team (CDT3) had been flown by C130 transport to clear the Kuwaiti ports of Mina Ash, Shuaibah, Mina Doha, Al Qualai ah and Shatt-al-Arab of unexploded ordnance and the deadly Iraqi-manufactured LUGM-145 mines.

Working under the filthy black pall of the smoke from burning oilfields, Nolan and his companions laboured day after long day in incredibly dangerous conditions to make the ports safe for shipping. Unexploded missiles, plastic explosives, mines, IED's and all manner of discarded military junk littered the silt covered harbours. They even encountered a sunken Iraqi minesweeper loaded with scores of armed mines.

The explosive devices were far too numerous to be dealt with by conventional methods of disarmament. Each device had to be physically manhandled to a safe location where it could be detonated.

Every moment was potentially life-threatening but as a member of Australia's Special Forces, this was what the twenty-two-year-old, fit, strong, naval man had spent a combined total of seventy-eight weeks training for.

Although the task was gruelling, everything had proceeded safely and according to plan. The camaraderie that existed in the clearance team gave the divers a tremendous buzz that only those tasked with dangerous missions understood. Having trained, lived, played and worked together, they were like brothers, and like brothers they knew each other's strengths and weaknesses.

Or they thought they did. Then they received a radio call from the HMAS Sydney's own clearance diver, Chief Petty Officer Christian (Chris) Smart. 'Please meet me at Shatt-al-Arab. We need your help in the Straits of Hormuz.'

Having gathered their equipment, Nolan and his fellow CDT3 members took off for the Kuwaiti harbour in their Zodiac to keep a 1300 hour rendezvous with the Sydney's Seahawk helicopter. They arrived just in time to see CPOCD Smart jump from the chopper, a huge grin splitting his swarthy features. 'Great to catch up with you blokes,' he told them shaking hands. 'I've got a bugger of a job for you.

'During our blockade of the Gulf we've been conducting routine aerial patrols over the Straits of Hormuz looking for stray mines that might have floated from the Karun River. As you no doubt know,' he elaborated, 'the Karun is the confluence of the Tigris and the Euphrates and provides Iraq's only access to the Gulf. Because it was of such strategic significance to them, they mined it heavily and when they knew they were going to lose the war, they let tens of thousands of gallons of crude oil into the river from their oilfields near Basra. A lot of the mines have floated down the Gulf adding to the nightmare created by the worst oil spill in the world's history.

'We've been disarming mines as we find them but now we've discovered something far worse than a few LUGM-145s with 200 pounds worth of explosives inside. It seems Iraqi minesweepers have put a line of half-submerged barges across the shipping lane in the Strait.

'This is a new tactic that we've not encountered previously and we'll need to exercise extreme care until we know what we are dealing with.

'The water's pretty dirty in the area because of all the oil and stuff that's been stirred up since the war but my little CD team aboard the Sydney's had a look using our side-bar radar. That's how we've determined that they're barges with some new sort of IED attached.

'Each barge is tethered to a concrete anchor-block and we suspect they're packed not only with explosives but with oil so we cannot just blow them up. Obviously that would create another environmental catastrophe, releasing thousands of tons of crude oil which would wreck fragile and unique reefs and ruin valuable fishing grounds for the Gulf states.

'The barges must be physically inspected to determine if the charges can be disarmed. If they can, it is your task to do so and then to attach lines and marker buoys so they can be removed.

'Now, we need to get moving, so any questions you have can be put to me aboard the chopper.'

The CD team loaded their equipment on board and they set off without further ado to the Sydney where Smart had arranged for a FIB, (Fast Insertion Boat) to take them to the dive site.

Smart informed them, 'You blokes are recognised as being the navy's best clearance diving outfit and you've got more experience at dealing with the unusual than I have so I'll stay on board the Sydney and have my crew ready should you need back-up. One of my junior guys, Able Seaman Jim Yeoman, will look after the FIB while you go to work.'

They were soon hurtling across the choppy water of the Hormuz at breakneck speed. They manoeuvred their FIB into position above the first explosive barge, and left Jim Yeoman to look after it.

After conducting the usual safety checks, Nolan and his five companions descended into the murky water. Although poor visibility was something they were used to, the degree of difficulty multiplied exponentially with each metre that their vision decreased. For that reason each diver was tethered to his companion so they formed a line that would sweep by compass bearing over the target area. Once encountered, the semi-submerged, mined barges would then each be examined minutely by touch until the type of explosive device and its trigger mechanism was established.

In the new age of multi-skilling each diver had been trained to disarm almost any type of device. They had also been encouraged during their training to come up with new and ingenious improved explosive devices (IEDs) of their own design to ensure their expertise was not limited solely to conventional ordnance.

However, disarming something cunningly contrived to include any number of anti-tamper devices is never a simple task. In a dirty, oily sea with a swiftly moving current or tidal flow, dealing successfully with such a device borders on the impossible.

'Possible contact with target,' Brad, Nolan's dive buddy reported through his radio equipped full-face mask.

'Roger possible contact. Team leader, from team one, over?' Nolan called their search team leader.

'Team one, from team leader. Roger that.'

Immediately, the six man team stopped searching. Hanging suspended about five metres below the surface they waited while Brad felt for a suitable anchor point to attach them to the first barge. This was an essential measure that would prevent the current sweeping them away. Having successfully fastened a strong nylon cord to a conveniently positioned eye bolt which had probably been used to lower the barge below the surface, the other team members fanned out and began describing the results of their search. With their conversations recorded on the surface, it would enable future search teams to have a better idea what to expect.

In addition, if the worst happened and they blew themselves up, there would be a better chance of learning what went wrong.

Something's wrong here, Nolan thought worriedly, if a passing ship is supposed to blunder into this thing and set it off, what activates it? Unlike conventional

Iraqi mines, there are no Hertz horns on this thing.

The painstaking fingertip search took eighteen agonising minutes before Brad discovered the barge's explosive device.

It was like nothing any of them had ever encountered. A steel cylinder measuring approximately a metre in height by eight hundred millimetres in diameter, it appeared to have been constructed from a section of oil pipe-line. One end was welded to the barge's steel deck while the top was fitted with four threaded circular metal plugs. Nolan guessed these were for filling the device with explosives and the arming mechanisms.

They milled around the improvised barrel bomb, each diver taking it in turns to examine their find. They agreed unanimously with their team leader's assessment. 'We'll need to use the X-ray gear to try and determine what's inside. It's too risky to unscrew the plugs. There's bound to be an anti-tamper device fitted somewhere.

'Let's continue our examination of the rest of the barges and see if they're the same as this one. We'll return later with the X-ray equipment.'

Unclipping their tether, the six divers spread out and followed their original compass bearing, swimming the twenty-five or so metres until they encountered the second barge. They repeated the method they'd used earlier to construct a word picture for the recording equipment on the Zodiac. Everything seemed to be going smoothly for the first few minutes.

Then it all went horribly wrong.

Feeling their way over every square centimetre of

the barge's barnacle-encrusted surface, they decided to leave the barge's deck until the last. Because they anticipated finding a clone of the earlier device, they wanted to ensure first that there no unpleasant surprises attached to any of the other surfaces. They discovered nothing remarkable.

That was until they began inching up one side toward the barge's deck.

'Team leader from team three.' There was no mistaking the concern in the team three diver's voice.

'Team leader receiving, go ahead team three.'

'Team leader we seem to be caught up in a whole mess of monofilament line. We'll need a few minutes to extricate ourselves.'

'Roger that. All teams stop where you are. Teams one and two, please acknowledge, over.'

'Team one received.'

'Team two, roger.'

As the team three divers slashed and pulled at the fine nylon net that had somehow become wrapped around them, there was a dull thud.

With sound travelling five times faster under water than on land, it was impossible to know from where the noise had come. What was more concerning was the unmistakeable nature of the noise.

Some sort of device had just detonated.

The water around the divers filled suddenly with an immeasurable tangle of cloying, clinging monofilament netting. There seemed to be no way to get free. So dense was the cunning device that the divers were completely immobile.

As the nylon enmeshed him, Nolan somehow

managed to appreciate the ingenuity of the trap's Iraqi inventor. He also realised this was much more than an anti-tamper mechanism. It was an evil and cunning device clearly designed by someone who had anticipated the use of clearance divers to deactivate the minefield.

When the first divers became ensnared their efforts to get free activated an explosive charge that hurled the nylon trap over the entire clearance team. Coincidently, the explosion had also knocked out their radio system. Even if it had not, the percussion had burst their eardrums, rendering them all temporarily deaf. Now the CD team could no longer communicate with each other. Not only were they virtually blind in the turbid water, they were disorientated and had lost each other's moral support.

They must now work independently to try and save themselves.

Fighting to stave off the panic that threatened to overwhelm them, the navy divers hacked and cut at the nylon, oblivious as to the fate of the remainder of their team. Although tethered to his dive buddy, Nolan could not see him in the gloomy sea. He could however, feel the lifeline jerking as Brad struggled to extricate himself. Instead of reassuring him, the lifeline was impeding his efforts. He slashed the cord with his diving knife and concentrated on his escape.

It seemed hopeless. No sooner had Nolan cut away a section of the material than more tumbled in to fill the gap. While they each wore oxygen re-breathing equipment because it did not emit the tell-tale bubbles associated with conventional scuba gear, from the surface there was no way of knowing the team's exact location. However, there was one thing in their favour. Because they were less than five metres from the surface there was no danger that they would run out of life-giving air any time soon.

As he sawed at the nylon, Nolan still worried about the nature of the trigger mechanism used to deploy the mines. *They obviously aren't timed. They aren't set off by impact. Could they be detonated remotely by radio? No! No one's going to just sit and watch them and wait for a ship to come in range. There has to be another method.*

Nolan could think of three possibilities. None was pleasant.

Perhaps they exploded when the vibrations created by ship's propeller reached a pre-set intensity. Maybe they were magnetic and reacted to the presence of a large metallic mass like the steel hull of an oil tanker. Or, maybe they were fitted with some sort of sonar device that re-bounded radio waves from approaching ships.

Whatever the case, they would all be blown to smithereens if a ship came with range while they were caught-up against the suspended explosive oil-filled barge.

Another thought occurred to Nolan. Why had the Iraqi inventor of the mined barges bothered to construct a device that did not simply blow up the barges when the clearance divers became caught? The answer leapt into his head immediately. Because he wanted to kill almost irreplaceable members of the Special Forces, thus delaying attempts to rid the area of mines. Such an attack would demoralise all clearance divers, whatever their nationality; a major coup for the Iraqis.

But that was not going to happen. They would free themselves and their Zodiac crew would keep shipping away. Wouldn't it?

What Nolan and the other divers did not know as they struggled to cut themselves free was their FIB surface tender had its own problems.

When Jim Yeoman heard the distinct but relatively minor explosion of the net's activation system he knew something had gone horribly wrong. Unable to make radio contact, he waited for several minutes, expecting the dive crew to surface or to send up a safety sausage, the inflatable nylon tube used to mark the diver's position and signal that help was required. When that did not happen he radioed the Sydney and after providing a quick SITREP, requested instructions.

CPOCD Smart responded, 'Remain in the dive zone. We will send a back-up team immediately!'

While the HMAS Sydney had alerted shipping of the minefield, not all vessels monitored their radios as diligently as they should, or if they did understand the warnings, they deliberately chose to ignore them.

The gunboat from the Iranian Navy was one such vessel.

In a sabre-rattling display of hostility, the Iranians who were resentful of the West's shipping embargo decided to threaten the clearance divers by encircling them with guns bristling. It mattered not that the Straits of Hormuz were international waters. With the Iranians having already made several false claims over violation of their sovereignty, and on one occasion illegally

123

detaining and imprisoning coalition sailors, they relished another chance to flex their muscles.

Meanwhile, five metres below the choppy waters, Dick Nolan's numbed eardrums could just hear the sound of the approaching Iranian gunboat. As the growl of its powerful engines grew steadily louder, he feared the boat's presence spelt trouble.

Shit. If they get too close, they might set off the mine. I need to re-think my situation pretty quickly 'cos this just isn't working, he decided.

When the net at first cascaded over him, he had been pressed against the barge's steel hull running his hands back and forth over its surface. The net had not come between his body and the barge but had cascaded over his back and down beneath him.

What if I try sliding downwards? Surely, when I reach to bottom of the barge, the area beneath it will be clear?

Instead of fighting the nylon, Nolan slowly turned himself so that his back pressed against the barnacled steel surface. Even doing that was difficult. The nylon snagged his equipment. The only way to escape was to slip out of the re-breathing equipment's shoulder straps, turn his body and cut the gear free. Keeping his mouth piece in so that he could continue to breathe, he hit the quick release clips and executed an about face.

After unhooking the tangled mess from the equipment, he moved it carefully behind him and put it back on. Gripping the nylon he was now able to use it to pull his body slowly deeper.

Now he was in a much better position to tackle the nylon Nolan's progress toward freedom accelerated.

Praying that his dive companions had come to the same conclusion and that they would meet below, he noticed that his wetsuit was no longer scraping against the marine growth that covered the barge's exterior. He had reached the clear space beneath the hull.

There was no sign of the other divers.

As Nolan expected, the nylon curtain only fell so far. He was now able to swim beneath it and return to the surface. However, the din from the approaching craft was now cacophonic.

Expecting to be blown apart at any second, Nolan finned rapid upward.

His head broke the surface. He rotated his body frantically. *Where is the FIB? What is that other boat I can hear?*

After his emergency call to the Sydney, Yeoman spotted the familiar hull-down shape of a fast attack boat moving at speed across the strait toward his position. It appeared to have emerged from a small cove where it had obviously been watching them. Knowing the fundamentalist Islamic nation loved any excuse to postulate, he knew immediately it was one of the numerous Iranian gunboats that plied the Iranian coastline. He did not relish being the subject of an international incident.

'Jesus, what do I do now?' he muttered.

Firing up the FIB's powerful engines, he decided to give the divers a few more seconds before taking off to outrun the Iranians. With his hand on the throttle, he swung the nose of the FIB in the direction of the Sydney and reached for the radio handset. At that moment, a black, rubber-clad head broke the water about fifty metres away. The lone diver gave the internationally recognised "come and get me" signal and began blowing his whistle to attract Yeoman's attention.

But Jim had already spotted him. Shoving the throttles hard forward, he hung onto the FIB's helm to prevent himself from being thrown backward as the big semi-rigid hull almost leapt from the water in response. Reaching the clearance diver, he shoved the engines into reverse to arrest the FIB's progress.

Nolan grabbed the boarding line and hauled his body on board yelling, 'Go! Go! Go! Get the fuck out of here!'

Jim Yeoman hesitated. 'What about the others?' he asked incredulously. 'We can't leave them behind.'

Nolan could see the able seaman's mouth moving but he still couldn't distinguish his words. Nevertheless, he guessed and responded accordingly. 'If we don't go now, they'll be pickin' our guts outta the water with a sieve. Hit the gas!'

It is often said that hindsight is a wonderful thing. Looking back later, Richard Nolan knew he'd panicked. Instead of leading the Iranians away from the minefield, the FIB's frantic flight across the Hormuz's waters caused the Iranian skipper to try and cut them off.

The Iranian gunboat altered course, right across the minefield.

Like an erupting geyser, a gigantic column of boiling water shot skyward, lifting the gunboat several metres into the air. Breaking apart like a flimsy toy, bits of burning wreckage fell back into the churning sea. What remained of the gunboat's shattered hull quickly overturned and slipped beneath the windblown straits.

The huge black mess of oil that followed the tremendous explosion reminded Nolan of the boiling pools of volcanic mud he'd once seen in New Zealand's Rotorua. Blackened bodies littered the water. Covered in thick gelatinous black ooze it was impossible to tell whether they were Iranian sailors or the unfortunate clearance divers whom Nolan had deserted.

A pall of smoke from the burning oil rose above the disaster. The lifeless bodies were engulfed by the yellow flames quickly dispelling any thoughts the two navy men had of rescuing survivors.

Nolan felt sick with despair and self-disgust. If only he'd thought to head *across* the gunboat's bow instead of running *away* from it, he might have bought his mates the time they needed to escape. Instead, he had killed them as assuredly as if he'd detonated the mine himself.

The incident made headlines around the world. The media lauded the actions of CPO Nolan CD and Able Seaman James Yeoman, hailing them as war heroes. Further worsening his own self-loathing, Richard Nolan deliberately neglected to enlighten the resultant Naval Board of Enquiry as to the panic he'd felt. Neither did he reveal his fatal blunder of running away.

The only surviving witness to the tragedy understood that, as a mere able seaman, he was unlikely to be believed if he contradicted the word of the highly esteemed clearance diver. Biting his tongue, James Yeoman accepted his active service medal and bravery award, vowing one day to reveal the truth.

The chance to share his burden came sooner than he'd expected. However, he would have to wait much longer to see the clearance diver brought to retribution.

Suspecting that the navy had not wanted to delve too deeply into the incident, James Fleming wondered about several inconsistencies in Nolan's account and he decided to conduct his own private inquiry. As an intelligence officer, he thrived on information and knew incidents such as this often provided valuable leverage on which he could capitalise later.

Burdened by his own guilt at not standing up to Nolan during the heat of the moment, James Yeoman was only too happy to talk to the man from ASIO. 'The gutless bastard should be court martialled. He ran away and let his mates die,' he opined bitterly.

'Just keep it under your hat,' Fleming told him. 'When the time's right, Tricky Dicky will get his just desserts.'

Chapter Nine

Jambali was nervous. He'd been in Canberra for a month since the Australian Prime Minister's assassination and he still did not know who or what his target would be, for his contact had not got in touch.

As a dedicated jihadist, Jambali wanted to ensure he could move quickly when his orders eventually arrived. Waiting until the last minute to reconnoitre the target area did not seem a good idea, so with a camera slung around his neck he'd played at being a tourist visiting all the major public buildings including the Mint, the Australian War Memorial and both the Old and New Parliament House. Mingling with the noisy throngs of Japanese, American and Singaporean tourists he had even taken several guided tours, taking great care to alter his appearance as much as he could each time.

Scouting around the city had not only given Jambali something to take his mind off the thought that he would probably never see his family again, it had allowed him to pinpoint security cameras and plot the movements of the AFP Protective Service guards.

Unlike his home country, Australia never experienced much in the way of political unrest or terrorism so he laughed at the complacency of the officers tasked with protecting iconic buildings. They lounged about and gossiped; some with their shirts hanging out and their jackets unbuttoned. He thought them a slack looking bunch with their pot bellies showing their general overall lack of fitness. To Jambali, they gave the appearance of being a half asleep bunch of time-servers who posed no resistance.

Jambali laughed scornfully to himself at the declining standards of discipline of the West's law enforcement agencies. Nevertheless, he was careful to alter his appearance each day. One could never tell. Instead of merely going through the motions, one zealous or security conscious individual among the pack of complacent drones might actually be watching.

It would not do to be hauled in for questioning before he even knew what his mission was.

Elsewhere, in each of Australia's capital cities, other JI jihadists went through the same sort of pre-mission jitters while they anxiously awaited their orders. Each JI disciple knew Australian and Indonesian intelligence agencies worked closely together in the fight against terrorism. They all understood too, that a coordinated operation of this magnitude had had a lengthy gestation involving considerable financial outlay and intricate planning. Although eager to see Australian blood spilt, they were determined not to let impatience jeopardise their cause.

Meanwhile, as guests of Matthew and Catherine McCarthy at The Lodge, John and Mary McCarthy underwent an entire gamut of mixed emotions as they discussed their lucky escape from the Perth fires. Still amazed and grateful at escaping the bushfires which had killed so many, they also rejoiced over Matthew's appointment as prime minister while at the same time lamenting Connor Bowker's assassination and the disturbing trend of international events.

'It's wonderful to know you're safe,' Matthew told his parents. 'We saw the news bulletins and thought you'd both been killed. Then your phone call came through and we both cried in relief.

'While you were driving to Canberra I flew to WA and had a firsthand look at the disaster. I can't get the images of all those burnt out homes, cars, schools and shopping centres out of my mind. I really feel for those poor people and for the fire fighters and police who have to dig through the rubble looking for human remains.'

Mary McCarthy shook her head as she tried to clear the still vivid picture of the leaping, roaring flames as the firestorm had engulfed their vehicle. 'It is the most dreadful way to die, Matthew. To think the same thing will happen somewhere every year is just too terrible to contemplate. Something has to be done to ensure such a horrendous disaster never happens again.'

'Instead of each state conducting its own investigation, I've requested a national Royal Commission into Australia's bushfires. We need a nationwide approach to dealing with this issue and it seems all the state premiers agree for once,' Matthew told them. 'We have to seriously consider how to make it safer for people to live in forested areas.'

'Well, councils could start by ensuring communities have alternative escape routes. Do you know, in some Perth Hills shires they've blocked roads off, leaving many folk with only one way out? If the fire gets between householders and their escape path, as it obviously did this time, they're trapped. I've written to our local council and the fire brigade several times on this issue but they just kept putting it on the backburner. No pun intended.'

Concerned at the direction the conversation was

taking, Catherine McCarthy changed the subject. 'Are you going back to live in the hills when this is all over?'

'No,' John replied firmly. 'Mary and I discussed it on the long drive over here. There's nothing back there for us now and there's too many raw wounds that will never heal. We need a completely new direction and purpose. Besides, how can you run the country without us?' he added jokingly.

Matthew grinned. He knew his father was building up to the question of his involvement in his security. 'You can stay here at the Lodge as long as you like. You could both do with a bit of pampering. The staff will give you both the VIP treatment.'

John's weathered features expressed mock disgust as he surveyed the plush surroundings. 'I don't think I could take too much of this pansy-looking decor. It would turn me bilious. I think we'll find out own place as soon as we can.'

Catherine McCarthy agreed with her father-in-law. 'You're right. The previous incumbent's taste and ours are diametrically opposed but Matthew won't let me spend a cent. He says every prime minister's wife spends a fortune of the taxpayer's money on needless refurbishment and we should just put up with it but I'll tone it down, even if I have to get out the paintbrushes myself.'

'I'd love to help, Catherine,' Mary announced eagerly, her still-handsome face lighting up.

John snorted derisively, 'Imagine the fun the media and the political cartoonists will have with the idea of the prime minister's wife and his own mother hanging off ladders with brushes in hand, spilling paint everywhere as they daub the hallowed walls of the Lodge.'

'Why shouldn't we? Catherine replied indigently. 'At least if they're picking on us, they'll leave some other poor bugger alone.'

They all laughed. 'Seriously Dad,' Matthew said bringing them back to reality, 'I think there is a role for you as my personal security adviser. I don't need a well-developed sixth sense, or special intuition to tell me that Stormy's men are going to need a special kind of help in dealing with security issues. Although that ASIO Director General Jim Fleming seems pretty smart, he doesn't have a clue who killed Bowker. And with Al Qaeda and Jemaah Islamiyah just itching to make a statement, he and his men have their hands pretty full. I could do with someone with your talents to look at the big picture.'

John McCarthy looked a little concerned. 'I need to be brought up to speed. Will the Federal coppers and ASIO talk to me?'

'Yes, but you'll need official status. You'll need a "Top Secret" security clearance. I've already spoken to Commissioner Knight and apart from the allegations of nepotism, which I'm sure we can live with, there shouldn't be a problem. When would you like to come on board?

'Yesterday,' the older McCarthy replied. 'We can't afford to waste time.'

'What about house hunting?' Mary wanted to know. 'We can't sponge on the taxpayers forever.'

'Darling, I am under no illusions as to a man's role in such matters. It's the woman who chooses which house to buy and in what area. As long as it's quiet and there's a cold beer in the fridge at the end of the day, we blokes would be happy living in a cave. You suss out a few places you think will suit us both and I'll have a look at your short list and we'll select the one we both agree on then.'

'You men,' Mary responded, 'you always take the easy way out and leave all the hard work to us. Whenever we've bought a place in the past I've tried to choose somewhere I know you'll be happy.'

John McCarthy winked at his son. 'She's a great little sheila, your mum. At least she's not objecting to me going back to work.'

'Fat lot of good that would do me,' Mary responded. 'Besides it's better than having you moping around under my feet all day.'

John McCarthy, former police inspector turned private investigator, and the Federal Police Commissioner Stormy Knight met the following day at FEDPOL headquarters. McCarthy was surprised at the warm reception he received. In his experience most cops were territorial and considered the organisation to which they gave their allegiance the only one of any worth. All other police forces were considered second rate and their representative were treated with condescension. Freelance investigators were like security guards; they did not even rate a place in the law enforcement pecking order.

He expressed his surprise to the commissioner.

'John, I've worked in two state police forces as well as overseas. I cannot afford to be parochial. Besides, I've done a little checking into your background.'

'I'd be surprised if you didn't. It's all pretty humdrum ancient history stuff though.'

'On the contrary, you had a pretty colourful career in the New Zealand police; making detective sergeant after only five years, always serving in specialist squads such as the Police Diving Squad and Armed Offenders.

'Well, that's just because I get bored easily,' John grinned.

'You also figured in some pretty major murder investigations and became a very proficient prosecutor,' Stormy continued to John's embarrassment.

'I never really took to court work. Too stressful,' he interjected hoping the commissioner would stop trying to stroke his ego but it was to no avail, Stormy was determined to demonstrate that he'd done his research.

'In 1981, you resigned after fifteen years and moved to Western Australia where you decided against joining the WA police in favour of setting up your own security consultancy firm until the government of the day decided to separate the Protective Service component of the Federal Police and form the Australian Protective Service in 1984. I am puzzled why you decided to join as a new recruit. The pay was pretty lousy and it was an experiment which many thought was destined to fail, but for some reason you saw a career opportunity where others interpreted carving off the guarding component of FEDPOL as a cost cutting move intended to get rid of the deadwood in our mob.'

McCarthy knew an explanation was in order so he endeavoured to explain. 'Under the new arrangement the government was able to save massively on the wages bill by paying protective service officers such lousy money compared with coppers who were doing the job previously but I liked the idea of being part of a new highly specialised security agency.'

'Why didn't you join the Federal Police itself?' Knight wanted to know. 'We would have welcomed you with open arms.'

'I would have had to come to Canberra, and at that time it didn't suit my family arrangements,' John replied. *My word*, he thought, *Stormy's certainly done his homework.*

'Even so, guarding illegal immigrants and Defence Establishments was hardly an inspiring career for someone with your abilities.'

'Let's say, I had a vision for the APS that at the time, it did not even have for itself. There were some very high calibre individuals among the new recruits and I could see a lot of raw talent just waiting to be tapped and channelled into developing a niche as the Federal Government's premier security body. Some of us saw the potential for the APS to become the equivalent of America's secret service.

'I remember having a discussion along those lines with the then Director when he visited Perth and putting my views to him.' McCarthy chuckled at the recollection. 'It was bit risky someone at the bottom of the ladder telling the big boss how to do his job but I could see he was a public servant with no experience in running a quasi-police organisation. Really, he was out of his depth.

'Although he did not share my vision he was polite enough to listen. Then he told me I should reconsider my choice of career because my vision just wasn't going to happen. I replied, "Oh, I think it will." He just walked away shaking his head but fortunately, others in the outfit shared my view and managed to gradually steer him in the right direction.

'One such person was a fellow called Klaus Schmidt; a former West German border guard, who like most of us joined at the bottom. Werner's talents were recognised under the public service merit-based system and the APS which desperately needed entrepreneurs, almost immediately made him business manager. He was a real firebrand, a man with enormous intellect, imagination, vision and amazing listening skills.

'One of Werner's first moves was to tour all regions and milk ideas from the rank and file as to the future direction of the fledgling service. I was lucky enough to have Werner listen to my views and how they should be implemented. I told him that the first thing the APS hierarchy needed to do was to separate the Western Australian from South Australia's command. It was ridiculous having someone in Adelaide, two-thousand kilometres away, running the WA operation. He obviously agreed because he almost instantly appointed WA's first regional commander and made me his project officer.

'I had an absolute ball from then on. My new boss was a true entrepreneur. Anything and everything was open for discussion.'

'In fact, you were put in charge of establishing APS counter terrorist measures at all major airports and five years after joining you became Regional Commander, Western Region, a pretty impressive feat by anyone's standards.

'Instead of withering on the vine as everyone expected, the APS became very successful and I'd say a large part of that success is attributable to you. I don't think I'd be exaggerating if I said you could have ended up running the entire APS. In fact, if you'd stuck with it when it again became part the Federal Police, you could have been sitting in my chair now.

'I am curious as to why you would forsake such a promising career?'

John McCarthy laughed. 'You know, the funny thing is, I always suspected the wheel would turn the full circle and the two organisations would reunite. But I don't think I could ever have become commissioner. I am too outspoken and I would have been too old and cynical to be accepted by the time the merger happened. Besides, I didn't want to give up the Perth climate and lifestyle for the cold, bleak Canberra winters. Funny isn't it, that I'm finally here after all?'

Stormy Knight leant back in his office recliner looking puzzled. 'So you resigned in 1992 and set up your own private investigation and security consultancy company which you ran until just recently. You weren't exactly idle there either. If I remember correctly, Last Resort Investigations and Security won several major government contracts and captured a large slice of the fraud investigation work for major insurers.

'What I don't understand is why would you sell off LRIS at its peak?'

'Easy. I just got tired of working my tail off for thankless insurance executives who issued ridiculous ultimatums and set impossible deadlines. We'd often put in long hours gathering overwhelming evidence that proved fraud only to find they would never prosecute, even in the most blatantly criminal cases. The best they would ever do was to cancel the perpetrator's policy and refuse to pay the claim, leaving the crooks free to just move onto another insurer. They'd open a new policy, conveniently forget their duty of disclosure and then it would all start over again, whereas if the insurers had had the guts to prosecute, it would have acted as a deterrent and kept premiums lower. It was all very frustrating.'

Stormy's expression softened. 'A little like the revolving door situation with criminals and the justice system. Sorry to appear as if I'm putting you through an inquisition John. It's really none of my business. I want you to be aware that I respect all you've achieved and I guess I am just curious as to why you made some of the choices you did. I am also terribly sorry for the tragic events that brought us together but I am very happy to have you here and I think Matthew's proposal to appoint you as his personal security advisor has real merit.'

McCarthy sighed. 'Thanks for saying so. I just hope I haven't been out of circulation for so long that I've become irrelevant. Would you be prepared to have someone spend some time bringing me up to speed? If so, I would like to conduct a full protective security risk review and compare my results with the existing FEDPOL VIP security management plan for protecting Matthew, Catherine, Daniel and Sienna.'

Stormy nodded. 'Of course; it's always helpful to have a second opinion, especially since we haven't had time or the personnel to re-evaluate security arrangements since the assassination. In fact, you can sit in tomorrow when Chief Superintendent Colin Burrows briefs me on the progress on the investigation into the Bowker assassination and then our Intel people will give you a rundown on the organisations and individuals we're keeping our eye on.

'I've also arranged for you to be appointed as a special constable. As such, you will have legal standing and arrest powers.

'ASIO is rushing through your security clearance which shouldn't be a problem because you've previously been cleared to the highest classification.'

Stormy stood up, signalling that the meeting should finish. 'What say I see you here tomorrow at 0900 hours?'

'Thank you for your understanding and cooperation commissioner,' McCarthy said, offering his hand. 'But, don't tell me ASIO still have my records after all this time?'

The Commissioner grinned knowingly. 'Director General Fleming keeps a pretty comprehensive data base.'

++++++++++++

Chapter Ten

Tired and dispirited, Jambali returned from one of his scouting trips to find a small sealed envelope had been pushed under the door to his hotel room. His spirits lifted instantly as he stooped to pick up the plain white generic envelope from the hotel carpet. Turning it over he noticed that it was unmarked and had been sealed with adhesive tape. As he slid the blade of his pocket knife under the envelope's flap he guessed the author would have been careful not to leave any DNA or fingerprints on the cheap, mass produced paper. He fumbled excitedly with the folded note which appeared to have been produced by an ink jet printer.

The one line message written in Indonesian said simply, "*Meet tomorrow, 10.30 am at the Plastic Boomerang.*"

A quick check of the Canberra telephone book showed the Plastic Boomerang to be a busy internet cafe within walking distance of his hotel. Jambali remembered passing the premises during his many sorties and knew it was popular haunt of backpackers. He guessed it had been chosen as a rendezvous because anonymity would be virtually assured among its cosmopolitan clientele.

The following day he arrived fifteen minutes early. Choosing a table at the rear of the bustling cafe, he ordered coffee and sat where he could watch the door through a haze of marijuana smoke and observe his fellow patrons who were mostly in their late teens or early twenties. Mostly scruffy and obviously short of cash, they ignored him as they babbled noisily in at least half a dozen foreign languages, smoking or earnestly tapping away at computer keyboards or their iPads.

Expecting a face to face meeting, Jambali became impatient and anxious when half an hour after the appointed time no one had approached him. Undecided whether he should leave, he watched a buxom, Germanic-looking waitress making her way along the tables gathering dirty crockery. Without making eye contact, she paused beside his chair long enough to drop something on his table as she passed. Looking down, he discovered an identical envelope to the one left under his door the previous evening. However, this envelope was bulkier.

Jambali glanced furtively around the cafe looking for whoever had no doubt paid her to deliver the envelope. Everything appeared as it had a few moments ago. No one made eye contact with him. He had no way of knowing who had delivered the envelope but it was obvious that someone had been watching him.

Realising he was not supposed to have face to face contact with the other Jemaah Islamiyah operative, the young JI terrorist ripped open the envelope. Emptying the contents into the palm of his hand, he discovered an ignition key and remote locking device attached to a computer generated note. The note said simply, *"White Toyota van across the street."*

Jambali paid for his coffee and stepped into the tree-lined street, glancing furtively about to see if he was being watched. Although there were a number of vehicles occupying nearby metered spaces none appeared to be occupied. A scattering of pedestrians walked in both directions unaware of the unfolding drama. Directly across the road the ubiquitous white Toyota delivery van waited beneath the autumn-red canopy of maple trees.

Finding a gap in the traffic, Jambali crossed the street, pressing the button of the remote control as he did so. He pressed the button a second time and was relieved to see the yellow blinker lights flash, signifying he had indeed found the correct vehicle.

Although he doubted anyone was watching, Jambali did his best to appear relaxed as he slid behind the steering wheel and casually inspected the vehicle's interior.

The windowless rear compartment of the van was empty. There was nothing in the glove box or the door pockets. Checking the centre console, the would-be terrorist discovered a cheap pre-paid mobile telephone. As he inspected the device, scrolling through its memory in search of dialled numbers or previous messages he knew he would find nothing.

Suddenly the telephone rang. Surprised, he nearly dropped it. He pushed the button to answer, noticing that the call originated from a private number. Jambali put the phone to his ear. 'Yes?' he responded hesitantly.

'Listen carefully,' an unaccented female voice intoned quietly. He guessed she was young, choosing to picture a beautiful Balinese girl as she continued speaking. 'Just answer "yes," to each question unless you do not understand something, in which case you should just say, "no." Do you understand?'

'Yes.'

'When you return to your hotel, pay your bill and book out. Make sure you remove anything from your room that might be used to identify you. That includes cleaning every surface that you might have touched. Do not leave fingerprints or anything which might contain your DNA. Do not leave any rubbish in the bins and make sure you leave nothing of yourself behind. Do you understand?'

'Yes.'

'Now, memorise these directions. Do not write anything down.

'Do you know the road between Captain's Flat and Queanbeyan?'

'Yes.'

'When you leave Queanbeyan, the road will take you across a bridge over the Molonglo River. Check the vehicle's odometer reading so that you will know when you have travelled exactly twenty-two point four kilometres. Do you understand?

'Yes.'

'On the right side of the road, you will see a rusty oil drum that used to be a letterbox. There is an old sagging wooden gate to a dirt track. If there are any other vehicles using the road when you get there, or if by any chance anyone sees you arrive, drive on past and return later. You must not be seen.

'The track leads off into the trees and will take you up into the hills about one kilometre. Make sure you shut the gate behind you. Do you understand?'

'Yes.'

'At the end of the track you will find a disused farmhouse. The property is owned by an investor who lives in the city. Nobody goes there and the farm is no longer operating. You will not be visible from the main road. Nobody will know you are there. You will find food and water in the house. You will also find certain other things.

'You will know what to do with these items when you find them. Do you understand?'

'Yes.'

'Act quickly for we all must be ready to move when the time is right. Wait at the farm house. Check the mailbox each morning because that is how we will contact you.

'Do not keep this telephone or use it again. Remove the SIM card and destroy both it and the telephone. Do you understand?'

'Yes,' Jambali replied. His palms were sweating as he realised the caller had severed the connection.

Jambali understood the time had come to put his bomb-making skills to the test. Everything he needed would be waiting for him at the deserted farmhouse. 'Allahu Akbar,' he whispered as he started the van. He prayed it would not be too long before his target was revealed to him.

++++++++++++

Chapter Eleven

As John McCarthy drove his Nissan through the gates of the Lodge the young female uniformed APS officer on duty waved a cheery greeting. On impulse, he pulled to the side of the driveway and wound down his window.

'Good morning, Mr McCarthy,' the guard called as she swung the heavy wrought iron gates across the driveway. Blowing into her gloved hands and stamping her feet against the chill of the first frost for the season she joked, 'It's another lovely day in paradise.'

'It's good to see someone so alert and cheerful looking after the gates,' McCarthy called. 'How long have you been on shift?'

The young woman walked across to his vehicle. 'All night. I'm doing a double shift. The guard who was supposed to come on at 0700 hours rang in sick and we're short staffed.'

McCarthy noticed a name badge on the officer's heavy nylon bomber jacket. 'That's a bit of a worry Officer Thompson. How can they expect you to be alert, let alone stay awake? It must be a pretty boring job.'

'It's Annette. No, actually I enjoy meeting all the VIPs. And the prime minister is always so down-to-earth. Besides, I swap over with the guard patrolling the grounds and get to wander around and talk to the staff.'

'Annette, I am going to be taking an in-depth look at security. Experience has taught me it's good to speak to people on the ground if you want an unbiased opinion. You work with the system every day and will no doubt know how it can be improved. If I tee it up with your bosses, would you be prepared to give me a hand?'

'You bet!' Annette exclaimed. 'It's about time. We've all been saying how the security needs to be upgraded. If someone knew what they were doing, they could take over this place and hold the prime minister and his family hostage. With just two of us on duty, we couldn't do much to stop them if they were really determined and organised.

'The other thing that worries me is how vulnerable the PM is when the Commonwealth car comes in or goes out the gates. Once he's mobile it's probably okay because he's got an armed escort and they always vary the route he takes.

'Everyone laughs at me. They tell me I am suffering from an overactive imagination, but I can see how easy it would be for a suicide bomber to ram the PM's car, shoot him or blow him up.'

McCarthy looked horrified. 'After Connor Bowker's murder, I guess we've got to think that anything's possible. I just hope Al Qaeda's not thinking along the same lines as you Annette.'

As John McCarthy drove to FEDPOL headquarters for his briefing session, he could not dispel from his mind the dreadful scenario Annette Thompson had drawn.

Jesus. This is Australia, for God's sake, not Afghanistan or Iraq! Surely things haven't got that bad? McCarthy shuddered as he realised the dreadful answer to his own question. Nothing should be discounted since the death of Connor Bowker.

Reaching the FEDPOL building, he handed his newly issued identification card to the officer guarding the reception area.

'We've been told to expect you sir,' the burly constable answered as he issued McCarthy with a colour-coded security pass. 'Someone will escort you in a moment. But first, please empty everything from your pockets.'

McCarthy grinned inwardly, wondering, why do so many young cops nowadays seem to think they have to shave their heads, get tats and pump iron?

The gorilla-like FEDPOL constable placed McCarthy's belongings in an envelope. With the confidence of someone who had performed the same task innumerable times, he ran a hand held metal detector over McCarthy. Locking the envelope containing McCarthy's belongings in a locker behind the desk he announced, 'You can collect your things on the way out sir. They'll be safe with us.'

A smiling WPC approached him across the lobby. 'Mr McCarthy?' He nodded in response. 'Please follow me.'

After they wound their way through the labyrinth of highly polished vinyl and faux-wood panelled corridors, the WPC knocked on a padded door before pushing it open. 'Please go in sir,' she directed, leaving him without further ado.

Half a dozen business-suited men seated around an enormous teak conference table turned in unison as he made his way into the room. Glancing quickly at his surroundings, McCarthy guessed the windowless room was a heavily sound-proofed electronic dead zone that was probably swept regularly for listening devices.

'Sorry for all the rigmarole John,' Stormy said,

standing up from his place at the end of the table. 'We can't afford to be too careful these days. Everybody entering this room goes through the same procedures to ensure nothing said can be recorded. We like to be able to give opinions and toss ideas around freely in here without being inhibited by the thought that what's said might come back and bite us on the bum later.'

McCarthy nodded in understanding. As the Commissioner introduced him to the room's other occupants he felt overawed that the country's leading law enforcement officer would so readily permit him to be privy to what was obviously going to be a sensitive discussion.

'Gentlemen, this is John McCarthy, the prime minister's personal security advisor. Mr McCarthy is a highly qualified security professional and former high ranking police officer who has agreed to come out of retirement and take on this new portfolio.

'John, this is James Fleming, ASIO's Director General.'

McCarthy met the security chief's penetrating stare. As he shook the man's pudgy, limp hand he sensed animosity. Fleming gave a politician's smile and said, 'I hope I can be of service to you in your new and important role.'

Pompous arsehole, McCarthy thought. There's something about this man that says "don't trust me."

'This is Chief Superintendent Colin Burrows,' Commissioner Knight said as he moved to the next man. 'Colin's in charge of the investigation into Mr Bowker's murder. He's going to give us a run down on how things are going.'

After Fleming's flaccid handshake and insincere greeting, McCarthy found himself warming to the thickset, gruff Burrows who gripped his hand like a vice.

'Welcome aboard, John. When the boss briefed me on your background I remembered you. Of course I was only a lowly ranked uniform sergeant at the time but you're the bloke who was put in charge of organising counter terrorist first response at airports when the government took it off FEDPOL. There was a lot of ill-feeling in our ranks at the time and we didn't think you guys had what it takes but I must say you did a pretty good job.'

'It's good of you to say so. I'm just glad the politicians woke up and corrected their mistake. There's no way something so important should be handled by a body that lacks full policing powers. Anyway, that's all ancient history. I just hope everything's working in the best interest of the travelling public.'

'We like to think so, although there's always room for improvement,' Stormy interjected as he directed McCarthy's attention to the next man. 'This gentleman is Detective Inspector Graeme Clews. Graeme is in charge of diplomatic and consular protection and prime ministerial security. Graeme can answer any questions you might have about security arrangements for guarding of the Lodge and Kirribilli House and the general protection of the prime minister. But first, I think we should get down to the briefing. You two can get together later.'

McCarthy's and Clews' handshake was perfunctory. Clews who had been dubbed with the unlikely nickname of "Curly," was a lanky blue-eyed man in his forties with a shiny bald head and protruding ears that looked like wing nuts on a bowling ball. He did not smile and McCarthy sensed understandable resentment at an outsider being allowed to intrude on his domain. Knowing Clews could make his life very difficult, he vowed to win the detective over.

'The two gentlemen whom I have yet to introduce are Assistant Commissioner Bob Baldwin from the New South Wales Police and Deputy Assistant Commissioner Tom Fordham from the Victorian Police,' Knight concluded. 'In an inquiry of this scale we obviously need cross border cooperation and I am grateful for the presence of both Tom and Bob.

'Now I'll ask Colin to give his report.'

Picking up a remote control from the conference table, Burrows remained seated as he activated a DVD player and plasma television set. 'The footage you are about to watch was taken by a Channel Seven cameraman who was covering former Prime Minister Bowker's address in Martin Place at the time of his assassination. The cameraman was located on a cherry picker behind the stage so the footage is a bird's eye view of the crowd.

'We have other footage taken from two other television cameras but they were situated behind the crowd to film Bowker and the other politicians. Although their recordings will prove invaluable when we finally bring the offender to trial, this particular footage you are about to see gives us the first real breakthrough. Unfortunately, the photographer was completely unaware what was happening behind the

151

crowd at the time of filming and it wasn't until he got back to the station and downloaded the images that he realised he'd captured the actual shooting on his camera.'

Spellbound, they watched as the most shocking political tragedy in Australia's history unfolded. High above the festival atmosphere of brightly coloured banners, balloons and bunting, the highly amplified voice of Connor Bowker's last words reverberated in the microphone.

The camera lens zoomed down past the prime minister's expensive coiffure to the faces of his enthusiastic supporters. An eclectic representation of Australian society hung on every word. A young girl of about two hoisted onto her father's shoulders waved an Australian flag with one hand while from the other an ice cream cone dripped a sticky mess down her father's shirt. Skimpily-dressed, mini-skirted teenage girls smiled and waved streamers like cheerleaders at a football match. Grey-haired pensioners wore the sceptical expressions of those who had heard a thousand broken election promises. Pushed to the front of the crowd, a paraplegic man in a wheelchair sat with his arms folded. Pregnant mums with toddlers clinging to their skirts held mobile phones aloft to capture the prime minister's image for posterity. Office workers clutching cappuccinos mingled with leering labourers goofing-off from nearby building sites. Dressed in ubiquitous stubbies and steel-capped boots, they stood out from the usual rent-a-rabble who frequented any excuse to stir trouble.

As Bowker's address gathered momentum the roar

of a jumbo blocked the sound as the camera panned over the crowd toward the cenotaph and the GPO. In the distance, traffic stuck in the paralysis of the morning rush hour formed unbroken lines across a city intersection. The orange-tinged glow of the sun rebounded from the canyon walls of high-rise buildings and the camera operator retracted the lens.

Burrows' voice interrupted the deceased prime minister's commentary. 'This is our first glimpse of the killer,' he commented as he held the image. 'Look up near the top left corner of the screen.'

Following his direction, they peered at the shadowy entrance of an office building. The blurred image of a hobo could just be seen. Frozen momentarily by the digital technology, he had apparently just arisen from the ground where a ragged dirty bedroll was lying beside a sandstone pillar.

Burrows pressed the remote again. The tramp reached down to the bedroll and pulled something from within its folds. Tucking whatever it was under one arm he then removed a second item while Connor Bowler outlined his vision for a cleaner, more sustainable way of life.

The bum's hands moved at lightning speed. The two components became one. The unmistakeable shape of a rifle barrel steadied against the corner of the sandstone pillar. Sunlight glinted briefly as the assassin took aim.

'Jesus, didn't someone sweep the area before Bowker arrived?' Stormy exclaimed.

'I am sure they would have,' Assistant Commissioner Baldwin replied, quickly flying to the defence of the N.S.W. Police. 'This bugger probably

153

snuck in with the crowd.'

Unfortunately, the camera moved away and the sniper was no longer visible. Oblivious to the hidden gunman, the cameraman was again concentrating on the crowd's reaction to the prime minister's speech until Bowker's dying scream filled the crowded room, chilling even the most hardened policeman to the bone.

For a split second the cameraman continued filming the crowd. Then, realising from the stunned looks on people's faces that something had happened, he swung the lens to focus on the podium. From his vantage point, the figures many metres below resembled the digitally constructed images of a violent video game. The broken body of the PM, the plump, dowdy figure of his wife kneeling and the rapidly spreading crimson stain appeared surreal.

The camera lens retracted again as with the presence of mind of a seasoned news professional looking for a scoop, the operator searched for the unknown killer. The sandstone pillars came into view again. This time there was no sign of the bum or his bedroll.

Panning frantically across the now scattering mass of humanity, the cameraman was unaware he had already captured the killing.

As the camera swung wildly across the plaza, Burrows froze the image again. 'There goes our man,' he said quietly. 'Top of screen, you can just see the bastard before he turns the corner.'

The assassin was little more than a blurred mass of pixels. However, from the colour and shape of his silhouette McCarthy and the others in the room knew without doubt that it was the same person captured a moment before as he assembled the murder weapon.

'We're trying to see if the images can be enhanced,' Burrows told them turning off the television. 'But we're not that hopeful. Still, we hope that this will give us enough to identify the make of the murder weapon and someone will remember seeing this guy close up.

'There is little doubt that this was a professionally planned hit. While the killer was probably disguised to look like a homeless psycho type, we feel sure he would have ditched the murder weapon and his disguise at the first opportunity. It might be a waste of time but we've got a big team going through all the garbage bins in the inner city area.

'It's a mammoth task with about as much chance of a successful outcome as trying to hit the moon with a slingshot. You've no idea how much crap is generated by the Sydney metropolitan area each day.'

'Colin, has it occurred to you that the killer might have been picked up by vehicle shortly after the hit?' Tom Fordham asked. 'He may even have had a getaway vehicle stashed up an alley.'

'Both are possibilities and we can't discount them. However, we don't think that's likely because a homeless bum being picked up or getting into a vehicle and driving off would arouse suspicion and someone might remember. It's more likely that he slipped into a nook nearby, changed his appearance, dumped the murder weapon and his disguise and then simply blended in with the crowds. Needless to say, we're exploring all scenarios and acting out reconstructions for each one which we'll play on prime time television in the hope someone will come forward with useful information.

'The prime minister has authorised a reward of five million dollars. That might just provide the incentive for someone with vital information to come forward. Meanwhile our taskforce which comprises coppers from the ACT, New South Wales, Queensland and Victoria is continuing to haul in underworld figures, registered informants and anyone else we can think of with a motive.

'Frankly, we've been overwhelmed with calls from the public, from psychics, and it seems every nutcase running the street wants to confess or claims to know who's responsible. Unless we get a major breakthrough soon, this is going to drag on for a long time to come.' Burrows turned to face the ASIO chief. 'I am hoping the spooks can offer a ray of sunshine. Jim, have your mob managed to prioritise a list of the most likely groups behind this?"

McCarthy could not understand why he was suddenly interested in the ASIO man's reaction to the question. Perhaps his instinctive distrust of the chief spook triggered his curiosity or perhaps it was his years of reading other people's characters that enabled him to feel when things were not quite as they should be. Whatever it was, he found himself studying Fleming's facial muscles and body language.

Although the incident lasted a mere second, the ASIO director sensed the burning power of McCarthy's gaze. Unable to resist, he cast a furtive glance in the older man's direction before looking quickly away. It was doubtful that anyone had seen the exchange and Fleming's expression did not alter as he lumbered to his feet.

'It's common knowledge that many people would like nothing better than to see the Labor Government forced to backtrack on its environmental policies. Opposition is not limited to groups within our shores. Our major trading partners as well as countries hungry for our natural resources feel threatened. For instance, China has an insatiable appetite for coal and minerals. Nuclear powers want our uranium and our nearest neighbour Indonesia is eying off the oil and gas fields in our northern waters.

'Labor's opinion that Australia must stop being an enabler of the world's major polluters and its insistence on halting uranium exports quite frankly threatens the ambitions of other nations. Its Zero Carbon Energy Bill threatens major manufacturing nations who fear the spread of Australia's example. Imagine if too many other countries adopt the Australian Government's thinking. Consumerism would almost become a thing of the past.

While this may well be necessary for the long term survival of all humanity, it obviously undermines and shifts existing wealth and power bases. Frankly, the new Labor's policies are seen by many as a form of extreme left-wing socialism. The fact that so many people have become believers, shows how effective public education programs can be and there is widespread concern that what I term eco-socialism or Australia's unique version of McCarthyism will spread across the globe.'

Flipper Fleming paused long enough to cast an accusing glance in John McCarthy's direction. 'Don't misunderstand me, I have an open mind on the topic of global warming and I am just trying to say it as I see it. However, Australia now has more enemies than ever before.'

John McCarthy remained poker-faced but he couldn't help thinking, *I think I know where your loyalties lie too, mate.*

Disappointed at McCarthy's lack of indignation, Flipper continued his discourse. 'Inside our borders there are many wealthy and powerful groups and individuals who have too much to lose to allow the implementation of McCarthyism. By one means or another, they will try to force a new election.

'Australia's political environment is now as shaky as that of the worst banana republic.'

'In conclusion, if you are looking for suspects for Bowker's murder, those with motive, means and opportunity are just too numerous to single out any one group. Nevertheless, I have endeavoured to compile a short list based upon the assumption that the assassin was hired by an individual or organisation based in Australia.'

'Why do you make that assumption, James?' Stormy wanted to know.

'Because I think external enemies are adopting a "wait and see" approach in this instance. With Bowker, a long term and savvy politician, there was always the possibility of him caving in if he thought he would lose at the polls. McCarthy on the other hand, is not a politician. He believes he has a mandate and he is almost fanatical in his zeal. He will push through at almost any price because his beliefs are more powerful than his self-interest.

'However, because his policies are such a radical departure from traditionalist thinking, other nations expect and hope that the new Australian Government will simply implode, saving them the worry of initiating action to bring down the government.'

With a deeply furrowed brow, Stormy ran his fingers through the grey upside down brush of his hairdo. 'That's a very vivid and worrying picture that you paint, James. Do you want to give us the list of the most likely contenders for Bowker's murder?'

'I'd start with the MSWU. Keith Sutton is perhaps Australia's most infamous union thug. He would only have to hint to his brainless band of steroid-abusing heavies that he wanted Bowker removed from the equation and a lot more than one of them would have jumped at the chance.'

Bob Baldwin expressed surprise. 'There's little doubt that they've fitted concrete boots to quite a few people over the years, but do you think Sutton's bruisers have the intelligence to pull something of this scale?'

'Sutton's bruisers as you call them would not need to plan it. They would only have to have been schooled in what to do. Monkey see, monkey do. The other possibility is, the MSWU brought in a professional hit man.'

'If we get enough evidence, we'll ask for a warrant to intercept their telephones,' Baldwin suggested.

Flipper smirked and tapped the side of his nose with his index finger. 'I don't think you need to go to that trouble, Assistant Commissioner.'

'Christ, I wish we had the freedom to do the things you guys just class as part of your usual routine. I should have known you'd be one jump ahead. So, who else is on your list Director Fleming?'

'I think we also have to look closely at the likely political heirs within the Labor movement. Jack Hammond is probably next in line for the throne if McCarthy goes although Helen Knox is a close second.' Seeing the incredulous looks on the faces of his audience, Flipper held up his hand, halting an outburst of anger. 'I know what you're going to say. Jack Hammond is too much of a gentleman and thoroughly liked by both sides of politics, but do we really know anybody that well? He's been sitting waiting in the wings for years and if it wasn't for all this hyperbole surrounding climate change, he would have been prime minister by now. It's no secret that he wants the top job and that he feels hard done by because Bowker got it and now it's gone to McCarthy. Although Hammond pretends to tread the party line on climate change, he's let his real views slip in supposedly private discussions with those close to him.

'Don't forget Hammond's roots. He was a big-wig lawyer representing the Transport Workers Union and their members stand to lose their jobs if and when McCarthy starts taking trucks off the road.'

'I just don't see Jack Hammond resorting to murder,' Stormy replied, shaking his head. 'I've known Jack for donkey's years and consider him a personal friend. He's been a great ally of the Federal Police and a first-class treasurer. Nevertheless, I'll take your advice and we'll see if we can do some discreet checking of bank records to ascertain if there have been any mysterious money transfers, although he would be too smart to get caught that way.'

'Don't forget the size of the stakes,' the ASIO chief reminded him. 'It's amazing how money and power can change people.'

And I bet you'd be an expert on that subject, John McCarthy mused silently. *You think everybody is as scheming and manipulative as you are.* Then, a sudden thought occurred to him. It was out of his mouth before he could stop himself. 'What about Senator Bacon? He's done a lot of ranting in the media and in parliament against Labor's policies on climate change. There have also been rumours flying around for years linking him with organised crime.'

Fleming hid his annoyance well. Although the mention of the Boar's name did not surprise him, indeed he expected someone to suggest Bacon as a possible suspect; he had not expected it to come from someone whom he considered an outsider.

Although Fleming felt sure no one knew of his and Bacon's association, he was not about to arouse suspicion by too readily flying to the senator's defence. 'That's a credible suggestion Mr McCarthy. I am glad you raised it. In fact, my department is well aware of the rumours and the senator's reputation and we're looking into that possibility already. We have nothing to suggest Senator Bacon is anything other than the founder of Shriver Pharmaceuticals and he has clearly fulfilled all obligations to disclose his involvement to parliament so there is no conflict of interest. Should we come up with even the most tenuous link, we will pass the information to Commissioner Knight without delay.'

McCarthy decided to ignore Fleming's patronising

manner. 'I would like to know why Senator Bacon has such a rabid hatred for the prime minister. It seems to go beyond the normal acrimony associated with political differences. It is as if his personal position is somehow jeopardised if the climate change initiatives succeed.'

'I think I can answer that,' Stormy interjected. 'Senator Bacon has spoken out strongly against the joint state commonwealth drug taskforce and the extension of police powers allowing cross-border action on illegal drugs. His position is that it is in breach of the Australian Constitution and is a thinly disguised ploy by the Commonwealth to further erode the powers of state governments. There has always been fierce opposition toward the centralisation of political power.'

McCarthy grinned inwardly. He couldn't help wondering if it wasn't more likely that Bacon's rumoured underworld empire was threatened by the widening of police powers. *But would the senator resort to killing the country's top politician?*

Fleming seemed to be struggling to contain his frustration at no longer holding centre stage. He sat down heavily. 'As I said before, we have innumerable suspects and it helps to understand why that is the case and why it is impossible to compile an actual list.

'The situation we now face is akin to a revolution. While most people think they understand the ramifications of McCarthyism and the polls say society is ready to accept an entirely new way of thinking and living, the social upheaval will be enormous. Families will have to relocate to find work; many people will have to retrain, every one of us will have to rethink how we live, work, travel and play.

'We all know change is never easy to accept and the changes advocated by Labor are about as drastic and far-reaching as they can be. Thousands will have to undergo painful changes and that can cause tremendous resentment among individuals who may have struggled to become successful only to find everything they've worked for destroyed virtually overnight.

'People are scared. And when people are scared they sometimes become dangerous.

'Put yourself in the shoes of many shareholders, small business people and the heads of large corporations who find the profitability of their various enterprises under serious threat unless they somehow adapt to the new world of sustainability. Can you blame them for wanting to defend their position?

'While many will become very rich by capitalising on the boom in sustainable technologies, it is inevitable that others will become dinosaurs.

'While most folk accept that if we are to survive, change is necessary and inevitable, there are perhaps hundreds of thousands who do not.' Fleming shook his head. 'It is no wonder that people choose to bury their heads in the sand and hope it will all go away.

'Now, I believe Mr McCarthy would like a run down on the terrorist threat.

'The greatest threat to Australia from overseas terrorists comes from Jemaah Islamiyah.

'With a current membership of anywhere between five hundred and several thousand, JI was originally founded in 1993. It has a jihadist vision and wants to establish an Islamist state encompassing Brunei, Indonesia, Malaysia, Singapore, the southern

Philippines and southern Thailand.

While factions within the organisation differ over how to achieve the goal of an Islamic state, a group within JI called "the Bureaucrats" would like to concentrate on building a military capacity large enough for an Islamic revolution. On the other hand, splinter groups allied to Al Qaeda have resorted to bombings, the most infamous in recent times being the 2002 Bali bombings that killed over 200 people. Of course, there have been many other attacks, such as, the 2003 bombing of the Marriott Hotel, the 2004 attack on the Australian Embassy and the two recent bombings of hotels in Jakarta.

'Umar Patek is thought to be the current devil incarnate behind the bombings following Nordin Muhammad Top's death, although we still believe Abu Bakar Ba'asyir is a major facilitator despite Indonesian courts exonerating him from involvement in the 2002 massacre. Patek was arrested for Al Qaeda-related terrorist activities in Pakistan but he escaped and fled to the Philippines where he was very active. We understand that he's being harboured by JI in Indonesia and has now taken charge of terrorist attacks although JI itself is very coy on who heads their group.

'Some JI members admit links to the late Osama Bin Ladin and his successors and JI is known to have helped fund the 9/11 attacks and provide safe havens for Bin Ladin's operatives.

'Now as to the threat JI pose to Australia, we have no intelligence to suggest that they plan attacks on our shores in the immediate future. Of course, that could all change in an instant.

'Although Al Qaeda has known sympathisers in Australia, mainly among the Middle Eastern communities, we also have no intelligence at this stage to suggest that Al Qaeda is planning attacks in this country. Nevertheless, we cannot afford to let our guard down. Terrorist groups are becoming increasingly sophisticated and are learning how to stay beneath the radar.

'There could well be sleeper cells from either Al Qaeda or JI just waiting to strike at any time.'

Fleming concluded his address by answering a number of questions from those present about the types of improvised explosive devices used by suicide bombers. He then showed a number of graphic pictures of the aftermath of various terrorist attacks around the world. Although in his former role as a counter terrorist expert McCarthy had been no stranger to pictures of violent bloodshed, he'd not experienced the carnage first hand. The images strengthened his resolve to do everything in his power to protect his family.

'What a sorry old world we live in eh?' Stormy remarked as he escorted McCarthy to his office after the meeting had concluded. 'It seems we're damned if we don't take action to tackle climate change. On the other hand, dealing with it creates its own nightmares. Globally, we're only a sprat in a pond filled with sharks. The most powerful nations of the world seem hell bent on becoming increasingly richer and even more powerful, focussing almost exclusively on the global financial crisis while we go it alone on climate change. What hope is there?'

'We have to remain optimistic and pray other

nations will come to their senses in time.' McCarthy replied. 'There is no other option. I am enormously proud that my son has the courage to show such leadership and I feel duty bound to use my knowledge and training to ensure he lives long enough to guide Australia along a path of humanitarianism and sustainability.

'Commissioner, while the meeting was underway I couldn't help wondering why Matthew wasn't there. Wasn't he invited?'

'Yes, but he told me it's important that his presence doesn't inhibit what is essentially police business. He knows I'll keep him and his cabinet abreast of developments. In fact, I have a meeting scheduled this afternoon. In the meantime, John, if there is anything more I can do to help you with your new job, please let me know.'

Forty-five kilometres away, in the deserted homestead, Jambali stared at the sealed plastic Amophos fertiliser bags, the plastic buckets filled with nails and ball bearings and the diesel drums piled against the back wall of the rickety outhouse at the rear of the sagging main building. Although he felt elated at the prospect of striking a blow against the much-hated Australians, he had wondered how the dozen bags of fertiliser could be delivered effectively against any of the potential targets. His sorties around Australia's capital city had shown all the iconic targets to be protected by heavy bollards, or large concrete, shrub-filled troughs that although serving to beautify the city, also provided effective barricades against car bombs.

Although it would be an easy matter to detonate a device in a crowded shopping precinct or business district, he doubted that his masters would receive sufficient satisfaction from mere random slaughter. Effective and devastating as it would be in a country that hitherto had not experienced major terrorism within its borders, the destruction of a building such as the Australian War Memorial, the Mint or even Parliament House would reverberate around the world. *So what is the plan?*

He hurried back to the house and began searching the cupboards. Like the rooms, they were all empty. Where else to look? His eyes travelled to the ceiling and he ran to the hallway in search of the small trapdoor he knew would be there. The plasterboard square was soiled with hand marks and the spider's webs festooning the cracked water-stained ceiling had been disturbed recently.

'How am I going to get up there?' Jambali muttered. His short stature ensured the old fashioned three-metre ceiling was well beyond his reach. Running outside again he looked anxiously for some way to gain the extra height needed. Deducing whoever had hidden the remaining bomb components would not have wanted them discovered accidently by curious children or someone else stumbling into the old house, he guessed they would not have left a convenient ladder behind.

Rummaging in the long grass of the neglected vegetable patch he produced a number of stout but weathered tomato stakes. He stacked these in the hallway, then returned to the old vegetable garden and selected two railings from the fence that been left untouched by ravaging white ants. A second search of the shed produced some fencing wire and a pair of rusty pliers. Thirty minutes later Jambali's makeshift ladder leant against the hallway.

Scrambling into the ceiling space, Jambali sneezed as a century's accumulation of dust and grime assailed his nostrils. Tiny shafts of light lanced downward from the rusting corrugated iron roof providing just enough light for him to make out thirty or more blue plastic containers stacked against the roof trusses. Jambali's frown creased in puzzlement. Each box resembled a domestic kitchen waste bin but there were a couple of points of difference. The bins were identically labelled but in the dim light he could not read what the labels said. Shuffling in a half crouched stance, he made his way carefully across the timbers. A large cardboard box with its flaps tucked closed sat beside the bins.

Jambali's fingers shook with excitement as he prised open the flaps. Feeling inside the box, he identified the familiar cylindrical shape of electronic detonators, square 9 volt batteries, coils of insulated wire and other electronic components which he guessed would turn out to be timing devices. The box also contained an envelope, photographs and several sheets of paper.

Leaving everything but the envelope in the ceiling he dropped back into the sunlit hallway so he could read his instructions. The would-be terrorist's eyes lit up and he chuckled. *I have to build ten bombs, not just one. But what are the plastic bins for?*

He soon found the answer in the intricately detailed plan that was so daring, imaginative and audacious that it might just work.

Jambali could not wait to get started assembling his deadly cargo of improvised explosive devices.

The deadline was in ten days' time.

++++++++++

Chapter Twelve

Matthew McCarthy could not help feeling a little guilty. The azure sea, cloudless skies and warm sun should have helped dispel the disquiet leaving his post at such a crucial time had caused. Common-sense told him the few hours doing what he loved would recharge his batteries and equip him much better to deal with the responsibilities of his office. Still, it didn't feel right.

'So what's the dive plan Dick?' he asked, as his personal protector and dive buddy throttled back the big twin Mercury outboards.

They'd juddered across the wind ruffled surface of the sea for the past hour after setting sail from a small picturesque south coast fishing hamlet. The sudden quiet was a welcome relief from the roar of the engines. The deep V of the aluminium hull settled back into the water. The outboard motors settled into a purr as they idled toward a rocky outcrop liberally coated with guano.

The shriek of indignant gulls almost drowned Matt's words as the birds rose, whirled and swooped in clouds around them. The unmistakeably ammoniac stench of seals wafted across the water and flabby, awkward ebony shapes slipped into the waves. Approximately 500 metres from their position another boat bobbed gently as two black-clad figures moved busily about its deck, clearly readying themselves for their incursion into the ocean's depths. The familiar blue and white dive flag fluttered from a flagpole atop the aluminium vessel's cabin.

Ever interested in boats and their various designs, Matthew recognised the craft as a New Zealand manufactured Swiftcraft, an extremely popular and seaworthy aluminium vessel sometimes chosen by volunteer sea rescue groups for its ability to handle the roughest conditions. Peering against the sun's glare he tried to distinguish the boat's registration number but was unable to do so due to some dark substance smeared across the numerals.

Dick Nolan's voice distracted the younger McCarthy from his curious study of the other boat. 'This spot is nicknamed Thunder Rock by local divers. There's the wreck of an early unnamed barque on this side, although it's mostly indistinguishable from the surrounding reef. On the other side there's a much better preserved dive site of the old steel-hulled coastal trader, the S.S. Fairy Queen. I've dived on both sites before and I am sure you'll enjoy them Matt.'

Nolan still felt awkward calling the country's top politician by his first name but McCarthy insisted on informality when away from the high pressure world of Canberra's bureaucrats.

'What is the deepest we will have to go?' Matt asked, as he unfurled the blue and white dive flag and propped its end into one of the rod holders atop the sturdy boat's half cabin.

The federal policeman directed the boat's nose carefully toward the coordinates on the craft's GPS, at the same time studying the echo sounder. 'There she is,' he exclaimed suddenly, forgetting to answer McCarthy as he pointed to the sharp peak on the instrument's tiny screen. 'That will be the old steamship. We'll come back around over her and you chuck out the anchor when I give you the nod.'

McCarthy could see from the depth indicator that the ship lay in approximately twenty-two metres of water. 'We'll dive on the steel ship site first 'cos that's the deeper of the two wrecks,' Nolan told him. 'There's a swim-through about twenty metres long at the western side of Thunder Rock and that will put us straight onto the barque. She's in roughly eighteen metres and about fifty metres away from the Fairy Queen so we can easily swim back to the dive boat again either on the surface or come back along the bottom depending on how much air we suck. I reckon we should pick up a few lobsters in the crevices if you want.'

'Sounds great, Dick.' McCarthy nodded toward the other boat. 'It looks like our friends over there are concentrating on the old barque site. Is there much of a current for us to be concerned about through this area?'

'Not that I've encountered previously. Right, chuck the anchor over now.'

Australia's PM and the navy-diver-turned-policeman leant against the boat's gunwales as they donned wetsuits and the remainder of their dive gear as their boat rocked in the slight swell. Nolan was not surprised by the prime minister's muscled physique. Since he'd been appointed to personally guard the other man he'd been required to accompany him on his daily 10 kilometre run through the Canberra streets and knew the prime minister regularly pumped weights in the small gym at the Lodge.

Peering over the side, McCarthy felt the pre-dive

exhilaration every diver experiences at the thought of plunging into gin-clear waters on a perfect day. Suddenly, he felt his spirits lift even higher. *What could be better than this?*

'Dick, I usually like to throw floating line out the stern, just in case we have trouble swimming back against the current. Particularly as we have no boatman to pick us up if something goes wrong.' McCarthy was mildly surprised that the veteran diver had not thought to take this basic safety precaution.

'Just testing to see if you'd remember,' Nolan joked, trying to laugh off his obvious oversight. *You won't be needing it mate. You won't be coming back anyway!*

With fifty metres of nylon rope and a couple of makeshift floats hanging languidly in the ocean behind their craft, the two divers went through their pre-dive checks. McCarthy set the lapsed time bezel on his dive watch and signalled to his companion that he was ready to go. Nolan raised his right hand, his index finger and thumb forming the universal signal "okay" and the two men rolled backward simultaneously into the water.

With the boat's hull separating them, they swam to its bow and the anchor rope where they again signalled "okay", duck-diving in unison to begin their descent.

Although Matthew McCarthy was a seasoned diver with over a thousand dives under his belt Dick Nolan seemed just at home in the water as he was on land. Whereas McCarthy had to pause several times during the descent to equalise the pressure in his ears, Nolan's descent was swift and seamless. Schools of bait fish swirled about them, and thick bull kelp waved to and fro on top of the reef which dropped sharply either side into deep trenches where little light penetrated.

McCarthy was surprised to find a large octopus staring balefully from the anchor around which it had wrapped its tentacles as if to claim it as a prize. Nudging the creature with his crayfish loop he managed to persuade it to swim away so that he could ensure the anchor's flukes would not pull free as their boat rose and fell with the swell. Several large reef sharks swam lazily by, showing little interest in the human intruders. Although McCarthy had studied the ocean's life forms intimately he never tired of its miracles. Gesturing to Nolan, he paused to enjoy an enormous stingray's watery flight, likening it to some interstellar spacecraft gliding gracefully over a jungle covered mountain range.

Dick Nolan pointed into the trench to the divers' left and they swam on down, marvelling at the hundreds of crayfish lining the long crevices, as if on display, their feelers twitching inquisitively at the alien vibrations created by the diver's rising air bubbles and the flap of their rubber fins. Ignoring the much prized marine delicacy they peered into the gloom, searching for the wreck of the Fairy Queen.

McCarthy was the first to spot the vessel's weed encrusted hull. Nature was rapidly embracing the steel leviathan and although its outline would eventually be indistinguishable from the barnacle-encrusted rocks comprising the reef there was still no problem discerning the vessel's shape.

The ship had settled on its keel. Weed festooned her railings and the tangled mess of her broken superstructure spoke volumes about the torment she'd endured during her encounter with the jagged rocks of the storm-lashed reef. Twisted and split asunder by the pounding waves she'd spilled her guts across the ocean floor as if disembowelled by some mad, axe-wielding giant.

Although earlier divers had picked over the submerged debris in search of trophies, the wreck site was now protected from further plunder by maritime laws and provided no shortage of fascinating relics. Ancient wine bottles, their corks still intact, littered the seafloor along with numerous dinner plates, and an amazing assortment of pottery, shoes, hand tools and other strange junk at whose purpose they could only wonder.

After prodding and poking among the strange clutter for several minutes they swam to the huge opening in the ship's massive belly. Switching on their powerful torches both divers peered into the threatening black void of the ship's interior, planning their path carefully before entering to avoid being snagged by the seemingly limitless array of jagged obstacles that once comprised the engine room and holds.

As a naval demolition expert Nolan was better acquainted with the ship's internal layout so McCarthy willingly relinquished the lead. He checked his dive computer, contents gauge and watch, noting their depth and elapsed time. A mere 15 minutes had passed since they'd left the boat and at 23 metres they were well within safety limits. Although Nolan seemed to know what he was doing McCarthy withdrew a ball of strong twine from his catch bag. Tying one end to a convenient anchor point, he allowed the string to unravel as they moved deeper into the ship's belly. This simple precaution would ensure they could easily find their way out from the confusing labyrinth of passageways.

Port Jackson sharks flitted away, posing no threat but obviously not happy at the intrusion. An enormous crab paused in its sideways shuffle across the steel slatted engine room floor to raise its claws defiantly. Although they tried not to disturb the layer of fine silt covering everything, the water soon became turbid. Nolan gestured upward and they followed a sagging steel ladder through a hatchway to the next level where a catwalk ran along the ship's side. Doors to cabins hung open, revealing bunks and lockers of what had once been the crew's accommodation. Here they found the water clearer. With shafts of eerie greenish light lancing through a line of grimy portholes they were able to extinguish their torches. They peered into cabins but finding nothing of interest, Nolan gestured that they should make their way back. McCarthy willingly agreed, hoping his companion's intention was to re-enter the ship from its superstructure and explore the bridge and wheelhouse which promised to be more interesting.

McCarthy led this time, winding up the twine as they retreated. He glanced behind him several times, anxious to ensure he did not break one of the basic principles of safe diving; never lose sight of your buddy. For some reason, the former navy diver seemed to be taking his time. Although he returned McCarthy's "okay" gesture he dropped further and further behind.

The marine-scientist-cum-prime-minister swam down into the murky bilges and engine room, switching on his torch again to light their way. The torch beam penetrated approximately one metre into the suspended silt particles and he was glad to have the string to follow. It was now no use looking to see if Nolan was following, the water was far too murky and he was forced to trust that the navy diver's experience would stand him in good stead.

A dark shape moved across the limited periphery permitted by McCarthy's face mask. He turned his head quickly, hoping to catch a glimpse of whatever lurked within the gloom but he could see nothing. An icy chill ran along his spine and discovering his breathing rate had increased, he told himself it was just an illusion. Consciously slowing his breathing to conserve his precious air supply he glanced at the luminous dial of his heavy Seiko dive watch and was surprised to discover they'd now been below the surface for nearly 45 minutes. His contents gauge showed he'd consumed over half the single bottle strapped to his back.

Without warning something whacked heavily against the air tank, ricocheting into the inky blackness with a resounding metallic clang. Shocked, McCarthy whirled around in the cavernous engine room. *What the fuck was that?*

Something flashed mere metres away. Blinding pain made him scream although the sound was lost in a mass of bubbles. He looked down to his abdominal area and the source of the pain. A long steel spear shaft had penetrated his wetsuit. Although he could not see the spear's barbed point he knew it had gouged a deep wound across his hip. Something dark and oily looking curled from the wound. It took a moment for his shocked brain to register that he was bleeding profusely.

Knowing he was in serious trouble McCarthy pulled his dive knife from its sheath. His cray loop was useless as a weapon and he let it sink into the muddy bottom. He quickly realised that one spear directed his way may be attributed to a careless spearfisherman not properly identifying his target, but a second was no coincidence.

At least two divers shared what may yet be his tomb. There was no doubt they meant to kill him.

Yanking the spear free, Matthew dropped it and whirled and backed against something solid to face his attackers. Clamping his left hand over the wound in an attempt to staunch the blood flow he was just in time to see a pair of black rubber fins disappearing toward the only way out of the old wreck.

Of Nolan there was no sign. Beginning to feel light-headed, McCarthy hoped his assailants had either assumed they'd completed their mission and fled or were not prepared to take on an extremely angry knife-wielding opponent. The third option that they were lying in wait was not worth thinking about, he must get to the surface and tend his wound lest he die from blood loss or, worse still, the sharks returned to finish him off.

His air supply was now dangerously low. He couldn't risk waiting to see if Nolan would arrive to assist him. Abandoning his string winding, he used the strong cord to pull himself toward the exit, his head swivelling from side to side and the knife clenched between his teeth. A ragged circle of light ahead loomed. He had almost reached the exit. Drawn by the smell of blood, a trail of inquisitive fish followed closely.

Please God, let me get safely to the surface.

Careful to control his ascent, McCarthy followed the speed of the smallest bubbles from his regulator as they rose, wobbling like miniature jellyfish. He sucked the last dregs of air from his regulator and although under normal circumstances he knew he could survive on the residual air within his lungs as it expanded with his ascent, the pain was too intense. Struggling to stave off the panic, from somewhere within his foggy brain he remembered the tiny emergency "pony" bottle meant for such emergencies. He reached for the valve and air flowed instantly into his mouthpiece.

As Matthew's head broke the surface he realised he was still some 50 metres from the boat. That distance was nothing to an able bodied fit swimmer but to him it seemed like a mile.

The distant scream of an outboard motor drifted across the waves. Matthew inflated his buoyancy vest and rolled onto his back. He looked toward the noise. The aluminium hull of the Swiftcraft raised a V shaped white plume as his two would-be assassins disappeared toward the horizon.

Dropping his weights and catch bag, he abandoned his air tank to conserve his energy for the swim and slowly made his way to the dive boat. After what seemed an agony-filled eternity, he reached the transom. Grasping the stern ladder he gasped for breath and mustered the remnants of his flagging energy to climb back into the boat. Suddenly, a head popped up beside him.

'Where the hell have you been?' McCarthy gasped as Dick Nolan pulled his mask down around his neck and stared at him.

The policeman blinked. 'What do you mean? What's going on? Where's your gear?' he enquired.

McCarthy suppressed his rage. 'For God's sake just help me get aboard. I've been shot by a bloody spear gun.'

Nolan quickly shed his dive gear and attached it to the trailing safety line before leaping up the ladder into the dive boat. 'Give me your hand,' he said leaning over the stern. Grasping McCarthy's proffered hand he hauled him into the boat.

'Fuck, boss, you're a bloody mess! What do you want me to do?'

Matthew realised he must remain conscious. If Nolan was mixed up in the assassination attempt as he suspected he might decide to finish the job while there were no witnesses. 'Give me my bloody mobile phone,' he ordered.

Nolan hesitated for a moment before fetching the prime minister's iPhone from the cabin and handing it to him.

'Don't worry about trying to deal with my wound,' Matthew growled. He still hung onto his knife and held it threateningly. Jabbing 999 into the screen he held the phone to his ear with his free hand. 'Just get the bloody engine going and get me back to shore as quickly as you can,' he muttered as he waited for the emergency operator. Having identified himself and provided a brief description of events he felt safer, knowing an ambulance would be waiting for them when they returned.

This bastard's not going to try and kill me now he

knows there'll be some very awkward questions to answer.

Propped at the back of the boat where the ride was smoother, McCarthy fixed his gaze on Nolan's back as he focussed his attention on driving the boat. The roar from the big outboards rendered conversation impossible. In any case his befuddled mind had enough to do dealing with the pain and remaining conscious until the paramedics could deal with his injuries. He thought briefly about phoning someone with whom he could share his suspicions. That's all they were after all. Nolan had only to deny involvement. What did he have? Nolan's tardy diving practices could be easily explained. The water was murky and they'd become separated. Some lunatic diver had fired his spear gun without identifying his target. The fact that there had been two spears and they weren't attached by the usual cords to the weapons was extremely suspicious but there was no connection that he knew of between the Federal policeman and his attackers. No, he'd wait until they got back before requesting that Nolan be removed as his bodyguard and a full investigation into the incident mounted.

That was, if he survived

Clamping his hand tighter over the wound in his side, McCarthy gritted his teeth against the pain and fought the waves of nausea that threatened to engulf him.

++++++++++++++

181

Chapter Thirteen

The cordon around the crime scene immediately following Connor Bowker's assassination had been unprecedented in size. Although the crowd fled and few witnesses remained on the scene, the New South Wales Police Force knew it must do everything its resources would allow to assist its federal counterparts. Cops attending low priority jobs were ordered to immediately stop what they were doing and get themselves to the scene. Leaving skeleton staff to provide only the most essential services, they came from all over the state. Leave was cancelled, deskbound officers were ordered back into the front line and the plea went out for all other states to assist. The response resulted in the biggest manhunt in Australia's history. The crime scene extended over most of Sydney's central business district, effectively shutting down business activity, and creating major damage to both the state and the national economy. While most corporate leaders and citizens bore the inconvenience stoically the force's commander and the state government realised they could only keep this up for so long.

Chief Superintendent Colin Burrows as the operation commander faced a logistical nightmare in coordinating such a mammoth operation. For once the professional jealousies, territorialism and rivalry between state and federal agencies were put aside. Scotland Yard and the FBI offered to send their top investigators. Because the Americans had firsthand experience in handling politically-motivated assassinations, Burrows had no qualms accepting whatever help he could get. The new prime minister declared a national state of emergency and ordered the country's defence forces to assist with transporting police and resources from across the nation. Service personnel took on the task of manning barricades and providing accommodation and feeding the thousands of personnel now involved in the operation.

Every attempt was made to seize all CCTV camera footage. Processing the images was another matter. It would be slow and tedious. The police rounded up Sydney's vagrants from emergency shelters, squats, parks, railway stations, alleyways, beneath bridges and a myriad of haunts, to be questioned. The Salvation Army, Red Cross and other agencies established food distribution points for the homeless on the fringe of the crime scene and the police raided those. Prostitutes, drug dealers and society's other criminal flotsam was quizzed and the incentive of the $5,000,000 reward waved under their noses.

With the barricades established on every thoroughfare and the crime scene frozen, nothing moved in or out of the CBD without being checked first.

This included the city's massive quantities of rubbish. The filthy, unenviable task of painstakingly sifting through the city's detritus was delegated to State Emergency Service personnel. Rubbish bins and skips in the immediate vicinity of Martin Place they searched immediately but rubbish containers from further afield were photographed in situ and labelled with their exact location before being transported to a nearby car park to be emptied and the contents thoroughly examined.

Sorting through apparent leads, blatant lies and

misinformation is all part of the tedious, boring routine police work associated with any major criminal investigation. The qualities of a good investigator include optimism, stubborn, meticulous perseverance, knowledge of the workings of the criminal mind and a certain natural intuitiveness that cannot be taught.

Although Burrows' team comprised the best the country had to offer, the top policeman knew luck also played an important role. The first breakthrough came three weeks into the investigation with a phone call from the S.E.S. Commander, Gareth Holman. 'I think my boys and girls have got something you'll want to see,' he announced. 'It looks like we've discovered the components from some sort of high-powered rifle.'

Burrows could hardly contain his elation. He wanted to see this for himself. 'Okay, don't touch anything until I get down there,' he ordered, grabbing his uniform jacket. 'Get the forensic teams down to the sorting yard now,' he told the uniformed sergeant assigned to assist him. 'And have my driver bring the car around the front.'

Ten minutes later Burrows had pulled on his gumboots and overalls and stood amid the reeking piles of rubbish. 'Since we spoke I've had all bins from the same alley collected over there.' Holman, a sixty-something ex-military type, gestured toward several garbage bins and a huge, green graffiti-covered metal skip.

'Where did they come from?' Burrows asked.

'It was some grubby unnamed laneway off George Street about 750 metres from Martin Place. Come over here and I'll show you the exact location on the city map.'

'Good work Gareth!' Burrows exclaimed. 'Forensics will take over searching this lot. Let's hope you've found a real treasure trove. I bet our man thought he'd got rid of the evidence and no one would think to search through rubbish so far from the shooting.'

Dragging hand carts loaded with their equipment across the bitumen, the forensic team got stuck in, methodically removing each item of rubbish for photographing and bagging. It did not take them long to strike gold.

As soon as the first rifle components began emerging from the bins, Burrows had summoned George Page, the Federal Police's top ballistics expert, a diminutive, moustachioed former S.A.S. armourer and weapons instructor who lived and breathed firearms.

'The weapon is a Sauer 202 takedown rifle fitted with a laser sight,' Page reported. 'This one was also fitted with a Sauer muzzle break to reduce recoil and muzzle flash. It fires a .357 magnum round from a 5 capacity magazine which was ample for the task. The entire thing is designed to be collapsible in a few seconds. In other words, it's the ultimate weapon for the modern day assassin.'

'There's something unusual about the bolt.' Burrows cupped his chin in his hand. 'I know what it is,' he declared suddenly, clapping his hands together. 'The bastard was a left!'

'I wondered if you'd spot that,' the little weapons expert said. 'There can't be many professional left-handed hit men. It should help narrow the field considerably.'

'As long as he is a pro,' the police superintendent mused.

'Oh this bloke knew his trade all right. You can be sure of that. I bet it hurt him to part with a gun like this. He obviously weighed up the chances of being caught red-handed against disposing of it and decided we'd never find it and it would end up in landfill. With any luck we can narrow down where the weapon came from originally even though the numbers have been filed off.'

Colin Burrows was ecstatic but experience had told him to suppress any excitement. Too often apparently good leads ended against a brick wall. 'Okay, George. I'll leave that side of things in your hands.'

Jambali was feeling very weary. He'd been working non-stop for the past few weeks assembling his not-so-little toys. He did not want to miss the deadline. D-day was the next day and although he did not know when the special vehicle that was to be used to deliver his bombs would arrive, he knew it was going to be a very busy day for him. He looked forward to joining his fellow martyrs in paradise.

'Allahu Akbar! Death to the puppets of the Great Satan,' he shouted aloud in his native tongue.

'Quiet my friend! You never know who is listening,' a voice answered.

Jambali spun around to face the owner of the voice. The youthful face of one of his fellow countrymen smirked at him from the doorway. He had not heard a vehicle arrive, or the man's approach, and he was taken completely unawares. He instinctively grabbed for a long fine-bladed screwdriver he'd been using moments earlier to tighten the terminals on the last of his makeshift bombs but relaxed as the man put his hands together and bowed in the traditional sign of greeting and respect.

The new arrival sported a thick crop of black hair. He had a small, luxurious, equally dark growth extending to a point about six centimetres beneath thick sensual lips. His rather broad and very prominent nose made any introduction unnecessary. Jambali knew the man had recently escaped from Tanjung Gusta prison along with 200 criminals and three suspected members of a notoriously vicious extremist organisation. He could not recall the group's name but knew its leader, Toni Togar, a Jemaah Islamiyah sympathiser, was on Indonesia's most-wanted list.

It was also no secret, that in order to fund their jihadist networks, Togar and Jemaah Islamiyah were inextricably linked to Indonesia's organised crime gangs who sold methamphetamines and other illicit substances. They had recently extended their reach and profited handsomely by smuggling drugs on fishing boats to Australia and selling them to bikie gangs with nationwide distribution networks.

During his brief time in Canberra, Jambali had recognised the name Shriver Chemicals from its on-running, prime time television campaign for popular cold and flu remedies. He knew the company was a huge employer in Indonesia and benefited enormously from that country's cheap labour. Jambali had heard many rumours that Shriver was responsible for manufacturing huge quantities of illicit drugs.

How very ironic for an Australian company to be

paying for the slaughter of its own citizens.

'I am Nibras Als Arab, also known as Amir Als Wawan. Please call me Nibras.' The young jihadist's deep brown eyes fixed Jambali with an intense stare.

'I know who you are,' Jambali replied, bowing deeply. 'I am very honoured.'

'I have come to Australia to personally take charge of this most important and historic mission to strike at the very heart of these decadent western pigs.

'I have also brought you the vehicle you will use tomorrow.' Nibras held up a set of vehicle keys attached to a Ford badge. He dragged a wooden chair across the bare boards and sat down. 'Let us discuss the plan to make sure you understand exactly what it is you must do.'

'Of course, but may I first ask some questions?'

'I am happy to satisfy your curiosity if I can, my friend, but some things cannot be disclosed. If you don't know, then you cannot be made to reveal our secrets to the authorities if you are captured.'

'I would never talk,' Jambali cried indignantly.

'Everyone talks if the right methods of persuasion are used. Do not make the mistake of thinking that the Australians would not resort to very persuasive methods. After all, they sleep with the Great Satan whose agents are experts. Now quickly, what is it you want to know?

'Why aren't you coming with me tomorrow? There is so much for one man to accomplish alone.'

'Aren't you up to the task?' Nibras' bushy eyebrows jumped toward his hairline like two caterpillars that had just been electrocuted.

'No, no, you misunderstand,' the bomb-maker cried. 'I am just saying that you have great knowledge and experience when it comes to hitting our enemies where it hurts. There is much I can learn from you.'

'Have you forgotten that you are going to paradise tomorrow, my dear friend? The knowledge will do you no good in this life, and after tomorrow, you will have done your duty to God and will be able to enjoy your just reward. Besides, you have been well trained and especially chosen. We know you are up to the task. Do not lose faith in yourself now.

'The other reason for not coming with you is that I am a wanted man, and too well known. Allah's work will not be completed by this one blow at Australia's heart. The real jihad is just beginning and I cannot risk being captured again.'

'Nibras, I am eager to know how you got into Australia without being recognised?'

'Ah, that is one of the things I cannot tell you but we have established our channels and have a network of good friends who are faithful to our cause. I cannot put all that at risk.'

Nibras smiled to himself as he remembered how easily he had bypassed Australia's border protection measures. The island nation's vast northern coastline was for the most part unprotected. It had been a relatively simple matter to land at night from one of the simple wooden Indonesian fishing boats that were so abundant in the seas between the archipelago and Australia. Two Jemaah Islamiyah operatives, a man and a woman posing as Asian tourists, had met him at the prearranged rendezvous on a remote coastal beach. The jihad organisation had financed the hire of a six-berth motor home from a well-known company and was perfect for the task. With overseas tourists hiring the Winnebago-type vehicles all the time, they were unlikely to arouse anyone's curiosity. Needless to say, anyone checking the couple's credentials would come to a dead end.

He'd sat in the vehicle's rear for most of the trip, watching the mostly uninteresting scrubland roll by the windows. The straightness of the road and the long distances between towns staggered him, as did Australia's vastness and small population.

Despite the lack of civilisation, there was a seemingly endless stream of aging couples driving motor homes, or towing luxurious caravans, touring the country and he could not understand how they funded such expensive vehicles or paid the exorbitantly high prices for the fuel these gas guzzlers required.

While his mind wandered and he'd been bored for much of the long trip through the Outback, he thought of his extended family and how they were always destined to work long hours, always struggling to earn a few rupiah in order to survive.

It's not fair for these Australians to have so much wealth and all this empty land that could be used to raise crops or cows, goats and pigs. It should be shared. In fact, it is our duty to Allah and Islam to take it from these greedy, decadent infidels!

Except for the huge, ever present road trains that thundered along the long, lonely highway, driving at night was simply too dangerous. While these leviathans could continue day and night, choosing just to smash over any creature careless enough to get in their path, the bloated carcases of kangaroos and wandering cattle littering the roadside provided ample warning to anyone thinking of driving after sunset.

The trio had not used caravan parks during the four day trip, choosing instead to stop overnight in one of the many free camping spots provided along the way. When space permitted, they parked well away from the many vehicles that flooded into the clearings each afternoon. Whenever friendly, garrulous baby boomers, ever eager for company, approached them at these overnight stays, they pretended not to understand English, smiling politely and shaking their heads stupidly. This act never failed to drive away even the most determined of the infidels.

When it became necessary to refuel at one of the few small towns or at a roadhouse, Nibras remained out of sight. His travelling companions always paid with cash so as not to leave a trail. They made it to Australia's capital city unscathed and his companions dropped Nibras at the Canberra safe house before returning to the Northern Territory to pick up the next jihadist operative.

This method of bringing jihadists to Australia was proving very effective and Jemaah Islamiyah would soon establish a sizeable terrorist network within Australia's borders.

"I shall ask no more questions.' Jambali felt chastened and wondered why the budding mastermind of terrorism did not also disguise his appearance.

The other man seemed to know what he was thinking. 'I do not change my appearance. It is unnecessary. I move only at night and its blackness is all I need. Now, let us get down to the specifics of our great plan and then I will help you load the fruits of your labour into the van. I must be gone long before daylight.'

The two men talked late into the night, going over the details again and again. Nibras made Jambali recite every aspect of the plan in great detail, quizzing him as to how he must act, the uniform he was to wear and the way he was to behave. They role played various scenarios so Jambali could demonstrate his acting ability when it became necessary to speak to the Australians or their police and security. The "what ifs" went on and on for hours until both men had satisfied themselves that they'd covered every possible contingency.

Finally, Nibras stood up, stretched his rail thin body and announced, 'Wait here. I have something for you.'

Slipping outside to the waiting van the terrorist leader returned a moment later with an overnight bag from which he withdrew a small sleeveless vest and spread it on the table.

The hair on Jambali's neck seemed to stand on end despite knowing about the backup plan should anything should go awry.

Courage! I must have courage, for this is my duty to Allah.

Pockets had been sewn onto the front and back of the simple cotton garment. Thin wires ran from each pocket to a small pouch designed to fit on a trouser belt. He'd helped make the suicide vests back home and knew the pouch contained the battery pack and a spring-loaded pressure switch that would simultaneously activate the plastic explosives in each of the vest's pockets.

Jambali's hands began to sweat. His big moment was drawing closer.

Nibras fixed his dark eyes on his visibly anxious recruit. 'You know what this is for. You and I are about the same size so I know it will fit. You must wear this under your uniform tomorrow. The uniform is very loose-fitting so there is little danger of the vest being seen.

'Under no circumstances are you to let them arrest you. If you cannot continue your mission, take as many of the Australians with you as you can.

'May Allah be with you,' Nibras declared and embraced the bomber. 'We will meet again one day in paradise. Now, let us load your little surprises into the van. You must then get some sleep so you are fresh for the morning.'

Jambali did not reply. He knew sleep would be impossible.

The two Indonesians carried the ten seemingly innocuous plastic containers to the waiting Transit van, stacking them securely in the rear.

'One last thing,' Nibras instructed. 'These obviously weigh more than they would when they are empty. It is therefore vitally important to carry them so they appear very light.

'I have practised this,' Jambali replied. 'It will be no problem to me.'

'Good.' Nibras jumped into the Toyota van Jambali had first used and called out the open driver's window,

'Do not forget to set the timers to ensure every bomb explodes simultaneously at 3.00pm tomorrow!'

John McCarthy was impressed. He'd just completed a full inspection of the 40 room Georgian style mansion and its 18,000 square metres of landscaped grounds. Built in 1927 as a temporary measure to house Australia's prime ministers until such time as a residence more fitting the status of the country's political leader could be constructed, the Lodge had housed successive prime ministers for eighty years. Extensively renovated and remodelled, the residence also boasted state-of-the-art security systems incorporating closed circuit television cameras, biometric security, high fences, shatter-proof windows and a safe room in case of terrorist attack.

However, John McCarthy was not satisfied.

As a highly-trained security professional and former policeman, McCarthy senior understood only too well that even the best security measures had loopholes and could be breached. It was just a matter of finding the weaknesses in the Lodge's defences, and to do that he adopted the mindset of a would-be terrorist intent on wreaking maximum havoc, or the alternative of someone who simply wanted to take the prime minister's life.

In other words, in order to catch a crook one must think like a crook.

McCarthy's theory that good security entails surrounding what must be protected with layer upon layer of protective measures, a bit like an onion, saw him start at the perimeter and gradually work his way inward to the greatest asset, the Lodge's inhabitants.

The famous wrought iron gates equipped with their brass padlock and guarded by armed protective service officers provided access to a hedge-lined gravel driveway leading to the elegant, white main building with its wisteria-covered pergolas and many balconies. The perimeter fence was not easily climbed except by the most determined intruder. The video surveillance added deterrent value but the extensive shrubbery and trees in proximity largely negated the latter's effectiveness. McCarthy felt sure motion sensor would be of little value whenever a slight breeze blew. In his opinion the security management plan placed too much reliance on the vigilance of patrolling guards. He knew from experience that human beings employed on boring repetitive work could be easily circumvented.

The protective service officer detailed for gate duty on the first day of his survey was a good example of the type of individual one would not want protecting the lives of those nearest and dearest to him. At approximately 240 kilograms the man needed to be nearly two metres in height to approach anywhere near the ideal body mass. Instead he was a mere 175 centimetres. The bulging gut hanging over his belt threatened to burst his shirt buttons, while the accoutrement belt containing his Glock pistol was precariously close to sliding down the wharf-pile-sized thighs any moment.

Slouching against the wall with both hands stuffed in the pockets of his rumpled trousers, the man's vacant gaze suggested an intelligence level only slightly higher than Neanderthal man.

McCarthy's eyes flicked momentarily to the guard's name badge. 'Long day is it, Constable Lloyd?' he enquired, making no attempt to hide his sarcasm.

The lights came back on in Lloyd's eyes as he realised his career prospects might be in jeopardy. Shifting his weight onto both feet with cumbersomeness reminiscent of a sloth, he attempted a degree of professionalism. 'Good afternoon sir. I am a little weary. I think my blood sugar levels might be down a bit. Sorry if I didn't see you coming but you must have snuck up on me. I don't think I know you. May I see some identification?'

McCarthy produced his newly-acquired identity card bearing the Federal Police logo and his photograph and held it under the man's nose.

'Special Security Advisor to the Prime Minister,' the guard read, his eyebrows shooting heavenward. 'I am sorry Mr McCarthy, they told me you'd be prowl... I mean, having a look around. I hope everything's all right?' Clearly, the guard had not made the connection between McCarthy's name and that of the prime minister.

No it's not, you worthless tub of lard!

'Is Annette Thompson on duty today? She seems a very alert and efficient officer.' McCarthy couldn't help placing emphasis on the "she".

Chastened, the fat man's eyes flashed his resentment. 'Thommo's been reassigned to other duties. The brass seems to think she's wasted here. It's just me, Keith Sturt and Brian Kavanagh. They're on ground patrol,' he added.

'You're it then,' John McCarthy said.

'Waddya mean, I'm it?'

'I need someone to answer a few basic questions about security.'

'I don't know if I am allowed to provide information. It's the old need to know thing.' The guard tapped his bulbous nose and grinned. McCarthy could see the man was attempting to assert some authority.

'Well, Constable Lloyd, I suppose I'll have to go over your head. Before I do, tell me, what do you think my job title actually means. Do you think I am just some low-level public servant running errands for the prime minister? Has it not occurred to you that I might possess *some* authority and have been assigned by persons in high office?'

The penny dropped at last. 'Oh fuck! I've stuffed up big time haven't I?'

Normally an empathetic and competent manager of men under his command, McCarthy could not abide the man's slovenliness toward his duties and appearance. 'You might say that. I know discipline, pride in one's appearance and work ethic has taken a slide over the years but you would be the worst example of a law enforcement officer I have ever encountered. You lounge around looking like a bag of shit with your brain in neutral when you are supposed to be protecting one of the most important and iconic buildings in this nation, not to mention the lives of the country's prime minister, his family and all the decent, honest folk employed here. You and those who assigned you to this post are a disgrace to the AFP.'

'Oh, that's a bit harsh. What would you know about doing a job like this? Nothing ever happens. It's so bloody boring.'

'You know nothing about me, so I'll enlighten you a little.

'I've plodded the beat in all weather, meticulously shaking bloody door knobs, night shift after night shift, back in the days before two-way radios and cell phones. I've frozen my arse off on stakeouts, sometimes for weeks on end with nothing happening but I managed to stay alert. I've guarded murder scenes, governors general and other dignitaries so they could sleep soundly in their beds. I've plodded around deserted airports, immigration detention centres, and commonwealth establishments on twelve hour shifts.'

At the periphery of his vision, McCarthy noticed a slim Asian man who happened to be walking by pause and stare briefly toward the gates of the Lodge. Something about the man's behaviour and body language did not seem quite right; however he was too angry at Lloyd's slovenliness and dismissed the man as *just another tourist.* Refocussing his attention on the PSO he continued his tirade, 'The job is what you make it, Lloyd. You can choose to switch off and be bored to tears, or you can adopt the attitude that you're here for a very good reason and stay alert. You do that by dreaming up various scenarios and role playing them in your mind so you will be ready when or if something does happen. You do that by making a promise to yourself that no one will ever catch you napping. You do your best to ensure nothing happens on your watch without you knowing about it.' John McCarthy pointed to Lloyd's bulging gut. 'You do that by taking pride in your appearance and physical fitness and every small but essential detail of the job you do, such as making it your business to know your beat intimately and by looking for ways to improve things. So, don't give me your bullshit.'

'So, are you going to report me?'

'What do you think?' John McCarthy growled. Swinging on his heel, he walked away, leaving the other man to ponder his future.

The following morning, the federal police commissioner ushered McCarthy senior into the small lounge area adjoining his offices and motioned for him to sit opposite in a leather recliner chair. Worried that FEPOL's security boss might get his nose out of joint, John had requested the commissioner to ensure Graham Clews also attended his briefing.

Clews, who had been staring out the window, turned but remained standing as McCarthy entered the office. His shiny billiard ball-like head nodded a somewhat curt greeting as he returned McCarthy's hand shake a little reluctantly.

'I am sorry I haven't had time to get together with you yet Graham.' McCarthy smiled, hoping to placate the Detective Inspector. 'Things have obviously moved much faster than either of us could anticipate and I thought the best way to get ahead of the play was for the three of us to get together and work out a plan.'

Clews sighed. Like most successful career policemen he was a pragmatist. The prime minister's father had obviously earned the commissioner's respect and obstructing the former kiwi copper would not be a good career move. 'I'll be interested to hear any suggestions you might have, John. After all, we both want the same thing.'

After ordering his aid to fetch three coffees, Commissioner Knight smiled at his subordinate and the prime minister's father. 'It's nice to see you again John and I know you two will get along. When you get to know each other you'll find you have much in common.

'John, I look forward to reading your final security report on the Lodge after Graham has looked at it. I am sure you'll do an excellent job but obviously something's bothering you for you to call this meeting with us so urgently. What is the problem?'

'Thank you for making time in your schedule Commissioner, I appreciate that you're a very busy man,' John McCarthy replied. 'I am very concerned that there will be another attempt on my son's life. It's obvious from the reports in the newspapers that he's stirred up a hornet's nest among the unionists and big business with his refusal to back down on his environmental reforms.

'By the way, have you had any leads or break through on the assassination?'

'We're playing things pretty close to our chest but between we have some good leads. Colin's insistence that all the garbage from the area around the crime scene be sifted by his teams really paid off.'

'How so?'

'We now have the murder weapon. We know the shooter was left-handed and we've lifted DNA from the clothing he ditched after the murder. We've pulled in CCTV footage and actually have some good images of him both before he ditched evidence in the alleyway when he was disguised and after he ditched it.

'At least, we're ninety percent sure it's the same man we've captured on camera coming out of the alley. Less than three minutes had elapsed between the vagrant going in and a fellow dressed as a business man exiting.

'Unfortunately, we weren't lucky enough to get any prints off the weapon, which didn't surprise anyone, but we've got sufficient to put together an identikit image of the suspect. We're about to go public in the hope someone will know him.'

'That's fantastic news! I just hope he hasn't taken off to some country with no extradition agreement with Australia. Do you have any further leads as to the hit-man's employers?'

'Unfortunately, the possibilities seem endless at this point but we've prioritised the list and we're hoping the five million dollar reward will provide the incentive for someone to start singing.'

'What about the murder weapon? Any luck there?'

'Ah, that's a different story. I don't want to disclose the exact make and model of the weapon but suffice to say bolt action rifles designed for left-handed people are very rare,' the commissioner declared, a small triumphant smile playing around his mouth.

'From your obvious enthusiasm I am presuming that the rifle was specially made and not modified afterward,' McCarthy replied. 'Sorry, it's none of my business. I guess I just can't contain the old copper in me. Let's switch to why I am here.

'My complete review of the Lodge's security and that of the prime minister and his family will probably take about two weeks. Unfortunately, I believe we can't afford to wait that long and need to implement certain measures immediately.'

Clews frowned and placed his coffee cup carefully on the table beside him. 'This sounds rather ominous.'

Sitting back in his chair the commissioner glanced from one man to the other. 'I'm listening, John. What are your main concerns?'

McCarthy decided to sugar coat the pill he was about to deliver. The last thing he wanted was for Clews to think he was questioning his competency. 'From my preliminary inspection I am largely satisfied with the technology Graham has in place. The biometric system is state-of-the-art, as are the motion detectors and the high resolution colour cameras. I think more could be done to beef up the perimeter protection systems, such as creating a floodlit no-man's land all the way around the fence line.'

He hurried on as Clews began to object. 'Of course, I know Graham has had his hands tied by those who regard aesthetics as more important than security. I also realise that creating an additional security buffer would adversely impact on some of the beautiful trees and gardens and I'll give that aspect in-depth consideration before making any recommendations that are likely to upset the heritage people. I may be able to come up with a satisfactory compromise.'

Clews smirked. 'You've no idea what a pain in the arse the bastards can be.'

'I think I do Graham. I had similar problems when I tried to implement a security plan for Parliament House in WA. Anything that the politicians considered inconvenient ended up with me being mentioned in

Hansard.

'Anyway, that can wait; my main concerns need an immediate resolution so I'll outline what they are.

'Yesterday, I spoke with a certain Constable Lloyd. I suppose you know him?'

The detective inspector grunted. 'Actually I do. Let's say he's come to my notice on several occasions for the wrong reasons.'

Stormy Knight cupped his chin in his hand thoughtfully. 'I seem to remember recommending disciplinary action against the man. 'Wasn't he the idiot who kicked the Governor General's dog?'

'Yeah, the fat bugger was guarding Government House and didn't realise the Governor General was in residence at the time. The dog took an instant dislike to someone intruding in its territory and kept yapping at Lloyd's heels. The silly bugger yelled at it to fuck off and kicked it. He got a real shock when the Governor General's wife came out of the house and called the dog off.' Clews laughed. 'Any one of us would have felt like doing the same thing under the circumstances but when you're looking after security for the Queen's representative you have to be a bit more circumspect.'

Enjoying the joke, McCarthy thought sharing a similar experience would help cement his relationship with the two federal policemen. 'That reminds me of a similar incident in New Zealand years ago. A probationary copper with the unlikely nickname "Whitebait Guts" got into the lift at Christchurch Police Headquarters one day with a rather short stocky bloke whom he didn't recognise. This bloke looked Whitebait up and down and said, "You're pretty skinny to be a cop." Whitebait returned the scrutiny and said, "At least I'm not a short-arsed little fat fucker like you."

'Steam almost came out of the other bloke's ears. He said, "How dare you call me a short-arsed, fat little fucker. Do you know who you're talking to?"

'Whitebait knew he'd put his foot in it in a big way but he said, "Why should I care who you are?"

'The other bloke replied, "Because son, I am Chief Superintendent Gideon Tait, the District Commander and you are now ex-Constable whatever your name is. Hand me you ID card."'

The three men chuckled. 'What a bloody idiot,' the commissioner said, shaking his head.

McCarthy decided it was time to become more serious. "Harold, I am relieved to hear that you know this man. I was far from impressed by his appearance, his attitude or his ability to be part of the team protecting the nation's political leader and the Lodge itself.'

'What was he doing?'

McCarthy produced his iPhone and brought up the first in a series of images on its screen. 'Lloyd didn't see me take these or he'd be even more worried than he is.'

As the commissioner thumbed through the images his frown deepened. 'I see what you mean. Not exactly a deterrent presence is he?'

'No, and the other thing I am worried about, apart from his ability to respond, is the lack of protective service staff or police at the Lodge. I would have thought the current high level of alert would justify a stronger presence.'

'What are the minimum numbers you think

necessary?'

'I believe there should be at least two of your best Protective Service personnel on the gate at all times. I would like to see a dog section officer and one other uniformed member inside the grounds and two patrolling outside the perimeter.

'One of Constable Lloyd's criticisms, namely the boring nature of the work, is very valid, not that I told him that! For that reason, personnel should be rotated frequently and if possible, randomly, so that the changeover is unpredictable.'

'I can see sense in that. The crooks couldn't work out when there would be another team visiting to swap over and it would also help keep our people on their toes.'

'Exactly my thinking. I also think there needs to be some sort of fitness criteria and even psyche testing for the Lodge guards and the personnel protection detail. On that note, I came across one officer who did impress me the other day and wondered why she'd been moved from the Lodge.'

'What's her name? I'll look into it.'

'Annette Thompson. She struck me as being just the sort of person one would want keeping an eye on things. She's clearly alert, intelligent and imaginative. I can really see her going places.'

Knight leant forward and jotted some notes on a pad resting on the coffee table between them. Sitting back, he chewed thoughtfully on his pen. 'I've been concerned about the decline in physical fitness and the lowering of our entry standards to accommodate the equal opportunities lunatics. Like so many employers, we've been victims of political correctness gone wrong and the overarching fear that we'll be sued for unfair discrimination. The bloody world's gone mad!'

'Harold, surely you can apply aptitude and physical fitness testing; after all it's a matter of national security.'

'You're quite right John. I've only been in the top job for six months but it's time I took a stand on this particular issue.

'Commencing immediately, Constable Lloyd and all those of his ilk who don't measure up will be reassigned to non-essential duties and subjected to strict medical reassessment. If, within a reasonable time frame, they don't reach the optimum standard of physical fitness, or pass psyche examinations designed to test their aptitude, they'll be offered the choice between a redundancy package or being transferred to somewhere like Afghanistan, Cairo or Beirut.

'Unfortunately, in the past, diplomatic and consular protection has been regarded as the dumping ground for those unsuitable for front line policing. It's also been somewhere to put officers who are getting near retirement, or carrying some sort of injury or health problem. In other words, VIP protection has become the dad's army division of the federal police.

'We've got away with it because the threat levels have been low until now but terrorism has clearly arrived on our shores and having worn out old has-beens or lazy time-servers guarding the nation's assets and its leaders is no longer satisfactory.'

John McCarthy nodded enthusiastically. 'What's needed is a change in the culture and thinking so the

DCP people establish a reputation as an elitist group. I suggest you start with a name change. Run a promotional campaign stressing the need for new recruits willing to undergo specialist training and rigorous testing regimes along the lines of the S.A.S. Make those in the current DCP unit reapply for positions in the new unit, or send them back to front line duties if they don't want to go through the training course. That way, you'll attract the right type of people and build a special group with strong camaraderie and team spirit.'

'I'll take steps to instruct that these measures are to set up as soon as possible. We've got some excellent training instructors who have special services experience. I am sure they'll just love to throw a course together, although we'll have to make do with what we've got until we put enough people through the training.'

'I think you'll find all the good officers in the ranks, including those in supervisory positions, will breathe a huge sigh of relief. My experience is that anyone who takes pride in the job is embarrassed when their fellow officers let them down. Good people very quickly become demoralised and disillusioned when the system doesn't discipline the recalcitrant ones, or get rid of the dead wood. It was the lack of discipline and poor selection processes that were responsible for my resignation way back in 1992.'

The commissioner's discomfort that his beloved organisation had been found wanting was obvious so John McCarthy changed tack. 'Well, perhaps this incident with Jerry Lloyd will turn out to be a blessing in disguise. FEDPOL should be grateful that it now has a commissioner at the helm prepared to bring about changes for the better.

'Thank you for listening to me. I really appreciate it.'

Stormy smiled. 'It's okay John. If I can't stand a little criticism I don't deserve to hold my position. What other matters needed to be dealt with immediately?'

'I am worried about the very real threat posed by suicide bombers, drug-crazed malcontents and other loony tunes. The front gates at the Lodge are insufficient to stop a vehicle ramming its way through and crashing into the house. You will no doubt recall several recent episodes where vehicles have been used as weapons against courthouses and police stations. The same thing could easily happen at the Lodge and it doesn't take much imagination to conjure up the carnage a truckload of explosives could do. I think it would be wise to install retractable bollards, or some other retractable barrier sufficient to withstand a large, heavily-laden truck.

'The other issue is the vetting of visitors. Now I know everyone who enters the gates must have a security clearance, or they are escorted by one of your officers, but too often vehicles are simply waved through without being checked. That happens because the staff on the gate have either become complacent, or they have become overly familiar with delivery persons and drivers.

'Checking passes and kicking arses is boring and tedious work, so it's normal for people to develop friendships and to start trusting those they encounter on a regular basis, however it is a recipe for disaster. We must get the message across that nothing and no one should be taken for granted. Given the current high threat level, I would recommend every vehicle be given at least a quick going over, including checking the underside by mirror to ensure it's not carrying an I.E.D. I would also suggest that staff randomly target a minimum number of vehicles each day and give them a thorough search. Even that is insufficient. Again, experience has taught me staff will take short cuts, especially when it's getting close to a meal break or time to knock off. For that reason, they need to be kept on their toes by the occasional and random placement of a simulated I.E.D. in vehicles passing through the gate.'

The commissioner shook his head in amazement. 'You're a sneaky bastard aren't you?'

'Not really. We just can't afford to have anyone let their guard down and knowing there are consequences for doing so is the best way of ensuring optimum performance. You should also provide incentives for staff to do the right thing.'

Stormy nodded. 'The old carrot and stick approach eh? I'll get someone onto it right away John. Obviously all these things won't happen overnight but those that can be implemented immediately will be and the others will receive the highest priority.'

The meeting over, the two men shook hands, both satisfied with the strong bond of mutual respect and liking they'd established. However, as McCarthy left FEDPOL HQ, he felt almost overcome by a nagging feeling of disquiet. Images of his grandchildren's happy, innocent faces flashed before him.

I just hope we're not too bloody late with all this.

As John McCarthy made his way back to the Lodge to continue his security survey, his mobile telephone vibrated. Reaching into his jacket pocket he pulled out the iPhone and glanced at the caller ID before answering. 'Hello Mary my darling, what gives?'

His wife's voice quivered agitatedly, 'John, something terrible has happened. How far are you from the Lodge?'

McCarthy's heart sank. Mary was not easily upset so he knew it must be bad news but he attempted to keep his voice calm. 'About five, Mares,' he replied. 'What's the problem?'

'Matt's had some sort of diving accident. They're flying him to the Canberra hospital. I'm on my way there now with Catherine.

'Oh God, John, they say he's been shot with a spear-gun.'

'I'll meet you there darling. Try not to get yourself too worked up. These things usually get exaggerated and Matt's a pretty tough character. I'm sure he'll be okay.'

McCarthy dug the keys to his government Commodore from his pocket, jumped in and spun the car's nose toward the Canberra hospital. 'Why is it that the bloody traffic lights always seem against you when you've got to get somewhere in a hurry?' he muttered as he overtook an ancient Volvo hugging the centre line. Glancing at the driver as he passed he cursed the hat-wearing old fart bent over the steering wheel for his selfish disregard for other road users. 'Bloody geriatrics!' he growled. 'Doesn't he ever look in his rear vision mirror?'

John arrived at the hospital just as the Westpac rescue chopper sank gently onto the helipad. TV crews and journalists milled around the hospital entrance, protesting noisily at the police cordon barring their access. He flashed his ID badge at the burly sergeant in charge who immediately cleared a path for him through the journalists. Striding rapidly to the emergency department he found Catherine and Mary waiting, white-faced.

The prime minister's gurney rattled down the corridor surrounded by paramedics and white-coated hospital staff, one of whom ran alongside pushing a drip stand from which hung a red blood transfusion bottle and one containing what John McCarthy presumed was a saline solution. Blood soaked the white sheet draped over his son's lithe form.

Dread washed over John McCarthy and he grasped his wife's and daughter-in-law's hands.

As the gurney passed, Matthew lifted his salt-tousled head from the pillow and grinned weakly. 'It's okay folks, just a little argument with a spear-gun. I'll be fine. Come in as soon as I'm cleaned up and I'll tell you all about it.'

When Stormy Knight received the news of the attempt on Matthew McCarthy's life he wasted no time in suspending Federal Agent Richard Nolan and appointing a replacement. While he knew the police union would claim one of their numbers was being victimised, he cited the special agent's failure to carry out his duty to protect the prime minister as sufficient reason to remove him from his post while the internal investigations unit conducted a full investigation. Despite the lack of concrete evidence directly linking the policeman to the assassination attempt, he could not afford to take chances until the nation's second biggest manhunt for the two rubber-clad figures that had left the scene in the Swiftcraft were found and either exonerated Nolan or confirmed his involvement.

While shares on the Australian stock market tumbled at the news of an assassination attempt on the country's leader so soon after Connor Bowker's murder, Fairfax- and Murdoch-owned newspapers had a field day. Television stations fell over each other as they attempted to gain access to the prime minister and hear his story firsthand. They resorted to all manner of subterfuge and tricks to get into the prime minister's hospital room. One enterprising journalist even donned a white coat and stethoscope and posed as a doctor, earning a tongue lashing from the police for his trouble.

No matter how determined they were the media was thwarted at every turn by Stormy Knight's men and John McCarthy. The latter, being determined that no one would get near his son, maintained a vigil at his bedside until he was satisfied that whoever replaced Nolan as his son's personal guard was beyond reproach. Starved of hard facts, the media did what they always did under such circumstances; they filled their pages and news programmes with rumour and speculation, overriding the usual soapies, cooking shows and morning gossip sessions transfixing the gullible, ever-sensation-hungry nation.

'For goodness sake, get me out of here,' Matt

pleaded to his family as they gathered around his hospital bed the day after his admission. It was so good to see Daniel and Sienna after his close call. Daniel had started university recently and was endeavouring to follow in his father's footsteps as a marine scientist, while sixteen-year-old Sienna had political aspirations and followed her father's new career avidly. Sienna was a dead ringer for her mother and was already learning that superb looks were not always an asset because her father's position meant she now had to fend off the amorous advances of Canberra's up and coming young hoi polloi looking to add the prime minister's daughter to their list of conquests. At the moment she was reclining beside her father, her arm draped protectively over his shoulders. She had always been Daddy's girl and knowing her father had nearly died rattled her.

Matthew shuddered as he thought how those he loved most almost had to deal with the tragedy of his murder. 'I feel okay now and I just want to go home and get on with the job.'

'You've only been in hospital for a day Matthew,' Catherine McCarthy scolded, gesturing toward her husband's heavily bandaged torso. 'You've had a close shave and you need time for that nasty wound to heal.'

Eighteen-year-old Dan grinned proudly at his father. 'You know Dad, it's pretty cool having a father who's prime minister of Australia, but it's even better having a dad who's also a hero.'

'I'm hardly a hero, son. I can tell you I was pretty damn scared when I realised those other divers were out to kill me.'

Although Matthew McCarthy had lost nearly two

litres of blood, he'd been incredibly lucky. The stainless steel spear shaft had passed through his side, narrowly missing a kidney and vital arteries. 'They're quite neat wounds really, one in the front and one at the back. I'll be right in a day or so and I'll be much safer and happier at the Lodge.'

Pushing the uncomfortable hospital chair away from the bed Catherine let go of her husband's hand and stood up. 'I wish you'd never taken on this job.' She sighed resignedly. 'I don't want my husband to be in the world's history books as the second prime minister in Australia to be assassinated.'

'They won't get a second go. Dad and Stormy will make sure of that. Just get me home so I can be with the people I love and away from the media until the feds catch the bastards!'

++++++++++++++++

Chapter Fourteen

However he viewed his situation, Dick Nolan knew he was in serious trouble. Resolutely maintaining his silence while he considered his options, he went to ground, choosing a small hotel in the pretty Snowy Mountains town of Tumut to hide from his pursuers and FEPOL's internal investigators. Staying out of sight in his hotel room, he availed himself of room service, keeping abreast of events via the small television set as the media searched determinedly for him in the hope of securing the interview of the decade.

The media's persistence was the least of the federal agent's problems. Topping his list was his concern as to how soon the ASIO chief would move to eliminate him from the equation.

He knew full well it was just a matter of time.

Second was the grim spectre of spending years behind bars, pilloried and branded as one of Australia's most reviled criminals.

I wonder if I can broker a deal; immunity from prosecution and a new identity under witness protection in exchange for "Flipper" Fleming? Or, perhaps I can get a false passport and head to Vanuatu or somewhere that doesn't have reciprocal extradition laws with Australia.

Nolan suddenly smashed his fist into the wall. Whatever happened he knew he'd never see his wife or his son and daughter again.

'Fuck bloody Fleming, the slimy, conniving bastard,' he swore, pacing the room. Catching sight of his wrathful countenance in the dressing table mirror, he paused and stared hard at reflection. 'Dickie-boy, maybe it's time for you to do what you should have right at the start of all this!' With that, he hauled his suitcase onto the bed and began packing.

One week later, Senator Bacon paced the floor of his penthouse, berating the perspiring ASIO boss.

'Jesus, you've stuffed up this time, you stupid bastard. Nolan's been missing for a week now and God knows what he's up to. You better fix this up bloody quickly, before they find him, because when they do, he'll take you down with him!"

Fleming stared back morosely. 'What are you worrying about; he doesn't know the connection between us so you're in the clear. It's me who'll go down for this if he squeals. Besides, you can hardly blame me for the mess. Nolan set this up but you supplied me with those two dickheads who were supposed to do the actual deed when he told me he couldn't do it on his own.

'For Christ sake,' Fleming continued ranting, 'They should have been able to finish him off. They had him in a confined space, they had powerful, gas powered spear-guns, and, he was at point blank range. Apart from that, Nolan should have completed the job when both their shots missed.'

'Shouda, coulda, woulda!' the Boar stormed. 'I'm not interested in excuses. What I want to know is how you intend to sort this out. What are you gunna do if Nolan decides to sell you out, because at the moment that's what I'd do if I were in his shoes. And knowing you as I do James, you'll also cave in if you think you can save your own arse by dobbing me in. So, do I need to go into damage control mode?'

The ASIO boss shivered despite the room's warmth. He had no doubt what the senator meant by the words "damage control". The man had vast and unscrupulous resources at his disposal and would not hesitate to use them as he had during the Vietnam era when he was consolidating his criminal network. Fleming responded sullenly, 'I'll handle it personally.'

Bacon's top lip lifted in a snarl. 'Well you better do it soon and make sure you don't bugger it up. Fuck off out of my sight and don't come back until you've got some good news.'

'Sometimes being the prime minister has a few perks attached.' Matthew McCarthy grinned at his family as the RAAF Blackhawk clattered noisily in its ascent from the hospital's helipad. 'It feels great to be out of that place and it'll be even better to get home and bunker down.'

'It's one way to avoid the media pack I suppose,' Catherine responded, gazing down at the sparkling waters of the man-made Lake Burley Griffin. 'Tourists pay a fortune for a scenic flight like this.'

Matthew never tired of the view and pointed to where the placid Molonglo fed into the lake. 'Dad tells me the Molonglo wasn't always the pleasant meandering stream that it is today. It used to be a toxic sewer of heavy metals back in the 1950s.'

Surprised, Catherine's beautiful, blue eyes widened. 'Why was that?'

'Ah, time for little local history lesson.' Matthew grinned. 'The river's source is at Captains Flat, roughly 40 miles away. The Flat as it is called today wasn't always just a trendy place for yuppies and retirees. It grew up around a very productive gold and copper mine after minerals were discovered there back in the convict era when bullock drays were the popular method of transport.

'Most people these days have forgotten the significance of the apostrophe between the n and the s in Captain and unlike when I went to school its now been dropped from the signs and maps because they don't know how the town got its name.'

'Okay, Mr Prime Minister-know-it-all-smarty-pants, I can see you're just dying to tell me, so how did the town get its name?'

'Well, the bullock teams that carried supplies to the miners and the sheep farms in the area during the gold rush of the early 1800s used to follow the river until they got to its source. Once there, they'd unhitch their animals and let them graze on the lush grass growing on river flats before heading back again. Every bullock team had a lead animal. One particular bloke's lead bullock called Captain became a common sight as it grazed and the locals dubbed the area "Captain's Flat".'

'You made that up just now!' Catherine exclaimed disbelievingly.

Matthew was indignant. 'I swear it's true. Dad went to school at the Flat briefly when he was growing up, so he ought to know.

'Anyway, getting back to the pollution problem; in its heyday Captains Flat had a population of over two thousand people. Like most mining towns it was pretty rough. The emphasis was on profit and the mine owners didn't care much about potential environmental problems. The mine tailings just used to be heaped up at the river's headwaters as a handy way of damming the river. Unfortunately, those tailings contained heavy toxic metals, including lead.

'During the winter of 1954 heavy rains caused the dam to overflow and burst. Huge quantities of contaminants flowed into the Molonglo killing everything, including thousands of acres of lush grazing land along the river banks.

'It took many years for the river to recover. In fact, I wouldn't be surprised if there are still high lead concentrations in the river mud at some of the popular swimming holes.'

'How horrid. Did the mine ever compensate the farmers or do anything about repairing the damage they'd done?'

'As far as I am aware, they got away scot free. The mine petered out in the 1960s and the Flat died along with it. Most of the buildings were pulled down until folk looking for a tree change or cheap land rediscovered it in the 1970s.'

Matthew gripped his wife's hand affectionately, 'I'll have to take you out there, Catherine. Being the history buff that you are, you'd love it.

'The old buildings at the Foxlow sheep station on the way there are worth looking at. Not so long ago the station required an entire team to run it. They employed carpenters, tractor drivers, jackaroos, stockmen, mechanics, gardeners and even a book keeper and a groom who all lived there with their respective families in houses supplied by the station. Nowadays, thanks to technology, outsourcing and modern farming methods, the entire 18,000 acres is run by one man.'

The Blackhawk turned and flew low over the nation's capital which presented a spectacular sight from the air. Surrounded on three sides by eucalypt covered hills, the carefully planned city sparkled in the bright afternoon sunshine. Today, there was a bluish tinge to the slopes resulting from vapours rising from the many gum trees that were gradually making a comeback after the disastrous fires that ravaged the city and surrounding forests during 2003.

Until the calamitous fires that drove John and Mary McCarthy from Perth, the Canberra fires had been the worst in Australia's history, having killed four people, injured 490 others and destroyed 500 homes. Matthew's face became grim as he recalled the most recent devastation in Western Australia and the seemingly endless spate of cyclones that seemed to plague Australia's east coast in recent times. The assassination of Connor Bowker and the attempt on his own life only served to vindicate his decision to press on with environmental reforms.

The global warming wombats cannot be allowed to win, he mused to himself. If we don't take a stand now, these short-sighted morons who think only of profit and care nothing about humanity will be the world's undoing.

Constable Annette Thompson was somewhat bewildered. For some inexplicable reason she'd been transferred to traffic after a brief stint at the Lodge and while she wasn't going to complain about spending her days with a speed camera and copping abuse from Joe Public, she shared most of her colleague's dislike for doing duties most considered to be the worst type of policing. So, it was good to be reassigned to the Lodge once more. She felt proud and honoured to guard the nation's top politician and the members of his family, who she was sure were genuinely decent, down-to-earth people.

Annette had joined FEDPOL at twenty-four, after six unsatisfying years in the Australian Army, where, after being subjected to seemingly endless sexual harassment from her male counterparts and the lesbian factions, she had decided the military life was not for her.

Had she been butt-ugly, things might have been different, but her vibrant personality, sapphire-blue eyes, almost flawless complexion, golden hair and looks reminiscent of Jennifer Hawkins had attracted jealous taunts from her straight colleagues, unwanted advances from the dykes and relentless sexual innuendo from her male counterparts, regardless of their rank.

She had soon learnt the hard way that to seek redress through official channels resulted in further bullying and only served to damage one's career prospects. There were simply too many from the old school that still refused to accept woman in the front line, despite the government's push for sexual equality in the Services. It was better not to rock the boat. Left with the options of becoming some dyke's plaything, the regimental bike, developing a hide like a rhinoceros and shrugging off the boorish behaviour, or getting out, Annette chose the latter option.

While she hadn't been immune to sexual discrimination in the Australian Federal Police, the national law enforcement agency had much more enlightened views and effective mechanisms in place for dealing with the misogynistic dinosaurs. It also helped to be the sole offspring of man who had in his day been a fairly high ranking and well respected police officer.

Annette loved the heritage listed building, its splendidly peaceful gardens and the sense that her presence was valued by the house's occupants, especially John McCarthy whom she'd been told was responsible for her return and had obviously taken on board her suggestion to improve security as well as implementing other much needed measures.

The police presence at the Lodge had been doubled and Annette was almost overjoyed to find she no longer had to tolerate the objectionable John Lloyd. In fact, the Lodge detail now consisted of a younger, fitter breed of personnel. While some of them were mere rookies they were paired with a more senior officer and their enthusiasm and alertness more than compensated for their lack of experience.

Detective Chief Inspector Graham Clews had personally chosen the new guard. He'd taken the trouble to visit each shift on the job pulling no punches as to his expectations. 'ASIO and our own intelligence sources are of the opinion that there is a very real threat to the lives of the prime minister and his family. In fact, a terrorist type attack may be imminent.

'Do not labour under the illusion that Australia is

immune to the type of extremism you read about in the Middle East and Indonesia. It is not. We have entered a new era, as evidenced by Prime Minister Bowker's recent assassination and we need fit, alert and suitably trained officers to counter those who would threaten the very stability of this nation.

'You have each been selected because you are considered by your previous supervisors to have the potential to form part of that unit. However, your posting to the new V.I.P Security Protection unit is a stop gap measure until we can build a new, highly-trained unit. Over the next few weeks you'll each be put through an especially rigorous training programme during which you'll learn new skills and be tested to the limits of your endurance. If you don't measure up, or if your heart and soul is not in the job, you will simply return to general duties.'

The address by Clews had been carefully crafted to instil a sense of pride, elitism and spirit de corps and not one of those chosen had declined the opportunity. Clews had surprised Annette by taking her aside. 'You have the prime minister's father to thank for your return to the Lodge, Constable Thompson. I don't know you well enough to make a judgment but you obviously impressed him so please don't make me look a fool for choosing you on the say-so of an outsider.'

'I won't sir. Was there any reason why I was moved from here in the first place?'

'Let's say, you were a square peg in a round hole and leave it at that,' Clews responded cryptically and walked away.

I bet it was because the old farts who've treated this

Alan Greenhalgh

place like an old men's home for so long felt I threatened the status quo. Thank God, John McCarthy was able to shake things up!

+++++++++++++

Chapter Fifteen

Jambali could feel the sweat trickling in a steady stream from his armpits despite the morning chill. He felt as if there was something alive slithering in his bowels. He'd not slept after Nibras left, tossing and turning on the thin piece of foam he'd spread on the floor of the derelict cottage until the cawing of crows and the cackle of kookaburras signalled it was time to get moving. He sluiced his face and hands with rainwater from the tank outside the back door and then knelt on his prayer mat facing Mecca for his morning prayer ritual. He knew this could well be his last day on Earth and he begged Allah for strength and guidance in his attack on the infidels.

The ritual finished, Jambali hastily stuffed himself with some instant noodles and then went about the business of setting timed incendiary devices to destroy the house after his departure, thus removing all trace of his activities. By the time anyone noticed the fire and summoned the local bushfire brigade it would be too late to save the house. His next move involved peeling the blank white magnetic sheets from the sides of the Transit to reveal the sign written livery; "Sanilady Mobile Personal Hygiene Services".

Nibras had explained during the previous night's briefing how the jihadist group had purchased the company and operated its franchises along Australia's east coast twelve months previously as part of a carefully thought-out plan to attack Australia for its role in the Iraq and Afghanistan wars. Each of the franchise's employees had been totally unaware of the terrorist group's intentions, innocently taking on casual driving jobs until being summarily dismissed from employment and replaced by jihadists immediately prior to the date of the planned attacks.

Jambali strapped his canvas suicide vest beneath the loose-fitting pink Sanilady uniform, grimacing at having to demean himself in such a way. *What self-respecting man would dress in pink and collect the disgusting items disposed of by women? he wondered.* Consoling himself with the thought that it was permissible to do almost anything if it meant he could strike a blow for Islam, he fired up the Transit's diesel motor and set off for Canberra.

His first call was Australia's War Memorial. Driving right up to the public entrance he wondered if anyone would challenge him. However, apart from the initial glance, most people turned away and paid him no heed. In fact, they avoided him as if he were a leper. It was obvious from their facial expressions that they were embarrassed to see a pink-uniformed man collecting used sanitary products from women's toilets. Jambali smiled. So effective was the ruse that he doubted that any one of them would be able to describe him later. Even the war memorial's attendants looked the other way, giving him unhindered access.

Just in case an observant guard noticed that the supposedly empty container was heavier than the full ones Jambali removed, he had decided at the last moment to use a hand trolley.

The first drop went without a hitch. His previous

sorties into Canberra's iconic attractions had not been a waste of time. During the previous night's briefing with Nibras he had proudly demonstrated a sound knowledge of the layout at each of the ten target sites and he was able to complete the task within minutes.

One down, nine to go.

'Do you and George want to take your lunch breaks now, Annette?' Neville Carter, Annette's supervisor enquired. 'Steve and I'll look after the main gate until you get back and then we'll take our break.'

'What about Trevor and Neil?' Annette wanted to know, referring to the two constables patrolling the grounds.

'They can spell each other. We can make do with just one in the gardens during the lunch break.'

'Okay, thanks. See you in thirty minutes.' Annette was looking forward to her break. She'd bumped into Sienna McCarthy during a stint patrolling the grounds earlier and the prime minister's daughter had suggested they enjoy a sandwich together. Although strictly speaking it was against protocol Annette sensed Sienna's loneliness and agreed. With a scant half hour's break, she did not want to waste a moment and hurried up the driveway to her rendezvous.

She found Sienna waiting for her. An outdoor table shaded by a large umbrella was set up with a silver tray containing an ornate china teapot and a variety of tasty-looking club sandwiches. 'This looks lovely, Sienna. Thank you for going to so much trouble.'

Sienna smiled, pleased and happy for the chance to chat with someone who was really not that much older than her. 'I made them myself. The kitchen staff was a bit put out that I wouldn't let them make our lunch but I can't get used to being waited on hand and foot.'

'How is your father now?' Annette hoped Sienna didn't think she was prying but she was genuinely concerned that Matthew McCarthy had nearly been killed. Although she didn't know Richard Nolan personally, she knew he'd been suspended. As in most police forces, the rumour mill worked overtime whenever one of its number's behaviour was under question.

Sienna's eyes brimmed with tears. 'He's recovering well but Mum wishes Dad had never got into politics and she's pretty angry with him for putting his life at risk over his beliefs. I just hope all this doesn't drive them apart.'

Annette squeezed Sienna's hand sympathetically. 'I am sure they'll be okay. It can't be easy for her you know.'

'I just can't believe someone would want to kill Dad for trying to do something that's so crucial to the planet. I am so proud of him and I want to be just like him. Most people don't appreciate how dire the situation is. Dad is convinced that the world has reached the tipping point regarding climate change. If the world's major polluters don't take action now it will be too late to avert a major catastrophe.'

As they were chatting, Annette noticed a diminutive Asian man in a flowing pink shirt wheeling a hand trolley up the driveway to the staff entrance of the Lodge. The vehicle in which he had arrived was reversed up to one of the still-open gates, its diesel engine idling quietly. The stocky Neville Carter with his swept back Brylcreamed hair and his younger, slimmer offsider Steve Blackborough were lounging beside it, engaged in some sort of casual conversation. Annette felt annoyance. *Lazy buggers are probably talking about the bloody cricket when one of them should have escorted the Sanilady man.*

Annette watched as the man entered the building and did not hear what Sienna was saying at that moment. Apart from the man not being accompanied by a FEDPOL officer, she wondered why his shirt was so baggy and why he'd need a trolley to shift a plastic bin weighing no more than a few kilograms.

'You're not listening to me Annette. What's wrong?' Sienna sounded peeved.

'Oh, I am sorry Sienna. I guess I am just being silly. I am a bit worried about that man but it's probably nothing. What were you saying?'

'It's just the guy changing over the sanitary bins, silly. What harm could he do? They've been coming here every week since we moved in. Anyway, I was just saying how I feel as if I am a prisoner here. I know it's a beautiful building and all the guards and precautions are necessary, especially since Mr Bowker was killed and they tried to murder my dad, but I can't go anywhere or do anything without a bodyguard trailing along with me.'

'I know it must be hard for you Sienna but Australia has well and truly lost its free, innocent lifestyle. The days of politicians being able to mingle freely with the people or members of their families retaining their anonymity have sadly gone forever.'

Sienna sighed. 'I guess I'll adapt in time. I'll have to anyway if I want to follow a career in politics.'

Annette watched the Asian man come back out of the house wheeling his trolley on which sat the white plastic sanitary bin. The man seemed to be in a tremendous hurry, almost jogging as he made his way back to the white van. He opened the van's rear doors, threw the bin in the back, hurriedly slammed the doors and clambered behind the steering wheel. As he did so his shirt rode up revealing a bulky strange-looking vest underneath. Annette had glimpsed a dozen or so sanitary bins lying haphazardly inside the vehicle. Some of the bins were lying on their sides as if no attempt had been made to stack them. Considering the unsanitary nature of their contents this seemed very strange.

Annette leapt to her feet and ran across the lawn shouting to the driver. 'Excuse me. Stop there will you. I need to speak to you!'

The van's driver looked at her, alarm registering on his face. Instead of waiting for her to reach the van, he slammed the driver's door and gunned the engine.

Alerted by their colleague's shouts Neville and Steven moved to block the van from leaving, holding up their hands as they signalled the driver to stop. The van's driver clearly had no intention of complying with the police officers' directions. The rear tyres squealed as they bit into the bitumen. The engine roared as the driver slammed the accelerator pedal to the floor.

Neville leapt to one side, reaching for his pistol as he did so, but the driver's side wing mirror caught his arm, spinning him around. Steve wasn't quite as quick. As he attempted to jump to his right the van struck him with a sickening thump, knocking him backwards.

Annette watched in horror as the front wheels ran over the unfortunate policeman's lower torso. Her pistol was now out of its holster. She stopped running. Bringing up her left hand she adopted the firing stance, legs shoulder width apart, arms extended and knees slightly bent. Aiming at where she imagined the driver's seat to be she fired two rounds in quick succession. *Double tap!* She fired two more rounds. The van swerved wildly and mounted the kerb, coming to a halt against the perimeter fence.

I've hit him!

Running towards the vehicle Annette noticed Steve's inert, crumpled form lying on the road. Neville had regained his feet and with his weapon drawn was shouting shrilly at the driver to get out of the vehicle. She could see the man slumped over the steering wheel, blood running down his face. Suddenly, he turned his head and sat up, a strange twisted grin splitting his thin features.

Some primeval instinct told Annette to throw herself flat on the roadway. Curling herself into a ball, she tried to shout a warning to Neville as she clamped her hands over her head but it was too late. A blinding flash of light accompanied by immense heat swept over her, followed by a thunderous, deafening noise that filled her ears and then, everything went black.

Annette slowly regained consciousness. *Why am I lying on the road? What is that smell? Why is it so hot? Why is it so quiet?* Turning her head, she stared uncomprehendingly at a blazing pile of twisted metal. Somewhere in her brain the thought that this unholy mess had once been a motor vehicle struggled to the front of her conscious mind. Blackened debris littered the roadway outside the Lodge. The famous wrought iron gates now hung, twisted crazily, from their supporting pillars.

As the full horror of what had just happened dawned on her, Annette looked for her fellow officers. Steve Blackborough's body still lay where it had fallen but she could not find Neville. Struggling to her feet Annette could now just make out the sound of approaching sirens and realised the blast had deafened her.

Looking back toward the Lodge building, Annette hoped Sienna was unharmed and breathed a sigh of relief to see the prime minister's daughter running toward her, her mouth moving as she shouted silently.

'Go back Sienna, please,' Annette yelled. She did not want the girl to see what she had just glimpsed; pieces of human torso, arms, legs and entrails hanging from the perimeter fence. Something blackened and grotesquely burnt and vaguely familiar lay on the road outside the gates. *My God, it's a head!*

Sienna's concern for her policewoman friend overrode anything else. Blood was streaming down Annette's face, her uniform was almost in tatters and her face was ghostly pale. Realising her friend had been deafened by the explosion Sienna put her mouth close to Annette's head and shouted. 'Annette, what can I do to help?'

Annette barely heard Sienna's words but her brain was operating at top speed now. 'Stay here and wait for the first responders. I've got to get up to the house now.'

'No. I'll come with you.'

'No Sienna. It's too dangerous to go back to the house. I think that man put a bomb in there and it could go off any moment.'

Sienna started to protest.

'No, you must stay here so you can alert the authorities that there may be other bombs planted all around the city.'

Not waiting to argue, Annette turned and loped unsteadily toward the house where various personnel milled confusedly around in the driveway. 'Everybody, please go down and assemble on the main lawn right now. Please wait there until we can account for everybody.'

The urgency in Annette's voice coupled with her dishevelled appearance and the terrible explosion was sufficient to galvanise the group into action. John McCarthy came running down the stairs closely followed by the entire McCarthy clan, including the dressing-gowned prime minister, as Annette ran inside.

'Jesus, Annette, what happened?' John cried.

'A suicide bomber just detonated a device outside the gates. He's killed two of our officers and I think he's put an I.E.D. in the ladies' toilet downstairs. It's highly probable that he's also planted other devices around the city before he came here.'

John McCarthy did not wait for further explanation. He glanced at his watch, instinctively noting the time; 12.35pm. 'Okay, let's get everybody out,' he responded and ran to the front entrance where he hit the button for the evacuation siren, activating the whooping tone which was accompanied by a pre-recorded voice on an endless tape. 'This is a bomb threat warning. Please evacuate the building immediately and move to the assembly area.'

Turning on his heel, John McCarthy ran back up the stairs with their beautifully, crafted balustrades, shouting to Annette as he did so, 'I'll make sure all the upstairs rooms are clear. You check downstairs and I'll meet you outside.'

Having cleared the house, the elder McCarthy joined the stunned evacuees on the lawn, well clear of the main building. Annette was providing a SITREP to police HQ via her two-way radio and he beckoned her to join him away from the main group. 'Yes sir,' she said impatiently. 'I know that's a huge task and FEDPOL doesn't have the resources but you must get the New South Wales police and the army to help or there could be a major disaster. Yes, that's right, every major government building, including Parliament House. Yes, they all need to be evacuated. There's probably I.E.D.s in every one of them. Bloody idiot!' she muttered, releasing the button on her microphone. 'I am having trouble getting them to take me seriously.'

'Annette, you have done an amazing job. I take you very seriously after what's just occurred. Tell me why you think there might be other attacks imminent.'

Sweeping her dishevelled hair out of her eyes with a bloodied hand, Annette quickly outlined her theory while McCarthy listened, appalled. 'Let's see if I can help to speed things up.' he said grabbing his phone and punching in the direct number to Stormy Knight's office.

Moments later, all over the nation's capital, sirens wailed as the War Memorial, the Mint, Parliament

House, embassies, consulates and government offices almost simultaneously activated their evacuation procedures. The N.S.W. and Federal Police bomb squads pooled resources and began checking high profile targets in the Australian Capital Territory.

First on FEPOL's list was of course the Lodge, and the bomb squad arrived within minutes of the suicide bombing and began setting up while the fire brigade worked to extinguish the still-blazing Transit Van. John McCarthy fervently hoped there'd be some useful forensic evidence remaining after the scene had been doused with foam and trampled by their boots.

The McCarthys were whisked away from the Lodge to the relative safety of a Canberra hotel, except for John McCarthy. The old policeman in him had been revived and he worried that potential terrorist attacks might be more widespread than Annette theorised.

What if they've targeted places other than the nation's capital?

John shared his concerns with Curly Clews when he arrived at the Lodge to see the devastation first hand.

'Let's see what the bomb squad find,' the detective chief inspector replied as the two men watched the bomb squad officer make the long, slow and lonely walk to the prime minister's residence.

'Graham, I don't believe you should take any chances. By the time they dismantle the bomb, if it is a bomb, it will be too late to send out the necessary warnings. I know it will create mass panic but I'd suggest you consult your list of likely terrorist targets and advise them to take the precaution of evacuating immediately!'

'Jesus, John. Do you know how big that list is? Christ, it covers everything from the Sydney Harbour Bridge and the Opera House to the Lucas Heights nuclear reactor, every bloody defence establishment, international airports and each city's water and power supplies.'

'I don't see that you have any alternative mate. Can you live with yourself if I am proved correct?' McCarthy replied quietly.

'Fuck. And if you're wrong, the media will have a field day.'

'And if I am right and you don't do anything... what then?'

The senior policeman's face was ghostly white now. 'You're right of course. I'll ring the commissioner and ask him to make the announcements. It has to come from him or no one will take it seriously,' he added, striding off towards the nearest police vehicle.

Looking like some weird, alien being in his heavy protective suit and helmet mounted camera the bomb squad officer carried X-ray equipment which he would use to examine the sanitary container in one hand and a small toolbox in the other. 'I am now inside the Lodge and making my way to the toilet.' Relayed from his helmet microphone, the officer's voice was muffled by his heavy helmet. The hiss of the cool air pumping through his suit and his laboured breathing as he struggled against the cumbersome suit could be heard in the background as McCarthy watched the images relayed to the squad's CCTV screen.

'These blokes have to be crazy to do this job,' McCarthy remarked to Graham Clews as he glanced at his watch. It was now 1.10pm and he recalled his time in the APS when that service first established its bomb appraisal teams. There had been no shortage of applicants and each one had undergone psyche tests to determine their ability to handle the highly stressful work. McCarthy and his fellow officers had been amazed when the psyche examiners approved one particular applicant whom McCarthy had always considered mentally unstable due to the man's penchant for playing mind games and a preoccupation with violent computer games. After consideration they concluded he had managed to trick the examiners but McCarthy had continued to worry that someone so potentially dangerous had been armed with the knowledge and skills to wreak havoc if he ever ran off the rails. Aside from this particular individual, McCarthy had been amazed that anyone would voluntarily don an uncomfortably-hot, heavily-armoured suit, knowing that while it would provide some degree of protection in the event of an explosion, they ran the risk of losing their unprotected hands which had to be uncovered to retain dexterity needed to ply the bomb squad officer's trade.

The bomb man's inspection of the suspected I.E.D. revealed nothing unusual from the exterior, but the X-ray images confirmed the bin was stuffed full with what was presumed to be fertiliser, a detonator, some sort of anti-tampering switch connected to the lid and a small battery powered clock. Had they not suspected the presence of other similar devices elsewhere in the city the bomb squad would have used its robotic device to extract the bin, transport it to a safe area and fire a shotgun blast into the bomb's innards which would either detonate the device harmlessly, or disable its mechanism, rendering it harmless. However, knowing when the device was timed to explode was crucial so they chose the much more dangerous option of gaining access to the bin's interior.

It was almost 2.00pm by the time the experts bypassed the bomb's anti-tamper switch and disconnected the circuitry. A wire connected to the clock's hour hand and the clock face showed the device would detonate at 3.00pm.

McCarthy had been correct when he suggested there'd be mass panic when the warnings went out. The list of potential targets was huge and the resultant disruption was massive. The major airports in Sydney, Melbourne and Brisbane cancelled flights and diverted incoming planes to secondary airfields or interstate. Streets had to be cordoned off, government buildings, defence establishments, embassies and consulates, major power stations, iconic buildings such as the Sydney Opera House, the Governor General's residence and Kirribilli House were all evacuated and searched. Nine other explosive devices all contained in Sanilady bins were discovered in Canberra, six in Sydney and another five in Melbourne.

Unfortunately, by the time everyone responded, there was insufficient time or resources to deal with all twenty I.E.D.s, let alone the innumerable and now-suspicious sanitary bins left at lower profile targets.

At 3.00pm twenty devices exploded. Although no lives were lost, there was widespread damage and the disruption to business activities would cost the country countless millions.

Nibras and his jihadists were overjoyed. Images of his smirking face claiming responsibility for inflicting a savage blow to the previously safe and peaceful country appeared on You Tube shooting him to an equal ranking with the late Osama bin Laden as one of the world's most notorious terrorists.

As the nation's leader, Matthew McCarthy knew Australia's security had been shattered by what was a well organised and heavily funded attack. Despite his own still painful injuries, he reconvened parliament and ordered a nation-wide state of emergency for the first time since the Second World War. State and Federal police forces, Customs and Border Protection, the RAAF, Army and Navy, the Australian Security Intelligence Service (ASIS) and ASIO were all summoned to an emergency meeting to formulate a plan to hunt down the terrorists and close the gaps in Australia's northern borders.

Federal and State Police raided Sanilady's small Sydney head office only to find it abandoned and any records destroyed. The Transit vans used in all the attacks were found abandoned and burnt out at various locations, but the company's employees who had been sacked the day before the attacks began coming forward to tell how they'd been duped. They were angry and willing to provide whatever information they could, including descriptions of those who had hired them.

While these initial inquiries served to confirm Nibras' and Jemaah Islamiyah's claims of responsibility for the attacks, the jihadists had planned their escape route well, vanishing by the same means they had deployed to breach Australia's border security. FEDPOL immediately sent officers to Indonesia where the police in that country were eager to assist in bringing the perpetrators to justice. Experience showed this would not be an easy task with so many JI sympathisers willing to shelter Nibras and his cohorts whom they proclaimed heroes.

+++++++++++

Chapter Sixteen

Sitting in an anonymous hire car at a remote lookout in Sydney's Blue Mountains, Helen Knox looked at her watch for the fourth time in as many minutes. The sun had set several hours earlier and it was now dark and cold.

She had to be very careful. If anyone knew who she was meeting it could prove disastrous but she'd used this place before and was confident of remaining undisturbed. Being too far from nearby towns to attract canoodlers and well off the beaten track, the lookout was ideal for the purpose.

Hurry up. You're late!

She looked at her watch again and debated whether to risk using her mobile phone to check if her associate was still coming. No, too risky, she decided.

She was still seething that the Labor powerbrokers had bypassed her in favour of Matthew McCarthy as Connor Bowker's replacement and now the botched attempt on McCarthy's life and the shocking terrorist attacks had done nothing to improve her chances of winning the top job. Indeed, McCarthy's survival had served to make him even more of a folk hero, not only that but the nation now seemed to be infatuated with the entire McCarthy clan.

However, Helen Knox was a very determined woman with very rich and powerful friends who needed her to succeed. She was not going to admit defeat so easily.

About time!

The deputy prime minister released her frustration by thumping the dashboard as the headlights of an approaching car lit up the trees. Its tyres crunching on the gravel, a big Mercedes coasted to a halt beside Knox's Falcon. The quiet beat of its powerful engine ceased and the headlights faded and died. The vehicle's interior light glowed briefly, but it was sufficient for her to identify the sole occupant who was clearly not going to come to her.

Bloody typical! Mohammed must go to the mountain for the mountain will not come to Mohammed, she thought wryly.

Opening her door, Knox pulled her elegantly tailored coat around herself. She hunched her shoulders against the cold as she hurried the few paces to the other vehicle. Slipping into the passenger's seat she closed her door pausing briefly to enjoy the satisfying click of the vehicle's carefully engineered locking mechanism. *Not like the bloody Ford. I've always got to slam its door.* She welcomed the air conditioned warmth but wrinkled her nose against the pungent stench of the man's cigar. Glancing in the vanity mirror on the back of the passenger's visor she patted her famous blonde coiffure back into place before turning side on to face the other occupant.

The Mercedes' driver, a short, stocky florid-faced man with piggy eyes and thinning grey hair, lifted a pudgy hand from the steering wheel. The cuff of his expensively hand-tailored suit rode, up revealing a solid gold cufflink engraved with the initials M.W. as he reached over and shook Knox's hand.

'Hello again Helen, I thought when we met next I'd

be congratulating you, not commiserating over the turn of events.'

Knox swallowed her annoyance at the other man's failure to apologise or offer any explanation for his lateness. She realised it was his way of showing her who was boss and knew she had no choice but to accept his little mind game.

As the major shareholder of Walker Coal and Iron Pty Ltd, a major exporter of Australia's coal to China and India, Mal Walker paid her handsomely to ensure nothing happened in parliament that would jeopardise coal exports.

'I thought you would too, Mal,' Helen replied bitterly.

'The question now is where do we go from here? McCarthy appears to be armour plated and to have nine lives.

'We simply cannot allow McCarthy's climate change bill to pass through parliament, so I hope you've got another plan.'

Knox's anger swelled to bursting point. 'What do you suggest now, hemlock in his tea?' she snarled. 'You come up with something. My hands are tied. There's no hope of parliament blocking the new legislation. Labor's majority in both houses guarantees that the bill will have a clear run. The Greens can't block it, the Independents might be persuaded to vote against it, if we could do a back room deal, but even then, the Nats and the Libs wouldn't have enough votes, so I don't see any alternative but for the man you used to get rid of Bowker to have another go.'

'He's long gone. Security is too tight around

McCarthy now for us to risk another shot.' Mal Walker smiled but there was no humour in his expression. 'No pun intended,' he added.

'All I can think to do right now is to throw some ideas around and see if something emerges that we can build on.'

'A brainstorming session?'

'Yes. For a start, we're not the only ones who want to see McCarthy's plans stymied. Normally your company and the miners' union are at loggerheads but thousands of ordinary folk will have to be retrained, either in developing and supplying renewable energy, or in other fields if coal exports cease when McCarthy shuts down the coal fired power stations. Those families who have to relocate to find new jobs will face tremendous upheaval. There will be a knock-on effect for businesses built around coal mining. Entire towns could become deserted. Apart from all that, China and India aren't going to be very happy either but I suppose they'll just buy their coal from other countries that will be only too willing to capitalise on this ludicrous situation.'

'We know all that,' Walker responded impatiently. 'But McCarthy seems to have done a pretty good job of convincing most of the voters that it's for the long term good of the nation and that the government will compensate all those affected.

'At the end of the day, I will not countenance my companies being shut down and my shareholders taking a hit. Many of them are already selling their shares and reinvesting in renewable energy stocks.'

'Perhaps we have to counter attack on many fronts,

instead of trying to find one simple solution.'

'What do you mean?'

'For a start, you could mount a major advertising campaign to discredit the government's climate change policy. The Bush government was pretty good at that sort of thing as I recall. Tell the public that shutting the power stations and stopping coal exports is unnecessary because clean coal technologies and carbon capture and storage will remove the pollution from burning coal.'

'We both know that's a long way off Helen. In fact, I doubt that it will ever be financially viable.'

'Joe Public doesn't have to know that. Get your scientists to convince the masses that it's just around the corner and Australia will be able to sell the technology to China and India. Muddy the waters. Confuse the public. Sow doubt in their minds.'

The mining magnate clamped a fat cigar in his mouth and looked thoughtful as he lit it with the dashboard lighter. 'We *can* do that, in fact we *will* do it. Maybe we can plant a few good shit-stirrers among the miners and rile them up enough so they march on Canberra. We can also remind them that Australia's contribution to greenhouse gases is less than two percent of the global total and stopping pollution in this country will make little difference.'

'You can also go back to the hoary old chestnut of reminding the public that when the sun doesn't shine and the wind doesn't blow their lights will go out without coal-fired power stations. Get them worrying about blackouts and the resultant disruption to their lives.'

'Not many people swallow that one these days.

Technologies have advanced to the stage where energy can now be stored to provide base-load power twenty-four-seven. The combination of hot-fractured-rock-thermal-power, tidal, solar and wind can actually provide for the country's power needs. The new thin-film photo voltaic polymers have substantially reduced the cost of solar panels making them very cost-effective. In fact, they could be a real threat if the government decides to pursue that option.

'No, what we have to do is sell the idea that there will be a severe economic recession if the country loses the income from its coal exports. We'll tell them we'll lose our triple A credit rating and their kids will be saddled with paying off a massive debt and there'll be colossal unemployment. Somehow, I don't think we'll win that argument though.'

The air in Walker's Mercedes was becoming thick with rank-smelling cigar and Knox fumbled for the button to wind down her window. 'Well, perhaps we can get the bill put on the backburner,' she coughed. 'Talking of pollution, are you trying to kill us both with that stinking thing?'

Walker examined the end of his cigar and looked offended. 'It's the finest Cuban tobacco. Don't be such a princess. Suck it up!' he sulked. 'What do you mean about putting the bill on the backburner?'

Knox's thin lips parted slightly revealing incredibly white and even teeth. She fixed Walker with the famous killer stare she used on her political opponents as she smiled knowingly. 'Well the government's got its hands pretty full at the moment dealing with this terrorist attack. If we can somehow stir the pot a little more,

McCarthy and those who support him will be too busy to worry about climate change.'

'Ah, you've been holding back on me Helen. Come on, out with it.'

'Today, I had a little visit from a certain FEDPOL agent attached to the Close Personal Protection Unit who has just been stood down and wanted to strike a deal to save his hide. He had a very interesting tale to tell concerning our top spook and the very colourful Senator Bacon who has been the subject of nasty rumours concerning the illicit drug trade for years.'

'Do you mean that bloke who was diving with McCarthy when he got shot?'

'His name's Richard Nolan. He was a navy clearance diver who won a bravery award in the first Gulf War. After leaving the navy he joined the Federal Police and later became a sergeant in the Close Personal Protection Unit until they appointed him as the prime minister's personal bodyguard.

'It seems that Sergeant Nolan has been hiding a dirty secret and he's not the war hero everyone thinks he is. The incident which resulted in him being awarded medals for bravery was in fact, a fiasco that resulted in the deaths of five of Nolan's dive buddies. The poor sod's suffered from a guilty conscience for donkey's years and couldn't wait to get it all off his chest.'

Walker stubbed out his cigar. 'Okay, but what's this got to do with Fleming and Bacon?'

As the mining expert listened enthralled, Knox explained how the ASIO boss had learnt about Nolan's dubious past and used this information to blackmail the policeman into faking a diving accident to get rid of the prime minister.

'Fleming thought he had Nolan over a barrel, but Dicky Boy decided to put his own investigative skills to good use and see if he could somehow turn the tables on Fleming.

'As a federal agent involved in drug operations and spying on the Mr Bigs of the underworld, he has acquired a pretty good handle on how to use listening devices, plant GPS trackers, tap telephones and hack into computers. What's more, he didn't need to use FEPOL's spy gear because these days, anyone can buy some pretty scary stuff on the internet.

'Nolan got himself a whole swag of the stuff and went to work. He put a camera on Fleming's house, a GPS tracker on his government car and a tap on his private phone. He then sat in his car nearby for several nights to see if anything eventuated.

'He struck lucky on the second night when Fleming got a strange late-night telephone call from someone who didn't identify himself wanting to set up what was apparently a regular meeting.

'Nolan was surprised when the ASIO chief didn't use his official vehicle but instead left the house on foot, however, he stayed in his car, kept the light off, and followed Fleming to a garage not far from his house where Fleming keeps a second vehicle.

'Fleming drove off with Nolan tailing him and they ended up at the Milsons Point Tower where Bacon has his North Shore penthouse. Fleming is apparently a frequent visitor, because he had an electronic access control card to the basement car park. He drove in and parked and then went up in the lift. He was completely unaware that Nolan had slipped through the security gate on foot. Nolan apparently raced up the stairs and managed to listen in to their conversation using a directional microphone and a digital recorder. He came up with enough dirt on both men to put them away for years and before he left, he planted a bug in the wall of Bacon's apartment which has continued recording every meeting held there between Bacon and his criminal associates.

'While Nolan had managed to out-spook the top spook, it was too late by then to use the information because he had already tried to kill McCarthy. In other words, he found himself holding a tiger by the tail,' Knox concluded.

'Mmm, *very* interesting,' Walker responded. 'Everyone's suspected for years that Bacon's a crook but why would the ASIO boss want to have anything to do with him?'

'Well, here's the really interesting bit. While it's no secret that the two men served in Vietnam at the same time, few people know that Bacon used to be Fleming's platoon commander. We all know Fleming survived the Battle of Long Tan but he was also being blackmailed by Bacon.'

'Bloody hell!' Walker exploded. 'What does Bacon have on Fleming?'

'It seems our chief spook is a closet homosexual and while that's no crime these days, it was back in the Vietnam era when Bacon learned of Fleming's sexual proclivities. He filled the young sapper with alcohol and drugs and engineered a tryst with a male prostitute so he could blackmail him into doing anything he wanted. He had Fleming in his pocket then and he's never let him go since.

'When Fleming came back from Vietnam he was recruited by ASIO and worked his way up to the top, while Bacon used the proceeds of illicit drugs to start up Shriver Pharmaceuticals, which is now a multinational drug company. There have been rumours circulating for years that Shriver also churns out and distributes illegal drugs but if they do, they cover their tracks pretty well.

'When Bacon became a Labor senator, he had to declare his interests in Shriver and remove himself from Shriver's board but he's still the majority shareholder.'

'Well bugger me! Shit Helen, this is huge. But I still don't understand why Bacon would want to get rid of McCarthy.'

'You obviously don't follow what's happening in Canberra closely enough, Mal, or you'd know one of McCarthy's reforms involves the Commonwealth Anti-Illegal Drug Bill which aims to provide state police forces with sweeping across-border powers to deal with the illegal drug trade.

'McCarthy has declared drugs a threat to national security, which they are. He is also setting up a national anti-drug task force to crack down on organised crime. The task force will have access to company taxation records, the ability to tap telephones and the power to compel anyone to give evidence. The Act also places the onus on suspected drug dealers to justify their earnings.

'Bacon is worried that his distribution networks will crash and the investigators will manage to work their way back up the chain to him.'

'Surely, someone in his position would have covered his tracks, or be so far divorced from the front line that they can't touch him?'

'It only takes the right person, Fleming for instance, to cut a deal in exchange for immunity from prosecution and his empire will come crumbling down. If Dick Nolan can find out what Bacon's been up to, others can too.'

Mal Walker whistled. "Phew, it seems that our top spook has been out-spooked. Your Mr Nolan must realise he's in a very precarious position. Even if Fleming and Bacon don't know he's running around with information that can destroy them, Fleming already has sufficient reason to silence Nolan.'

'He knows that, and he's pretty scared. I've got to make sure he's kept out of danger until we work out what we're going to do with this.'

'What you've told me has the potential to create the biggest scandal since John Kerr sacked Gough Whitlam. McCarthy will have to sack Bacon from the Labor party, but there will be many questions asked as to how Bacon could carry on his criminal activities undetected for so long and how Fleming could get to the top of ASIO with such a dubious past. Everything else will certainly pale into insignificance for quite some time.

'But all this happened before McCarthy came on the scene, so I don't see how it's going to help us.'

'I've thought about that,' the deputy prime minister replied smugly.

'I bet you have, but before you tell me what you've got in mind, what are you doing to keep your Mr Nolan on ice in the meantime?'

'I've suggested to him that he do a bunk, but remain in touch by email and his mobile, because I can't personally hide him anywhere. He is supposed to let the Federal Police know his whereabouts at all times and when he doesn't physically report to police headquarters they'll start a search and cut off his money supply. He had about five grand of his own money and they're paying him while he's on suspension, but they'll freeze his bank accounts and cut off his salary the moment they think he's flown the coop, so he'll soon run out of funds. I've given him another twenty grand to go on with from our slush fund. I thought it was a good investment, considering the information he has in his possession.'

'No problems, Helen, twenty thousand is just petty cash when you consider the billions at stake. What about his family?'

'They're completely in the dark. They will think the worst of him but he reckons his marriage will be over whatever happens, so his family become collateral damage.'

'So what's the plan? How are you going to break the news and how will you go about it without implicating yourself?'

'I've told Nolan to hang onto the tapes of the conversations between Bacon and Fleming until I give him the nod. He'll then contact Sixty Minutes to arrange an interview at a secret location during which he'll hand over the tapes. The nation's already reeling from the terrorist attack and the breaching of our borders. Add this scandal to it with the right political spin and we can make the McCarthy government look totally inept. You know what the media is like with tall poppies. They'll be only too happy to crucify him if it sells newspapers or increases TV ratings. When the time is just right and I am confident I've got the numbers, I'll challenge McCarthy for the leadership and that will be the end of your problems.

'I haven't done anything yet because I thought I'd wait until we had this chat but I'd like to do it as soon as possible. So, what do you think?'

Walker's eyes all but disappeared in the folds of his fleshy cheeks as he cackled happily. 'If you can pull it off it's brilliant, Helen. The sooner the shit hits the fan the better for us.'

+++++++++++++++++

Chapter Seventeen

With a pneumatic hiss, the frost-covered lids of ten missile silos slid opened simultaneously. The obscene phallus-like, gunmetal grey nuclear Taepodong-3 rockets nestling in their shafts were all but invisible under the leaden clouds concealing a scythe-thin moon. Vapour rose ethereally from the launch tubes beneath which a vast and complex subterranean network of tunnels crisscrossed the mountain's innards. Fifty metres away, in the high tech missile control centre, the North Korean leader and his generals stood stony-faced, watching the banks of television screens as the countdown began.

Based on the earlier limited range and less accurate Taepodong-2 rocket, the Taepodong-3 was considerably larger and possessed the capability to carry a substantial nuclear warhead, or chemical, biological and conventional weapons to anywhere within mainland America with considerable accuracy. The extremely deadly new intercontinental ballistic missile now spearheaded North Korea's ability to strike against the nation it considered had oppressed it for too long.

Only days earlier, North Korean troops had massed at the border with its southern neighbour. Mobile ICBM platforms equipped with the earlier, shorter range Taepodong-1 and Taepodong-2's had been trundled out and aimed at South Korea, Japan and Australia's northern coastal towns of Darwin and Broome. However, because the impoverished nation often resorted to such sabre rattling displays of its weaponry, no one paid much heed. Why would they? Kim Jon-Il and his late maniacal father, Kim Il-sung had done this countless times and most likened the situation to fat, spoilt rich kids playing with their toys. Nobody really believed the baby-faced despot would be sufficiently insane as to actually fire ICBMs at other countries.

After decades of sanctions, during which North Korea had survived by starving its people and selling weapons to Iran, Syria, Libya, Sudan, the United Arab Emirates, Yemen, Pakistan and other politically unstable regimes using its companies Hap Heng and Komid, Kim had declared to his generals that he'd had enough of being pilloried and lampooned by Western Nations. He'd also had enough of the United States and other countries imposing sanctions and stopping food shipments in a bid to bring his repressive regime to heel.

Kim knew sanctions would never work because the country possessed substantial natural resources, including iron, zinc, copper and lead and with better management of its farmlands it could feed itself. In addition, China, the country's closest ally and trading partner, could not afford the consequences of North Korea's economic collapse and chose to counter the effects of American sanctions by supplying whatever North Korea needed to survive. Nonetheless regardless of the consequences to his country's twenty-three million citizens, many of whom had been severely brutalised, starved and repressed, he was determined to show the world that his country was a force to be reckoned with.

It was time to teach the world a lesson.

When Genesis satellites in stationary orbit above the

DPRNK detected changes in the images being continuously relayed to the Pentagon, the U.S. Submarines *Ulysses* and *Neptune* and the giant floating city that was the nuclear powered aircraft carrier *Louisville*, they immediately raised the alarm. Respective officers of the watch aboard all three ships literally hit their panic buttons. Telephones were lifted from cradles by shaking, adrenaline-fuelled hands and nervous calls made to the United States' senior military leaders, alerting them to the imminent threat. These never sleeping commanders tasked with the role of the world's nuclear watchdogs then unsealed nuclear attack contingency plans and quickly reminded themselves of the procedures to follow.

Was this the real thing or just another false alarm? The next minutes would tell.

Sirens wailed throughout South Korea and as its crisis-hardened citizens scurried to the country's fallout shelters, nervous fingers twitched on the triggers of the South's anti-missile systems. Patrolling fighter and bomber pilots swallowed the rising bile of fear and anxiety as they prepared to retaliate, each well-schooled as to what their response must be.

Russian and Chinese satellites had also detected Kim Jon Il's brinkmanship and both countries immediately began preparing for the worst.

In his White House bedroom, the U.S. president dropped the omnipresent secure telephone back on its cradle with a laconic, "I'll be right there!" For the umpteenth time since becoming president, Clement Turnbull wondered why he, or anyone, would take on the most stressful job in the world, a job that aged presidential incumbents faster than the most virulent cancer. Wrapping a robe around his agile, pyjama-clad form, the Panther joined the Security Service detail waiting outside his bedroom for the short but rapid walk to the White House Situation Room.

Oh, dear Jesus, please don't let this happen!

Reaching the Sit Room, President Turnbull was not surprised to find General Bayliss, CIA Director Jerry Robson, Rear Admiral Sandover and a bevy of top military commanders already waiting for him. These dedicated warriors never seemed to sleep and all made a point of beating their commander-in-chief to the Sit Room whenever there was crisis of national security or a major disaster demanding the president's intervention.

Adopting the persona of the never-stressed, ice-cool man of decision, Turnbull willed the butterflies in his acid-laden stomach to settle as he addressed the crowded room. 'Okay, give it to me in a nutshell.'

General Bayliss cleared his throat, a pulse above his right eye throbbed visibly and he fixed the president with his steely grey eyes as he spoke. 'Mr President, we've gone to full alert. Kim Jon Il seems to have completely flipped this time. If you look at the screens please sir, you'll see the satellite images of the North Korean's Chongjin area shows twenty missile silos opened only minutes ago and it's clear from vapour emissions that their ICBMs are all primed ready for launch.

'There's also been unprecedented activity on the border with South Korea and at all North Korean military establishments. The North Korean navy has sailed from the seaports of Nampho, Rajin, Chongjin,

Wonsan and Hamhung and they've sent aloft much of their air force. In addition, our drones show that their mobile ICBM launch platforms are all manned and they appear to have locked onto targets. Pyongyang, Kaesong, Sinuiju, Wonsan and Hamhung, Nampho and Rajin are all blacked out but our satellites have detected large convoys of military vehicles moving southward.

'Mr President, I think we should get in first and hit Chongjin and key other targets before Kim Jon-Il unleashes hell on us, South Korea, Australia and Japan, or we might not be able to stop mass slaughter.'

Turnbull could feel the sweat trickling down the middle of his back. With 1.21 million personnel, the North Korean army enjoyed a budget of eighteen percent of the nation's GDP and was the world's fifth largest military force. The rogue nation also possessed substantial stockpiles of chemical, radiological and biological weapons and had the capability to deliver these anywhere within a radius of six thousand kilometres. Its BM-25 long range ballistic missiles could strike targets up to fifteen hundred miles away and its conventional weaponry would not be easily defeated. If its troops crossed through the demilitarised zone into South Korea the South would be hard pressed to stave off the invasion.

The ultimate decision was his to make but guidance from these highly trained, battle hardened veterans of at least two recent wars would help lighten the enormous burden of the president's decision.

'What's the general consensus?' he inquired quietly.

One by one, his middle aged warhorses committed themselves with either simple but grim-faced nods or a brief, "I agree, sir."

'Mr President, please wait a few more minutes.' Secretary of State, Colin Polanski cried in alarm. 'Kim is just doing what his father did so many times before. They know we're watching and they always pull back at the last moment. It's bound to be just another attention seeking ploy.'

The Sit Room erupted noisily as the doves and the hawks squabbled for ascendency.

'Holy bloody hell, man, grow a spine, we can't afford to take the chance,' Bayliss thundered. 'We're playing with the lives of millions here. We don't know how many nuclear warheads each of those Taepodong-3s might carry but we must assume that they have several and each one can be aimed at a separate target.

'Let me remind also you that ICBMs go through three basic stages after launch; the boost stage, the mid-course stage and the re-entry stage. The boost stage, which is the initial launch phase, lasts about three to five minutes before the rocket reaches its sub-orbital flight path and a speed of approximately four point three miles per second.'

Bayliss paused momentarily to let the sheer speed of the missiles register in everyone's brains before continuing. 'The mid-course phase which takes approximately twenty-five minutes maximum, comes next. During this phase the rocket can release several warheads, each aimed at a different target. Re-entry is the final stage and by then the warheads are travelling at approximately two point five miles per second, which is simply too fast for small anti-ballistic missile systems to be of any use. The ICBMs also release penetration aids consisting of aluminium balloons, chaff or full scale warhead decoys making them very difficult to intercept.

'There are only three systems capable of intercepting ICBMs; our Terminal High Altitude Area Defence, or THAAD, Russia's ABM-4 Gorgon system and China's recently developed high-altitude Fan Ji-3 interceptor.

'Russia and China aren't going to take action against North Korea! In fact, they'll probably rub their hands together with glee. We are the only ones who will put a stop to this madness. We have to hit them *before* they launch, if we are to be sure of minimising casualties!'

'I am not playing with anybody's life,' Polanski retorted. 'If you're all wrong and you push the button you'll start World War III. Iran and Syria will see this as an opportunity to launch missiles at Israel, the entire Middle East will erupt and who knows what China's going to do? Can't you see you're playing right into Kim's hands?'

'Gentlemen, please, settle down,' the president commanded, his voice cutting through the hubbub of dissent. The room fell quiet.

'Get President Hu Jianto on the phone now. Surely, he can talk some sense into these lunatics. The Chinese don't want this any more than we do. And someone make the phone calls to the Japanese and Australian PMs for me. Tell them I've got my hands full but I'll speak to them personally as soon as I get a chance. In the meantime, if any of those Taepodong-3 rockets move, hit those goddam sons of Satan with everything we've got!'

Apart from the aid who was trying to contact the

Chinese president no one spoke. All eyes were glued to the television monitors and every word and action in the next few minutes would be recorded.

Flopping into an easy chair, the president rubbed a hand across his face and wished he'd taken the time to change out of his pyjamas and gown.

I feel like a patient in a geriatric hospital. Is this how history will remember this moment, a black president in his night attire trying to avert World War III?

'Oh my God. Oh fuck, they've really done it!' The shrillness of the voice was like acid in the air. No one wanted to believe what was happening and there were simultaneous gasps of disbelief before their training kicked in.

There was little the president could do now. It was time for his warriors to take over. Sick to the stomach and in awe of what was unfolding, he stood at the back of the room, listening to the now business-like commentary and trying to decipher from the unfamiliar military jargon exactly what was happening. Although there was no sound from the satellite images relayed to the Sit Room's television monitors the sight of the missiles rising from their silos was sickening.

Seemingly in slow motion at first, the sleek, evil shapes had emerged from their subterranean nests. The white-hot flames blasting from each missile's tail appeared almost solid. The long aluminium tubes, emblazoned with the North Korean flag, seemed to stand on the dancing column of their flames, before winning the fight against the forces of gravity and blasting vertically into the stratosphere at an ever increasing rate. Great clouds of dishwater-grey smoke enveloped the scorched earth around the silos and Turnbull could imagine the thunderous noise and the earth-shaking power needed to send these evil harbingers of death into a sub-orbital flight path.

The Panther wondered how megalomaniacs like Kim Jon-Il convince their generals to unleash their dogs of war, knowing they were consigning their nation to suicidal and calamitous destruction. It seemed inconceivable that anybody would breach nuclear nations' long-held doctrine of mutually assured destruction (MAD) that was based upon the rationale that no one would attack another if his own annihilation was guaranteed. However, that thinking should have been revised with the advent of the suicide bomber who believed that by destroying the infidel he would be assured of a place in paradise.

Moving to sit beside a young naval lieutenant whose job appeared to be keeping a hand-written log of events as a back-up to the electronic record, he asked the man to provide him with a commentary. To the president, the lieutenant appeared little more than a scrawny kid who still had traces of teenage acne on his pale, hatchet face.

Keeping his eyes fixed the screen in front of him the lieutenant paused briefly before responding, his prominent Adam's apple bobbing. Despite his young age, he understood the need to address the president in layman's terms, for although the president was commander-in-chief of the United States' military might, he was after all, a civilian with no military background or training. 'Mr President, the North Koreans have fired off ten Taepodong-3 missiles. As far as we can tell at this stage three are heading toward Japan, two toward Australia and another three toward the United States' mainland. We're not sure where the other three are going but it looks like they're trying for Britain, France and Germany.

'They've also fired an unknown number of Taepodong-2s from mobile platforms at Seoul and other South Korean targets. The South Koreans have already retaliated with their Patriot and Aegis anti-missiles-systems but we expect major casualties, sir.'

'Is the North using nuclear warheads on their Taepodong-2s?'

'Sir, so far the ones fired at South Korea all appear to contain conventional explosives but we think the Taepodong-3s are nuclear equipped.'

'What response has there been from the Ulysses and the Neptune?'

'Both the Neptune, which is located in the Yellow Sea, and the Ulysses, which is in the Sea of Japan, have responded by firing SM2MR and Harpoons at key North Korean military targets. We anticipate knocking out most of the T3 ICBMs they've launched in the first strike sir. We should also be able to take out the rest of their T3 silos before they launch a second wave.'

'What are our chances of knocking down *all* their Taepodong 3s before they reach their targets?'

The young lieutenant looked extremely grim. 'Our ICBM intercept facility in Alaska should stop anything from hitting Japan, the States and Australia sir. Unfortunately, we can't do anything about the ICBMs fired at Europe.'

The president swore under his breath. 'The fucking

Germans and the Poles are going to wish they hadn't blocked the Bush administration's proposal to provide Europe with ICBM defences back in 2007.'

The young lieutenant blanched as the reality of the commander-in-chief's words hit home. 'I neglected to mention Mr President, that the North Koreans have also fired a Taepodong-2 at northern Australia. Our Alaskan intercept facility should be able to get all three missiles sir.'

Should? But what if just one of them gets through?

'What's your name, son?'

'Lieutenant Ross Jaworski, sir.'

'Ross, tell me, does Australia have any warships in the area with anti-ballistic missile capabilities?'

'Sir, the destroyer H.M.A.S. Darwin is currently in the South China Sea and one of their submarines, the Dechaineux, is on joint manoeuvres with the Indonesians in the Timor Sea. The Dechaineux has McDonnell Douglas Sub Harpoon Block 1Bs with active radar homing and the Darwin has Harpoon and SM2MR missiles. However as the general said a moment ago sir, ICBMs such as the Taepodongs simply travel too fast for the Harpoons or the SM2MRs to be of any use.'

'Have the Australian ships launched any missiles against North Korea?'

'Not yet Mr President.'

'Are they aware what's going on?'

'Yes sir. The U.S. Defence Department has briefed them and they've gone to battle stations. Also, on your instructions, the necessary advice has gone out to the leaders of Japan, Australia, Britain, Canada, New

Zealand and all NATO countries.'

'Let's hope the Aussies get their ass into gear soon,' the president muttered as he wondered whether the Australian Navy's woefully small but well-equipped fleet could respond to a full scale ballistic missile attack.

'Yes, sir.'

'Mr President,' someone announced, 'President Hu Jianto is coming to the 'phone now, sir. I'll switch the call through to your desk now.'

Turnbull had met and spoken to the Chinese president on several occasions and while he prided himself on being able to read most people, he found the recently appointed Chinese very difficult to read. As he took the phone from the naval rating who'd initiated the call he was well aware that every word spoken by either man would be recorded. The conversation would also be analysed and dissected later. Every nuance, expression, emotion and pause would be psychoanalysed and the armchair critics would judge him mercilessly. To hell with them all, he decided.

'President Hu, I am sure you're aware that Kim Jon-Il has attacked the South and launched missiles at Europe, Japan, Australia and the United States?'

The softly spoken voice of his Chinese counterpart responded in almost faultless, accent-less English, 'Please believe me Clement when I tell you we had no prior warning that he would do this. We previously asked the new North Korean leader not to do anything to endanger the negotiations for re-unification of both Koreas but he is a headstrong, young, and I am afraid, somewhat stupid and impetuous man.'

'Well, he's probably started World War III because

we've had no choice but to retaliate. As you are no doubt aware, we cannot intercept the missiles he's aimed at Europe and we can only pray they malfunction before they reach their targets. His missiles will slaughter thousands in South Korea and there's not a damned thing I or anyone can do to stop him.

'I need assurances from you sir that China will not side with North Korea while we try and stop this madness spreading.'

'I have tried to contact President Kim from the moment our satellites detected their weapon silos opening but the country has severed its international telephone network and they're not responding to radio and television broadcasts. I am afraid their beloved leader will take no notice of us but I will keep trying.'

'Please do sir. I suggest we maintain contact meantime.'

'I shall, but time is of the essence, so I must go now and do what I can to contain the situation,' Hu Jianto replied cryptically and terminated the call.

'Fuck, what was the use of that? I still don't know what the Chinese are going to do. Let's hope they don't make things any worse.'

Due to the time difference, Matthew McCarthy was at work behind his desk in his Parliament House office when he received the call from the White House Situation Room. As with the American President, he wondered why anybody would aspire to the nation's executive office. Dismissing such thoughts as self-indulgent, he immediately telephoned his chief of defence, Brigadier John Watson, a squat, tough-looking man with the face of a pub brawler and a pair of sparkling blue eyes.

Despite his appearance, Watson was an extremely intelligent individual. He was also a great military tactician with a well-developed sense of fair play. As with most top ranking militarists he had his own well-established communication channels and was already well-apprised of the situation.

'I was just about to pick up the phone and call you, Prime Minister. I've taken the liberty of instructing the country's armed forces to fully mobilise. While we are now obviously at war, I need your approval to instruct the commanders of Darwin and Dechaineux to launch Harpoon and SM2MR missiles at North Korean targets. The yanks are going to need all the help they can get,' he added.

Matthew McCarthy did not hesitate despite the momentous consequences of the decision. 'Yes, do whatever it takes, John. I am recalling parliament and I will announce on the midday news to the Australian people that we are now at war with North Korea. How do you rate our chances of coming through this unscathed?'

Watson's gravelly voice was matter of fact. 'If the yanks can't stop the Taepodongs with all their high tech anti-ballistic missile facility in Alaska, I don't like our chances.'

Like most military men, Watson had scant regard for his political masters and he couldn't help adding, 'If previous governments hadn't cut defence spending and had taken notice of the recommendations in the last White Paper, we'd have our own effective ICBM defence system in place now. We did try to warn the government not to place too much reliance on America's Alaskan intercept facility.'

'Mate, I know your views on national security and believe me, despite the enormous cost, I agree, but it's too late for griping about it now. We've just got to rely on the US to save our bacon.'

'Which amounts to crossing our fingers and hoping, I am afraid,' the brigadier responded. 'If those missiles headed our way get past the Alaskan counter ICBM defences we've got about twenty-five minutes before we're all vaporised.'

'Do we know yet what they've targeted?'

'It looks like they're planning to hit the communications base at Exmouth and the RAAF base at Tindal.'

Exmouth had previously been a key United States military communications base that had become obsolete due to rapid advances in technology. The Americans had returned it to Australian control and it had been re-equipped to monitor all South East Asian and Middle Eastern telephone, radio and internet traffic. In short, it eavesdropped on other countries in an attempt to detect and identify threats from terrorists and organised crime networks.

The second target, Tindal, was located in the Northern Territory and now housed the RAAF and a sizeable United States Air Force contingent. It was designed to counter potential military strikes from China, Indonesia and North Korea. The latter country had objected strenuously to Australia granting the Americans the right to locate military aircraft within relatively easy striking distance of its shores and retaliated by making both installations key military targets.

'Prime Minister, there is insufficient time to evacuate personnel at both installations. I have warned them of the imminent threat because I think it's the moral thing to do and those who can fit into the limited space in the shelters are bunkered down. I have also requested all aircraft at Tindal to take to the air just in case. They are awaiting further orders. The Americans have already mobilised their Tindal-based fighter and bomber squadrons and those with the capability will help mount a counter attack against North Korean targets.

'While the next half an hour will be crucial, I suggest you also move to the War Office into the nuclear shelter beneath Parliament House. The defence chiefs and I will join you there to direct proceedings.'

Despite her duplicitous and ruthless, scheming nature, Helen Knox was flabbergasted by the news of the North Korean attack as she hurried to the fallout shelter beneath Parliament House. While she viewed her government's policy on climate change as politically suicidal and had wished for an effective way of stymieing it, she would never have wished for a full scale nuclear attack as the solution. Still, having the country at war was like manna from heaven.

Provided they all survived.

She was sure that Matthew McCarthy would now be far too busy to pursue what she and Big Business considered a lunatic agenda. Convinced she could keep the threat of the scandal concerning the ASIO chief and

Senator Bacon up her sleeve as an ace to play if all else failed she pondered the financial implications of the unexpected change of events.

Wouldn't Australia now need its coal more than ever? Surely McCarthy couldn't afford to countenance closing the coal mines? How would the Middle East react to Kim Jon-Il's insanity? Would the Islamic world now see this as an opportunity to attack the West? If oil supplies dried up wouldn't the need for coal be crucial to the war effort? Wouldn't Australian industry have to gear up to meet the demand for weapons, aircraft, ships and various forms of military transport? On top of all that, wouldn't Australia's minerals be in great demand by the rest of the world as it struggled to re-build after the destruction of war?

Knox decided Walker, the unions and the mineral resources sector should be very pleased with this turn of events.

Reaching the purpose-built crisis room deep beneath the uniquely distinctive structure of Australia's Parliament House, Knox found Matthew McCarthy, his Cabinet and members of the opposing political parties already assembled to wait the result of Kim Jon-Il's missile launch.

In this time of genuine crisis, everyone had agreed to put aside their political differences in the best interests of the nation. Naturally, there was immense tension within the room which was filled with top military personnel, politicians and essential hangers-on.

Despite the short time lapse since the Taepodong-3s had taken off into their respective sub-orbital flight paths, reports of the enormous damage had already come in as a result of the shorter range Taepodong-2s fired at South Korea. Seoul and several other major cities had taken direct hits before the South had been able to retaliate. Casualties numbered in their thousands, buildings had been reduced to smoking piles of rubble, roads ruined and bridges toppled into waterways.

Fortunately, the Taepodong-2 rockets fired at Japan had been hopelessly inaccurate, falling harmlessly into the sea. Nevertheless, Japan's response had been swift and deadly. Its naval and air defence forces had immediately launched a barrage of missiles at DPRPNK targets, knocking out many key military installations.

Acknowledging his ignorance of matters military, McCarthy called upon the no-nonsense brigadier to explain the situation pertaining to the world's capacity to counter intercontinental ballistic missiles. While the knowledge would not alter their plight, it would help pass the time while they awaited the incoming Taepodong-3s which were now mere minutes away.

Watson's understanding of all forms of weaponry proved encyclopaedic. 'It's fairly common knowledge that during 1979 the United States of America, the U.S.S.R. and China signed the SALT II treaty prohibiting the deployment of weapons of mass destruction from being placed in orbit. Which was just as well because the Soviets had plans to launch nuclear weapons into orbit. If they'd manage to get away with doing so they would have had the capacity to destroy any target on Earth whenever they chose to activate an orbiting warhead.

'As you know, former President Regan's Strategic Defence Initiative had included plans for knocking down ICBMs using laser beams and kinetic kill vehicles consisting of small non-nuclear rockets to be fired from satellites to destroy ICBMs or satellites carrying WMDs. Regan's SDI program fell outside the SALT II treaty and other treaties prohibiting the launch of WMDs into space.

'Experts disagreed on the feasibility of using laser technology; however we do know a small laser was developed and used successfully to destroy the model of a satellite as long ago as 1983. In fact, one expert maintained it was possible to develop a satellite no bigger than an office desk equipped with laser technology which would have the capacity to render the entire Soviet missile program useless.

'As far back as 1986 the United States developed non-nuclear, satellite-based, high velocity tungsten missiles that would detect and destroy missiles without any external guidance. Unfortunately, the SDI met considerable opposition from within the U.S. due to its exceptionally high cost. It was strongly opposed by the U.S.S.R. for obvious reasons. Other countries also worried about SDI triggering another arms race. After the cold war ended there was no longer such urgency to develop these systems and SDI was abandoned in 1994.

'The official line is that no effective SDI hardware was ever manufactured for deployment but we know that is actually far from the truth. As well as having a stockpile of kinetic kill vehicles, the United States also developed a small satellite equipped with an electronically-powered, solid-state laser capable of destroying missiles, aircraft and satellites but as yet the U.S. hasn't put the satellite into orbit, choosing instead to conduct further experiments with laser beams fired from Boeing 747 aircraft. They've had varying success with these aircraft mounted systems but they are far from operational.

'Russia's ABM-4 Gorgon system is designed to counter ICBMs fired from America and China but the Russians could just as easily use their Gorgon counter ICBM system to neutralise missiles from other nations.

'Whether they have the time to reset their system, or have the will to intervene and negate the North Korean ICBMs for the common good remains to be seen but it's in nobody's best interest to have the planet contaminated by radioactive fallout.

'China's recently developed high-altitude Fan Ji-3 interceptor also has the capability but the same questions arise. Will they intervene, or will they see this as an opportunity to gain ascendency over America?

'I guess we'll all know in the next twenty minutes,' the brigadier concluded.

'What about radioactive fallout if the ICBMs are destroyed in flight? Won't that still pose a significant threat?' someone asked.

Watson's voice was devoid of any emotion as he replied. 'That is largely dependent upon the altitude at which the missiles are destroyed. A weapon detonated in the air has much lower radiation than a weapon of comparable size detonated close to the ground; however, meteorological factors and the yield of the particular warhead have a profound effect on the contamination levels. For that reason, all anti-ballistic missile systems aim to incinerate the warheads before re-entry into the atmosphere. The danger then is from the Kessler Syndrome.

'The Kessler Syndrome is a situation created from the destruction of a nuclear warhead in space resulting in thousands of radioactive particles orbiting the Earth. These particles of radioactive space debris would be in acute danger of colliding with and knocking out satellites and preventing any further space exploration.

'On the other hand, if a nuclear warhead is destroyed in the Earth's atmosphere, fallout radiation decays relatively quickly with time. However, the radio-biological hazard of worldwide fallout is essentially a long-term problem because of the potential accumulation of long-lived radio-isotopes (such as strontium 90 and caesium-130) in the body from being ingested in foods containing the radioactive materials.

'Nevertheless, this hazard is less pertinent than local fallout, which is of much greater immediate operational concern. After three to five weeks most areas become fairly safe for travel and decontamination but no one wants higher levels of radiation than currently exist, because in the long term, the incidence of cancers, deformities and thyroid problems will rise as any contamination spreads worldwide.'

As a member of McCarthy's Cabinet, Deputy Prime Minister Helen Knox listened to the brigadier's dissertation with growing alarm. Suddenly, the bleak prospect of a nuclear winter offset the huge potential financial benefits resulting from war. The downside of McCarthy's strategies for combating climate change paled into insignificance and she shuddered visibly.

Beware of what you wish for.

Studying the prime minister's face, Knox could not help her grudging admiration for the man. A newcomer to the cutthroat world of politics he'd been thrust unwillingly into the role of Australia's leader, yet during the few weeks since Bowker's assassination he'd had to deal with far more crises than any prime minister since the Second World War. He'd narrowly escaped death and was still recovering from the wounds inflicted by a spear gun, terrorists had tried to kill him and his family, his parents had nearly died in the recent disastrous Perth bushfires, he and his family were forced to adopt a siege mentality for their own safety, he was facing mounting opposition to his government's climate change policies, the world was on the brink of another Great Depression, and now, he was leading the nation into war. Despite all this, Matthew McCarthy retained his composure. Others seemed to draw from his strength and for once, Knox questioned her own capacity to handle the role of prime minister should she be successful in bringing about a leadership spill.

When the time comes to challenge him, he'll be no pushover, she decided.

Little did she know that Matthew McCarthy's calm outward appearance belied his inner turmoil; a thousand thoughts raced through his brain as he watched the countdown to the world's potential Armageddon and worried about his family's safety. He desperately wanted to be with them and while it wasn't possible, there was some consolation in knowing that his father would do everything within his power to ensure their safety.

What happened in the next few minutes would

determine whether or not the world would be changed irrevocably.

+++++++++++++

Chapter Eighteen

Despite the terrorist attack on the Lodge being thwarted, John McCarthy was convinced more than ever that the aging building did not offer adequate protection for the nation's leader and his family. Apart from that, the entire area was now a major crime scene under intense media scrutiny and there was simply no privacy for Catherine, Daniel and Sienna. After inspecting security precautions at the prime minister's Sydney residence of Kirribilli House, he concluded that they should all relocate until the Lodge could be brought up to the required standard. Matthew would of course remain in Canberra during the week to attend to matters of state and commute to Sydney each weekend.

Satisfied that he'd done all he could to help them settle in, John decided to pay a visit to FEPOL's Sydney headquarters and catch up on the ongoing investigations into Connor Bowker's assassination and the attempt on his son's life.

He was disappointed to find there had been little progress in tracking down Bowker's assassin, or the people behind it. He was even more surprised to learn that the suspended federal agent, Sergeant Richard Nolan, had simply disappeared and while Federal Police investigators were trying to track him down, they had so far been unsuccessful.

John decided it was time to brush up on his own investigative skills and make a few discreet enquiries.

Figuring he needed to learn all he could about the man so he could get inside his head, he started by delving into the former navy diver's background which entailed a trip back to the National Archives in Canberra.

The RAN records section of the National Archives was at first reluctant to disclose any information, citing the Privacy Act as its reason for non-cooperation. Although he knew he was probably overstepping his brief, John McCarthy produced his Federal Police identification and Top Secret security clearance and explained that his inquiries related to national security but it was his title of prime minister's personal security advisor that seemed to do the trick of opening doors to Richard Nolan's personal record.

It made for fascinating reading. Richard Nolan was the only child of an unremarkable, working class couple, who had at the time of his recruitment to the navy, resided in Ingleburn, a suburb on Sydney's western fringes. He'd attended Campbelltown High School where he'd always been among the top five students in his classes. At the tender age of seventeen he'd joined the RAN. and attended and excelled at his basic sailor training at HMAS Cerberus in Victoria before being posted to the navy's combat and security division.

After a period at sea, during which he'd undergone weapons training, he'd applied to become a clearance diver and successfully completed the training with high distinction.

Clearly a man who'd found his niche in life, Nolan met and married his wife Jenny in 1990. The couple had produced two children, Trevor and Jasmine, who McCarthy calculated must now be around twenty-three and twenty-one years of age.

By the time Nolan was deployed in 1992 to the first Gulf War in Iraq he'd attained the rank of Chief Petty Officer and was considered one of the navy's top clearance divers. He'd left the navy shortly after being decorated and in 1993 had chosen to pursue a career in the Australian Federal Police.

McCarthy knew the former navy man had served the police for twenty years. During this time he'd not blotted his copybook and seemed to be content to remain at the rank of sergeant and pursue his love of sport diving in his spare time. Background inquiries prior to his selection as the prime minister's personal bodyguard showed no debts, a solid marriage and no worrying associations, religious beliefs or affiliation with any particular political party.

In other words, he was the epitome of a solid, reliable citizen.

As far as the former New Zealand policeman was concerned Nolan's record raised more questions than it answered. Why would a decorated war hero and ranking federal agent with an exemplary record covering so many years suddenly turn bad? It just didn't make sense. There had to be something in his past and someone clearly had some sort of a hold over the man.

There seemed little point in talking to Nolan's senior officers to find out who could exert such powerful control that he could persuade Nolan to become involved in a plot to kill the prime minister. His record was filled with their admiration and praise. No, it had to be someone much closer to the man.

Inspecting newspaper accounts of Nolan's very public award for bravery, McCarthy wondered what had become of the other man depicted in the photographs of the medal ceremony, Jim Yeoman.

McCarthy studied the photos intently. Whereas Nolan appeared proud and happy to receive his medals, Yeoman looked as if he'd rather be someplace else. The body language between the two men was contrary to what one would expect from two individuals who had together cheated death. In the entire series of pictures Yeoman appeared to be doing his best to distance himself from Nolan and in one or two shots where he appeared in the background when Nolan was being interviewed he was actually scowling at the other officer.

His curiosity further aroused, John McCarthy requested Yeoman's personal file. The archival clerk, himself a balding, middle-aged former naval veteran was only too happy to oblige, commenting, 'I feel sorry for this bloke. The death of his mates really knocked the crap out of him. The poor bugger ended up with post-traumatic stress disorder (PTSD) and they pensioned him out of the service.

'I believe he's got a drink problem and now lives the life of a hermit in some backwater somewhere.'

That "backwater" proved to be Clarence Town, a small rural settlement with a population of less than eight hundred residents in the Hunter region of New South Wales. Yeoman's personal file also showed that he'd been divorced, had refused psychiatric treatment and subsisted on his Veterans' Affairs pension.

I better pay this bloke a visit, McCarthy decided.

Feeling a bit like a yoyo, he returned to Sydney and decided to drive to Clarence Town without telephoning first. It seemed better to take the gamble that Yeoman would not be home than risk being rebuffed at the outset and losing the element of surprise.

Situated just west of the placid Williams River, the sleepy but picturesque town proved a welcome respite from the hubbub of Sydney and the recent turmoil surrounding the terrorist attack and his son's near-death experience. It was easy to see why the rolling green hills, historic buildings and laidback lifestyle would attract someone seeking to bury the past.

McCarthy's GPS took him right to the door of an ancient, weather-beaten wooden cottage with a sagging front veranda and an overgrown jungle of weeds and cotoneaster trees. Parking his hired Commodore in the driveway behind a battered Hilux ute, he made his way to the open front door, noting the overflowing ashtray on a 1960s style rattan table standing beside a worn-looking canvas deckchair. Several empty overturned gin bottles littered the bare boards and others glinted dully among the weeds.

Taking a deep breath he rapped on the peeling woodwork with his knuckles and called out, 'Anyone home?'

'Who the fuck wants to know?' a gruff, asthmatic voice responded testily.

'It's okay, I am not selling anything mate. I just want a quick word.'

'If you're a bloody bible-basher you better bugger off before I put me size ten up your arse,' the house's occupant grumbled as he shuffled to the front door.

Pre-warned as to Yeoman's alcoholism, John had not expected someone in the peak of health but the man who came to the door was clearly on the path to self-destruction. Despite being of a similar age to his former navy boss, Yeoman was a rail-thin, mid-height character and typical of most chronic alcoholics, had no visible backside and a pair of spindly, wasted legs. He had clearly not shaved for weeks and his tobacco stained teeth were in great need of a dentist's ministrations. His hacking cough was ample evidence of advanced emphysema.

McCarthy produced his business and identification cards and proffered his hand which Yeoman ignored suspiciously. 'The prime minister's personal security advisor eh? What the bloody hell brings you all the way out here to see someone like me?'

'Matters of national security. I believe you might be able to help me with some information. May we go inside?' John gestured to the cottage's dim, sour-smelling interior.

'Don't have many guests. Better sit out here. I'll getcha a chair,' Yeoman muttered. Retreating inside, he dragged an ancient, badly scarred bentwood chair from the interior, positioned it next to his deckchair and flopped into the canvas seat with a thump. 'Park your bum sport and tell me what the hell this is all about.'

McCarthy brushed a layer of dirt from the chair and sat down. 'I take it you've heard about the recent attempt on the prime minister's life?'

'Ah, I'm beginning to see why you've come to see me. You want to know about bloody tricky Dicky Nolan, the gutless, yellow bastard.' The former able seaman hoicked and spat over the veranda rail to emphasise his hatred of the other man. 'I read the bastard's run off. Doesn't surprise me. He's a collection of shivers looking for a spine to crawl up.'

Sensing he was on the verge of some interesting revelations concerning Nolan, McCarthy knew the other man needed little prompting to tell his story. 'Jim, it sounds like you and Dick Nolan aren't the best of mates. Do you care to tell me about it?'

'I've been waiting for twenty years for that bugger to get his just desserts. I went to that fucking wanker, Fleming with the information just after it happened 'cos no other bastard would believe me but he just told me to sit on it. Fucking sit on it! The prick's ruined my life. Just look at me! I've got fucking PTSD. Me nerves are shot to pieces, I can't sleep, can't hold down a bloody job and me missus has deserted me.'

'Jim, you're a bloody war hero for God's sake. You deserve better. What did Dick Nolan do to ruin your life?' McCarthy had not missed the reference to Fleming and wondered could this poor, miserable specimen be referring to the ASIO chief? He'd ask the question when the opportunity presented itself but Yeoman had already embarked upon his story and it was best not to interrupt him.

Just as quickly as he started talking, Yeoman suddenly stopped, 'Hang on a moment cobber, I need a drink and a smoke 'cos this is going to be a long chat. I hope you've got plenty of time.'

After getting slowly to his feet, the ailing alcoholic re-entered the house, returning a few moments later with two glasses and an unopened bottle of Gilbeys' gin. Although McCarthy hated the stuff, sharing the man's liquor seemed the best way to gain his trust. He listened incredulously as James Yeoman described how the divers had been ensnared in the crudely effective Iraqi trap, how he'd rushed to rescue them from the Iranian gunboat and how Nolan had ordered him to run for safety.

'Christ it was horrible.' Tears coursed down Yeoman's cheeks. 'There were bits and pieces of our blokes scattered all over the surface of the ocean. That stupid bastard should have led the gunboat away from the mine; instead he caused it to try and cut us off and killed five of me mates.

'He was also responsible for the deaths of the Iranians. Shit, they were only ordinary blokes following orders just like us. Even if we'd sat tight and let them capture us it would have been preferable to what happened. They might even have helped rescue our boys.'

'You're not to blame mate. You were taught not to question orders during battle.'

'You think I haven't told myself that a thousand times? It doesn't help. I keep seeing all that blood and gore in the water and thinking of those poor sods tangled up in all that nylon shit wondering if they were going to drown or be blown up.'

'You mentioned that you tried to tell your side of the story but no one wanted to listen. What happened there?'

'The brass wanted to put a positive spin on what happened. They love good publicity and nothing's better than pinning a few medals on war heroes to get that. When they insisted on turning a blind eye I didn't know what to do but then, along comes this Fleming joker. He was the head of ASIO. Still is as far as I know. He wanted to know my side of things and I thought, at last, here's somebody who'll listen and do something about it, but he convinced me I should shut up and he'd take care of it.

'I haven't heard from him since. Did he send you to talk to me?'

McCarthy wasn't about to reveal that he suspected Fleming might be behind the assassination attempt. 'No, Jim. I am just trying to get a handle on how Dick Nolan's mind works.'

Yeoman was a drunkard but he was no fool. 'Don't you think it seems rather coincidental that tricky Dicky is implicated in a plot to kill the prime minister and that Fleming is the only other person to know about his shady past?'

'I intend to get to the bottom of this, Jim but to do that, I need you to maintain your silence a bit longer. Can you do that?'

'Loose lips sink ships. I've kept me trap shut for twenty years, so I guess I can keep it shut a bit longer if I know retired Petty Officer Richard bloody Nolan is going to get his comeuppance.'

As John McCarthy embarked on the two hundred kilometre return drive to Sydney, he pondered how to proceed with this earth-shattering revelation. Why would James Fleming want to kill Australia's prime minister? Had he also been involved in Bowker's assassination? It all seemed rather farfetched. Fleming was himself a war hero and although McCarthy had taken an instant dislike to the public servant, he wondered what the head of ASIO had to gain by such a heinous crime.

Nolan could answer that question. But was he still alive? If Fleming hadn't already got rid of the federal policeman to shut him up, could McCarthy find him if others hadn't? If he did find him, could he induce the AFP sergeant to reveal his side of the story?

McCarthy sighed. *Oh well, I guess I need to go back to Canberra and have a few words with Jennifer Nolan.*

No 10 Carmichael Street, Deakin, proved to be an unprepossessing brick and tile bungalow with immaculate gardens, located in a whisper-quiet, leafy street in the Parliamentary Triangle. McCarthy guessed the house was worth close to $900,000 and he couldn't help but wonder whether the Nolans owned their family home outright.

Jenny Nolan answered his knock somewhat warily and he guessed she'd been hounded by journalists and probably by FEPOL's internal investigations unit. An attractive brunette in her mid-forties, the federal agent's wife was expensively attired in designer jeans and a figure-hugging cashmere sweater. She'd clearly just re-done her makeup and brushed her chestnut hair in readiness for the appointment which McCarthy had arranged ahead of time. Showing him into a pastel blue lounge room tastefully furnished with a white leather sofa and matching recliner chairs, she invited him to sit.

McCarthy glanced around the room noting family portraits on a sideboard. A photograph of Dick Nolan and his son and daughter taken in front of the Sydney Opera House showed them with their arms around each other's shoulders grinning at the camera. Going by the ages of his children the photo had been taken recently.

Jennifer Nolan noticed the direction of his gaze and commented, 'That was taken before Richard was transferred here to Canberra to the close personal protection unit. He was so proud and happy.'

'You have a lovely home here Mrs Nolan. I am sorry that everything seems to be going so badly for you.'

'Yes well, I don't see how I can help you Mr McCarthy. I've already told the gentlemen from the internal affairs section, or whatever they call it, I don't have any idea where my husband is and I haven't heard from him since he was suspended from duty.'

'Please call me John. Mrs Nolan, I am not here to make your life any more difficult than it already is. I really do appreciate that everything that's happened; including the allegations that your husband is somehow involved in an attempt to murder the prime minister must be extremely distressing for you and your family. I would like you to hear me out because I believe Richard's life is in danger.'

Jennifer Nolan's carefully pencilled eyebrows shot up. 'Why do you think that? Who would want to harm Richard?'

McCarthy decided to chance using the woman's first name in the hope that a less formal atmosphere and a little more empathy for her plight might crack her defences. 'Jenny, what do you know about Richard's navy career? Has he ever opened up to you about what *actually* happened in Iraq?'

'He didn't like talking about it. I think it brought back too many painful memories. He did lose some very close friends you know.'

'Yes, I do know. I know he was also awarded the bravery medal and the medal for distinguished service. I know he was hailed as a hero at the time and the incident in which he was involved was without doubt, very traumatic. It called for split second decisions and extraordinarily good judgment when he was under extreme duress. Now, this is all conjecture on my part but I suspect Richard believes if he'd responded differently those other men would still be alive. He's carried an enormous burden of guilt for the past twenty years but I sincerely believe most people would have reacted just as Richard did. Unfortunately, the navy didn't help by giving him the counselling he deserved and needed at the time to get over the incident. They just wanted a hero to pin medals on. Richard probably went along with it because the alternative was too terrible to contemplate. He found himself painted into a corner and couldn't see any way to get out of it without destroying his reputation. Of course, the longer it went on, the more he had at stake, such as his marriage, his family and his new career. I also think others have used Richard's guilt over his handling of the situation to get at him to do their bidding.'

Jenny Nolan appeared to relax a little as she leant forward and fixed her eyes on his. 'How do you mean?'

'I've read his personal file and the official version of events. I've also spoken to one of his compatriots who gave me a completely different account.'

'Was that Jim Yeoman, because Richard told me the incident disturbed the balance of his mind and not to believe anything he said.'

'As a matter of fact it was but I have sound reasons

for believing Able Seaman Yeoman's version of events.'

'And what are those reasons? You surely can't believe that Richard would be involved in a plot to assassinate Prime Minister McCarthy.'

'It seems very likely that someone in a very high position was blackmailing your husband. I can't reveal that person's identity because I am only just beginning to uncover some very dirty goings on which is bound to involve very powerful people.' McCarthy suddenly changed tack. 'Do you still love your husband Jenny?'

'Of course I do. Why do you ask?'

'I think Richard is running scared. He is ashamed of what he's done and he probably believes he's lost everything. I don't know what his state of mind is or what he's likely to do but he's a desperate man in extreme danger. Those behind the plot to kill my son will want to silence Richard. It is imperative that we find him for his own protection.'

'Oh God.' Jennifer Nolan's face paled and her hands shook. 'I don't know where he is. How are we going to find him and what will happen to him when we do?'

'We can start by you giving permission to go through Richard's things. Has he taken his car?'

'No, it's still in the garage.'

'Does he have a home office or study?'

'Yes.'

'Has he used his bank accounts lately?'

'Just after he was suspended he withdrew several thousand from our savings account but he hasn't touched the account since.'

'Has he been in touch with Trevor or Jasmine?'

'No, this is most unlike him. They're worried sick.'

'All right, I want you to check his wardrobe and make a list of the clothing that's missing. It might give us a clue. While you do that, I want you to try and put yourself in his shoes. You know better than anyone how his mind works. Think, were there any times when he wanted to be left alone? What sort of places did he like to go? Was there somewhere special?'

'He loved anywhere by the ocean, especially if there was good diving to be had.'

'Has he taken his diving gear?'

'No, it's still in the garage.'

'Okay, I think we can scrub that idea. Were there any towns he particularly liked?'

'He loved the skiing towns, Thredbo, Mount Hotham, Falls Creek, Tumut, Bright, anywhere with lots of trees and fast-flowing creeks.'

'Good, that's a start. Now, if you don't mind, let me have a look around.'

John McCarthy started with Nolan's study. He rummaged through the filing cabinet and desk. He emptied the wastepaper bin and examined its contents, he pored over Nolan's diary. His desktop computer had been seized and Jennifer told him her husband had taken his laptop computer and a tablet device with him and he knew the internal investigators had probably already covered the same ground but he hoped he'd find something they'd missed.

He then moved to the garage where he discovered one end had been partitioned off to form a small workshop. It was here that he got his first surprise. The federal agent was obviously into electronics in his spare time. However the nature of the equipment really raised McCarthy's eyebrows.

There were several pinhole surveillance cameras, GPS tracking devices, directional microphones, tiny digital recording devices, various handheld video cameras, devices for unearthing bugging equipment and an array of apparently innocuous everyday computer hardware. There were even bedside clock radios, pens and other paraphernalia which would have made James Bond drool. *Well I'll be damned. Our Dicky boy has been doing some serious spying in his spare time. I wonder what he's been up to?*

Unfortunately, there was no footage on any of the cameras and no audio on the digital recorders so McCarthy moved to Nolan's car, emptying the console and the glove compartment and the door pockets. He looked under the seats, in the boot and even under the dashboard, but Nolan was obviously fanatical about his car and apart from a small notebook stuck under the driver's side sun visor he found nothing of interest. The notebook did not contain so much as a shopping list and McCarthy was about to replace it when he remembered indentations left by someone writing on the previous page could be read by a test using an electro-static detection apparatus (ESDA) or by applying oblique or glancing light to the furrows of the indented writing and then photographing the pages. The former technique was far more reliable but was not something to be done by an amateur. Contrary to what fiction authors often claimed, rubbing a soft lead pencil over a page to bring up the indentations from a previous page did not work and was in fact the quickest way to destroy any image.

Satisfied that the notebook's cardboard cover would protect any indentations left on its pages, he placed it in his pocket and returned inside to see what Nolan's wife had come up with.

The list of missing clothing compiled by Nolan's wife was unremarkable, consisting of a selection of mainly casual attire, one suit and some running gear. There was some cold weather gear consisting of jackets and pullovers but Nolan had left behind lightweight cotton shorts and T-shirts, so McCarthy deduced the disgraced federal agent had probably not gone to the hotter parts of Australia. While they were into the summer months, towns such as Bright and Tumut could still get fairly chilly so there was some likelihood he'd chosen one of those in which to hide out.

There was nothing more he could do at Nolan's home and because McCarthy's official position as the prime minister's security advisor and the status of special constable entitled him to carte blanche use of Federal Police resources, he headed off to FEPOL's Canberra offices to seek help from the forensic section in examining Nolan's notebook using their ESDA. While he did not expect to find anything of importance, it was worth a try.

The procedure for recovering indented writing proved complicated but very interesting. He watched as the forensic technician applied Mylar film over the page of interest and utilised a vacuum device which drew through a porous bronze plate pulling the film into contact with the paper. The technician then waved a high voltage electrically charged wand repeatedly over the Mylar.

'It works like this,' the technician explained. 'The document and the Mylar become electrically charged. Now, when I cascade a black toner-like powder over the electrically charged document the toner is strongly attracted to the static electricity and is retained on the film's surface in accordance with the amount of residual static charge that's present at any given surface point. The areas of the document containing higher static electric charge retain greater portions of the toner resulting in a deposit of toner aligned with the indentations in the paper. It's sort of the reverse of putting thin paper over a coin or a medal and then rubbing charcoal or graphite over the surface to bring out the image of the coin. There, see? You can now read what was written on the page.'

'That's amazing,' John responded. 'Now, how do you preserve the images for evidentiary purposes?'

'We do two things. We photograph the image and we also preserve it by placing an adhesive backed clear plastic sheet over the cellophane while it's still held in place by the ESDA's vacuum. The quality of this image is fairly good and I dare say it's even good enough to make a comparison with the author's own handwriting.'

'Great work. I will need to preserve the chain of evidence, so I'd like copies of the photos and I'll get you to ensure the original documents are labelled and secured in the evidence room.'

McCarthy left the building feeling both elated and extremely concerned. Dick Nolan's reasons for writing down the private addresses of James Fleming, the Director General of ASIO, and Senator Philip Bacon remained a mystery but McCarthy's alarm bells were

293

ringing very loudly indeed and the discovery presented him with a real quandary. While he knew he should hand everything over to the Federal Police, he really didn't know how far the corruption had spread. Who could he trust? Clews seemed beyond reproach but he was too low in the pecking order and would feel duty bound to hand the information to FEPOL's internal affairs investigators. His gut instinct told him Stormy Knight, the commissioner, was straight but if someone at the ASIO Director General's level was implicated in an assassination plot, who else was involved?

For the moment at least McCarthy decided to play his cards close to his chest. One thing he did know and that was finding and protecting Richard Nolan was now his main concern.

+++++++++++++

Chapter Nineteen

Eight hundred and fifty kilometres above the Earth, the Chuangxin-3, Shiyan-7 and Shijian-15 satellites had been orbiting quietly since blasting into space simultaneously from the Taiyuan Satellite Launch Centre in North China's Shanxi Province on 20 June 2013. At that time, the Chinese government's official news release had declared all three satellites were intended solely for research and communication. However, despite being signatories to several space treaties banning the presence of WMD from being placed in orbit, China had gambled that no one would find out that the payloads on their satellites included the latest anti-ICBM technology, which they'd been trialling in secret since the U.S. had abandoned its Star Wars program. The world's most populous nation had been going all out to gain complete control of space. It now had the technology to capture other satellites and remove them from orbit, destroy orbiting satellites with kinetic kill vehicles and destroy any ship, aircraft, or surface-based military target from space.

It now also possessed satellite-mounted, laser technology with the capacity to shoot down any nation's ICBMs before they re-entered the Earth's atmosphere.

While most nations wondered about China's motives, the People's Republic of China did not want and could not afford the consequences of a widespread nuclear holocaust. By launching his nuclear equipped Taepodong-3 ICBMs, Kim Jon-Il had incurred the wrath of his greatest ally, forcing China into a situation where it either revealed its duplicity by breaching an important international treaty, or it allowed the destruction and radioactive contamination of much of Europe, Japan and Australia. China also knew that nuclear contamination from North Korea's missiles would eventually spread worldwide and endanger its own citizens. It had no choice but to act.

All three satellites responded to commands from the Taiyuan control room. Their extremely powerful laser weaponry was the fruit which had resulted from years of hacking into the U.S. SDI initiative and laser weaponry tests conducted from Boeing aircraft. In addition, other satellites equipped with retractable mirrors also responded, opening umbrella-like reflective shields to enable the Chuangxin-3, Shiyan-7 and Shijian-15 craft to bounce their lethal beams in any direction.

As all ten of North Korea's T3 missiles transitioned into the sub-orbital flight path stage of their journey, each of the three satellites zeroed in with pinpoint accuracy. Each satellite selected which of the missiles it would destroy. Then, on command from the control centre, millions of volts of electrical energy were converted in an instant and concentrated into immensely powerful, lightning-like solid state infrared energy beams which they then released across the vacuum of space.

Despite travelling at many times the speed of sound, the North Korean missiles were no match for the invisible force aimed at them. When struck, the T3 missiles simply melted and imploded into thousands of tiny particles of radioactive space debris which would orbit well below the many communications and weather satellites on which the Earth now depended. While the

Kessler effect was an unfortunate outcome preventing the launch of new satellites, the debris cloud would re-enter the Earth's atmosphere within a few weeks. During re-entry the debris particles it would burn up, resulting in only miniscule amounts of radiation reaching the Earth's surface.

Despite China's intervention, thousands of South Koreans perished when Taepodong-2s penetrated that country's missile defences. However, the counter attack was swift and without mercy. Equipped with guided Rim III missiles, weighing over seventy tonnes and nearly eight metres in length, Japan's Maritime Self-Defence force let loose a deadly barrage on North Korean targets. Japan's rockets were accompanied by similarly lethal Harpoon missiles from Darwin, Dechaineux, Ulysses and Neptune. More RIM IIIs fired from South Korea's fleet of Sejong and Chungmugong Yi Sun-sin-class destroyers then joined in the carnage, resulting in an unavoidably high casualty toll among North Korea's long-suffering citizenry.

Much of the North Korea's key infrastructure was obliterated in the massive bombardment of the first strike. DPRNK troops poised to flood into the South were virtually annihilated by the South's artillery and more missiles before they had time to cross the no-man's land dividing the two Koreas.

While Kim Jon-Il had certainly attracted the world's attention, he and his impoverished nation paid an enormous price. Unaware whether his missiles had hit their targets and rendered impotent by the might of his enemies, the baby-faced despot and his equally-crazy bloodthirsty generals fled across the border into China, anticipating refuge. While their formerly closest ally waited with open arms, there would be no sanctuary, only enormous anger and the wrath of a nation possessing an appalling human rights record.

Sixty years of posturing, during which the peoples of North Korea had starved under the oppressive and fanatical communist rule ended virtually overnight. Leaderless, bankrupt and demoralised, the shattered remnants of the North Korean army happily capitulated. Families, who had not seen loved ones for decades, were able to reunite – if they had not been killed in one of the shortest and arguably most vicious wars of all time.

While the U.S.A. Russia, Japan and European nations had been shocked to discover that China now ruled space, there was little criticism levelled at the communist nation.

'At least we know the doctrine of MAD works,' the U.S. president announced. 'While we are disappointed that China chose to launch its weapons of mass destruction in defiance of the treaties it had signed, we must be grateful that their technology was able to save the world from the apocalypse that the maniacal North Korean regime sought to unleash.

'We must also hope that the cataclysmic destruction of the North Korean nation and the deaths of so many of its people, will serve as a lesson to Iran and other nations harbouring nuclear ambitions that they too, will pay a dreadful price should they resort to the use of nuclear, chemical or biological weapons.

'That said, the U.S. cannot afford to play second fiddle to the might of China. Neither can it count on future Chinese leaders acting as responsibly, or as expeditiously, as the current government of the Peoples' Republic of China did in this instance. Neither can we sit back; assured that China will come to our rescue should another nuclear-equipped, lunatic regime attack those nations who seek to live in peace.

'It is often said that the price of freedom is eternal vigilance. If America and its allies are to maintain the freedom they treasure so much, they must learn from the past twenty-four hours. We must never again let our guard down as we did when we abandoned America's Strategic Defence Initiative at the end of the Cold War, mistakenly believing that we were no longer threatened by another nation's military might.'

In a pointed reference to China's treachery President Turnbull added, 'Clearly, we were also mistaken, when we believed in the honesty and the goodwill, of those nations who had signed international treaties banning the use of weapons of mass destruction. While the current Chinese leader did the right thing in this instance, a less sober and responsible leader might very well have taken a different view. Had this occurred, the consequences would have been too horrible to contemplate. The past twenty-four hours has taught us not to rely on treaties. Treaties are obviously only effective for as long as the goodwill and honesty of the nations who sign them lasts.

'If we are to guarantee our future security and our freedom, we must surpass the capacity of China's weaponry. We have no alternative but to re-activate America's SDI program as a matter of the highest priority.'

What Turnbull did not add was his hopes that the new arms race would become America's economic saviour.

++++++++++++++++++

Chapter Twenty

Canberra's streets were in gridlock. Flooding to the national capital in their tens of thousands, miners, truckies and many whose livelihood depended upon coal exports blocked the streets, waving placards and chanting raucously. Led by Keith Sutton, the human tide flowed along Commonwealth Avenue eventually sprawling across and invading the vast lawns surrounding Parliament House.

Extraordinarily well-equipped and organised with military efficiency, the demonstrators had come prepared for the long haul. Declaring they would not move until the McCarthy government promised to abandon environmental reforms that would spell the death of the coal industry, they had established everything they needed to sustain themselves. There were mobile toilets, food kitchens, generators, lighting, sound systems, seating and staging, caravans, motor homes, tents and even long haul trucks equipped with sleeper cabs.

Mal Walker and other coal industry representatives had made massive anonymous donations to the unionists to fund the demonstration. Taking out lengthy, eye-catching advertisements in all major newspapers, and using Twitter, Facebook, and other social media, Walker's misinformation campaign went into full swing. As Knox had predicted, Walker had found no shortage of scientists who happily accepted the attractive remuneration packages in exchange for declaring that global warming actually benefited the Earth's population by enabling high food production.

Running against the IPCC's recent declaration which said climate change was ninety-five percent anthropogenic, these scientific mercenaries attempted a scare campaign by bamboozling the populace with statistics and citing past incidence where supporters of the climate change theory had got it wrong.

The demonstrators had timed their protests well. Parliament was sitting each day and Matthew McCarthy hoped to pass the necessary reforms to assure the nation's transition from fossil fuels to renewable energy sources. By blocking access to the House of Representatives they would endeavour to ensure the bill's supporters would be unable to vote. Nevertheless, the prime minister was determined to ensure the democratic process proceeded unhindered and called upon the Federal Police to provide politicians with unimpeded access to the iconic building.

For Liberal Party Leader, Brian Caldwell, a wealthy former barrister from the elite Sydney suburb of Vaucluse, the demonstration presented a golden opportunity to attack his opponent. Considered by the battlers to be a self-opinionated womaniser who mainly appealed to the blue-rinse set, Caldwell was nonetheless a consummate politician. However, for the moment, it suited the unionists to embrace the familiar, suave middle-aged man who appeared on the Parliament House forecourt grinning broadly.

When the cheering died down Caldwell took hold of a loud hailer and began haranguing the prime minister. 'I congratulate you all for rallying here today to express your displeasure at a government which seems hell-bent on destroying your jobs and Australia's economy. While the rest of the world seems to be taking active steps to combat the worst global financial crisis since the Great Depression, Prime Minister Matthew McCarthy is focussing on dealing with a problem that many scientists claim is nothing more than an enormous myth. I will go further by suggesting climate change is actually a conspiracy perpetrated by business interests and individuals who stand to profit from renewable technologies and from trading in carbon credits.

'McCarthy and the Greens would have you believe that the terrible bushfires that devastated Canberra, Victoria, New South Wales, Tasmania, and most recently, Western Australia are connected to climate change. They will try and blame climate change for the cyclones and the floods that wreaked so much havoc in Queensland. Well, as far as I am concerned, they're talking through their hats. This country has always been subjected to droughts, floods, bushfires and cyclones and always will. Dorothea McKellar said as much in 1908 when she wrote her famous poem, "My Country".

'Over the past century there has only been a miniscule increase in atmospheric temperatures and to suggest this increase is responsible for bushfires, cyclones and floods is frankly nothing more than a load of crap.

'Just like his unfortunate predecessor, this prime minister is clearly incompetent and unfit to run this great nation. In fact, one could say, the entire Labor Party is incompetent and dysfunctional. They have allowed national security to decline so badly since they've been office that assassins have managed to kill this country's leader and almost pulled off a second attempt on his successor. We've seen terrorists infiltrate our borders and target our most iconic buildings. Australian was a safe nation free from terrorism and political unrest until the current government took over office. Now we live under a reign of terror and financial uncertainty while the prime minister fiddles with his hare-brained schemes involving unproven technologies.

'There's no doubt Matthew McCarthy's television documentaries were interesting and entertaining. He became famous because of them. However, he used scare tactics to con the Australian public into believing tackling climate change was far more important than building a strong economy able to withstand the financial storms and international pressures created when other nations default on their loans or go to war with each other.

'Matthew McCarthy will send this country bankrupt if he continues down the current path. Coal exports are worth over forty-seven-billion dollars annually. Coal is Australia's second biggest export earner. We cannot simply cut off such a huge source of this nation's wealth. In addition, Australia will lose the respect of other nations who depend upon our coal and mineral exports. They will retaliate by closing their markets to us and for what? Refusing to export coal to Japan, South Korea, China, India and other nations will not force those nations to change their ways because Canada, Africa and the United States will happily step in to maintain supply resulting in much dirtier coal being burnt than at present.

'Stand up for your jobs. Stand up for the Australian economy. Stand up for secure borders. Stand up for

Australia's reputation as a responsible nation and trading partner. Let this government know today that you're not going to allow them to destroy everything for which you have fought so hard. Thank you.'

The mob roared and clapped their approval as Caldwell turned and re-entered the building. FEDPOL, who had just finished mustering its resources, moved in. Uniformed officers with full riot gear and supported by police dogs, formed human wedges to push through the thousands of angry unionists determined to block their path. Spat upon, struck with placards and fists and pelted with anything handy, the riot squad ran the gauntlet. Swinging and stabbing with their batons, they beat their way toward the parliament's massive glass doors. As fast as they cleared a path for other officers to begin linking arms and forming a human barricade, the crowd surged to fill the space.

From somewhere behind the shouting, screaming mob a Molotov cocktail thrown at police lines burst, showering the booted feet of the policemen and women with glass fragments and burning petrol. Set alight, one officer fell to the ground where his attempts to extinguish the flames by rolling were thwarted by brutish thugs within the crowed who kicked him mercilessly. As his fellow policemen went to his rescue more petrol bombs landed, setting the Parliament House forecourt ablaze. The flames did not discriminate between demonstrators and law enforcement officers. People ran screaming in flames and the resultant mayhem only served to fuel the mob's anger.

Curly Clews who had the unenviable task of overseeing public order, seized the brief moment of crowd confusion to order the use of chloropicrin (CS) gas. The riot squad donned gasmasks and unclipped its teargas grenades. Raising a teargas launcher often referred to as a Federal Gun to his shoulder, one officer knelt and aimed the stubby barrel of his weapon at those who were throwing petrol bombs from behind the rioters. With a dull thud, the heavy rocket left the tube. Its tail fins opened as it soared above the melee leaving a smoking, ash-grey trail in its wake. Landing with a clatter on paved surface, the missiles burst and rolled, engulfing the careless idiots in a choking, acidic cloud of gas.

The canine section then moved in. With German shepherd dogs snapping and snarling excitedly on long leashes they allowed their animals to cover a wide arc where they sank their fangs into the backsides and limbs of those who weren't fast enough to escape their savagery. Arrest squads then moved in, manhandling anyone who had not fled. Handcuffed with nylon cable ties and hauled to paddy wagons waiting behind the scenes, they were photographed and their details recorded on purpose-designed mass arrest cards.

Eventually, the police restored order and forced the remaining demonstrators away from the forecourt back to the sweeping lawns where they milled around confusedly.

Watching from her vantage point in Parliament House, Helen Knox forgot she was one of the main instigators of the scene unfolding below and expressed her horror to those around her. 'My God, has it come to this? I never thought I'd see the day where we'd have to resort to the tactics of a police state.'

While others agreed with her, the demonstrators had left the police with no alternative. Always the meat in the sandwich of dissent, several officers had suffered horrendous burns. One had a broken arm and many were bruised and battered.

More defiant than ever, Keith Sutton mounted the podium where he used a loud hailer to angrily denounce the police and blame them for the violence. Simon Wjotosiack, the President of the Australian Council of Trade Unions and the head of the Transport Workers Union, Joe Murphy, spoke next, adding further fuel to the fire. Thugs moved among the crowd handing out propaganda leaflets and urging the protesters to begin a chant, taunting McCarthy to address them.

From the comfort and security of his Newcastle office, Mal Walker watched the scene on television. 'It couldn't have gone better,' he commented to his office staff. 'That should end McCarthy's honeymoon period and shatter the public's love affair with our greeny prime minister.'

Never one to walk away from conflict, the Irish blood in McCarthy's veins reached boiling point. 'There's a bloody rent-a-rabble element in that mob out there that have gone out of their way to incite a riot. I am guessing that Keith Sutton and his cronies did not have the brains, or the resources. I bet people like Mal Walker and others within the coal industry cooked this up. I think I need to address the crowd.'

'What? Don't you think that's foolish? You'll only set them off again and the police won't be able to guarantee your safety.' The speaker was McCarthy's finance minister, Phoebe Swan, a fiery lesbian and women's liberationist with the classic short spiked haircut and mannish features.

'I think it's worse if I don't show my face. They'll think I am just cowardly.'

'No one will think that, Matt, particularly after what you've just been through.'

'Physical courage and political courage are worlds apart. Besides, I didn't have much alternative did I? It was just a case of survival instinct kicking in.' The prime minister thought for a moment before adding, 'I'll send a messenger to Keith Sutton via the journalists out there inviting him to debate me on the issues in front of the crowd.'

Matthew McCarthy's ploy of using the media was a clever one. If the union leader refused to debate the issues about which the demonstration was focussed he would look weak and incompetent. On the other hand, the prime minister was taking an enormous gamble that the already rancorous mob would not erupt yet again.

Knowing the ball was in his court, the wily Sutton put the question to the crowd anticipating they'd howl the idea down. 'The prime minister wants to come out and argue his case. He wants a public debate but he's asked me to guarantee he'll be heard. Do you want to listen to any more of his fairy tales?' he bellowed.

'No!' they roared in response.

Joe Murphy, who was well known for his ability to take on the most competent of speakers and twist their words until they became tongue tied and confused, grabbed the bull horn. 'I say, give him a chance. I'll shoot down any argument, fact or statistic he comes up with and show this government's Zero Carbon Energy

Bill as the most dangerous, socialist piece of legislation ever introduced into parliament, so come on people, let me put an end to this once and for all.'

Sutton cast a doubtful look Murphy's way. 'It's Matthew McCarthy, qualified marine scientist, public celebrity and TV star against Joe Murphy, the knuckle-dragging battler made good. I really don't know, Joe.'

However, it was now too late. The crowd were baying for blood. 'Okay, let's see what the bugger's got to say,' one stocky miner yelled.

'Yeah, let Joe sort him out,' someone else yelled.

Murphy addressed the mob once more. 'If I am going to debate Prime Minister McCarthy we need to do it in a civilised fashion. There have been too many people hurt already today and it will serve no purpose if we howl him down. The prime minister has agreed to answer questions from the floor. He's also suggested Tony Jones adjudicate. I've spoken to Mr Jones and he's agreed. Let's have a vote on it. I ask those of you in favour of the debate going ahead at 1.00pm today; to remain standing and those who are against the idea, please sit down.'

Several minutes of confusion followed. No one wanted to take the lead and people looked uncertainly at each other trying to gauge what the majority would do before making up their own minds. Half a dozen or so of Sutton's heavily tattooed minders endeavoured to influence the mob by parking their ample backsides on the grass. A few protesters decided to sit down but most remained standing. And then, some that had been sitting changed their minds and got back to their feet when they discovered they were in the minority. Eventually, it became clear that the debate would proceed.

At 12.55pm a dozen Federal Police officers formed a phalanx and escorted the prime minister to the stage which had been set up during the intervening period. Veteran ABC broadcaster and political commentator, Tony Jones, immaculate in his dark grey suit, patent leather shoes and striped shirt, climbed the steps to the stage, his silver-grey hair glinting in the sunlight like spun silk. Jones greeted the prime minister and Murphy. The two verbal combatants then shook hands before seating themselves to face the expectant crowd. Enjoying the limelight Jones then addressed the hordes, a broad smile playing across his handsome features.

'Ladies and gentleman, we've seen some terrible things happen here today and it's patently obvious that the issue of climate change has caused everyone's passions to run very high. I am sure the last thing anyone wants is for there to be a repeat of this morning's violence. The prime minister has very bravely and generously agreed to come before you to discuss the issues at stake. Nothing will be gained by shouting him down, so I ask everyone to please let the participants in this debate speak without interruption. We'll toss a coin to see who speaks first.'

Murphy won the toss and elected to speak first. There was resounding applause from the unionists as he stood to present his case.[2] Always popular with blue collar workers for his down-to-earth style Joe Murphy spoke eloquently and passionately for fifteen minutes

---

[2] For those interested in the science behind climate change the argument put by Joe Murphy is set out in full in the penultimate page of this novel.

without interruption. Amazingly the mostly low-brow audience hung on his every word until cheering, wolf whistles and a standing ovation greeted the conclusion of Murphy's speech. With a self-satisfied smile, he gathered his notes and sat down.

Jones waited for the applause to dwindle before speaking. 'Joe Murphy has put a very strong and well-articulated argument against the government's climate change reforms. It will be very interesting to see how the prime minister responds.'

As Matthew got to his feet and moved to the podium among considerable booing and jeering someone tried to get the crowd to commence slow handclapping. Smacking a gavel loudly, Tony Jones soon stopped this protest, reminding everyone that the debate would be cancelled unless they complied with the agreed rules.

Matthew thanked him and began his address. 'I would like to begin by expressing my sympathy to those who were injured in this morning's protest. It's always upsetting when a few irresponsible individuals mar peaceful demonstrations because you have every right to be here and to express your opinions and your displeasure at the government's policies. I would like to thank you all for giving me the opportunity to speak and to answer Joe Murphy's assertions.'

Matthew's youthful good looks, warm smile and charisma as the producer of Your World soon had the majority of the crowd almost eating out of his hand. He countered Murphy's arguments easily as he calmed their fears over job losses and economic recession.[3]

---

[3] Matthew McCarthy's answering speech based upon the

'Lastly, this country has abundant sources of renewable energy,' Matthew reminded everyone. 'It has the technological knowhow and most of its citizens have the will and the courage to do what must be done to adapt and to survive the greatest threat mankind has ever faced.'

Pausing for effect McCarthy played his trump card. 'Many of you are parents and grandparents and I am sure you care about the type of future your children and grandchildren will inherit. If we don't take meaningful action now, some day in the not-too-distant-future our grandchildren will come to us and ask, "Granddad, or Grandma, what did you do to stop this terrible thing from happening?"

'If that dreadful day comes, I want to be able to look my grandkids in the eye and reply honestly, that I did everything I could. What will you say?

'Thank you for listening. Now, I am happy to answer any questions.'

A momentary hush followed the prime minister's speech. He had almost expected the crowd to begin heckling him and hurling abuse but the import of his words had clearly struck a chord.

While many people raised their hands seeking further clarification, the prime minister had heard every argument against climate change and successfully defended his position with little effort. Joe Murphy on the other hand, tried to bluster his way through, resorting to personal attacks and snide remarks which

opinions of the world's top scientists can be viewed at the end of this novel for those who wish to increase their understanding of climate change.

only served to weaken his position.

Like the spoilt birthday-boy whose balloon had been pricked, Keith Sutton began interjecting as he saw the ground slipping away. 'The prime minister's arguments are nothing more than carefully prepared propaganda. Don't be swayed by this bullshit. He and his tree-hugging cronies don't care about you and your families; they stand to make millions from renewable technologies.

'When have politicians ever kept their promises? Stand firm people. Show this mob of wankers that you're not going to let them take your jobs away without a fight!'

With that, Sutton's union heavies began chanting, 'Lies and bullshit. Save our jobs,' but the crowd refused to take up the call and began drifting away desultorily, whereupon Jones wound up the debate.

Swearing, Mal Walker turned off his enormous flat-screen television. 'Damn it. I knew this wasn't going to work. Those bloody Neanderthals, Sutton and Murphy are no match for McCarthy.' Picking up the telephone he called Helen Knox's private number.

'Well Helen, it looks as if we'll have to resort to Plan B.'

'Yes, I've been watching the entire circus from the Parliament House forecourt. The crowd's dispersed now, leaving Sutton and Murphy's lot with egg on their faces.'

++++++++++++

313

Chapter Twenty-One

Flipper Fleming knew he was taking an enormous risk. However, his position as the head of ASIO with all the attendant benefits was on the line, as was his reputation and freedom if he didn't pull a rabbit out of his hat. While the stakes were high, he'd gotten himself out of some very tricky situations previously and felt sure he could do so again.

After much thought and a very sleepless night, he selected three of his most trusted, but not necessarily brightest agents, and ordered them to a briefing in his spacious office in Canberra's Parliamentary Triangle. Looking at them now, arranged in a semi-circle in front of his desk, they reminded him of penitent schoolboys who'd been summoned to the headmaster's office for a telling-off.

A skinny twenty-five-year-old with the unlikely name of Greg Winterbottom sat to Fleming's left, picking at imaginary fluff on his crumpled chinos. His too-long hair framed a peaked-looking face that always wore a slightly bemused expression. A typical geek, Winterbottom held a PhD in electronics but Fleming reckoned he was like many highly intelligent people and probably couldn't boil an egg for his dinner. Greg had an obsession with studying resulting in very limited social skills and he'd got into ASIO purely on the basis of his academic achievements.

Arockia Doss, or Rocky to those who struggled to get their tongue around his awkward first name, sat in the middle, fidgeting nervously. A Singaporean Indian, also in his mid-twenties, Doss was a prematurely balding, hyperactive individual with the annoying habit of unexpectedly switching from the current topic of conversation to something completely different, so that one never quite knew whether or not he was on the same wavelength. While Fleming knew Doss's I.Q. would qualify him to join the Mensa Society, he lacked the focus required for the good old fashioned plodding needed to be a good investigator.

The third person, Jenni Werner, whom Fleming always regarded as the token lesbian required by a world where political correctness overrode merit, was a dumpy, sallow-faced woman who dressed like a 1950s housewife. Deskbound most of the time, her penchant was research and she'd rarely ventured into the field.

Despite their quirks, all three agents had one important qualification in common; they usually did as they were told without asking too many questions. Handing each agent a folio that he'd personally prepared, Fleming instructed them, 'These are you operation orders. Please study them carefully. Keep the photograph but commit the information to memory and return the folders to me before you leave this room. It is very important that none of this falls into the wrong hands, or I'll have your guts for garters,' he threatened before commencing his briefing using the classic military style.

'Operation Velvet Glove is a highly classified, top secret, covert operation involving national security. It also has international implications and is the most important operation of its kind in Australia's history.

'Information surrounding the operation is on a purely need-to-know basis. We don't know who else is involved and the subject of the operation may have accomplices within law-enforcement agencies, so you are not to approach FEDPOL or any of the State Police forces unless you have my personal approval.

'Mission. Your mission is to locate Sergeant Richard Nolan, an agent of the Federal Police, and place him under surveillance.

'Situation. We have reasonable grounds to believe that the subject is directly connected with, and might even be the mastermind behind the assassination of Prime Minister Connor Bowker, the attempted assassination of Prime Minister McCarthy, and the attempted bombing of the Lodge and various other targets.

'The subject was until recently the prime minister's personal bodyguard. He is a former naval clearance diver who was highly decorated as a result of active service in the first Gulf War. During that time, he was involved in a very traumatic event resulting in the death of five fellow clearance divers.

'Although this man passed all the psychological tests needed for selection into the Federal Police Close Personal Protection Unit, we believe he recently began suffering belatedly from post-traumatic stress disorder as a direct consequence of his time in Iraq. This condition has seriously disturbed the balance of his mind, and has made him dangerously psychotic. Nolan is also suffering from a persecution complex and believes that Prime Minister McCarthy and McCarthy's father, John, are Marxists who are out to destroy Australia's economy and impose socialist rule. If that's not bad enough, the crazy bastard is also convinced that

ASIO and the Federal Police are controlled by communist agents.'

Fleming paused at this point to gauge whether his agents had swallowed this piece of blatant fiction, but nothing in the body language of the three suggested incredulity, so he continued. 'Nolan went to ground at the first opportunity after attempting to kill Prime Minister McCarthy, and despite intensive inquiries, the Feds haven't been able to locate him. His bank accounts haven't been touched, his car is still in the garage and he hasn't used his mobile phone. Telephone taps on his home-phone and his wife's mobile have so far yielded nothing and we don't believe he has spoken to his wife Jennifer or his two children.

'Now, Nolan had to hand in his passport to stop him fleeing, but this man is highly trained in undercover work and knows how to foil the system. There is little doubt in my mind that he'd have a number of false passports, driver's licences and credit cards in other names.

'Nolan might be psychotic, but he almost succeeded in his attempt on McCarthy's life. You will recall that he tried to make it look like an unfortunate scuba diving accident, but by sheer good fortune, both spears fired at the prime minister failed to hit vital organs.

'Public confidence in ASIO and the Federal Police has been seriously shaken by all three attacks and Richard Nolan must be located as a matter of the highest priority before he makes another attempt on the prime minister's life, or causes further embarrassment to the government, ASIO and FEDPOL.

'Richard Nolan is desperate and dangerous and we

believe he is probably armed and won't hesitate to shoot if he's cornered. For that reason, do not approach him and do not try to apprehend him.

'When he is located you are to place him under surveillance and notify me personally, regardless of the time of day. The hope is that he will lead us to Nibras and other members of his network. At that point, I will call on the appropriate law enforcement body to affect the arrests.

'Administration. I will be in overall control of this operation and you will report directly to me. Each of you will be temporarily assigned to head a team of ten agents whom you will select and brief and deploy as I have specified in the orders in front of you. Agent Winterbottom's team will cover New South Wales. Agent Doss, you and your team will be responsible for Queensland and the Northern Territory and Agent Werner will be responsible for Victoria, South Australia and WA.

'This is the defining moment in your personal careers. If you each carry out this operation to my satisfaction, your temporary promotions will become permanent.

'Before I discuss logistical arrangements do you have any questions at this point?'

Because ASIO officers are not authorised to carry firearms or to arrest suspects and must call upon the Federal Police or State Police Forces for assistance, Winterbottom, Doss and Werner looked nervously at each other. It was a moment before Winterbottom broke the awkward silence.

'Why do you think Nolan's connected to the attack

by Jemaah Islamiyah sir? Surely after his experiences in Iraq where he saw his mates die, he'd hate the Islamists?'

'Aaah, thanks for bringing that up. I forgot to mention this, although it's in the file in front of you. Nolan converted to Islam during his teens. He apparently had some Muslim friends who swayed his young and pliable mind that Islam is the only true religion and he renounced his Catholic faith to the horror of his parents.

'While being of the Muslim faith doesn't automatically make one a terrorist, Richard Nolan wouldn't be the first Westerner to change his allegiance or sympathise with the jihadists. Look at that fellow in America recently. He was a Muslim and an army psychiatrist for God's sake, yet he shot dead several of his fellow soldiers. I also believe Jambali and Nibras had to have had somebody with inside knowledge. They must also have had assistance getting into the country and remaining undercover. As a federal agent, Nolan knew how to bypass Australia's borders and he has intimate knowledge of security precautions at key government installations which were targeted by Jambali.'

Werner chipped in this time. 'Sir, why have you chosen us? There must be agents who are more qualified and experienced.'

'Unfortunately, Agent Werner, seventy percent of ASIO's one-thousand-seven-hundred-and-sixty officers has been recruited since 2002. We have a huge gap in experience. Those officers recruited before that time are mostly nearing retirement or unfit for field duty. I have to make do with the best I've got and you three represent that best. Now let's get down to the logistics.'

After sorting out aspects relating to costs, transport, equipment and other nuts and bolts issues Fleming concluded the briefing satisfied that the three agents would carry out their orders unquestioningly. All in all, he thought things had gone pretty well.

How fortuitous for Nolan to have converted to Islam, it really adds a ring of truth to my clever, if hastily contrived tale.

Knowing he had more to do than he could handle alone, John McCarthy pondered for some time whether there was anyone to whom he could turn for help. There seemed to be nobody he could trust or burden with what might well be nothing more than a preposterous conspiracy theory. *Christ, this is Australia. Things like this don't happen here. Who can I trust that won't think I am completely nuts?*

Like somebody shining a torch in a darkened room onto a portrait, Annette Thompson's face suddenly popped into the retired policeman's mind.

It was no wonder his subconscious mind had suggested Annette could be the one to assist him. She'd been playing on his mind since their encounter with Jambali but until now, he'd been far too busy to get in touch. He also knew she'd been directed by FEPOL's medical examiner to take annual leave and undergo trauma counselling despite her insistence that the best therapy of all was to keep busy. While he knew firsthand how traumatic incidents could return to haunt one in later life, John tended to agree with Annette's assertion, so knowing she'd be resenting her enforced idleness, he decided to pay an unannounced visit to her Deakin apartment and sound her out. She opened the door as soon as he pressed the intercom button.

'Mr McCarthy, it's so good of you to drop by. I saw you on the security camera when you pulled up out the front and I couldn't believe it was you!' she exclaimed. 'Come in and tell me the latest goss. I'm going stir-crazy sitting around home not knowing what's going on.'

'It's great to see you looking so well. I was more than a bit worried about you,' John replied, giving her a quick, fatherly hug before following her into her small, but tastefully furnished living room, his policeman's eye taking everything in at a single glance. It was the first time he'd seen her in civilian attire and despite the age difference; he had to admit she cut a very attractive picture in a simple, white, almost-diaphanous blouse, bare feet and figure-hugging blue jeans. With her hair pulled back into a ponytail and smelling of shampoo she wore just the right amount of makeup and exuded youth and vigour.

Settle down old fella, you're a married man and old enough to be her granddad!

'I like your apartment,' McCarthy remarked, lowering himself into a burgundy leather chair opposite the one on which Annette had perched herself. She tucked her slim legs beneath her in a typically feminine posture that would cripple most men. 'I see you've got a few mementos from your army days.'

Half turning in her chair to look at the oak dresser behind her, Annette responded. 'I did have some good times despite the grief the army gave me. Those are my passing out photos and I like to remember the few good friends I did manage to make before everything went pear-shaped. But you're not here for idle chatter, Mr McCarthy. What is it you want?'

Annette's tone was still warm and friendly but McCarthy was surprised by her no-nonsense perspicacity.

'That's what I like most about you Annette. You're very astute and you don't beat about the bush. Actually, I have stumbled on something that's very worrying and potentially explosive and I need someone to help me.'

Untangling her legs, Annette sat on the edge of her chair, her gaze instantly becoming intense. 'Okay, let me make us a coffee and you can tell me about it and why you think I can help you.'

McCarthy watched as Annette selected mugs emblazoned with the Federal Police logo and placed them under the spout of her automatic coffee machine. 'When I explain what this is all about, you'll understand. I am not pulling your leg. This is deadly serious. Unfortunately, by telling you what I know, I am putting you in a very awkward and dangerous position. So, if you feel you don't want to get involved, I'll completely understand. I'd like you to promise me that whatever decision you make, you keep this information to yourself. Unless something happens to me,' he added.

'Bloody hell, John, you sound as if someone's plotting to kill you,' Annette said, placing a tray with coffee, milk and sugar within his reach before sitting down again. 'John, I have the greatest respect for you. If you've had to come to me rather than the FEDPOL bigwigs, it must be something very serious indeed. Believe me; I'll do whatever I can to help.'

Her use of his first name had not escaped McCarthy. He relaxed, took a deep breath and plunged right in while the young policewoman listened without interrupting.

'...so, what do you think?' McCarthy concluded.

'Wow, that's the most incredible thing I've ever heard. There's one thing that bothers me though.'

'I am surprised you've only found one thing,' McCarthy joked. 'What bothers you, Annette?'

'Well, you haven't mentioned anything about telling your son, the prime minister. Don't you think he needs to know that the head of ASIO was behind the plot to kill him?'

McCarthy stirred his coffee thoughtfully. 'I guess I didn't want to heap any more problems on Matthew's plate. He's only been in office a short time and already he's had to deal with a nuclear missile attack that almost resulted in World War III, Australia-wide terrorist threats, and then the very bloke assigned to protect him tries to kill him. To top things off, the bloody redneck unionists decide to riot and throw petrol bombs at the entrance to Parliament House. I think he's got enough distractions for the moment without having to deal with a bloody treasonous director general of ASIO.'

'I know but what if something happens to you? Apart from Richard Nolan you're the only one who knows all this stuff is happening. And now, me of course, but who's going to listen to a lowly constable if they decide to knock you off as well, which they will do if they find out you're likely to blow things wide open.

Sorry, I'm rambling a bit. Anyway, what's your plan from here, John?'

'I want you to help me track down Nolan before Fleming and whoever else is mixed up in this silence him but there are too many places he could have gone and I can't check them all out on my own.'

'We can start telephoning all the hotels, motels and caravan parks now if you like.'

'No, Annette. That won't work. We need to actually visit all Nolan's likely haunts and talk to people face to face. It's not possible to build a rapport with people over the phone; most of them will just take the easy way out and fob you off.

'I think we should split the list that Jenny Nolan provided and flash Nolan's photo around. He'll be using an alias but he also needs wheels and he has to eat, so somebody will have seen him.'

'ASIO and the police are also looking for him. Won't they soon hear about it if we're out there asking questions? Small towns are full of gossipers.'

'We've got to take that risk. We'll try to keep it low-key so we don't raise too many eyebrows but we'll also make sure we keep checking in with each other. If you're ready, you can make a start. I'll head out to Tumut and the other towns down that way as soon as I've brought Matthew up to speed.'

'Before you go, what do you think Nolan was doing with all that electronic equipment in his home?'

'I can only surmise that he's been doing some serious eavesdropping. His bank accounts show he purchased the gear shortly after his posting to Canberra, so there has to be a connection to the assassination plot.'

'If Fleming's behind the attack on your father, Nolan might have been trying to get some dirt on him, sort of like life insurance,' Annette mused.

'You could be right.'

It being a week day, John McCarthy knew he'd find the prime minister at Parliament House, but he telephoned ahead to ensure his son could spare a few minutes before that day's parliamentary sitting.

'Sure Dad, it must be serious for you to want to come into this hornet's nest,' his son responded.

Unfortunately, convincing Matthew not to go straight to Commissioner Stormy Knight proved more difficult than John had supposed because of his son's unwavering confidence in the Federal Police commissioner.

'Jesus, Dad, if what you're telling me is correct; this is going to shake this country to its very core. I simply can't believe Stormy would be in cahoots with James Fleming. It's no secret that they hate each other's guts.'

John shook his head wearily. It felt like he was caught up in a weird nightmare from which he couldn't awaken. 'I know what you're saying Matt and I tend to agree. At some point we'll have to decide just who we're prepared to trust, but please let me do a bit more digging first before you go to Stormy. I don't want egg all over my face it I'm wrong and I don't like the consequences if Stormy does happen to be involved.'

'Shit, they've already tried to kill me, Dad. They won't hesitate to get rid of you and that young policewoman you've dragged into this when they know what you're up to. Is she the one who used to help guard the Lodge? I always liked her.'

'Matt, I've survived a lot of tricky situations over the years by knowing how to watch my back, and taking certain precautions has become second nature, so don't worry about me, I'm doing what I love. When it comes to Annette Thompson, she's a very capable woman who's already proved to me that she can take care of herself. That's not to say I don't feel really guilty dragging her into the situation and putting her life in danger, I do, but I've got to have somebody to help me and she fits the bill in every respect.'

Matthew McCarthy exhaled noisily. 'Bloody hell, how did we get ourselves into such a mess? I knew politics was a dirty business and I was prepared to put up with a fair bit if that's what it took to get real action happening on climate change but never in my wildest dreams did I imagine I'd be putting everyone I love at such risk.'

John McCarthy grinned and slapped his son on the back affectionately. 'You'll be right son. We McCarthys aren't going to let some bloody, geriatric horse's-hoof beat us, are we?'

Matthew smiled at his father's old-fashioned epithet for male homosexuals. 'You really are a bloody homophobe aren't you? The Labor party would be lost without poofters and dykes as you call them.'

McCarthy left his son's office to make his way back to his car. As he did so, he almost bumped into the deputy prime minister as she stormed down the corridor. Although Helen Knox recognised him, her icy stare bore through him and she ignored his greeting. Curious, John halted and turned to see where she was headed. Knox stopped at the prime minister's door, knocked once and barged in without waiting for permission, shutting the door with her trademark assertiveness.

Now there's a lady on a mission. She looks like she about to sink the knife into somebody's back. I hope it's not Matt's.

McCarthy shrugged and continued on his way. Had he known Helen Knox's agenda he would not have dismissed the incident so lightly.

Surprised at Knox's interruption, Matthew McCarthy half rose from his desk. 'Helen, you might be the deputy prime minister, but it doesn't give you the right to barge into my office,' he scolded. 'You know I'll see you any time, so why this sudden attack of rudeness?'

Knox appeared unfazed. 'Matthew, I make no secret of the fact that I think your appointment as PM was a grave mistake. You also know I voted against your environmental reforms when Connor was PM because I believe the party's committing political suicide by turning its back on the unions and their financial support. I went along with it because you had the numbers and I had no choice but I've now got information that will change all that. In short, I want you to stand down as PM.'

'What the hell are you on about Helen?'

'I have voice recordings of a private meeting between Senator Bacon and the Director General of ASIO. During that meeting they discuss your assassination. The tapes also implicate Bacon in the manufacture and illegal importation of illicit drugs. In fact, he's been up to his balls in illegal drug deals since the Vietnam War.'

Coming on top of his meeting with his father, the information lacked the impact for which Knox had hoped. She'd expected McCarthy to be speechless, giving her the chance to administer the *coup de gras* of asking that he resign. Instead, Matthew remained poker-faced.

'It confirms what I've just been told myself and although this is very shocking news Helen, why are you attacking me? I'm not responsible for the rotten apples in the barrel.'

'Maybe not but you are responsible for identifying them and throwing them out before they taint the rest. I propose to release the tapes to Sixty Minutes unless you stand down and walk away from your climate change reforms.'

Matthew could feel the anger building. *You back-stabbing bitch.* 'And why would I stand down Helen?'

'Because I plan to show you up for the incompetent, politically naive do-gooder that you are. Do you want to know how I'll do that?' Knox continued without giving McCarthy the chance to respond. 'Number one: there have been rumours about Bacon's seedy dealings for years. As prime minister you should have had him investigated, or at least insisted that he resign from office. Number two: Bacon's been blackmailing the Director General of ASIO for Christ's sake. Number three: Fleming and Bacon have plotted to assassinate you. For all we know, they may also have assassinated Connor Bowker. Number four: since you've been in office terrorists have managed to infiltrate the country's borders and attack its citizens. Now, every single Australian is worried sick that we'll have our own nine-eleven.

'You allowed this to happen on your watch, Matthew. If that doesn't show that you're unfit to run the country, I don't know what does.'

Matthew was incensed at the injustice of her allegations but Knox's ability to manipulate scandal-loving journalists was legendary. The Murdoch Press's anti-Labor newspapers, such as the Telegraph, would just love the opportunity to try and bring down his government. 'And you'd be prepared to destroy the Labor Party just to get at me?'

'If that's what it takes, but I don't think it needs to come to that. If you step aside, I'll do a deal with Bacon and Fleming. They can quietly resign and go off somewhere to enjoy the fruits of their ill-gotten gains. As a former prime minister, you'll retire with all the usual fringe benefits and a very healthy superannuation package and the Labor Party can get back to running the country the way it needs to be run.'

McCarthy's voice was ice-cold. 'And who have you discussed this with Helen?'

'I don't need to discuss this with anyone to know your biggest supporters will abandon you like rats leaving a sinking ship when the shit begins to fly. They are all political animals who care only about themselves.'

'In other words, they're just like you. Helen, I don't have the vocabulary necessary to express the contempt I have for you without resorting to obscenities. I am tempted to tell you where to go in the language that would put a wharfie to shame; however, you profess to be a lady so I won't. Instead, I'll ask you politely to pack up your office and tender your resignation, not only as deputy prime minister, but as a member of the Australian Labor Party. You are a disgrace to everything the party stands for.'

Knox's face split into a wide smile and she began to chuckle coldly. 'Now you're joking. Why would I do such a thing?'

Sliding open his desk drawer, McCarthy produced a small digital recorder that was obviously operating. 'I've never trusted you Helen. I knew one day you'd try to sink the knife into my back. When you barged into my office, I suspected that moment had come and turned this on. Now, I might not have had the presence of mind to do that, but for the fact my father alerted me to the Director General's traitorous activities. So, everything you've just said has been recorded. Not only that, but I also pushed the intercom button on my phone so my staff could hear what you had to say; providing me with ample corroboration should you wish to deny your treachery. Now, please get out before I lose control and do or say something I'll regret.'

Looking like an inflatable doll whose seams had suddenly split, Knox left the prime minister's office. Snatching up the telephone, McCarthy called his father and outlined what had taken place.

'You bloody beauty Matt. Well done, now we know what Nolan was doing with the spy gear and we've got the confirmation we need to put Bacon and Fleming in the frame. It's even more important than ever to find Nolan and get his tapes so we've got the evidence to confront Stormy Knight, or go to the Corruption and Crime Commission and have them both put behind bars.

'If Stormy's not involved, well and good; I'll be enormously relieved. However, if Stormy's tied up in this, I'll bet those two will sing like a couple of canaries if they think they're going down. But what about Knox; do you think she'll make further trouble?'

'I don't see how, Dad. The Day of the Long Knives is over for our Helen. By the time word gets around about the stunt she tried to pull, she'll be lucky if she gets a job as a dog catcher's assistant.'

'Just make sure your people in the office are sworn to secrecy. We can't afford Bacon and Fleming to know we're onto them.'

'It's okay. That bit about pushing the intercom button was just a bluff.'

+++++++++++

Chapter Twenty-Two

Four days after Knox's attempted bloodless coup, Richard Nolan began to worry. He'd not heard from the deputy prime minister since she told him to go to ground.

Despite doing what he could to change his appearance, Nolan knew it was only a matter of time before ASIO or FEDPOL tracked him down. If ASIO got to him first, he knew they'd stage his death to look like suicide. On the other hand, if FEDPOL found him, he'd be charged with treason and attempted murder. If that happened, he'd use his digital recordings to try and strike a deal that took Fleming and Bacon down with him, but he didn't fancy living out the remainder of his days in the isolation unit of a maximum security prison. As an ex-cop, someone was bound to get to him sooner or later. Powdered glass in his food, an overdose of heroin, it didn't matter; there were a dozen different tried and true methods for disposing of someone if his enemies were sufficiently determined.

Either way, he was doomed, unless Knox managed to bring McCarthy down so she could become prime minister. She'd assured him that when this happened she'd use his tapes to cut a deal with Bacon and Fleming allowing them to retire into political obscurity rather than subject the nation to an horrendous scandal. She'd then take steps to ensure he was able to leave the country unhindered and establish himself overseas with a new identity.

Nolan was tempted to forget about Knox's promises and to make a dash for freedom using one of his forged passports. However, despite altering his appearance significantly, he was not game to risk being picked up by the new facial recognition software that had recently been installed at Australia's international airports. Apart from that, he was well known to Customs and Border Protection officers throughout Australia.

His nerves were shot. He'd reasoned that it would be more difficult to find him in the seething metropolis of Sydney than in some tiny country town where tongues never stopped wagging but he was tired of being cooped up in the seedy Kings Cross hotel he'd opted for. Turning on the room's small television set, he tuned to Channel 24 which he considered provided the best news coverage and political commentary. As the screen lit up, a yellow banner emblazoned across the bottom of the picture blocked the lower half of some AFL sports star who was being interviewed over a multi-million dollar contract he'd just signed with a rival club.

"Deputy Prime Minister Helen Knox resigns suddenly amid rumours of a failed leadership challenge."

Horrified, Nolan rummaged in his briefcase and located Knox's business card on which she'd written the number of the mobile telephone she reserved for her behind-the-scene manoeuvrings. Cursing, when the phone rang out, he tried twice more before she answered with a terse, 'What is it?'

'Helen, I've just seen the news. What's going on?'

'Richard, you're on your own. I can't help you

anymore,' Knox replied flatly.

'What do you mean, "You can't help me anymore?" We had a deal. You at least owe me some sort of explanation.'

'I don't owe you anything Richard and if you try to say anything to the contrary I'll deny it. I've got my own problems now, so just bugger off!'

'Shit, the bitch has cut me off,' Nolan swore. *What the hell am I going to do now?*

Telling himself not to panic, Nolan sat on the edge of his bed and began taking stock of his situation. His only chance for salvation seemed to have evaporated with Helen Knox's sudden resignation. She'd been so sure that Matthew McCarthy would step aside rather than risk a scandal that would tear apart the Labor Party and ruin his reputation. She'd obviously underestimated the scientist and her plan for a leadership spill had backfired. There could be no other possible explanation for her unexpected political demise.

There were several things that could happen. A: he would skip the country using a fake passport and establish a new life somewhere overseas. B: the Federal Police would catch him in which case he'd be charged, undergo a lengthy court trial and then be imprisoned for many years. C: Fleming would use ASIO's resources to find him and dispose of him, either before he left Australia, or wherever he went overseas. In other words, if he wasn't found in Australia, he'd spend the rest of his life looking over his shoulder. D: he could make Fleming and Bacon aware of the incriminating evidence against them and use the recordings to negotiate a deal offering them the recordings and his guaranteed silence in exchange for his freedom. This latter plan had an obvious downside; there was no way he could trust the two men not to kill him once they got their hands on the tapes, so he'd have to keep copies for evermore.

Although Nolan was determined to die rather than risk capture, trial and incarceration, he would ensure Bacon and the ASIO boss both went down if Plan B came to pass.

Suddenly, the tiny digital recorder had become his most treasured possession. It was vital that nothing happened to it or the information it contained. After retrieving the device from a small rucksack containing his spy equipment, he began burning copies of the recordings to disks. Once he'd completed that, he'd make sure they and the recorder were placed in a safe deposit box. The key and instructions as to what should be done with the recordings in the event of his death would then be deposited with his solicitor without delay.

Nolan knew the Federal Police were unlikely to cut a deal if he was arrested. However, they'd be very interested in the recorded conversations between Bacon and Fleming and would immediately launch a full scale investigation which would undoubtedly culminate in the prosecution of the Director General of ASIO and the high-profile Labor Senator. He also realised, in order to prevent Fleming and Bacon killing him, he'd have to ensure both men were made aware of the recordings as soon as possible by sending them confidential letters warning that if anything happened to him, his solicitor would send the recordings to Sixty Minutes and Four Corners who would blow everything wide open.

Feeling much better now that he'd covered all bases,

Nolan bustled around his room preparing the necessary letters, packaging up the recorder and the disks. Once he was satisfied that the recorder was safe, he'd risk trying to leave the country, but not through any of the major international airports equipped with facial recognition technology and bristling with border protection officers, he'd choose a smaller international airport where the high-tech gear had not yet been installed.

Although it involved driving over five thousand kilometres, Port Hedland in the North West of Western Australia seemed a good option. The airport had only a small number of Customs and FEDPOL officers and they'd be unlikely to recognise him, or even consider he might choose that route to escape. Flights regularly left the hot, remote and dusty Pilbara town laden with FIFO workers heading to Bali. He'd book a return flight so as not to raise suspicions. On reaching Denpasar, he would then purchase a one-way ticket to somewhere in Europe, maybe Zurich, it didn't matter; he had plenty of time to work out a final destination.

Had the fugitive federal agent been aware that John McCarthy and Annette Thompson were also conscious of the recordings and were trying to pick up his trail, he would not have felt quite so confident.

Before leaving Canberra, McCarthy had phoned all the hire car companies. Well aware that Nolan was unlikely to use his own name and driver's licence, he'd faxed Nolan's photo to them all using an official Federal Police facsimile cover sheet to negate any concerns about privacy and requested each company to quiz its booking staff to see if anyone recognised the federal agent.

Surprisingly, he struck gold.

On her first day on the job in Avis's overworked airport office, a young female trainee clerk had been making her first booking when she was approached by a fit-looking man in his mid-forties requesting a hire car for an indeterminate period. Very nervous and petrified of making a mistake, the young clerk carefully examined the copy she'd made of her customer's driver's licence because she was anxious to ensure all the details and the photograph had been replicated satisfactorily before directing him to his vehicle. The man then paid in cash, which was unusual. She also wondered why he had had been in such a hurry and anxious to get on his way, so his face stuck in her mind, unlike the hundreds of bookings she'd made since.

'I'm sure it was the man you're looking for,' she told McCarthy over the phone. 'I've dug out the booking form and his photograph and I'll fax them to you, but he's given the name of Roger Gould. He produced a New South Wales driver's licence with 50 Sporing Way, Heathcote, as his residential address. I matched the signatures on the form with the driver's licence to make sure it wasn't a stolen licence,' she added defensively.

'It's okay, you did an excellent job. He'd probably practised the signatures.' *Or forged the entire licence.*

McCarthy thanked the young woman and telephoned Annette with the news. 'I've no doubt there's someone by that name living at 50 Sporing Way, Heathcote, but Nolan will have stolen some poor bugger's identity. However, I don't have the time to check it out and it won't help us much if I do anyway.

The car he's hired is a 2013 model, battleship-grey Ford Territory. It's a good choice because there must be thousands of them on the road. If Nolan's got any brains, he'll have swapped the licence plates but write down this number anyway.' McCarthy repeated the number and wished Annette luck, reminding her to keep in touch before severing the connection. *You bloody beauty. You've made your first mistake, Dicky Boy.*

Annette reckoned she could compile a tourist information book from the knowledge she'd acquired plodding around all the towns along the New South Wales south coast in the past week. Starting her search at Nowra she worked her way south through Sussex Inlet, Batemans Bay, Narooma, Eden, all the way to the tiny, picturesque holiday village of Mallacoota, cursing the endless procession of semi-trailers, the huge mobile palaces called fifth wheelers, enormous recently-purchased caravans and the expensive motor homes piloted by cashed-up grey nomads who all seemed determined to spend their children's inheritance before they died. She visited nearly every hotel, motel, caravan park, petrol station, supermarket, cafe, restaurant and B and B, flashing Nolan's photo, all the time hoping she'd not get into trouble with FEDPOL for unauthorised investigative work while on sick leave. She chatted with backpackers, hitchhikers, holidaymakers, road workers; in fact, anyone she thought might have noticed a handsome middle-aged man travelling alone.

It was all to no avail. Tired, lonely and dispirited she finally telephoned John McCarthy admitting defeat.

'You're doing great Annette. I can't believe you've covered so much ground in such a short time. I've had no luck either, so far,' McCarthy reported. 'Keep going until you get to the Great Ocean Road in Victoria. If you haven't come up with anything by then, give up and go home. In the meantime, I'll contact you if I come up with anything, but so far, I've worked my way from Canberra to Cooma, along the Monaro Highway all the way to Bombala and back up the Alpine Way to Jindabyne, Thredbo and Corryong. I am about to head up through Tumbarumba and Batlow to Tumut and I'll then work my way down the Snowy Mountains Road. Hang in there. I am sure someone will have seen him somewhere.'

It was exhausting work. The winding mountain roads were taking their toll on John's sixty-seven-year-old arms and shoulders, his back ached and he was rapidly coming to the conclusion that he was past doing this sort of gruelling police work when he pulled into Tumut's main street.

'I reckon you deserve a beer, Johnno,' he told himself as he nosed into a parking spot outside the first pub.

Perched on a tall bar stool, a frosty schooner of Tooheys Old registering the three huge gulps he'd taken in the frothy residual rings on the inside of the glass, he surveyed his surroundings. He'd entered the public bar from the street, failing to notice in his rush to quench his thirst that the hotel offered a number of rooms to aspiring guests. From where he sat he was able to look through into a well-furnished reception area where a portly, grey-haired man was in the process of accepting a booking from a couple McCarthy assumed were newlyweds from the starry looks they directed at each other. He waited until they picked up their suitcases and began making their way up the wide carpeted staircase before draining his glass and approaching the desk.

'Yes sir, may I help you?' the desk clerk asked, peering at McCarthy over a set of bifocals perched precariously on the tip of his nose.

John smiled disarmingly. 'You're a credit to the hospitality industry. It's nice to meet someone who still practises good manners. Over the past week I've got sick of spotty-faced adolescents young enough to be my grandkids calling me "mate". That is, if I could get them to leave their mobile phones alone long enough to serve me. Actually, I am looking for someone in connection with an investigation I am doing but I've been driving all day and I am absolutely knackered, so I'd love a room for the night, if you've got one to spare.'

The elderly maitre d' consulted his register. 'That's no problem at all. I've got a nice ensuite room looking out to the Alps for a hundred-and-twenty per night with breakfast included. Are you a private investigator, sir?' he wanted to know.

McCarthy guessed the clerk thought he was too old to be a serving policeman and assumed he'd chosen the career in which so many former law enforcement officers conclude their working lives.

Now is a good time to ask. This old bloke will remember Nolan if he was ever here.

'Actually I'm not. I am seconded to the Federal Police and I am looking for this man,' he replied, placing Nolan's photo on the desk.

The clerk's face remained inscrutable. 'If sir has some identification, I might be able to help. You'll understand that we have to respect the privacy of our guests.'

Eureka! He's all but confirmed Nolan's been here.

'Here's my ID and before you ask, yes I am related to the prime minister. I am his father, as well as his security advisor, but I need you to exercise the utmost discretion and keep the fact that I've been here to yourself, because if the media get to know, they'll splash it all over the papers alerting this bloke to the fact that I am looking for him. Now, have you seen him?'

'Of course I have. His photo's been plastered all over the telly and the Canberra Times. He thought he'd disguised himself by shaving his head, growing a beard and plastering himself with tattoos to look like a bikie, but after dealing with people all my working life I've become somewhat of an expert at spotting phonies. He was too clean and too well mannered, and he carried himself like a military man, rather than the thuggish persona he'd adopted. Apart from that, the hired Ford Territory he was driving just didn't suit him either. I'd have thought something like an F250 pickup or a four-wheel-drive ute would have been more appropriate.'

John grinned. 'Good on you Sherlock.' *It's a wonder you didn't add, "elementary my dear Watson" to that wonderful example of perspicacity.* 'So, your use of the past tense suggests he's no longer here?'

'That's correct. Mr Bateman, aka Nolan, booked out two days ago. As far as I can tell, he remained in his room for the entire ten days he was here and then paid his bill and took off.'

'I am not criticising you, but I can't help wondering. If you recognised him and knew the police were looking for him, why didn't you make a quiet phone call to your local gendarme?'

The clerk suddenly looked uncomfortable. 'Even if our local plod doesn't have the skills to track a bleeding elephant through a snow drift, it's not my place to do the police's work for them. Your man was here long enough to be found if they'd been doing their jobs properly.'

Knowing how easy it is for small town police officers to know who comes and goes on their patch, McCarthy tended to agree. In his opinion, liaising with local publicans and checking guest registers was elementary.

'Sherlock, I think it's more likely he twigged you were on to him and he offered you a nice "incentive" to keep quiet.'

'My name's not Sherlock, it's Anderson, and I don't take bribes,' the hotel clerk replied indignantly.

McCarthy suspected differently but pushing the issue further would be counterproductive. 'It's okay Mr Anderson, we'll catch up with him now and I won't tell him you spoke to me, so you don't have to worry. By the way, did Mr Nolan have any visitors, or did he make any telephone calls using the hotel phone?'

'No visitors and no calls. He could have used his mobile of course, and the hotel's got wireless internet, so he could also have used that laptop computer he was carrying to send and receive emails.'

'Okay, if I haven't got you too far off side I'll take that room now. One last question; which direction did our friend go when he left here?'

'He headed back toward Canberra.'

Had he known Nolan's true destination McCarthy's spirits would have soared. As it was, they nose-dived. He thought it was more likely that Nolan had headed to his home town of Sydney because Nolan possessed an intimate knowledge of that city and would know where to hide out among its three million or so residents. In addition, despite altering his appearance, the fugitive federal agent was simply too well known in Canberra and must have realised by now that his searchers would have learned of his small town haunts and would scour them thoroughly.

McCarthy concluded that the likelihood of locating the fugitive policeman had just diminished exponentially. He telephoned Thompson with the news and arranged to meet her back at her flat so they could re-evaluate their situation.

When it arrived at the Canberra GPO, the innocuous D4 envelope was placed in ASIO's private bag. At 9.00am a government courier delivered the bag to the security intelligence organisation's headquarters where the contents underwent the usual X-ray scans to which all ASIO's mail was routinely subjected. Along with hundreds of other letters, it then dropped into a large plastic tub to await sorting.

Had it arrived in the mail at most organisations, the ordinary-looking business envelope would not have raised anyone's eyebrows, but because there was no clue as to the who had sent it, ASIO's Grade 1 junior clerk who was tasked with collecting and distributing incoming mail looked at the envelope more closely, as he'd been trained to do. He noted the quality of the paper; not cheap and flimsy but thick, opaque and not easily torn or damaged by the rigours of the postal service. He also noted that the address; "Mr James Fleming, Director General of The Australian Security Intelligence Organisation" had been generated by a ubiquitous laser printer, and that the envelope also bore the warning; "Personal and Confidential" both front and back. However, what really attracted his interest was the fact that the flaps had been initialled and sealed over with adhesive tape as a final reminder that the contents were intended for the ASIO boss and no one else.

The clerk felt the envelope carefully and although he was satisfied that it contained only a single sheet of paper, he put it to one side. Although it was a very remote possibility, the envelope could still contain chemical or biological substances and further direction was required from his superiors as to whether it should pass through an electronic device designed for detecting biological agents such as anthrax or botulinum toxins. It then sat where he'd placed it for most of the morning before a supervisor eventually deemed it minimal risk and ordered it to be delivered to Fleming's Canberra desk. An email was then sent to the ASIO chief's mobile phone alerting him to its presence. However, because Fleming was in Sydney, it sat unopened until he arrived in Canberra two days later.

By this time, Richard Nolan was halfway across the Nullarbor on his way to Port Hedland.

Although he half expected Nolan to take the precaution of protecting the damning evidence against the two powerful men, the letter's content was the last thing Fleming wanted to read. He immediately contacted Bacon on his private number to set up an urgent secret meeting.

At approximately the same time as Fleming and Bacon were heading to their rendezvous, John McCarthy and Annette Thompson were sitting down at Thompson's town house to revise their strategy for locating Nolan.

'We're not going to find him if he's gone to Sydney,' McCarthy concluded. 'I think we've got to make him want to come to us.'

Annette looked puzzled. 'How are we going to do that? We can hardly post ads in the papers, or use the media without blowing the entire thing wide open. Fleming, Bacon and anyone else who's involved will go immediately into damage control mode and FEDPOL is going to ask a hell of a lot of questions as to why we're conducting a private investigation.'

'I've been thinking about that. There's one person who might know where Nolan is, or at least knows how to get in touch with him, and that's Helen Knox. Knox knows about the tapes, so Nolan must have approached her with intention of seeking immunity from prosecution in exchange for grassing on Bacon and Fleming.'

'Except, Knox tried to use the information for her own political advantage and it backfired, meaning she might not feel very favourably disposed toward you.'

'Well she's not going to come out of this smelling of roses when the manure starts flying and her deviousness is revealed. She's already left herself open to charges of being an accessory to murder. The way I see it, this is her final and only chance for redemption.'

A quick phone call to Matthew was all it took to get Helen Knox's private telephone number and home address. She made no attempt to disguise her animosity when he telephoned, but once he explained the precarious position her malevolent behaviour had created, she reluctantly agreed to speak with him and Thompson.

The involuntarily-retired former deputy prime minister's residence turned out to be a one hundred-and-fifty–year-old stone cottage set in the middle of a ten hectare hobby farm outside the once tin-pot town of Bungendore, approximately forty kilometres from Canberra. A former 1840s Cobb and Co. staging post, the town had undergone a revival, metamorphosing into a trendy village mostly inhabited by yuppie tree-changers, public servants and retirees looking for a quiet town not too far from hospitals and other amenities.

John nosed into the farm's Hurricane-wire front gate to the accompaniment of much dog barking. Two large, black and tan Dobermans appeared and bounded down the gravel drive bellowing their displeasure at the intrusion. Leaping against the wire, they snarled and slavered, their dark eyes menacing John and Annette.

'What other sort of dogs would a nasty bitch like her have? How appropriate,' John remarked as they waited while Knox appeared and called for the maniacal canines to retreat.

During John's previous encounter Knox had been attired in a dark grey business suit with her blonde hair expensively styled to soften the hard lines of her fifty-something countenance. Clad now in blue jeans, tan work boots, a chequered blouse, and with her hair pulled savagely back into a bun, any last vestige of femininity was gone and the former deputy prime minister looked every bit the hard-nosed man-hater she was reputed to be.

Knox swung the gate open, waited until they'd driven through, and then secured it by looping a galvanised chain through the mesh and over the head of a bolt jutting from the weathered-grey hardwood post. She then followed on foot to the house where she stood with her hands on her slim hips watching as they alighted.

'You're here under sufferance. Tell me what it is you want from me and then leave before I change my mind and set the dogs on you,' she all but snarled.

McCarthy lounged against the grille of his Commodore while casting nervous glances at the two dogs that were now lying in the shade, watching hopefully. He had no doubt that with one word from Knox they'd delight in tearing great chunks of flesh from the unwelcome visitors.

'That would only compound your situation, Helen, so I wouldn't advise it. You may not like us being here, but a little more civility and a lot less animosity from you is called for, in light of the fact that I can probably keep you out of gaol, if you cooperate. Now, may we go and sit down and talk like civilised adults, or do I walk away and put everything in the hands of the Crime and Corruption Commission?'

Knox exhaled noisily, releasing the pent up stress of the past ten or so days. She pivoted on her heels, slouched to her shady front veranda and flopped dispiritedly into one of several cane chairs. 'Okay, let's get on with it,' she growled.

The two investigators seated themselves opposite and John began. 'Helen, when did Federal Agent Nolan first approach you?'

'It was the day after he and your son had been diving. Matthew was still in hospital after the attack.'

'How did he make contact?'

'He just walked right up to me in the members' car park at Parliament House. I am sure he'd been waiting for me to arrive.'

'What were his exact words?'

'He said, "Ms Knox, I believe you know me, I am the prime minister's personal protection officer.'

'What did you say?'

"I said, "Yes, I know who you are. What do you want?" He replied, "I am in serious trouble and I need you to help me." I asked him why I should help him and he said, "I know you want to be the prime minister and I've got some information that will help you to achieve that, if you use it properly."'

'What did you say then?'

'Well, naturally, I wanted to know what the information was and how he thought it could help me.'

'And did he then tell you what the information was?'

'He said he had taped conversations between the Director General of ASIO and Senator Philip Bacon that implicated them in a plot to assassinate the prime minister.'

'What was your reaction?'

'You could have knocked me over with a feather. That sort of thing doesn't happen in Australia.'

'It seems it does now. Had you already forgotten that somebody shot Connor Bowker?'

'Of course not but I found it hard to accept that the Director General of ASIO and a long-standing Labor senator would plot to assassinate the Australian Prime Minister.'

'Did you ask how he came to be spying on Bacon and Fleming?'

'Yes, but he said it would take too long and the car park of the nation's parliament wasn't really the appropriate place for such a discussion in case Bacon or Fleming got to hear that he'd approached me, so we arranged a rendezvous that evening.'

'Where did you meet?'

'There's an old-fashioned drive-in theatre that's still operating in Queanbeyan. It's the ideal spot for clandestine meetings. I've used it in the past. You can sit in the dark and talk without being seen or overheard.'

John couldn't help wondering what other diabolical schemes Knox had been involved in and with whom, but he didn't ask. 'Did he bring the tapes with him and did he then give you the full story?'

'Yes. He told me about his navy days, how he'd nearly been killed in Iraq, how he was awarded for bravery and how he felt really guilty that his mates had hadn't survived because he made the wrong decision in the heat of the moment. Do you want to know what actually happened?'

'I think I've got a pretty good idea but I'd like to hear his version.'

Helen Knox's ability to recall Nolan's words was faultless and there were few variations between Nolan's version and what Yeoman had told McCarthy. John allowed her to finish before asking, 'Did he say why he didn't put the record straight at the time?'

'I think he was too traumatised and too afraid of the disgrace of being branded a coward. He let the lies go on for too long and it all just became too difficult in the end. He said he got out of the navy and joined the Federal Police in the hope he could put it all behind him. Unfortunately, Fleming got suspicious and unveiled the truth. He's a slimy bugger. He didn't do anything with the information at the time because he suspected as Nolan made his way of the ladder in his new career he'd have someone within FEDPOL he'd be able to manipulate one day.

'As it turns out, Fleming has a few skeletons in his own closet and he was in turn being blackmailed by Bacon. Bacon wanted to get rid of Prime Minister McCarthy so he blackmailed Fleming to do it.'

'Why did Bacon want to kill Prime Minister McCarthy?'

'It's all to do with Bacon being tied up in the manufacture and importation of illicit drugs. I don't know whether you're aware, but Bacon is the majority shareholder in Shriver Pharmaceuticals. His Indonesian factory apparently manufactures illegal methamphetamines as well as legitimate drugs. He has them smuggled into Australia and uses the bikie gangs to distribute them. Your son's National Anti-Drug legislation gives all police forces nationwide powers to pursue the drug dealers, manufacturers and distributors and Bacon is worried it will impact on his profits because it will shut down the bikie gangs' distribution networks. He's prepared to get rid of your son and anybody else who tries to push the bill through parliament.'

'Jesus, that's pretty extreme. So correct me if I am wrong, but I gather Bacon blackmailed Fleming to have my son assassinated and Fleming in turn blackmailed Nolan to do the actual deed?'

'That's pretty much it.'

'What's Bacon got over Fleming?'

'It goes way back to the Vietnam War when Bacon was Fleming's Platoon Commander. Even back in those days, Bacon was buying drugs from the Golden Triangle and smuggling them into Australia. Do you know how he was doing that?'

'No, but I hope you're going to tell me.'

'United States Air Force planes used to fly the bodies of American soldiers home to the States via Cairns where they'd stop to refuel. Apparently the drugs were packed into the coffins and I think he might have even hidden them in the bodies. The drugs meant for Australia were unloaded in Cairns and the rest went on to the States. Customs never thought to check the bodies or the coffins. I mean who would think for a moment someone would transport drugs that way?'

'And Nolan has all this on tape? It seems rather amazing that he'd manage to get so much detail from eavesdropping on their conversations.'

'I've heard the recordings. Fleming hates Bacon with a passion. Bacon despises Fleming and they goad each other at these meetings. In one session they were having a flaming row and that's where the stuff about Vietnam came out.'

351

'Going back to my earlier question, what prompted Nolan to begin spying on Fleming?'

'He wanted to find why Fleming wanted him to kill your son and he also wanted to know if anyone else was involved. It was his way of taking out some life insurance because he suspected Fleming would get rid of him so he couldn't talk. He also wanted a hold over Fleming in case things went pear-shaped.'

Annette listened to the interview in astonishment but her curiosity was getting the better of her and she chipped in before McCarthy could ask the question that was also bothering him. 'What about Connor Bowker's assassination? Was there any mention of Bacon or Fleming being involved in that?'

Knox appeared to pause momentarily before responding laconically, 'No.'

'Where are the recordings now?' McCarthy wanted to know.

'I don't know. I told Nolan to hang onto them until he heard from me. If he's got any sense they're locked away somewhere safe.'

'And if you'd managed to get my son to resign the prime ministership and take over, what were you going to do with this information?'

'I would have approached Bacon and Fleming with the evidence and given them the opportunity to resign. I hate drugs as much as the next person so I would have insisted Bacon shut down his illegal operation and donate a significant percentage of his accumulated wealth to drug rehabilitation programmes.'

'So you would have let them both go scot free?'

'The alternative would rip apart the Labor Party.

There'd be international outrage and a scandal of unprecedented proportions.'

'Do you have any reason to believe anyone in the federal or state police forces is implicated?'

'Not as far as I know, but you never know with people like Fleming and Bacon. They have a very wide reach.'

'Last question, do you know where Richard Nolan might be and do you have a telephone number or some other way of contacting him?'

'I have his email address and a mobile telephone number but I don't have any idea where he is.'

'Okay. I'd like those details please and I'd also like you to let me know if he makes contact with you.'

'He's unlikely to do that. I told him to bugger off.'

'I am glad you decided to cooperate, Helen. We'll leave you to get on with whatever it was you were doing.'

John nodded to Annette and they got to their feet in readiness to leave. Knox remained seated. 'I know I've made a mess of things,' she said softly. 'Women have to work twice as hard as men to get anywhere in politics and I've worked damn hard to achieve my ambition to become prime minister because I believed I could do a really good job, so it really hurt when I was bypassed by the party in favour of your son. My chances of ever achieving my goals seemed lost and when Nolan told me about the recordings, I let my resentment overrule common-sense because I truly believed my right to the top job had been stolen from me.

'I am so sorry. What's going to happen to me now?'

John stared at the slumped figure, struggling to

control his rising anger. *You're sorry all right. Sorry for yourself.*

'Helen, I can't promise anything. One way or another, you are going to pay for what you've done because when the truth comes out, as it assuredly will, your reputation and your credibility will be in tatters. I am sure when the charges are laid your decision to cooperate and the price you've already paid will be taken into consideration.'

As they drove away from Knox's hobby farm, Annette looked back toward the stone cottage. Helen Knox had not moved but someone had come out of the house and was bending over the former deputy prime minister and appeared to be comforting her. Bemused she observed, 'I thought Helen Knox lived alone.'

'As far as I know she does. Why do you ask?' McCarthy replied, glancing in the rear view mirror as they rounded a bend and the cottage dropped from view.

'Some woman came out of the house when we drove away. If I'm not mistaken, it was Phoebe Swan. Is it possible that she and Knox are in a lesbian relationship?'

'It would answer a lot of questions about Miss Locked-Box-Knox if they are.' McCarthy laughed.

'Bloody dykes and poofters seem to be taking over the world,' Annette sneered and then apologised. 'Sorry, I am letting my homophobia show.'

McCarthy grinned. 'Don't apologise. It's a relief to me to know some of your generation still has old-fashioned values.'

'Some would say we're just narrow-minded and maybe I am, because despite knowing they can't help the way they've been put together and after fending off all those bloody lesos in the army, my skin crawls and I feel physically sick whenever I see women kissing each other.

'Anyway, I think that cold-blooded bitch deserves to be locked up for what she's done. I don't know how you didn't go off your face, John.'

'Knox has the rest of her life to think about what might have been. She'll suffer enough for her treachery. It's far more important to bring Bacon and Fleming down. Especially Bacon, he's pure evil. When I heard about his involvement in the drug business, it really got my blood boiling because I know firsthand how much suffering drugs cause.'

Annette glanced quickly at the retired policeman. She realised she knew little about the McCarthys' private lives. Had there had been some sort of tragedy involving someone very close to the older McCarthy? A strong bond had developed between them so she felt comfortable asking, 'Was someone in your family an addict, John?'

Annette was not prepared for McCarthy's response. 'Yes, *I* was,' John announced, and then went on to explain how he'd been prescribed Septaphycine and other drugs for chronic fatigue and fibromyalgia. He elaborated on how Septaphycine was Shriver Pharmaceuticals' brand name for methadone, a dangerously addictive narcotic that trapped millions in a cycle of hopeless mental and physical dependency. How those who were addicted underwent adverse changes to their personality and how the drug affected thousands of families and ruined countless lives globally. He

355

explained the graphic details of his own struggle to break the chains of his enslavement to the drug and concluded with, 'I thought it was bad enough that people like Bacon are able make millions from addicting people to legal drugs, but that rotten bastard's been spreading the filth of illegal addiction across the world for years. Christ, when I heard the bit about him putting drugs into the body cavities of poor bastards who'd died fighting to prevent the spread of communism, I became even more determined to make sure he spends the rest of his life behind bars.'

Annette was shocked by McCarthy's story and couldn't imagine the horror he and his family had gone through. 'It must have been terribly hard for Mary to see you going through those weeks of suffering while you were breaking the addiction.'

'I think I had it easy compared with her. I don't know how I would have coped if I'd been in her shoes.'

'How do you suppose Bacon gets the drugs into the country?'

'I don't know, but I am wondering if perhaps he pays Indonesian fishermen to sneak into our waters at night and drop drugs along the northern coastline somewhere. There's literally thousands of kilometres of coastline, and our navy and customs boats can't possibly cover it effectively.'

'What's the plan now?'

'We'll try to contact Dickie Boy and get him to come in from the cold. We've got to get our hands on those recordings even if it means someone with sufficient power and authority promising Nolan that he won't go to prison.'

Unbeknown to McCarthy and Thompson, Nolan was by then three quarters of the way across the Nullarbor where mobile telephone coverage is almost non-existent. When McCarthy's attempts to contact Nolan failed, he composed an email letter suggesting to the disgraced federal agent that he would be wise to respond before Fleming's men got to him.

+++++++++++++

Chapter Twenty-Three

After his customary ten-kilometre morning jog around the sparkling waters of Lake Burley Griffin, Matthew McCarthy thanked his exhausted protective service minders and made his way to the Parliament House gymnasium for a thirty minute workout.

Although it was only 7.00am, Parliament House was already bustling with politicians, journalists and the usual army of public servants essential to the massive building's functioning. Although Matthew still considered the environment stultifying and largely divorced from the real world, the daily run was an excellent antidote because it provided the opportunity to chat with his protective service detail on a wide range of everyday matters that kept him grounded. After showering, he breakfasted in the members' dining room before making his way to his office for a briefing with Merv Barrett, his private secretary, on the day's schedule. An extroverted career public servant in his late twenties, Barrett was a dapper, highly intelligent individual. He was a great communicator and not easily cowed by the parliament's abundance of egocentric individuals and megalomaniacs; a trait that had resulted in the two men becoming firm friends.

After exchanging the usual pleasantries McCarthy asked Barrett to run through the day's schedule.

'You've got a caucus meeting at 9.00am. I've prepared and distributed the agenda as you requested. Because it's mostly fairly mundane stuff, I expect you'll get through it in about one hour. After that, I have scheduled a meeting at 10.15am with representatives of the Woods Hole Oceanographic Institution who are apparently approaching world leaders to try and garner support for iron fertilisation of the oceans as a way of combating climate change.'

'I know about WHOI. It's a private, non-profit research and higher education facility that's been around since the 1930s. They specialise in all aspects of marine science and education. Lately, they've been conducting extensive tests to determine if there is a link between the oceans' declining phytoplankton levels and climate change.'

'Aren't they the little marine bugs that form the basis of the marine food chain?'

'Correct, but they're much more than that. Phytoplankton is made up of many different organisms of which diatoms and coccolithophores are probably the most prolific. These microscopic creatures which look something like snails are important because they are the food on which krill and other marine species depend. As you know, whales and fish then feed on the krill. Diatoms also sequester carbon in their shells and produce oxygen essential for the survival of humans and other land-based creatures. It's sometimes said they are responsible for every second breath we take. When the diatoms die, they fall into the abyss, taking CO2 down to the sea floor in the calcium carbonate from which their shells are comprised. They lock up the CO2 for up to four thousand years.

'Our oceans are becoming increasingly acidic and this poses a major threat to the diatoms whose shells are essentially being eaten away by carbolic acid. The same thing is happening to our corals. Fifty percent of the

Great Barrier Reef has already been lost because of increasing ocean acidity.'

'Yeah, there's been a lot about coral bleaching in the news lately but I wasn't aware of the significance of these diatom and cocco thingies. So, let me get this right, if the diatoms die, the food chain breaks down and oxygen levels in the Earth's atmosphere decline?'

'That's the theory.'

'Bloody heck. So what's iron fertilisation?'

'It's still very controversial, but essentially, it involves spreading very fine particles of iron in the ocean to stimulate a phytoplankton bloom. Phytoplankton requires iron and silica to survive. Some waters are deficient in both iron and silica and some are only deficient in iron. It's little use depositing iron into silica deficient waters because the phytoplankton will just die, so you have to choose the right areas if you want the blooms to last. The Galapagos and the Arctic and Antarctic oceans would probably be good choices for a major seeding campaign.'

'Why is it so controversial? Is it because it's costly?'

'The cost depends upon the quantity of iron needed and that won't be known until more extensive trials have been undertaken. As an example, one kilogram of iron can result in the sequestration of up to eighty-three-thousand tons of carbon dioxide. A concerted seeding campaign could effectively offset all man's CO_2 emission and it could be financed by introducing a price on carbon of as little as seven dollars per tonne. However, problems arise due to the precautionary principle (PP) which states that if an action or policy has a suspected risk of causing harm, in the absence of scientific consensus, the burden of proof that it is not harmful falls on those who would take the action.

'On the other hand, and in my humble opinion, the precautionary principle doesn't apply, for the reason that man-made emissions could be said to be the action and iron fertilisation the remedial action necessary to address the problem. Nevertheless, opponents of ocean seeding are worried about creating toxic red tides or some other unnatural and catastrophic imbalance, but that's a load of codswallop. Volcanoes erupt all the time and distribute iron particles into the oceans, and they've never caused red tides, or had other harmful effects. On the contrary, the Mount Pinatubo eruption actually resulted in phytoplankton blooms that created a spike in the world's oxygen levels.

'There's another problem though. The London Dumping Convention of 2010, to which many nations including Australia are signatories, prohibits the dumping of wastes at sea. However, the treaty is non-binding, so if there was incontrovertible proof that there were no adverse effects from seeding the oceans it would be worth ignoring that treaty to try and reverse climate change.'

Merv Barrett grinned. 'I love this job because I can count on you to expand my knowledge base every day.'

'You're welcome to sit in on the meeting with the WHOI people if you like. It should be very interesting.'

'Thanks anyway, Matt, but I think all the scientific jargon you blokes use would have my head in a spin.'

'Don't sell yourself short, Merv. You're pretty

quick on the uptake.'

Matthew faced a barrage of questions at the caucus meeting over Helen Knox's unexpected departure. While he was itching to provide a full explanation and believed his team was entitled to know the truth, the time was not right. He explained that Knox's behaviour and the reasons for her resignation were the subject of an ongoing investigation. 'Suffice it to say she was a traitor who was prepared to bring down the Labor Party to fulfil a selfish political agenda. She came into possession of explosive information involving high profile individuals in key government positions. Revealing further details could prejudice an investigation that is likely to result in charges of treason and murder. I am afraid you are just going to have to trust me but I promise to provide you with a full explanation at the appropriate time.'

Caucus members were far from happy with the explanation with some even claiming that the prime minister did not trust them.

'I am sorry you feel that way,' he told them. 'However, you of all people should know that this place is as about as leak-proof as a sieve. You'll understand when the time comes why I can't afford to take you into my confidence. Now, let's take a vote on who should replace Knox as deputy prime minister.'

After the meeting, Matthew breathed a huge sigh of relief as he made his way to the WHOI meeting which would provide a welcome respite from political wrangling. He'd managed to extract a vow of silence from caucus members despite their displeasure, but because he regarded some of his colleagues as gossiping old women, he hoped they could keep their lips sealed.

The four WHOI scientists rose to their feet as one when Matthew bustled in. An eclectic bunch comprised of three men and one woman with ages ranging from mid-twenties to nearly eighty, they were at least amiable and clearly thankful that he'd found the time to meet them.

The group's spokesperson was an almost anorexic woman with steel-grey hair and very plain features who went by the unlikely name of Deborah Harry. Unlike her rock idol namesake she was totally without sex appeal.

'Prime Minister, thank you for taking the time to see us. Permit me to introduce my colleagues, Iain Somerville, Roger Bayzand and Stuart Bromley.'

Matthew shook hands with each of the group's members. He had read several papers published by Somerville during his CSIRO career and regarded the stocky octogenarian as one of the world's foremost authorities on marine ecology. Although he wasn't familiar with Bayzand and Bromley he did not doubt their competency despite their obvious youth.

'It's my pleasure. You've no idea what a relief it is to be able to talk about something other than politics. I've arranged refreshments which should be here in a moment but I am afraid I am on a very tight schedule because the parliamentary session begins soon, so I'd appreciate you getting straight down to business.'

Harry began by explaining how WHOI had just concluded a worldwide ten-year study into declining phytoplankton levels and the impact of rising ocean acidity on marine ecosystems. While Matthew was familiar with much of the data he was unprepared for Harry's final summation.

'...and so we have reached the incontrovertible conclusion that phytoplankton levels have in fact declined since 1950 by much more than the forty percent reported by other studies. In fact, phytoplankton is declining exponentially with each passing day. We are of the opinion that their survival has reached a tipping point and unless immediate action is taken, the entire marine ecosystem will collapse within twelve months.'

Stunned, Matthew wondered if the highly esteemed group could somehow be mistaken. Sensing his incredulity, Somerville stood up and began pacing as he spoke. 'Prime Minister, I know as a climate and marine scientist you understand the implications better than anyone.' Pausing, he placed heavy emphasis on his next sentence. 'This is not a mistake. The situation is dire. Far more dire than the crisis the world faced back in 1974 when the catastrophic consequences of unfettered use of chlorofluorocarbons on the ozone layer was discovered by Sherry Rowland and Mario Molina. We all faced extinction then and we face extinction now. The only difference is the time available to take remedial action. Unlike in 1974, we cannot wait thirteen years while nations debate whether or not to take action; we must act now.'

'What do you propose?' Matthew wanted to know, although he had little doubt what Somerville and Harry's action plan would be.

Harry took over from Somerville. 'Prime Minister, we have already approached US President Turnbull and the Secretary General of the United Nations, Ban Ki Moon. While they were sympathetic and promised to try and convene a world summit to address the problem, they could not seem to grasp the enormous gravity of the situation. You seem to be our only hope. You have become one of the world's foremost environmentalists and you are apparently the only leader with the courage to implement the economic and structural reforms needed to tackle climate change. While we know Australia will face enormous criticism, we want your government to immediately implement a massive iron fertilisation programme to stimulate phytoplankton regeneration in the Arctic and Antarctic Oceans and the seas around the Galapagos Islands.'

Matthew nodded thoughtfully. 'I thought that's what you were going to say. I just finished discussing this issue with my private secretary a couple of hours ago.'

'So is that a yes?' Harry asked hopefully.

'You have my personal support, but this is a decision that must be made in consultation with my Cabinet colleagues.

'I'll call a meeting with them tomorrow morning, but I'll need all the evidence you've compiled if I am to persuade them to go against the London Treaty, which, as I am sure you know, prohibits the dumping of wastes at sea. I also suggest you attend the meeting and put your case so there is no question of this being another one of my crazy brain waves.

'If my colleagues agree to go ahead with this seeding programme, as I am sure they will if you

365

present your case as succinctly as you just have, we'll need to move swiftly. We will also need to move covertly.

'You may wonder why I stress the need for secrecy, so let me explain.

'The problem you describe has arisen because of the twisted philosophy endorsed by the most governments that says nations and businesses must continually grow and expand. That thinking is simply insane because the world's resources are being consumed at nearly twice the rate that Nature can replace them.

'Unfortunately, there are many short-sighted and selfish individuals who either don't care about the survival of future generations, or who are too blinded by greed to accept the truth. These people will do all within their power to protect their interests as is evidenced by the recent assassination of Prime Minister Bowker and the attempt on my own life because of my government's attempts to change the current world philosophy to one of living sustainably and in harmony with the environment and each other.

'If these evil or misguided individuals are prepared to resort to murder to protect their own selfish interests, they will stop at nothing to prevent the seeding of the world's oceans.'

Somerville collapsed into his seat looking like a boxer who'd just fought the fight of his life. 'Thank you Prime Minister. We're sure this is our only known hope at this point. We're also sure that there will be no undesirable consequences, and even if there are, we can't make the situation any worse than it already is.'

The meeting with the WHOI delegation wound up with everyone agreeing to reconvene the next morning so Matthew's caucus colleagues could be apprised of the situation. Before they left Matthew reminded them again of the need for secrecy quoting Kitchener's wartime motto: "loose lips sink ships."

During the afternoon's parliamentary session Matthew passed a cryptic handwritten note along the front bench advising his team of the urgent need to discuss a highly confidential issue of major significance the next morning. With opposition members likely to attack the government over its Zero Carbon Energy Bill and its handling of the recent riots there was a distinct possibility that parliament would sit late into the night and this created considerable conjecture and grumbling with some MPs being worried about sleep deprivation..

'Suck it up,' McCarthy told them unsympathetically. 'When you discover what's on the agenda a few hours of lost sleep will pale into insignificance.'

Although it was nearly 11.00pm before parliament finally wound up for the night, the gravity of WHOI's findings and the enormity of the decision he'd been asked to make meant Australia's youngest ever prime minister was too keyed-up to sleep. He felt a desperate need to mull over everything with someone he could trust and debated telephoning Catherine to run everything past her but immediately dismissed the idea.

Although he knew his wife would not be upset if he woke her, Matthew could not be sure that someone wouldn't eavesdrop on the telephone conversation. Nolan's betrayal and the recent bugging of Fleming and Bacon's conversations had made him paranoid about trusting anyone and he'd come to realise how easy it was to invade another's privacy. For all he knew, a listening device could have been planted in his hotel room.

Had his father not been off hunting Richard Nolan, Matthew would have sought the older McCarthy's counsel despite the lateness of the hour. Instead, to the extreme consternation of his minders who were hoping for a quiet night, he donned his joggers and running shorts and set off on a gruelling run through the almost deserted Canberra streets.

As Matthew ran with his bodyguards in tow, he attempted to get his thoughts in order. If he and his government went ahead with the iron seeding programme and the WHOI report was subsequently found to be flawed, they would be politically crucified both in Australia and internationally and his attempts to bring the world to its senses on climate change would hit a brick wall.

Despite the London Treaty being non-binding, breaching it was not a matter to be taken lightly. Was there time to verify WHOI's findings? Was it also possible to collect the huge quantities of fine iron particles and secretly distribute them?

Surely someone would leak the news. And if that happened, unions and governments would be up in arms. Mining unions would probably refuse to dig the stuff out of the ground if they knew where it was headed. If he got the ore as far as the ports the wharfies would probably refuse to load the ships or permit them to leave whatever harbours they were to sail from.

Who would undertake the task of shipping the ore to the Arctic, the Galapagos and the Antarctic?

Would it be appropriate to use the Royal Australian Navy or should they look at private contractors? What would it all cost? When could they begin? How long would the programme take?

If they managed to pull it off, would it work, or would there be some disastrous and unforeseen consequences? What would happen if he refused to allow his government to implement WHOI's plan? Should he instead pressure other governments to come on board? Was there time to do this?

With all these questions still whirling around in his mind, Matthew suddenly realised he'd been running on autopilot for the past hour. He had arrived back at his hotel without even realising it.

The heavy revolving door began rotating automatically as he bounded up the marble steps and through the heavily carpeted foyer to the waiting lifts. He waved to the night-shift clerk manning the front desk and then thanked his AFP escort and wished them an uneventful night. After swiping his access card across the lift's card reader, he stepped into the mirrored compartment and studied his reflection as the lift doors closed with a soft hiss. His face looked haggard. He'd lost several kilos since being wounded and the weight of the prime ministerial office threatened to overwhelm him both physically and mentally.

Christ I miss Catherine. These bloody egocentric Canberra bastards are living in Lala Land. How did I ever let myself get talked into becoming a politician let alone PM? The answer came back as if from the ether.

Because there's no one else stupid enough to think they can save the planet, that's why!

The lift's car rose almost silently to the fourth floor which had been secured and set aside for his exclusive use while the Lodge was undergoing a re-fit. Matthew looked down at his feet, noticing his joggers were covered in grass and dirt. Realising he'd sprinted across a dew-soaked lawn during his run, he bent down and removed them so as to avoid leaving a trail of grass across the plush pile when he left the lift. When the stainless steel doors opened almost silently, he stepped into the deserted passageway. Some latent primeval survival mechanism instantly kicked in. He froze with one foot in the air. Goosebumps covered his forearms and the hair on the back of his neck stood up.

He should be alone. No one had authority to access the fourth floor, or his suite, unannounced, yet there'd been a strange noise. What was it? Had he just imagined it? Perhaps recent events had made him unnecessarily nervous.

You're being stupid. It's probably just something contracting in the cooler night air, he told himself and began to move toward his door.

Shit, there it is again. It's as if cloth brushed against a wall or a door. Yes, definitely. I'm not imagining it.

Adrenaline suddenly coursed through his veins as his brain activated the fight or flight response. Common-sense told him to take the safe course of action by retreating and calling for his minders to clear the prime ministerial suite. However, Matthew's curiosity and a fierce rage that had suddenly flared overrode his inner voice. He'd had enough of people wanting to kill him and felt a desperate need to vent his fury. He looked around for something to use as a weapon, but, as with most hotels, the vestibule and the passageway were almost devoid of loose objects, apart from an enormous vase containing a dried floral arrangement. Beating an adversary over the head with banksia nuts and dried waratah flowers wasn't likely to do him much good, so he moved to the suite's entrance and pressed his ear against the door. Complete silence now, although a chink of light showed beneath the door. He realised the room should be in darkness and the antennae of all six senses started twitching, telling him that danger lurked on the other side.

Should I try for a silent entry, or should I throw open the door and just burst into the room making as much noise as I can?

'Don't do either you silly bugger. Back off and go and get the Feds,' the little voice of reason implored.

Matthew slipped his shoes back on, reckoning going into confrontation barefooted was just asking for trouble. He then swiped his key card. The electronic lock winked green and there was a soft click. Hurling himself against the door, he slammed it back against the wall. Propelling himself into the room he barrel-rolled across the small sitting area hoping this would defeat any attempt to stab or shoot him.

'Right you bastard, you're in deep shit!' he roared as he leapt to his feet. Spinning through three-hundred-and-sixty degrees he took everything in at a glance.

Nothing appeared to be out of place and the suite was just as he had left it apart from fresh flowers in the vase on top of the smoked glass coffee table. The tan drapes covering the sliding door to the balcony were open as he'd left them. The screen of the wall mounted television set was blank. The four gold leather dining chairs were arranged neatly around the black highly-polished circular table. His laptop computer was still where he'd left it on the writing desk.

But wait. Something was not right. The computer's lid should be closed. Somebody had been looking at it because the little blue LED light for the hard drive was blinking and he could hear the soft whirr as the cooling fan prevented the device from overheating

Matthew glanced toward the bedroom. It was wide open and he could see that fresh, neatly folded towels had been placed on the foot of the king-size bed's light grey striped coverlet. A faint depression marred the bed's neatness where somebody had sat on the broad, dark-blue cloth strip decorating the lower half of the bed. A faint musky odour of sweat hung in the air intermingling with the room's normal smell of lavender air freshener and toiletries.

Crossing quickly to the ensuite bathroom, he assured himself there was no one hiding there, or in the wardrobes. It was impossible to get beneath the bed so he didn't bother checking. It was a strange time to think about such things but he suspected the inevitable fluff balls lurking beneath the bed base would shatter his illusions as to the hotel's housekeeping standards.

The tiny kitchenette was as neat as a new pin. The drawers were all closed and the tea and coffee sachets had been renewed.

The bastard must have left, but how? We're four storeys up. Shit, that's it! The balcony. He's hiding on

the bloody balcony! I thought I felt a slight draft when I opened the door.

With his back to the bench, Matthew slid open a kitchen drawer as he kept his eyes on the doorways. As he felt quietly among the contents, his eyes travelled toward the glass balcony doors watching for tell-tale movement. Through the almost sheer curtains lights from the semicircular swimming pool below flickered, reflecting ethereally on the glass safety screen surrounding the balcony.

Sure enough, one of the doors was slightly ajar.

Matthew's hand closed around the wooden handle of a heavy stainless steel meat cleaver and he moved toward the balcony. Hearing a faint noise emanating from the bedroom, he turned too late, realising his mistake. He'd forgotten the second door which provided access to the balcony from the bedroom. The intruder had slipped back into the bedroom and crept up behind him. Whirling about, he raised his left arm to fend off the attack. There was a puff of wind against his face accompanied by a swishing sound. Something crashed into his forearm. Pins and needles shot through the limb and he was knocked to his knees by the ferocity of the attack. A heavy object descended on his head. Stars flashed before his eyes. The cleaver fell from his grasp and as his vision clouded he glimpsed a pair of black canvas, rubber-soled combat boots, one of which was being drawn back as his assailant prepared to deliver a powerful kick to Matthew's upper body.

Knowing he was fighting for his life, Matthew managed to throw himself sideways. Rolling over and over in the cramped space, he covered his head with his forearms. His defensive roll halted by a red leather recliner rocker, he bucked and lashed out with both feet, striking the other man in the groin. His assailant grunted in pain, providing Matthew with a brief respite sufficient to enable him to scramble to his feet.

Sucking in great heaving gasps of air, Matthew half crouched and turned side on, his feet spread to provide stability and his fists raised. For the first time he was able to size up his opponent.

Matthew guessed the other man was in his mid-twenties. A heavy-set individual, well over six foot in height, his oriental features were heavily pock-marked. His lank, straight black hair was swept back from a high forehead and glistened with some sort of oily substance. Clad in a camouflage one piece paratrooper's overalls, he swung a black, aluminium baseball bat back and forth, his almost-obsidian eyes menacing.

'What do want?' Matthew croaked. 'How the hell did you get in here?'

In answer, the man emitted a low-pitched growl. Lunging and swinging the light but nonetheless lethal improvised metal club, he attempted to corner Matthew.

Diving headlong across the low coffee table Matthew crashed into the sliding balcony doors nearly knocking himself unconscious as his head struck the aluminium frame. The baseball bat swished through the air, striking him across his shoulders. Almost paralysed with pain he ducked his head and crash-tackled his adversary. As they fell to the floor Matthew wrapped both arms around the other man's midriff in a crushing bear hug.

Releasing his hold on the bat, the oriental clawed at Matt's face attempting to gouge his eyes out. Matthew sank his teeth in the other man's wrist. Blood spurted hotly against his teeth and the coppery taste filled his mouth. Spitting out the oozing red fluid that threatened to choke him, he drew back his head and smashed his forehead into the bridge of his opponent's nose, crushing bone and cartilage in a crimson spray of bloody snot.

Grunting and swearing, Matthew in English and the other man in something that sounded like Mandarin, they rolled around the floor, knocking over chairs and tables in the ensuing melee. Hanging on and tightening the vice-like embrace even further, Matthew continued to crush the air from his attacker's lungs. Used to doing fifty daily push-ups, his arm muscles were well developed and he knew it was only a matter of time before he began breaking the other man's ribs and perhaps even his spine.

The Chinese attacker must have realised the same thing because he began pounding the back of Matt's head, beating in staccato with iron-hard knuckles. Shaking his head against the excruciating barrage Matthew realised his strength was waning. His already battered body seemed to be telling his brain it could take no more. Releasing his grasp, he rolled away and staggered to his feet, looking down at the would-be assassin.

The Chinaman's fury remained undiminished despite his ruined features. Spitting blood and broken teeth, he leapt to his feet and charged again, emitting a bloodcurdling scream. As Matthew spun to the side he realised the other man was now clasping a lethal-looking stiletto in an underhand grasp.

Fuck, what next!

Grasping the overturned coffee table in both hands, Matthew used it to protect himself from the other man's deadly lunges. Although the table proved to be an excellent shield, it was too heavy and awkward to use as a weapon. Dancing around as if practising some sort of strange ritual, the two men faced off. Suddenly, his assassin swiped at Matt's exposed fingers, the stinging pain forcing him to let go of one side of the table.

With blood dripping onto the carpet from his damaged hand, Matt screamed like a demented peacock. Mustering his remaining strength he swung the coffee table back-handed as if hurling a Frisbee. As it spun across the short space separating the two men, the edge of the table struck the Chinaman on the side of his head. With a clunk that sounded like a hammer striking a watermelon his skull cracked open. Blood and gore spewed across the room. The killer's eyes glazed over and he collapsed in a twitching tangled heap. Staring down at the other man's body Matthew knew without doubt that his attacker would never move again.

Christ, I've just killed someone!

It seemed an eternity but in reality only a few seconds passed as Matthew struggled to regain self-control. His body was shaking now and he felt nauseas. He crossed to the toilet and vomited.

Someone was hammering on the door and shouting. Exhausted and giddy he limped around the failed assassin's corpse just as the door burst open. His protectors burst into the room their Glock semi-automatic pistols at arms' length. Behind them came the tactical response group looking somewhat annoyed that the CPU guys had beaten them to the punch.

'I think you blokes better find me somewhere else to stay tonight,' Matthew said with feigned calmness, 'Preferably, somewhere where I don't get uninvited visitors wielding baseball bats and stilettos.'

The shocked FEDPOL officers couldn't understand how anyone had breached their security measures. Matthew opened the balcony door and gestured. 'I wonder if that rope hanging down from the roof has anything to do with it,' he said sarcastically.

'Get me out of here so you blokes can do whatever you do when someone gets killed trying to commit murder.'

Although Matthew was aware that the investigating officers would immediately expect to get the full details of what had taken place, he was too shocked and exhausted to face their questions. He decided the circumstances justified a little officiousness.

'I've got a busy day tomorrow chaps and I need some sleep. You can come to Parliament House and get my full account of what happened tomorrow. Phone my private secretary and he'll arrange a time to suit us both. Now, I am going to have a shower. By the time I come out, I want to hear that you've found somewhere for me to spend the night.'

FEDPOL's emergency accommodation turned out to be the police barracks. Matt didn't care. If he wasn't safe there, he wouldn't be safe anywhere.

After he was shown to his room Matthew did not go to bed although he ached all over. His minders had wanted to take him to the hospital but he insisted he'd be all right. He'd packed a bag and bandaged his own wounds before leaving the hotel and made sure he had just the medication he needed to dull his aches and pains; a bottle of Johnny Walker Black Label. Instead of going to bed, he filled a tumbler with ice which someone had thoughtfully conjured up from the staff kitchen and poured himself a stiff shot.

After locating a small notebook containing the confidential telephone numbers of influential international figures, he made himself comfortable within easy reach of his laptop computer, and his mobile telephone. Checking his wristwatch he subtracted the sixteen hour time difference between Canberra and New York and discovered it was only 8.00am on America's east coast.

Too bad chaps, it's time for you buggers to begin earning your keep!

Matthew's first call was to a five-storey town house in Sutton Place, Manhattan, home to Ban Ki-Moon, the United Nations Secretary-General. A heavily-accented male voice answered after three rings and Matthew guessed the voice belonged to Ban's butler or some other human guard dog paid to fend off unwanted callers and cranks who had somehow discovered the confidential phone number.

Matthew introduced himself and explained he was ringing on a matter of extreme importance.

'Please, you wait. I see if Mr Ban available to take your call,' the voice responded politely.

Ban's familiar voice came on the line almost immediately. 'Prime Minister, it is a great pleasure to talk to you. It must be something very important for you to call me on my private number so early in the morning and so late at night for you.'

'Secretary-General, I apologise for ringing so early, however I have a cabinet meeting in the morning concerning a very grave situation affecting the entire world so I will not beat about the bush.

'I am calling you as a matter of courtesy. My government has been approached and asked to take a course of action which is very controversial and requires me to stick my neck out so I needed to consult you for your take on the issue. Before I say any more, may I speak off the record?'

'Ah, don't tell me, let me guess. You've been approached by the Woods Hole Institute over declining phytoplankton levels and they've asked you to authorise iron seeding of the oceans.'

Matthew was surprised. How could Ban know that? 'That's correct. I understand they approached you in the hope that the United Nations would pressure countries to rise to the challenge?'

'That is correct, Matthew. I wish it were that easy; however it will take many years to get sufficient votes for their proposal because the London Treaty on dumping waste at sea prohibits that type of action. Signatories to the treaty would need to vote on an amendment and I am sure they would want further studies done to satisfy themselves that such a programme would not cause further damage to the environment.'

'Secretary-General, are you aware of my qualifications and my previous career?'

Ban chuckled. 'How could I not be? I am one of your biggest fans, Matthew. I was also an avid viewer of your television documentaries.'

'Thank you, but I am not looking for kudos. I merely raised the subject because when I tell you that I agree with their conclusions and am seriously considering implementing an iron fertilisation programme you won't think I am acting hastily.'

'Matthew, should I become aware of that in my official capacity I would be required to caution you against taking a course of action that would breach the London Treaty on the dumping of waste products into the oceans. Of course, unless you provide me with an official notification of your country's intentions, I will deny having had this conversation with you.

'I agree that someone needs to act quickly. It was I who told the WHOI people privately to approach you because I knew they could depend upon you to do what must be done.

'I do have to ask though, have you read their report in full?'

'No, there simply hasn't been sufficient time, but don't worry, I will go through it with a fine toothcomb and I'll also ensure I have some of my former CSIRO colleagues examine the report before I make a final decision on seeding the oceans.'

'I am sure there is no need to tell you, but I will anyway. If you go ahead with this, you, your government and your country will receive much criticism. Some nations may even try to block your ships from carrying out the seeding, and you run the risk that sanctions may even be imposed on Australia's exports.

'Your major trading partners are already upset at Australia's plans to phase out coal exports, and there is talk that that was the reason behind Mr Bowker's assassination and the attempt on your own life.'

'Thank you, I am aware of that. WHOI's report has not been made public as yet and I have asked that they do not release it until we have completed a swift and covert seeding campaign. In other words, I am hoping that by the time the world knows there was a problem we will already have solved that problem.'

'I will not breach your trust, but please understand, Australia will pay a very high price if anything goes wrong and even if you are successful your country might be censured by the United Nations for breaching the treaty.'

'Secretary-General, I understand and respect your position and I thank you for your private support. In my experience, it is always the same when someone takes bold and courageous actions; succeed and you are celebrated as a hero. Everyone forgives and forgets your impulsiveness. On the other hand when one fails, one's friends run for cover and there is a rush to see who will hurl the first stone.

'I cannot stand idly by and do nothing if there is a chance of saving the planet.'

'I will pray for your success, Matthew.'

I hope the Panther is as supportive.

After considerable delay during which Matthew's call was re-directed several times, President Clement Turnbull finally came on the line. Just as he had with the secretary-general, Matthew apologised for the early telephone call and explained its urgency.

'Clement, I understand the WHOI scientists have already approached you but you told them the United States won't commit to a seeding programme in because you consider America would be in breach of the London Convention, is that correct?' As soon as the words had left his lips Matthew realised the president might think he was being accused of lacking political courage so he hastened to add, 'Given that the United States always seems to be the one who's asked to put its head on the chopping block whenever there's a new war or an international crisis, I can understand your reluctance. I can also understand that you're probably bombarded with scaremongers and doomsayers on a daily basis, but I am well informed on the subject of phytoplankton loss and its implications and I would like you take another look at their report and give it further consideration.'

'Matthew, I am in a very difficult situation at the moment. My new Medicare reforms have faced stiff opposition from within my own party due to the global financial crisis and I've just managed to get sufficient votes to ensure the bill is passed. I don't want to do anything that will jeopardise that and I fear if it becomes known I am using US resources in breach of the London Treaty that support will be withdrawn.'

Matthew was almost struck dumb by the flaws in the president's reasoning. *Bloody hell, the future of all humanity is at stake and you're worried about some stupid healthcare reforms? There won't be anybody to use those reforms if we don't take action!*

Matthew was so astounded that he automatically reverted to using the president's official title as he responded sarcastically. 'Mr President, it's rather stupid of me to expect that the president of the United States of America would understand the gravity of this crisis. I apologise. The lives of seven billion people and the future of all the life on this planet are obviously nowhere near as important as your healthcare reforms.'

'Who the hell do you think you're speaking to?' the Panther spluttered.

'Obviously not the man I'd placed on a pedestal as the greatest leader in the Free World. I won't bother you any more, sir, unless you come to your senses. Good night!' Matthew slammed the phone down, his blood boiling. How can somebody with so much political savvy and power be so blind? he asked himself.

+++++++++++++

Chapter Twenty-Four

Satisfied that there was nothing more he could do to find Richard Nolan, James Fleming busied himself with the mountain of paperwork that had continued to pile up in his in-tray. Because matters requiring his attention were simply piled on top of each other as they arrived in the tray, he upended the basket on his desk and began attending to items from the bottom of the pile. He applied the same practice to his emails, starting with the oldest message first, a habit that sometimes caused problems, especially if a later message updating the first escaped his attention.

And so, it was early the following morning before Fleming cursed his pedantry with a universally-adopted, four-letter expletive for missing the vitally important communication concerning the hunt for Nolan. Snatching his iPhone, he composed a text message to the operatives searching for Nolan:

> **The pigeon has flown the coop to Denpasar. He is now a different-looking bird. Catch him ASAP. Put him in a cage and then contact me immediately.**

Fleming examined the email from the Defence Signals Directorate again. While he cursed himself for not having read the message earlier, he congratulated himself for requesting that the directorate's very effective, electronic spy network flag Nolan's outgoing emails which had borne fruit and captured the former federal agent's message to John McCarthy.

Nolan's email disturbed him for several reasons. Firstly McCarthy and Thompson obviously knew about the recordings. Secondly, they had launched a private manhunt. Thirdly, they were hoping to negotiate a deal with Nolan that would bring him and Bacon down, and lastly, the pair now knew Nolan's approximate whereabouts.

Fleming was also puzzled. Why didn't McCarthy trust the Australian Federal Police? Did he think FEDPOL's hierarchy was in league with Bacon and him? Who else knew about the recordings? No doubt McCarthy had confided in the prime minister, but without hard proof, or Nolan's testimony, there was little they could do provided he got to Nolan first and offered him a deal he could not refuse.

The ASIO Director-General decided to gamble on the diligence of his investigators. Writing a short, hurried memo to his secretary, he advised her that he would not be contactable until further notice and instructed that his wife, and anyone else who inquired, was to be told he was on confidential business. He grabbed his briefcase, and a travel bag that he kept packed for such emergencies, and raced to his car, confident that his position as the head of ASIO would snag him a seat on Jetstar's 11.30am Sydney to Bali flight.

At least, McCarthy and the Feds aren't aware where Nolan is hiding, so I've got a good chance of getting the sneaky bastard before they do.

'Pack your bags, Annie my girl,' McCarthy instructed Thompson via his mobile phone. 'I've just got a reply from Dickie-boy saying he's in Bali and he's prepared to negotiate a deal, as long as we come alone.

'I'll pick you up in thirty minutes. We're on the next plane to Sydney. Unfortunately, we'll have to hang around Sydney for a few hours because the 5.35pm to Denpasar is the first flight with seats available.'

'Have you been there before?' Annette asked. 'I have, and I am not really looking forward to going there again.'

McCarthy was surprised. He thought like most young people, she'd have a love affair with the Indonesia's most popular holiday resort. 'No, I haven't had the pleasure. Why don't you want to go there again?'

'I was in Kuta during the 2002 bombings. I lost a close friend and the images of the carnage will stay with me forever. I am also worried the terrorists have been too quiet. I am frightened that they'll strike again soon.'

'Bugger, I didn't know that, Annette, I'm sorry. If you want to give it a miss I'll understand.'

'What, and have you bumbling around by yourself?' she pretended to scold him. 'You know you'd only stuff it up without me, so I've got no choice, have I?'

With up to thirty-three Sydney bound flights per day, it would have been a fluke if McCarthy and Thompson had arrived at the Canberra airport and bumped into the ASIO boss before his 9.55am Qantas flight lifted off. As it was, they missed him by a mere twenty-five minutes and by the time they landed at Sydney's bustling Kingsford Smith international terminal Fleming was already winging his way to Denpasar.

After checking their bags through, John McCarthy and Annette Thompson decided there was little point travelling into Sydney's CBD to fill in the afternoon so they made their way to the airport restaurant.

'My shout,' John announced. 'I hate the way every airport throughout the world assumes it has a license to rip travellers off and serve such lousy food.'

'At least it's marginally better than the plastic muck that passes for food that the airlines dish up to economy-class passengers,' Annette responded as they slid in behind a crowd of yabbering Japanese tourists who were queuing ahead of them.

After waiting nearly half an hour as the camera-bedecked mob ahead of them debated the merits of the various menu items, John and Annette negotiated through the chaos of over-crowded tables and carelessly placed luggage. Locating the only free table they cleared the detritus of spilt food and empty plates and settled down to a repast of dog-eared club sandwiches and rapidly-cooling coffee. John decided to quiz his companion about Denpasar and the Bali bombings.

'You must have been pretty young then,' he remarked.

'I had just finished Year 12. Like so many young people who finish high school, I went there with friends to celebrate schoolies week. As you know two-hundred-and-two people died, including eighty-eight Australians. A further two-hundred-and-two suffered horrific injuries.'

Annette's brow puckered as the memories and emotions flooded back and John wished he'd not raised the subject because he'd come to regard this young woman with the same fatherly affection he felt for his own kin. 'Sorry, Annie, don't go there if it's too painful,' he said softly.

The policewomen straightened her posture and with it her resolve. 'It's okay. I joined the military after that, because I hoped I could to do something useful toward ensuring evil bastards like Imam Samudra, Amrozi and Huda bin Abdul Haq couldn't spread their hatred and slaughter ordinary innocent people. God, how do people's minds become so twisted?'

'Now I know why you were so concerned about security at the Lodge when I met you for the first time.'

'If I hadn't had a dose of Bali belly, I would have been in the Sari nightclub when the bomb went off. Instead, I was yelling into the big white telephone in my hotel room when I heard the explosion. Somehow, I knew straight away what had happened. I ran down to the Sari Club looking for my friend Elizabeth. I never want to see such a horrible sight again. The television coverage of the incident was pretty graphic, but they cut out all the worst bits; the body parts everywhere, people screaming in pain, people on fire, people with arms and legs torn off, and the smell. I still have nightmares about it.

'Although I searched, I never did find Lizzy. There were people crying for help and I had to give up in the end and lend a hand. They dug poor Lizzy's remains out of the debris later and her family had to fly from Australia to identify what was left of her. Shit, I can't imagine how hard it must have been for them. So don't be surprised if I get a bit weepy and want to spend some time at the memorial paying my respects.'

'Until Jambali attacked the Lodge and JI nearly succeeded in blowing up so many other targets I only knew what I read in the papers and from watching TV. I made a point of doing a bit of research because I wanted to see if I could get a handle on who might have backed Jambali and Nibras. I knew there had to be a well organised and well-funded network with links in this country for them to nearly pull off such an ambitious and concerted campaign against Australia. I didn't realise certain individuals in Indonesia's police and military were implicated.'

'Yes, but they were never charged. In fact an Indonesian Air Force General who was arrested had to be released on the government's orders, but that bloody country is so corrupt that anything could happen.'

'I am still wondering who financed Jambali and Nibras. Al Qaeda's been pretty well decimated financially from what I hear, so they probably got their funds from somewhere closer to home.'

'Let's hope my Federal Police colleagues and the intelligence services get to the bottom of it.'

For the umpteenth time, Richard Nolan wondered if he'd done the right thing by answering McCarthy's email. After all, hadn't he managed to drive from one side of Australia to the other, book a flight using his forged passport, evade Customs and his fellow FEDPOL officers, fly to Denpasar, and then pass through Bali's security without incident? He was almost home and hosed as they say, so why risk blowing it all at such a late stage?

Although Nolan was filled with self-loathing, he knew the answer lay in the intrinsic decency and sense of fair play that he still clung to despite his involvement in an attempt on the prime minister's life and the events in the Persian Gulf that had initiated his downfall. His abiding love for Jennifer and their children and the prospect of never seeing them again also played heavily on his mind along with the fear they'd all be pilloried for his sins. So when McCarthy's email arrived, it fanned the flames of his blazing desire for forgiveness and redemption.

Knowing cheap air fares and Bali's low prices attracted so many Australians to the holiday resort, he hesitated to expose himself unnecessarily to the risk of discovery, choosing to hide out in his hotel room until he negotiated a deal with McCarthy, or headed to the Philippines for the next stage of his disappearance.

McCarthy had said he'd catch the 5.35pm flight from Sydney which arrived in Denpasar at midnight. Nolan had not revealed where he was staying or the name he was using, so McCarthy and Thompson were to book into a hotel and then send a text to set up the rendezvous. He was only moderately surprised when his phone announced an incoming message at 6.00pm.

"Perhaps they've snagged an earlier flight,' he mumbled as he checked the phone's tiny screen.

Got in early. Meet room 54. Aston Kuta Hotel.

Nolan checked the sender's number to ensure the message had come from McCarthy. Unfortunately, the simple precaution was useless. ASIO agents deployed by Fleming had already hacked McCarthy's mobile using a little-known and commercially available App that enabled them to then piggy-back the security man's telephone and not only capture incoming calls, but also send texts and telephone anyone at will using McCarthy's number.

Because the Aston was only a five minute walk away from his hotel, Nolan decided to head there on foot. A thunderstorm had just passed, making the streets slippery. With the humidity close to 100 percent his shirt stuck to his skin and the city's strange mixture of petrol fumes, overflowing drains, street-side food stalls and sweat seemed more intense than ever. Elbowing his way through the ever-present hawkers, he hurried to his meeting, eager to sort out the arrangements for his return to Australia.

So eager was he that he failed to notice the two men keeping pace with him on the other side of Jalan Kartika Plaza.

Turning right into Ji Wana Segara he located the hotel and slipped through the crowded foyer to the lifts, admiring the large, sparkling swimming pool around which the hotel had been built. He stepped out of the lift on the fifth floor and checked the room numbers to see which way he needed to go to locate room fifty-four. As he turned to head down the corridor, two men wearing tropical suits appeared from a room behind him. Glancing over his shoulder, he concluded they were guests making their way toward the lifts and took no notice as they passed either side of him.

Without warning the men spun around in unison. The man on his left applied a wrist hold on Nolan's right arm and the other clamped a hand over Nolan's mouth at the same time slipping behind him and seizing him in a headlock.

Taken completely by surprise, the federal agent was unable to break free from their grasp as they propelled him backwards into the room from which they'd just come. A third man pulled a bag over his head and then something pricked Nolan's arm. His vision blurred, his head swam, his legs buckled beneath him and he slipped immediately into a dreamless sleep.

'Got the bastard!' ASIO agent Rocky Doss grinned happily.

'Silly prick. It takes more than a change of appearance and a false passport to fool professionals,' the second agent responded, referring to how they'd bribed Bali's airport authorities to access incoming passenger lists and airport CCTV. They'd then compiled a list of all European males of a similar height and build to Richard Nolan who had travelled alone from Australia airports during the appropriate time frame.

While they'd almost eliminated passengers from Port Hedland due to its remoteness, Doss had insisted his team of six agents leave no stone unturned. Despite that, the list hadn't consisted of any more than twenty names; the most exhausting part had been talking to the hundreds of Denpasar taxi drivers and working through hotel registers to find their quarry.

'Yeah, and that email to McCarthy telling him how to set up their meeting made our job so much easier in the end.' Rocky smiled as he finished tying their unconscious captive's legs and wrists. 'Anyway, the big boss should be arriving shortly. Better send him a text saying, "Mission accomplished."'

As Flipper Fleming's flight taxied to the Ngurah Rai International Airport terminal, he switched on his mobile telephone and smiled in satisfaction as he read Arockia Doss's two word message. Taking his only item of luggage from the overhead locker he made sure he beat the other first-class passengers to the Boeing's forward exit door. When the door opened, he ignored the female cabin attendant's artificial smile and her expression of gratitude for flying with Qantas which had all the sincerity of a politician's election promise and made his way to the Hertz counter to collect his pre-booked rental vehicle.

Fleming was no stranger to the Indonesian province of Bali and the rapidly expanding city of Denpasar, whose population density of two million residents and municipal sprawl was roughly equivalent to San Francisco, and the ten minute drive to Kuta posed no problem.

As the Head of ASIO drew to a halt, the Aston's concierge saluted the obviously wealthy and distinguished-looking Australian. He accepted Fleming's generous tip with a small bow as he took the car keys and snapped his fingers, signalling for another employee to take care of parking the vehicle. Rocky Doss met Fleming in the hotel lobby and hastened to assure him he had already taken care of his boss's accommodation arrangements.

If Doss had expected any praise from Fleming he'd have been very disappointed. 'I hope you've got the bastard well and truly under lock and key,' was all Fleming growled.

Doss made the appropriate noises of reassurance and escorted the director-general to room 54 where Nolan had regained consciousness and was angrily sipping a glass of water.

Fleming glanced around the room, taking in the gaudy orange and red walls, patterned orange bedspreads covered in cushions and the ochre carpet. The room reminded him of a bordello and he wrinkled his nose in disgust. 'Christ, are you trying to make me throw up? Couldn't you have found something more Western? This joint looks like a fucking brothel.'

Doss, who could see nothing wrong with the decor, looked offended. 'You were right about him making wild claims, sir. He keeps raving on about his solicitor having tape recordings that will be released to the media and create an international scandal if anything happens to him. What is all that about?'

'That's none of your concern, son. I told you the man's a dangerous psychotic. Now, I want you and your mates here to leave me alone with Mr Nolan while we have a nice little chat.'

After the three operatives had left the room, Fleming switched on the large-screen television set and turned the volume to high. He withdrew a small electronic device from his briefcase and in answer to Nolan's inquisitive stare said, 'It's just a little white noise generator, Dickie, so don't worry. I might be paranoid but I don't want anybody else recording my conversations, you've done quite enough of that.'

'Arr, fuck off, Flipper,' Nolan spat. 'Things must be pretty bad in ASIO when you can't even trust your own blokes.'

'Trust, now there's a word you'd know nothing about. Your navy mates trusted you, and look where it got them. Still, Dickie, I am not here to talk about old times, so let's not squabble. It seems we have a little impasse that needs to be resolved.'

'You're up shit creek mate. The McCarthys know there's evidence in existence to sink you and Bacon, and if you do anything to me, you and your slimy mate will find yourselves in Long Bay, or some other less-than-cosy maximum security prison. By the way, did you know the death penalty still applies to treason?'

'Don't try that one on me. Remember I was a federal policeman and know full well the Death Penalty Abolition Act of 1973 abolished the death penalty for all federal offences and the last state to execute anyone was Victoria with the hanging of Ronald Ryan in 1967. Capital punishment was abolished by all states with New South Wales being the last way back in 1985. You know as well as I do, that in Australia life imprisonment is the maximum penalty the courts can apply. Only the worst murderers stay behind bars for the rest of their natural. It's a pity in a way, because if push comes to shove you'd be joining me at the gallows.

'However, it's not going to come to that Dickie-boy. You're going to instruct you solicitor to hand over the recordings and you'll then continue with your little disappearing act and keep your mouth shut.

'Without those recordings no one can touch us. The senator and I have been around long enough to know how to handle innuendo and groundless allegations. I get them all the time in my job.'

Richard Nolan was well aware of everything Fleming had said about capital punishment but he'd been playing for time. He tried another tack. 'You need to know I've made copies. I am hanging onto those, otherwise there's nothing to stop you having me bumped off at some later date.'

'No, Richard, you're going to make sure I get every last copy and you're just going to have to trust me.'

'I wouldn't trust you as far as I could kick your big fat poofter arse, you bloody turd-burglar. Those copies are my life insurance; what makes you think I'd give them up?'

Fleming sighed heavily. 'Tsk, tsk, such nasty language. Let me ask Dickie, do you love your wife and kids?'

Nolan's face paled at the implication. 'I don't care what happens to me. Keep them out of this or I'll make sure you and Bacon die the most painful and horrible deaths I can think of.'

'Dear me, Richard, you're in no position to threaten me, in fact, if I was a man who plays chess, I'd say this is check-mate, so I want you to draft a little letter to your solicitor instructing him to courier whatever it is he's holding for you to Phillip Bacon's apartment. Don't worry, I'll tell you what to say. Then,

I want your other copies. After that, it's just a matter of waiting until I hear from the good senator. It shouldn't take too long, you can go on your merry way and life will return to normal for the rest of us.'

++++++++++++++++++

Chapter Twenty-Five

Matthew was dreaming a beautiful, peaceful dream of sparkling, crystal waters, warm sunshine, seagulls cawing raucously and waves lapping against the hull of a cabin cruiser as he and Catherine made passionate love on the deck. He was kissing the honey-brown skin of her breasts and tickling her nipples gently with his tongue. She moaned in delight and grasped his manhood firmly with one hand, the other stroking his face.

They were somewhere in New Zealand, he thought. Probably the Queen Charlotte Sound because there was a ship gliding past. It looked like the old Wahine that had tragically sunk with the loss of so many lives during a terrible winter gale of 1968. He wondered how she was here now with passengers waving and cheering from her decks. Had they built a replica? No. There was no way anyone would ever give that name to a ship again. It must be a sister ship.

'Let's really give them something to cheer about,' he murmured to Catherine and slid into her.

Bang. Bang. Bang.

What's that noise?

Matthew opened his eyes slowly, wondering where he was. His head felt as if it would explode. A dull ache emanated from the base of his skull spreading upward to the top of his head. Sharp pains behind his eyes were as if someone were trying to poke his eyeballs out from the inside. His body felt as if he'd been run over by a bus. He groaned and closed his eyes again, hoping to slip back into the delightfully sensuous dream.

BANG. BANG. BANG. BANG.

'Prime Minister, excuse me for waking you. It's seven o'clock sir and you asked me to not to let you sleep in,' someone shouted from the other side of the door.

'Okay, okay. Thanks, I'm awake now. I'll be out in a few minutes,' Matthew croaked.

Making his way to the bathroom, he stood under the stinging spray from the shower, letting the water course down his face in the hope it would wash away the pounding in his head and the sour taste that filled his mouth. Scrubbing his teeth so furiously it was a wonder they didn't disintegrate, he popped three Panadol Osteo before dressing and making his way to the AFP mess hall only to find Stormy Knight was his breakfast companion.

'This is a pleasant surprise, Harold,' Matt greeted him with forced jocularity. 'Slumming it?'

The commissioner seemed unusually terse. 'You're proving a bit of a handful Matt. I heard what happened last night and thought it only proper I come and see for myself that you're okay.'

'Nothing a good feed of carbs and caffeine won't fix.' Matthew smiled as the two men slid in behind twenty or so police recruits lining up for breakfast.

Awestruck by such exalted presence the recruits stepped to one side in deference. Matthew grinned at them. 'No, you blokes carry on, thanks. The commish and I aren't queue jumpers are we, Commissioner.'

After filling their plates, Stormy steered the prime minister to a table that had been set aside for them, the clatter of the cafeteria guaranteeing they would not be overheard.

'So, have you got any news on the Chinaman?' Matt wanted to know.

'Only that he had just recently been hired to work in the kitchen. We searched his digs of course and printed his corpse and DNA tests are being carried out but I don't think we'll find anything on our databases. His passport's a fake. Shows him to be a student from the People's Republic of China which begs the question as to why the hotel was providing employment to someone who was clearly prohibited from working.

'They'll be in the manure with Immigration but that's the least of my concerns. We're tipping he was an assassin sent by the Chinese Government who are upset at the prospect of cessation of their coal imports. Of course, they'll deny it and I doubt whether we'll ever prove anything.'

'It seems there's an endless list of people prepared to bump me off. If I had life insurance the policy underwriters would be getting pretty worried.

'So, was I correct in assuming he'd abseiled down from the roof?'

'Yes. We found two karabiners and a nylon harness on the balcony. His choice of weapon seems a little unusual but we're speculating he wanted to make your death look like a robbery gone wrong.

'I've suspended the two close personal protection blokes who were on duty last night and demanded a full explanation from Curly Clews as to the inadequacy of the risk assessment on the hotel by his people.'

Matthew was horrified. 'You've what? For Christ's sake Harold, don't do that please. It's not their fault. Curly is a good operator and hindsight is a wonderful thing.' At this juncture Matthew felt he should offer some explanation as to why his father had not also conducted a threat assessment on the hotel but he didn't quite know how to account for John's absence without lying outright.

'Nevertheless, there will have to be a full enquiry. Speaking of which, we'll need a statement from you as soon as possible.

'Do you know you're even more of a bloody hero now? The media's dubbed you "Matt the Mauler".'

'Oh please,' Matthew groaned.

'Matthew, something else is bothering me.'

'What's that Harold?' Here it comes, Matthew thought.

'I haven't seen your father for a while. I thought he'd want to check out the hotel's security measures too. Is everything all right?'

Matthew hated himself for not taking the commissioner into his confidence. He knew Knight would be furious when he discovered he had sanctioned John's private investigation on the basis that both the head of AFP and ASIO might be corrupt. But until he learnt otherwise what could he do?

'Dad's actually attending to a personal matter for me,' he lied. 'Otherwise he would have checked out the hotel, but he'll be back on deck soon.'

Stormy wasn't going to be put off so easily. 'Why would he enlist Constable Thompson to help him? And why would they fly to Bali together?'

'Harold, I should have known your airport people would report on their departure and you'd hear about it, but I am just going to have to ask you to trust me when I say Dad is following up on something that's directly related to his role as my security advisor. I promise you, you will be the first to know the result of his investigation when the time is right.'

Harold Knight sighed heavily. 'Okay, Matt. I wouldn't like to think you don't have confidence in the AFP, that's all.'

'I think the AFP is Australia's finest law enforcement body and I have the greatest confidence in the organisation,' Matthew replied truthfully. *I wish I could be one hundred percent sure that statement includes its commissioner.*

Using decoy AFP and Commonwealth Government vehicles to confuse the waiting media pack, Matthew managed to gain access to his Parliament House office without incident. His bruised and battered face would be plastered over the pages of the world's newspapers and television screens soon enough.

Brushing aside his colleagues' concerns and curiosity over the night's events with a laconic, 'I am okay. You can read about it in the Australian,' he hustled his Cabinet together for a briefing by WHOI.

Harry and Somerville didn't disappoint. Armed with a very professionally prepared PowerPoint presentation which laid out the evidence coldly and without hyperbole, they left little room for doubt or conjecture. The consequences of rapidly declining phytoplankton levels would be calamitous.

'How much iron compound will be needed and how sure are you that this will work?' Phoebe Swan wanted to know.

Although Somerville had already covered this point, he understood many of his audience had been distracted by the sheer gravity of the situation and had probably not absorbed the finer details.

"Back in 1988 John Gribben was the first scientist to propose iron fertilisation. He published an article in the Nature Journal saying he was confident that it could be done without environmental damage.

'Gribben sowed the seed, no pun intended, and there's been a lot of work done since that time assessing the required quantities, the size of the particles, the best oceans for distribution, which by the way, must include high levels of silicic acid, and the manner of distribution.

'The quantities are miniscule in the scheme of things. In 1991, Professor Martin from our institute hypothesised that he could create another ice age with just half a super tanker of fine iron particles. While that may have been a spur of the moment exaggeration to make a point, it does illustrate that a comparatively small amount of iron distributed in the right locations can have a significant effect.' Somerville paused and peered at his audience over the rim of his glasses. 'We certainly don't suggest starting another ice age.'

'So, the cost is not astronomical then?' Peter Hamilton, the treasurer, inquired.

Debra Harry piped up, 'Fine iron particles are currently selling for as little as $133.50 per tonne. We estimate two-hundred-thousand tonnes of iron distributed across suitable oceans each year will restore all the lost plankton and sequester three gigatonnes of carbon dioxide each year.'

Hamilton tapped at his calculator. 'Professor Harry, I've calculated the cost per annum at two-hundred-and-sixty-six million dollars.'

'Yes, but please bear in mind the actual cost is dependent upon the actual life of the phytoplankton blooms, ocean eddies and currents holding the iron particles in suspension long enough for the blooms to take place, and the possibility of other marine species gorging themselves on the resultant phytoplankton before they can sequester sufficient CO2.

'But don't be put off by this please. As you know, it is only a matter of time before most countries agree to introduce a price on carbon which could be anywhere from $US5 to $US20 per tonne depending upon the costs associated with scrubbing, direct injection of CO2 and other industrial approaches for CO2 sequestration.

'When this occurs, Australia will be in the box seat to capitalise on a huge carbon offset market using phytoplankton sequestration. In fact, our estimates indicate that a full-scale phytoplankton restoration programme could reap between seventy and one-hundred-and-forty billion dollars per year.'

Somerville felt the need to get back to the issue at hand. 'Let's not get blinded by the financial advantages for your country. While they are potentially significant it is far more important to save marine ecosystems.'

'I am still not convinced,' McCarthy's defence minister, Angus Cameron, grumbled. 'Isn't there a significant risk of creating toxic red tides and other harmful algal blooms that could actually kill off marine species? And before you answer that, I understand that excessive levels of faecal matter may result from creatures feeding on large phytoplankton blooms. Won't this create an anoxic environment on the ocean floor and kill off creatures that exist there?'

Matthew was surprised at Cameron's knowledge and felt the urge to respond but held his tongue. His political cohorts had a tendency to forget that he was also a marine scientist and the answer would carry more weight coming from the WHOI experts.

'You are correct on both counts,' Somerville replied, 'But there would only be a problem if we conducted iron seeding close to the shoreline and this would be pointless. Fertilisation is only effective in the deep oceans where iron levels are insufficient for phytoplankton growth, so red tides and toxic blooms will simply not occur.

'As to the destruction of benthic, that is, bottom-dwelling sea creatures, this is extremely unlikely because it would entail removing the oxygen from thousands of cubic kilometres of benthic seawater beneath the bloom. Further to that, studies on major phytoplankton blooms resulting from dust storms have failed to detect any such deep water die-offs.'

'Australia does not have the ships capable of carrying the sort of quantities you're talking about,' Cameron observed. 'What type of vessels did you have in mind?'

Until now both younger WHOI scientists had merely listened and nodded. Now, Harry turned to Roger Bayzand and said, smiling, 'I'll defer to Roger on that point. He's our resident ship expert.'

Bayzand got to his feet and flicked his lank black hair away from his eyes. Unrolling a large chart which he hung from a tripod he cleared his throat and began talking nervously in a rather high-pitched voice. 'This chart produced by Lloyds shows two categories of ships: dry bulk carriers and crude oil tankers. We're interested in the dry bulk carriers for obvious reasons and there are six classes within that category. These are Handy, Handymax, Capesize, Very Large Ore Carriers, or VLOCs, and Ultra Large Ore Carriers, or ULOCs.

'VLOCs use your ports all the time. However, they have a capacity well above that needed so we'd suggest using three Capesize carriers.

'Capesize carriers get their name from the fact that they are incapable of using the Panama or Suez canals due to their size and therefore must pass around Cape Horn and the Cape of Good Hope. They carry between eighty thousand and one-hundred-and-seventy-five thousand tonnes.

'Of course, whether they are available or not is another matter. You may have to opt for several smaller ships of the Handymax class which have a capacity of seventy-five thousand tonnes dead weight.

'Distribution of iron particles in the optimum range of 0.5–1 micrometre or less can be undertaken using ordinary agricultural type vacuum blowers capable of drawing the particles from the ship's hold and scattering them across the surface of the ocean using wide spray nozzles at the rate of 104 tonnes per hour. This means each ship would have to remain in its target area for approximately one month during which time continuous monitoring would take place.

'The Southern Ocean should be one of the best sites for this program because diatoms, coccolithophores and foraminifera grow well under sea ice and form the very basis of the marine food chain. We anticipate whale and pelagic fish populations will also benefit significantly from increased krill production.

'Perhaps, given time, we might even restore the world's fish stocks,' Bayzand finished hopefully.

The more academic members of McCarthy's Cabinet pressed the WHOI scientists on the intricate details of the plan, however most could not be bothered with the complex mathematical equations, botanical names, references to circumpolar currents and thermoclines and other head-swimming data that formed the basis of WHOI's research. Happy to accept the information they'd been given, they gave their blessing to the programme and hurried from the meeting.

While most headed off to prepare for that day's session of parliament, Phoebe Swan had other things on her mind. Slipping away to a quiet corner, she speed-dialled Keith Sutton, a malicious glint burning brightly in her green eyes.

+++++++++++

Chapter Twenty-Six

McCarthy and Thompson's plane touched down on schedule at the Ngurah Rai International Airport. Just as Fleming had, John immediately turned on his mobile as soon as cabin signs signalled it was okay, hoping there would be a message waiting for him from Nolan.

'The blighter's probably gone to bed. After all, it is after midnight. We can't do anything until we hear from him in the morning so let's go to the Mandira Beach Resort, find our rooms and have a damn good night's sleep. I am sure he'll be in touch first thing.'

Having stayed at the Mandira previously, Annette knew the deluxe cottage suites with their high ceilings and huge picture windows overlooking the faux-tropical jungle which surrounded the huge starlight pool would take John's breath away. She was right.

'Wow. This must cost a bloody fortune,' John exclaimed as he threw open the door to his suite and took in the spacious bedroom with its king size bed and enormous en-suite.

'You wait until you see the rest of it. The food's out of this world too.'

'Pity, we're not on holiday,' John reminded her. 'I doubt we'll have time to appreciate such luxury.'

'Oh, you bloody old wet blanket,' Annette grumbled. 'At least you'll get an idea why so many people like coming to Bali and maybe I'll even convert you. I am sure Mary would love it.'

At the mention of his wife's name John's face fell. 'Poor Mare, she hasn't seen much of me lately. Maybe I will bring her here when this is all over. She deserves a treat after all she's been through. I hope she doesn't think you and I are having an affair, or something silly.'

'How long have you been married now, John?'

'Forty-five years. Why?'

'Well, I think I'm a pretty good judge of character and I'm sure you wouldn't have strayed in all that time, have you?'

'Of course not, I've got the best little missus in the world.'

'There you go then. Mary knows you well enough by now to trust you. Apart from that, she and I have had our little chats and she knows I don't go for old blokes.'

'Well, thanks very much,' John replied indignantly. 'Not so much of the "old" thank you.'

John woke at 4:30 the following morning. Although the night's black velvet blanket still swathed the city in a cool embrace, he knew the tropical sun would soon burst above the horizon, replacing the stars' twinkling beauty with its white hot fierceness.

Knowing he'd not sleep any more, he donned a pair of swimming shorts, strangely remembering a certain Australian politician made famous by his obscenely-brief swimming trunks appropriately termed budgie smugglers. He grabbed one of the hotel's huge, thirsty towels and slipped quietly outside to the vast, deserted pool where he swam laps for the next thirty minutes. He had just finishing towelling himself when Annette appeared from her adjoining suite clad in skimpy blue denim shorts, a sleeveless, bright-yellow, cotton blouse, already made up and looking gorgeous.

'What's the matter, old man?' she teased him. 'Why are you up so early? Did you wet the bed?'

'Bloody hell, you're beginning to show me about as much respect as my own kids,' he responded, promptly shouldering her fully-clothed form into the pool. 'See you at breakfast, you cheeky tart,' he called, sprinting to his room and locking the door, laughing like a teenager.

I might be a bit long-in-the-tooth, but there's plenty of life in the old dog yet.

John and Annette breakfasted early. She had taken her dunking with good humour despite having to re-do her hair and make-up, although she secretly vowed to even the score as they lined up to order. John went for the full Aussie breakfast of bacon, eggs, hash browns, beans and tomatoes while Annette chose a muffin and a fruit platter containing a delightful array of mouth-watering tropical fruits.

By 7.00am Nolan had not yet made contact so John decided to walk off the food before the pre-monsoonal sun and the humidity became unbearable. As soon as he stepped onto the pavement the street pedlars seemed to appear from nowhere and began pestering him. He increased his pace to a fast jog to avoid them. Two-wheeled vehicles were obviously the most popular form of transport. Buzzing everywhere like angry mosquitoes, they filled the already-crowded and chaotic streets. Shirtless westerner males accompanied by scantily-clad girls of all nationalities wandered aimlessly taking in the sights and occasionally pausing to barter for pirated CDs, copied watches and an amazing variety of other cheap paraphernalia.

While most people seemed unaffected by the constant cacophony of car horns, traffic noise, jabbering humanity, the preponderance of advertising signs and the confusing miasma of smells, John found the bustling resort almost overpowering until almost by accident, he stumbled onto Kuta's world-renowned beach.

While ten thousand or more of yesterday's tourists had churned the sand into a million miniature meteor-like craters, the beach was not yet littered with the almost-naked, well-oiled bodies that would soon make it difficult to find a clear place to sit.

John sucked in the tangy salt breezes wafting over the surf break to wash the polluted city air from his lungs before turning to make his way back to the hotel. Suddenly, he stopped. In his peripheral vision he'd caught a glimpse of a familiar, safari-suited figure in the distance. He turned instinctively to see if he could identify the man who appeared to have just completed an early morning walk. His jaw dropped.

Christ, surely that's not bloody Flipper Fleming?

The implications of the ASIO boss being in Bali at the same time as he and Annette hit him with a sledge-hammer-like blow.

My God, ASIO's located Nolan!

There was no cover, so John squatted on the sand to reduce his profile in case Flipper glanced back and spied him, but Fleming kept walking, increasing his pace as he disappeared into the crowded streets. Leaping to his feet, John sprinted to catch up. Realising Nolan was probably already in custody and would never make contact, it was vitally important that he track the other man in the hope Fleming would lead him to where Nolan was being held.

Just when he thought he'd lost his quarry, John spotted the taupe safari jacket and Fleming's grey, balding dome up above the shorter statured locals. Having no idea where he was, he looked around frantically for a street sign but couldn't find one.

Muttering apologies as he elbowed his way through the meandering tourists and omnipresent street sellers, he began to close the gap as the other man weaved his way purposefully through the jostling throngs, oblivious to McCarthy's presence.

His hands clammy with sweat, John fumbled for his phone, realising the need to let Thompson know where he was and alert her to the fact that ASIO agents were in Bali and probably had Nolan in custody.

Shit, no phone!

He slapped his pockets again, frantically wondering if he'd dropped it before it dawned on him that he'd left it in his hotel suite. Panic now threatened to overwhelm him and his heart was like a pile driver in his chest. Taking a deep breath, he struggled to regain his composure. How could he warn Annette? How was he going to maintain surveillance without back up? It was only by sheer blind luck that he spotted Fleming when he had. Now, so much depended upon following him to wherever it was he was holding Nolan.

Cursing softly to himself, John became aware that people were casting strange looks his way, no doubt wondering why a tall, sweating, agitated and elderly Western man was looking so upset so early in the day.

What a blow it would be to lose Fleming now, he thought as, like a ship making heavy weather against the current of a swiftly flowing river, he shoved resolutely through the chaos and the crush of humanity.

Balinese women with overloaded baskets of fruit and vegetables balanced precariously on their heads smiled at him coquettishly and he marvelled at their grace and composure. Squatting men with foul, unhygienic cigarettes hanging from their lips implored him to stop and sample all sorts of strange and exotic food. Rows and rows of chattering, twittering, and brightly-coloured birds in cages formed a thirty metre corridor either side. Monkeys with chains around their necks blinked sadly at him, as with little hands, they reached to pluck at his shirt. Ponging platters of fish turning rapidly foul in the heat seemed to abound, and there were stalls selling anything from handbags to cameras at miniscule prices. He'd never experienced such congestion and so many fascinating sights and wished he had the time to loiter but he focussed on his quarry and kept stumbling on in pursuit.

That he and Annette had little chance of springing Nolan from his captors never entered John's mind. He'd jump that hurdle when he came to it. Just finding where Nolan was being held would be sufficient for now.

You're a trained professional, John. You used to do this for a living. Remember? Yeah, right. That was forty years ago!

*Perhaps, Annette's right. I **am** an old bloke and this is a young man's game. I'm a bit like the dog that chased the tiger and then found itself wondering what it was going to do next when it actually caught it.*

Up ahead, Fleming turned the corner and John sprinted to close the gap lest his prey disappear down one of the many alleyways.

No, it's all right. There he is, just going into that hotel. What's it called? Where am I anyway?

There, in bold letters at last, a street sign announced: "Ji. Wana Segara" while above the hotel entrance neon-lit letters proclaimed: "Aston Hotel."

John signalled to a diminutive Javanese boy loitering outside the Aston's heavily-marbled lobby.

Doubtless, he was hoping to con rupiah from tourists by acting as their guide. Teeth glinting, his skinny brown face alive with his eagerness, the boy skipped hopefully over to where John was endeavouring to keep out of sight in the shadows.

'Yes, Mr? You want me guide you? I know Bali very good.' He beamed hopefully.

John pulled twenty dollars Australian from his wallet, and could have sworn that dollar signs momentarily appeared in the dark brown eyes. Twenty Australian dollars was well over two-hundred-thousand Indonesian rupiah; a fortune for a fourteen-year-old street urchin.

'Son, do you know where the Mandira Beach Resort is?'

'Of course, Mr Ozzie, sir. You want me take you there? It not far.'

John spoke slowly, sounding each syllable carefully. 'No. I want you to take this note to a lady. Her name is Annette Thompson. You give her the note and tell her I said she has to give you another ten dollars. You then bring her back to me and I'll give you another twenty, okay?'

'Fifty of the "Round Eyes" dollars? Man, I'm rich,' the boy shouted gleefully to himself in Javanese as he leapt in the air and bounded away, the orange note clasped firmly in his grubby mitt.

John fidgeted nervously, praying that Fleming or his men wouldn't spot him lurking across the street. He had no idea where they were in the hotel. They could be watching him right now for all he knew. Looking around for a better hiding place, he spotted a small open-fronted restaurant with tables, umbrellas and chairs spilling out on to the pavement half a block away. Although it wasn't ideal, he would be able to see when Annette arrived or if Fleming left the hotel on foot. However if the ASIO crew used a motor vehicle to remove Nolan, he would be very lucky to spot it, and powerless to respond anyway.

Finding a table close to the entrance, he ordered bottled water and explained to the pretty Balinese waitress using a combination of sign language and English that he was waiting for someone and would order a meal when his guest arrived. She smiled engagingly and wandered off to serve other customers while John gulped down the water thirstily and contemplated how he was going to pinpoint Nolan's exact location and the possibilities of rescuing him.

Half an hour elapsed before John spotted Annette holding the hand of the ragged Javanese boy whose smile couldn't have been any wider if he'd won Lotto. Wearing skimpy white shorts which showed off her long brown legs, a frilly, pink almost sheer cotton blouse, and with a white-leather shoulder bag slung over one shoulder, Annette looked every bit the carefree tourist.

The two arrived where John had been standing when he tipped the boy and began looking anxiously up and down the street. John indicated to the waitress that he was going to collect his friend and stepped out onto the street. The keen-eyed urchin, who was no doubt beginning to think he'd lost his other twenty dollars, spied the tall Australian immediately. Tugging at Annette's blouse, he began jabbering and pointing.

'What the heck's going on, John?' Annette wanted to know after the little fellow had scampered away with the balance of his loot. 'Little Freddy came banging on my door with your note and I got here as fast as I could.' Handing John his iPhone she scolded him gently. 'You ought to be more careful and make sure you don't go off without it next time.'

John ignored Annette's jibe about the phone. 'Little Freddy? Where'd that name come from?'

Annette smiled. 'I asked him his name but I couldn't get my tongue around it so I christened him "Freddy".'

'Little Freddy did a good job.' John nodded and then explained how he'd almost bumped into Fleming while he was walking off his breakfast, and his fears for Nolan's welfare.

'Bloody ASIO got to him before us. I reckon they've hacked into Nolan's email messages and they've probably tapped my phone somehow,' he reasoned. 'I think we need to turn our mobiles off just in case. We'll pick up a couple of pre-paids we can use in the meantime, but that's not my biggest concern; I'm more worried how we're going to get Dickie-boy away from them before they bump him off, or persuade him to hand over the recordings.'

'I've been thinking about that. Nolan might be a bloody idiot but he is no fool. I reckon he'll have backup copies as life insurance.'

'You're bound to be right but that snake-in-the-grass Fleming is likely to threaten to harm Nolan's family if Nolan releases the copies. I don't think

Fleming can afford to let Dick live. Once he's sure he's got the tapes, Dickie's life is on the line.'

'Maybe we should take the risk and call in the Federal Police, because this has all got out of our control now.'

'If we were still in Australia, I'd agree with you, but the Feds are pretty well hamstrung over here, and even if they could get here and take over, it would probably be too late for Nolan. No, I think we're stuck with the problem.'

'Okay.' Annette sighed. 'So what's the plan?'

'The first thing we've got to do is find out in which room Nolan is being held. After that, I am thinking of creating some sort of diversion so we can snatch Dickie, but I'm still working on that aspect.'

'This isn't Australia, John. Different rules apply here.'

'What do you mean?'

'Well, you're thinking Bali hotels will behave like Australian hotels. You're presuming that they won't, under any circumstances, give out the details of guests because of privacy and security laws, right?'

'Yeah. Even if they aren't constrained by legislation prohibiting them releasing the names of their guests they can't afford to compromise guests' security because the hotel's reputation is on the line.'

'Money talks here John. Hotel staff is on really lousy wages. If you offer the right financial incentive and convince them you're not a terrorist out to blow up the hotel, or something equally sinister, they'll tell you what you want to know, especially if they're also sure it won't come back and bite them on the bum.'

'Sounds like you've got it all worked out. What sort of dollars are we talking about here? I didn't plan on having to fund an overseas operation to take on ASIO; I just thought we were coming here to have a simple chat with Dickie and then fly home with him, and the recordings. My cash reserves are starting to run a little low.'

'Don't worry, it's small change. You saw how that kid, Freddy, was so over the moon at getting fifty bucks, which reminds me; you owe me ten but you can pay me later.

'You stay here; I'll be back in a couple of minutes. I'll dial your number and when we connect we'll keep our mobiles switched on so you can keep track of where I am and what I'm doing.'

Annette didn't go immediately to the Aston, instead, she headed into the maze of nearby street stalls. Although she'd never met Fleming or any of his ASIO operatives, Annette could not be sure that they wouldn't recognise her. If ASIO were now aware that she and McCarthy were hunting for Nolan, it was highly probable they'd at least seen hers and John's photographs and she'd look pretty stupid if she stumbled into Fleming or any of his people, so it was best to take some elementary precautions.

It didn't take her long to find what she was looking for and she emerged from the crowded market twenty minutes later wearing a long, brunette wig, and a flowing flowery-patterned Balinese sari over her shorts and blouse. She'd also ditched the shoulder bag in favour of a small bum bag which freed up her hands and kept her mobile secure and out of sight. Lastly, with a change of eye shadow, lipstick and blusher, she'd managed a convincing makeover which she felt sure would fool even her closest friends.

Entering the hotel's spacious, brightly-lit lobby, Annette admired an enormous white vase filled with a fascinating arrangement of twisted bamboo poles which protruded from a fern-like wreath encircling the top of the urn. Overhead, a huge, gold glass and crystal light fitting resembling an inverted flying saucer bathed the cavernous entrance with a soft golden luminescence. Approaching the ebony and gold marble reception desk, she noted that the hotel's lifts were a mere five paces to the right. From the overhanging mezzanine balcony, two men watched her with interest.

They've got ASIO-spook written all over them, she decided, hoping their interest had been precipitated by her slim, curvaceous appearance, and not because they'd blown her cover. Effecting nonchalance, she glided to the counter gracefully, despite her Nike sneakers and the inelegant bum bag worn around her midriff. Noting the handsome young Balinese receptionist's name badge, she adopted a damsel-in-distress persona and smiled imploringly.

The young man's eyes literally bulged and his mouth fell open at the sight of the drop-dead vision before him. He fell immediately in lust as he enquired, 'How may I be of assistance, miss?'

Annette batted her eyelids and leant over the counter making sure she gave the salivating clerk an eyeful of her sun-gold cleavage. 'Oh, I hope so, Joko. I am actually an employee of the Australian Department of Foreign Affairs and I've been asked to pass on a very important message to my boss who is in Bali on official business. I believe he is staying in this hotel. The trouble is, I don't know what name he's using, because he likes to travel incognito so people don't make a fuss over him. I've tried calling his mobile phone but it seems to be switched off and my office has lost his room number. I'm hoping if I show you his photograph, you'll be a sweetie and tell me what room he's in so I can pop up and deliver the message.'

While Joko ogled her, Annette reached into her bum bag. She switched on her mobile phone so she could show him the photo she had Googled earlier.

Joke bowed his head and studied the screen intently. 'I am sorry miss, the hotel rules prohibit me from giving out the names and room numbers of guests, but I can telephone the gentleman's room and ask him to come down to the lobby if you like.'

Annette was not thrown by Joko's response, which was just as she'd expected. Remembering John's advice she turned her 'phone off again quickly. 'No, please don't do that, Joko, he'll be mad at me and I'll get into trouble', she responded and began weeping gently. 'Oh dear, what am I going to do?'

The sight of the beautiful young woman in such distress, and the prospect of her career suffering simply because he'd refused to help her, were almost too much for the young clerk to bear. Torn between fears for his job and his desire to assist the vision before him, he hesitated.

Sliding her hand across the counter top, Annette gently patted the back of Joko's hand. With her free hand, she let him catch a glimpse the fifty dollar note folded in her fingers.

'I wouldn't want to get you in trouble. You're such a sweet young man. If you're *really* sure you can't do anything I'll just have to find another way,' she sniffled and turned slowly, as if to leave.

The thought of losing fifty dollars *and* having upset such an alluring creature brought the desired response. Joko opened the hotel register, pencilled a small cross beside one entry and then closed it again, leaving the pencil protruding from the page he'd marked. 'I have to slip out for a moment. I am sorry that I can't help you,' he apologised, giving her a wink.

Annette reached across to shake Joko's hand, slipping the fifty dollar note into his palm. 'Thank you. I am sorry if I've caused any trouble.'

When Joko turned his back to leave, Annette leant over and flipped the register open, noting the pencilled cross next to the name; "Brian Coogan, Room 54."

'Well done, Annette,' John congratulated her when she re-joined him at the restaurant. 'What happens if Joko sees Fleming and says something like, "Did you get the message from the young lady who was looking for you, sir"?'

'Think about it, John. He's not going to do that. He'll get himself in trouble for revealing a guest's details to a stranger.'

'I hope you're right; however we'll be in and out before they know what hit 'em so it might not be a problem.'

'Sounds like you've got a plan. You mentioned something earlier about creating some sort of diversion.

Were you thinking of doing something like setting off the fire alarms and then snatching Nolan in the confusion?'

'I thought about doing that, but I think the chances of success are too low and I don't like putting ourselves in a situation where it's highly likely that somebody will get hurt, or we end up getting arrested.'

'Well we can't just walk in, knock on Fleming's door, and say; "We've come to collect Dickie-boy."'

John grinned. 'Actually, that's virtually my plan, but pick your chin up of the floor before you trip over it. We're going to make sure Fleming and his lackeys can't refuse to hand him over.'

'How?'

John tapped the side of his nose with his finger. 'Listen in while I make some telephone calls and you'll get the gist of how this is going to go down in about thirty minutes from now.'

+++++++++++++

Chapter Twenty-Seven

With less than twelve months before marine ecosystems passed their tipping points, the Australian Prime Minister was acutely worried as to whether his teams would solve the logistical nightmare associated with the covert seeding programme in time.

First, they had to acquire the right type and size of vessel to distribute the iron particles. While there were ships available, they needed to be manned by Australian naval personnel because of the risk of foreign crews or civilians leaking information to the media. Then the masters and the crews of the ships involved would need to be compensated for the time their vessels were under Australian control. This raised insurance issues. How would they convince Lloyds to insure leased vessels without revealing how they were to be used?

Presuming they overcame those problems, naval personnel would then need to undergo familiarisation training.

Next was the problem of purchasing very fine iron ore. He couldn't just go to Gina Rinehart or Twiggy Forrest and buy the stuff. Treasury regulations and good governance demanded that they follow the tender process. It was one thing to breach an international convention but quite another matter entirely to spend public money without following due process so they would have to call for tenders anonymously and swear them to secrecy.

The successful tender would then need to be convinced as a matter of the highest priority to halt the normal production of export size ore and reconfigure equipment to produce microscopic iron ore particles. Questions were bound to be raised as to why the government needed two hundred thousand tonnes of talcum powder-size iron ore. Would they be able to maintain secrecy?

Once the ships arrived they needed to be especially equipped with agricultural blowers and their holds filled with the filthy black dust. Lastly, they needed to reach their target zones safely and distribute their cargoes within the time frame.

Had Australia come under a sudden attack from a foreign power the government would not have hesitated to adopt a war footing. Under such a scenario McCarthy would call for and receive bi-partisan support to defeat the common foe. Under the same scenario he could also call upon Australia's allies and invoke various defence pacts.

Unfortunately this was different. While he had no doubt the situation was equally dire, the young prime minister realised others would not share his government's view. Bi-partisan support was hardly likely to be forthcoming for an operation in clear breach of an international treaty. In fact, he would encounter massive opposition.

Neither could he call on friendly nations to come to Australia's aid. While the United Nations head, Ban Ki Moon, had supported him privately, the US President had run a proverbial mile.

Despite all this McCarthy was totally convinced that Australia was at war. Not a war where one could easily identify the enemy, but a war against the blind apathy of nations who simply refused to accept that the survival of all planetary life depended upon preserving the microscopic sea creatures that formed the very basis of the world's food chain and contributed to at least half the oxygen used by humans and other species.

If I am to win this war the entire operation is best handled by the RAN, he decided. They have the logistical skills, the manpower, the knowledge of the ocean currents, and prevailing weather conditions. They know how to maintain secrecy and how to work to deadlines. I am sure once the WHOI scientists explain who the foe is they'll come to the party. If not, they'll be given a direct unequivocal order.

Within days, Matthew convened an urgent meeting of Australia's top defence chiefs. Once again he requested the WHOI scientists to explain the gravity of the situation, outline the bold plan and stress the need for utmost secrecy.

Matthew wanted to hammer home the enormity of the situation so he leapt to his feet at the conclusion of WHOI's presentation.

'The world doesn't know it, but it owes much to the Woods Hole Institute for bringing this crisis to our attention. Nevertheless, as military people you are probably wondering why I've convened this meeting and why you've had to sit through a presentation concerning the imminent extinction of diatoms and coccolithophores.

'Bear with me because the reason for your presence will become abundantly clear in the next few minutes.

'Unfortunately, declining phytoplankton is only part of the problem faced by our marine creatures.

While I will shortly unveil a plan to deal with declining phytoplankton I need everyone to begin thinking how to solve another issue of equal importance to marine ecosystems and ultimately to human survival.

'That second issue concerns our heavily polluted oceans which are becoming riddled with plastic waste. In fact, some say there is an invisible island of plastic contamination twice the size of the continental United States in an area known as the North Pacific Gyre. For the uninitiated, a gyre is a rotating pattern of ocean currents.

'The North Pacific Gyre is a mess that has been aptly and sadly dubbed the Great Pacific Garbage Dump.

'The size of this toxic dump ranges from between seven-hundred-thousand to fifteen-million square kilometres, or 0.41 percent to eight percent of the Pacific Ocean.

'If that isn't bad enough, water samples taken from even the remotest of the world's oceans show four thousand microscopic plastic particles for every square kilometre of ocean. The situation is now so dire that there is no longer such a thing as a pristine ocean.

'Our oceans are now contaminated with potentially toxic chemical waste that poses a major threat to pelagic fish species because they consume substances such as biphenyl A, PCBs and derivatives of polystyrene. Of course this contamination then spreads through the marine food chain.

'Those of you who eat fish should be extremely concerned because you are undoubtedly ingesting toxic substances that may well cause various cancers, alter your DNA, or seriously damage your health in any number of ways.

'Studies to date indicate that eighty percent of this plastic waste originates from land. Much of it is washed into the oceans by major river systems such as the Ganges and major rivers from Bangladesh, Nigeria and other developing countries. Even the world's remotest beaches are now littered with man-made waste.

'The other twenty percent probably comes from shipping. As an example, a three thousand passenger cruise ship generates eight tonnes of solid waste per week and that waste ends up in the Great Pacific Garbage Dump.

'Every nation has contributed to the problem, yet so far no one has demonstrated the resolve to tackle the predicament apart from having nations sign the London Treaty prohibiting the dumping of wastes at sea. While there was nothing wrong with spirit of that treaty, it is nonbinding, and in my opinion is little more than a toothless tiger and a feel-good measure designed to con the public into believing the world is cleaning up its act when it clearly is not.

'In a minute I will also demonstrate that the London Treaty is actually counterproductive because it prohibits nations taking remedial action where such action entails introducing substances that could actually counteract the problems of waste and declining phytoplankton.

'While I am sure you're disturbed at the potential catastrophe the world faces, you are no doubt asking yourselves what this has to do with Australia's defence forces. Gentleman and ladies, it has everything to do with the defence of Australia because we are actually waging a fight for our survival.

'To demonstrate, cast your minds back to the 1970s, that's if you're old enough to remember when France conducted atomic tests on Muraroa Atoll in the South Pacific. During that period radioactive fallout threatened Fiji, Samoa, Rarotonga, Tahiti and New Zealand and, to a lesser extent, Australia. However, the rest of the world simply did not care, just as it doesn't care today about declining phytoplankton and the catastrophic effects of ocean pollution.

'One brave nation stood alone against the insanity of the French. That nation was New Zealand. It sent warships into the test site and through the statesmanship and heroism of a prime minister who was prepared to stare down the might of the French navy, and the New Zealand sailors who risked their lives, they forced the French to back down and in so doing prevented a massive environmental crisis.

'The entire world faces a similar situation today. And once again, nations simply don't care.

'Someone has to show courage and leadership. That someone will be us.

'Unlike New Zealand, we don't have a single clearly identifiable enemy we can confront. Our enemies are many. Some are faceless. Some are abstract and some even come in the guise of being our greatest allies. Unfortunately the latter have been blinded by short-sighted greed and apathy.

'We also face enemies on our home soil. These are ordinary, decent hardworking folk who probably regard themselves as patriotic Australians. However, they either can't bear to face the dreadful truth, or they are so misguided and misinformed that they refuse to grasp the fact that humankind is facing extinction, and so live in denial.

'My search for allies has been in vain. America won't help us. As insane as it sounds, internal issues are of greater concern to them than the survival of life on this planet. That other great institution of irrelevance, the United Nations, is hamstrung by the very conventions that are designed ostensibly to prevent environmental catastrophes.

'Next, Great Britain, India, China, Asia, Russia and European nations comprise a multicultural orchestra of Nero-like figures fiddling away while Rome burns around them. By the time they put down their violins and reach for the fire hoses we'll all be standing amid the ruins wondering what happened.

'The current situation can be likened to the 1960s and 70s when CFCs were widely used in aerosol sprays. The indiscriminate use of chlorofluorocarbons nearly destroyed the ozone layer that protects the Earth from harmful ultra rays. If it hadn't been for the actions of a few dedicated and determined scientists who went against popular opinion and companies with vested interest in the continued use of CFCs, life on this planet would have been wiped out.

'Despite the evidence of the harm being inflicted upon the world it took nearly sixteen years of lobbying before CFCs were eventually banned. In the meantime the hole in the ozone layer continued to grow and countless millions of people developed, or are yet to develop, potentially fatal melanomas. Finally, common-sense prevailed and the ozone layer began to recover, although it still opens up each year and exposes entire populations to the risk of contracting deadly melanomas.

'Unfortunately, diatoms, coccolithophores and other minute plankton can't afford to wait sixteen years for the world to come to its senses. These tiny creatures are on death row and we have less than twelve months to gain a reprieve.

'God willing, you gentleman of Australia's navy will avert the apocalypse. You will do this using several Handymax tankers to broadcast two-hundred-thousand tonnes of fine iron particles in the Southern Ocean, in the vicinity of the Galapagos Islands and in the Arctic Ocean. RAN ships will escort the tankers and deter any nation who opposes this mission to save the marine food chain.

'If our experts have done their sums correctly phytoplankton will regenerate to pre-crisis levels and in the process sequester three gigatonnes of carbon dioxide from the Earth's atmosphere. Marine species will bounce back and atmospheric oxygen levels will receive a welcome boost.

'After that, we'll tackle the Great Pacific Garbage Dump.

'Now, harking back to the main issue; if the unions get to hear of the iron seeding operation they will refuse to load the ships and try and prevent them from sailing. If that happens I propose to use the army to clear protesters from the wharves and load the ships.

'If we manage to clear our ports with the life-saving cargoes, we may even meet extensive opposition from the defence forces of other countries. We will call their bluff if push comes to shove.

'I have no doubt World Court will censure Australia for breaching the London Convention when it learns what we're doing. For that reason, we must act covertly and swiftly. However, if word leaks out and we are accused of breaching the London Treaty I will counter with the argument that the precautionary principle (PP) does not apply.

To refresh your memories the PP states that "if an action or policy has a suspected risk of causing harm, in the absence of scientific consensus, the burden of proof that it is not harmful falls on those who would take the action."

'Australia will argue that man-made emissions are the action that has created the decline of phytoplankton and iron fertilisation is a remedial action necessary to reverse the effects of man's actions.

'To put it crudely and bluntly, it is far preferable for this operation to be over and done with before shit has time to hit the fan.

'If everything goes to plan we'll prove this works. Any opposition will melt away as nations rush to capitalise on the billions of dollars to be reaped from carbon credits. The iron seeding programme will become an annual event that will mitigate the effects of global warming until such time as the world learns to live within its means.

'Ladies and gentlemen, mankind and the majority of life forms are staring into the abyss of extinction. If you believe in a god, go down on your knees and pray for Divine Intervention. God bless you all.'

While he had expected at least some scepticism, or even resistance from those assembled, the combination of WHOI's graphic presentation, Matthew's personal charisma and the respect he'd engendered in his short time as PM resulted in an unequivocal acceptance of what amounted to a call to arms. Even the tired old warhorses waiting for their metaphorical gold watches of retirement suddenly had a glint in their rheumy eyes and a renewed sense of patriotism burned at the prospect of becoming relevant once again. Here was something meaningful to fire up imaginations and provide the verve to dust off almost forgotten logistical and strategic skills. Ideas began flying back and forth and the meeting room almost seemed to pulsate with the palpable sense of urgency as the nation's greatest military minds eagerly coalesced with those of the world's top scientists.

Looking on from the sidelines Matthew was suddenly reminded of scenes from old Second World War movies where boffins and the top brass positioned replicas the country's forces against those of the enemy.

With the military's compulsion for assigning names to every operation, the iron seeding project was dubbed "Operation CO_2 Sequestration, which was quickly abbreviated to Operation CO_2S, or even more simply, CO_2S. However, naval commanders were not happy with the prime minister's suggestion that Australia lease or borrow the necessary vessels, instead coming up with a proposal to actually purchase several redundant Handymax class tankers lying idle at the ports of Rotterdam, Hong Kong and Panama.

Arguing that the vessels would become valuable assets when recommissioned as part of the RAN they convinced the government to dispatch marine surveyors to examine the seaworthiness and suitability of each vessel.

Thinking about it, Matthew had to agree purchasing the ships overcame insurance issues and secrecy concerns. Once renamed the three ships would provide a valuable adjunct to the Australian Government's humanitarian programmes when not being used on Operations CO2S. Although Opposition MPs would eventually raise questions over the acquisition of the vessels, Matt was confident he could stall them until the successful conclusion of CO2S.

And so eight weeks later, renamed and repainted HMAS support ships, Kiama, Exmouth and Stanley entered the W.A. port of South Hedland to each begin loading nearly seventy-thousand tonnes of 0.5 micron-sized iron ore particles.

Meanwhile, Phoebe Swan had not been sitting on her hands. Naturally, as a senior member of McCarthy's Cabinet she was fully apprised of developments and regularly kept Sutton informed.

Thwarted by the navy's purchase of the bulk tankers both Swan and Sutton realised that they could no longer rely on manipulating waterside workers, miners and truckies to stop the ore being mined, transported and loaded. Neither would they be able demand each ship's crew strike to prevent the vessels sailing. All the logistical aspects of CO2S had now become the sole responsibility of the military machine.

The situation called for a completely new strategy.

'Why did you take such a risk?'

Sutton was curious. The two had arranged to rendezvous on neutral territory; in this case one of Canberra's many carefully tended parks where they sat on a green slatted bench overlooking a heavily populated duck pond.

'What do you mean?' Swan replied, adjusting her large floppy-brimmed hat against the sting of the late spring sun.

'Well, while I'm grateful for the heads up on this silly bloody operation COTS, or whatever it's called, you've put yourself at my mercy. I could ruin your political career like that!' Sutton clicked his fingers to demonstrate. 'Of course, I don't intend to do that, but it would have been far safer if you'd just sent me an anonymous email.'

Phoebe's Swan's green eyes glinted malevolently. 'Let's just say, I don't like the way Matthew McCarthy is alienating the unions. I'm a traditionalist. I come from a long line of Labor supporters; my grandfather and my father both held key positions, first as one of Ben Chifley's ministers and my father as Bob Hawke's finance minister. They're both gone now but they'd turn in their graves if they knew how "green" the party's become.'

Sutton who loved winged creatures more than his fellow man had brought a bag of parrot seed with him. Magnificently-coloured Rosellas, pastel shaded pink and grey galahs and noisy snow-white sulphur-crested cockatoos strutted around their feet, with one or two more adventurous birds opting to perch on his shoulders and outstretched hands, sidling down his arms to feed from his cupped hands.

'You still didn't answer my question,' Sutton responded testily. 'This town's full of gossipmongers and polly-watchers and I am not referring to bird lovers like me. Word could easily get back to anyone from your side, or the Libs that you and I were seen having this little tete-a-tete and they'll link the meeting to the forthcoming furore when news of Cots becomes public.'

'It's called Operation CO2S,' Phoebe Swan corrected, ducking and recoiling in horror as a particularly brazen galah descended on her hat. She waved her arms in disgust to drive the beautiful birds off, imagining being infested with psittacosis or lice.

'Relax, Phoebe.' Sutton's laugh sounded like someone shaking a tin of ball bearings. 'Tourists pay a small fortune for this experience.'

'Well, bully for them,' Swan responded petulantly. 'I hate the bloody, nasty, vicious squawking things. They poop all over my car and drop pine cones on my tin roof as soon as the sun gets up. It's like bombs going off. They scare the hell out of me.

'Anyway, to answer your question, I don't really care if I'm discovered as the source of the leak; I want McCarthy destroyed, the way he's destroyed others.'

Sometimes Neanderthal in his grasp of the social niceties and certainly no diplomat, the unionist was no stranger to the foibles of humanity. 'I take it you're referring to him sacking your girlfriend, Helen?'

Swan's eyes flashed angrily. 'That's really none of your business. More importantly, how do we scuttle McCarthy's plan to dump all that iron ore into the world's oceans? I had thought we could orchestrate a nation-wide strike, but since he's turned it into a military operation that idea's gone out the window.'

Sutton shook his shaggy head in disbelief, resembling an Old English sheepdog with fleas. Scattering the last of the birdseed to the ducks that'd joined the avian banquet he brushed feathers and other detritus from his rumpled trousers. 'Is he really serious about the fish all dying just because some stupid little snails are apparently dying out? Surely something like that isn't going to mean the end of all marine life? The man's just a bloody psycho-scaremongering lunatic!'

Swan who had taken the time to read all WHOI's reports and conduct her own research was still too blinded by her hatred to care about the long term consequences. As with many people who discovered the truth was too bitter a pill to swallow she preferred to side with those who considered that mankind had exaggerated the world's environmental issues and would, in any event solve any issue with its technological expertise. Why would the decline in phytoplankton be any different? Why couldn't the little creatures' demise just be attributable to a natural phenomenon that Mother Nature would resolve herself?

'I think he's a dangerous alarmist who is about to trash this country's reputation, economy and international credibility. He'll make Australia the laughing stock of the rest of the world. We need to get rid of him before he turns Australia into a Third World Country.'

'Sounds a bit like the old joke; "how do you turn a big business into a small business? Give it to a Kiwi to run.' Sutton cackled at his own joke.

Swan smiled reluctantly. 'That's hardly fair. There are plenty of very wealthy, astute and successful New Zealand businessmen.'

'I guess we'll have to create a great big worldwide stink about McCarthy breaching that anti-dumping thing. Leak the plan to Hammond and his lot with the suggestion he take it to the United Nations and have Australia censured for using the oceans as a bloody big dunny.'

Christ, this is like talking to Cro-Magnon man.

'It's called, the London Treaty on Dumping Wastes at Sea, Keith. It's a non-binding agreement between nations which means they can't take any real action against Australia.'

'I know what "non-binding' means; don't fucking patronise me,' Sutton exploded as he bit off the end of one of his fat Cuban cigars. Fumbling for his matches, he lit the thick foul-smelling tube of nicotinic vegetable material. 'There must be plenty of nations who will take this as a personal affront to their fishing and whaling rights.

'What about the Japs? Wouldn't they like to get back at Australia for taking action against them in the world court over their so-called scientific whaling programmes?'

'I am sure they would. So would the Chinese, but no country will resort to actual military intervention and risk starting a war. They'll just make a lot of noise diplomatically and lodge a protest with the U.N. By the time the United Nations schedules a hearing Operation CO2S will be a fait-a-accompli.'

'We're not getting anywhere with this,' Sutton rumbled disconsolately. 'Where are they loading these ships?'

'I thought I'd told you that.' *Have you got bloody dementia, or what?* 'The ships are being loaded in South Hedland by Rio Tinto. Why do you ask?'

Sutton tapped the side of his nose and winked theatrically. 'Best you don't ask, Phoebe, my love. I think I can come up with a plan. Your job in the meantime is to stir up the mother of all stinks internationally and in the big house on the hill. Also, leak the operation to Hammond's lot and those feral bloody tree-huggers and I'll take care of the rest.'

+++++++++++++

Chapter Twenty-Eight

Nolan glowered at his ASIO guards. Fleming had the upper hand now and there was nothing he could do about it. He wondered where McCarthy and Thompson were and what they must be thinking. They'd probably conclude that he'd decided to renege on their arrangement, in which case they'd simply return to Australia, leaving him to Fleming's mercy.

Damn, I thought for a while things would work out and I could at least go back to Jenny and the kids and start a new life somewhere when all this dies down. It would have been good to see Fleming and Bacon get their just desserts. Now I am up Shit Creek without a paddle.

Although he'd had no choice but to write the letter instructing his solicitor to send the recorder to Bacon, Nolan thought he'd have another try at talking sense into his captors during Fleming's absence. While he had to agree that his tale sounded too farfetched, he had nothing to lose.

'Why don't you at least listen to me?' he asked Doss and the other man. 'Use your brains. Can't you see your boss is using you to save his own skin? I've told you what happened. I've told you I've got tapes that prove Senator Bacon and Fleming arranged the assassination attempt on Prime Minister McCarthy. Flipper's been in Bacon's pocket since they fought together in Vietnam. He was being blackmailed by Bacon and in turn he blackmailed me to set up the hit. I had no choice. He would have had my family murdered if I hadn't gone along with it.'

'Oh for Christ's sake, shut up, you mad bastard, I'm sick of listening to your raving. It's all bullshit. James Fleming is a decorated war hero. He's the head of ASIO and one of the nation's most powerful and highly respected public servants. There's no way he'd be implicated in something so absurd. Now shut up or I'll give you another little jab to put you to sleep again,' Doss growled as he fingered the hypodermic.

Nolan looked at his watch. It was now almost 11:00 am and fifteen minutes had elapsed since Fleming had gone to his hotel to collect the recorder, leaving him handcuffed and bound to a chair.

My solicitor should have received the emailed letter by now. Perhaps he is out of the office on other business. I wonder how long it will be before he packages up the digital recorder and couriers it to Bacon's apartment. When Bacon gets the recorder, will Fleming keep his word, or will he make sure I'm silenced for good?

Nolan's intestines churned as the sickening realisation that the ASIO boss would be a fool to let him live hit home. Knowing he obviously wasn't going to be able to talk his way out of his predicament, he decided he had to escape somehow before it was too late.

While Nolan sweated, McCarthy and Thompson watched the minutes tick down until their plan swung into action. Annette calmly passed the time playing games on her newly-acquired pre-paid mobile phone, but John fidgeted and paced back and forth.

The plan was undoubtedly audacious. Its success depended on almost split-second timing and a number of things coming together simultaneously. Although he had spent what seemed like an eternity on the telephone talking to various parties and getting assurances from them to play their part, he knew many things could go awry despite their guarantees.

'Aah, good,' John proclaimed in relief, as he spotted activity across the street. 'It looks like the advance party has arrived.'

Vans began pulling up outside the hotel's entrance. Some of the vehicles were emblazoned with the logos of local television stations. Others were the more sombre Black Marias used by local police. While helmeted and uniformed policeman spilled from the paddy wagons' doors and began tumbling into the hotel's foyer, TV crews and journalists scurried excitedly in their wake clutching cameras, recorders and notepads.

Striding across the street to join them, John unconsciously adopted the air of someone used to taking charge. Reaching the foyer, he identified the policeman leading the contingent; a slim, medal-bedecked, moustachioed Balinese police captain with a slightly officious manner.

'Captain Patika? I am John McCarthy; the man you were talking to on the telephone,' John identified himself as he offered his hand for Patika to shake. 'This is Constable Annette Thompson of the Australian Federal Police. Thank you for responding to my call.'

The police captain studied John intently, clearly weighing him up before he committed his men to this big Australian's wild scheme. Although he'd taken the precaution of calling the Australian Prime Minister's private telephone number which John had supplied during his call for assistance, he was still not convinced that it wasn't all some sort of crazy practical joke. After a moment's hesitation he accepted John's hand, shaking it politely. 'Mr McCarthy, I understand you are also a Federal Policeman?'

'Primarily I am the prime minister's security advisor; however I am also a special constable in the Australia Federal Police. Captain Patika, I don't mean to sound as if I am issuing orders because I realise Constable Thompson and I have no jurisdiction in your country, but we do need to move quickly. As I explained, the ASIO Director-General is corrupt. He is also holding an Australian citizen prisoner with no legal authority. Although that citizen is believed to have been involved in an assassination attempt on our prime minister, and is a fugitive from justice, he is in possession of evidence of major corruption involving a high-ranking politician. In fact, Director-General Fleming, the politician, and the man being held, are all involved in the assassination attempt. If we don't act swiftly, Mr Fleming may abscond and destroy the evidence of his corruption.'

Patika swivelled on his heel. Barking orders to this troops who deployed to secure the Aston's exits, he beckoned to half a dozen heavily armed officers to fall in behind. 'Show me the way, Mr McCarthy.' He bowed, motioning for John to lead the way. He was obviously relishing the prospect of having such a high-profile arrest on his CV.

In touch once more with the youthful vigour of his law enforcement days, John bounded up the stars, taking them three at a time. Reaching the fifth floor, he found Patika's men had already sealed that level and were waiting expectantly, their fingers resting alongside the triggers of their semi-automatic rifles which they held at the ready.

Striding to room 54, John glanced over his shoulder. Captain Patika and Annette were right behind, while the media pack who were essential to the plan's success had been allowed to gather at the end of the corridor and beyond the potential line of fire. Gesturing to one of his officers clasping a heavy battering ram, Patika nodded. The man swung the device with all the force he could muster. Its business struck the wood panelling beside the lock. The wood splintered, the lock gave way, slamming the solid-core door back against the wall. A stun grenade followed. Everyone covered their ears as its deafening blast shook the building and rattled the windows.

Shouting loudly, several Balinese officers barged into the room, their weapons covering all angles in what was obviously a well-rehearsed drill but there was no resistance from within, only a lot of moaning and groaning from the occupants whose hearing had been temporarily incapacitated.

Captain Patika stepped through the shattered doorway into the smoke-filled hotel suite. Turning, he smiled in satisfaction and signalled for John to enter.

With his hands rubbing his ears confusedly James Fleming got to his feet. The violent noise and unexpected intrusion by armed police had stunned him into stupidity and knocked him down behind a settee. Looking dazedly about him, he struggled to regain his senses.

The room's other occupants had not fared much better. Two ASIO men who'd been watching television looked frightened out of their wits. However, fearing they were about to be shot, they'd had the presence of mind to remain seated and they looked as if their lives depended upon touching the room's ten foot ceiling with both hands.

Gagged, handcuffed and bound, Nolan's eyes showed his relief as he struggled with his bonds.

John waited while Fleming's hearing returned. The ASIO man's mind was obviously working overtime as he struggled to regain his composure. At last, he found his tongue, directing his enraged rant toward the Balinese police captain while at the same time directing daggers at John with his eyes. 'What's the meaning of this? I am an Australian citizen. I am also a high-ranking civil servant and you have just created a serious diplomatic incident,' he roared. 'I'll make sure you pay dearly for this invasion of my rights and my privacy.'

Striding two paces, John shoved Fleming in the chest, knocking him onto his ample backside. 'Shut up, Flipper,' he snarled. 'Captain Patika has been asked by the Australian prime minister to arrest you and hold you in custody pending your deportation to Australia to answer to charges of treason, corruption and attempted murder.'

By this time, the media had gathered at the door. Cameras flashed, journalists scribbled furiously and camcorders recorded every word and action as McCarthy untied Nolan's bonds and released the handcuffs using a key taken from one of the ASIO agents.

'Where's the recording, Dick?' John wanted to know.

From the floor, Fleming chuckled. 'There are no recordings. Dickie-boy gave me some useless discs but I destroyed them. As for the digital recorder he reckons he left with his solicitor, well that should be in a certain senator's hands now. I'm sure that gentleman will report that there was nothing on it and everyone will conclude that this was just a scam by a poor, mentally-ill Muslim policeman with a beef against the Australian government.

'You've got nothing, McCarthy, and I am going to have your guts for garters. I'll sue you, Miss Goody-Two-Shoes, and your son, for all you're worth. I'll also demand and get a full public apology. By the time I'm finished with you all, the Labor Party won't be able to sack your son quickly enough. As for the Captain here, I reckon the Indonesian Premier will have him transferred to some remote island in West Papua to supervise the coconut harvest.'

Captain Patika cast John a worried look. John could see him beginning to kiss his career goodbye.

'I've still got Richard's verbal evidence,' he told Fleming, although his own confidence was beginning to wane. The ASIO boss was right about one thing; without the tapes there would be no chance of a conviction.

'No one is going to believe the lies of a disgraced lowly police sergeant against someone like me. I am a war hero. I am also the director-general of Australia's foremost security agency. I have an unblemished record and I can produce umpteen high-profile character witnesses. Nolan is a cowardly ex-naval officer who acquired a bravery medal by deception. He is also an attempted murderer. What chance do you think you've got with wild heresy accusations? You'll be laughed out of court!'

Richard Nolan rubbed his wrists where the handcuffs had left red welts. Fixing Fleming with a vexatious-filled stare, he announced quietly, 'I don't think so Mr Director-General.'

Walking over to where John was standing, he whispered in John's ear causing John to chortle with laughter.

'Captain Patika, I think you can take that low-life so and so away now and hold him for deprivation of liberty until we get deportation proceedings underway.'

'What the fuck did he say?' Fleming wanted to know.

John couldn't stop chuckling. 'I'll just let you sweat, Flipper. You'll find out eventually.'

Patika's men handcuffed the ASIO Director General and dragged him screaming abuse to the waiting prison van. When the media had departed with the biggest story of the decade, John turned to Nolan. 'I think you can share your little secret now Richard and then we'll take you to the airport. The RAAF VIP jet should be landing in about one hour to take us all back to Canberra.'

The federal agent sat down and his shoulders slumped. 'I am sorry. I've made a hell of a mess of things but I'll do whatever I can do to put it right and I'm prepared to take my punishment.'

'Oh, for goodness sake,' Annette said exasperatedly, 'you can say ten Hail Marys and one hundred Our Fathers for all I care. Just tell us what you said to John.'

'Dick is a Muslim, remember,' John reminded her.

'Well I'll throw bloody rocks at him if that's what he wants, but for fucks sake, are you going to tell me or not?'

'You better tell her, Dick, before she bursts her boiler.'

Nolan managed a wan smile. 'I didn't want to say this aloud while the media were listening because it would get back to Bacon and he'd kill off any last chance to convict Fleming and him but when I bugged Bacon's apartment, I left a six gigabyte memory bug there with a long-life battery. It should have everything that was on the recorder plus another nice load of incriminating stuff by now.'

+++++++++++

Chapter Twenty-Nine

Immediately following Fleming's arrest, John telephoned Matthew who immediately called in the Federal Police Commissioner and briefed him on events. As was to be expected, Stormy Knight was furious that neither of the McCarthys had trusted him and Matthew spent considerable time placating the commissioner and explaining that in light of the assassination of Bowker, the terrorist attacks and the attempts on Matthew's own life, he'd had no choice but to mount a private operation until he was able to determine the actual level and extent of Bacon's corrupt influence. Stormy eventually settled down when he understood the rationale behind the prime minister's actions and the two men discussed the urgent need to deal with Philip Bacon.

'John has advised me that there's still a recording device at Bacon's apartment. While I realise there could be problems with having the evidence admitted in court proceedings, I believe we need to move swiftly to secure the bug before Bacon finds it,' Matthew explained.

'I've no doubt the Teflon coated senator has already moved into damage control mode but I'll arrange the necessary warrants on his penthouse and parliamentary offices. I have already sent a team to seize the bug, his computers, files and anything that could be remotely connected to his criminal activities.

'Unfortunately, we don't know Bacon's current location so we can't arrest him at this stage. We're checking the airports to see if he's already flown the coop, which is on the cards; he must have known his day of reckoning would come eventually.

'If Flipper Fleming has been blackmailed by Bacon all these years as Nolan alleges, he must have been living under enormous pressure. Wriggling free from Bacon's clutches should actually come as an enormous relief and knowing him as I do, I think he'll sing like a proverbial canary if he thinks there's a chance of saving his own hide, or getting a reduced prison sentence.'

'I certainly hope you're right,' Matthew replied. 'What do you plan to do about Richard Nolan?'

'Nolan will go into protective custody under the witness protection programme as soon as he lands back on Australian soil. Only his minders will know where he's being held.'

'That should be any time soon. As you know I organised an RAAF flight from Denpasar. Fleming and the agents he manipulated are on board along with Nolan, John and Annette Thompson. The attorney general drew up Fleming's deportation papers and the Indonesian President was only too happy to cooperate in expediting his release into John's custody, especially when I explained that we should be able to close down the illegal arm of Bacon's drug operations in that country.'

News that the ASIO Secretary-General had been arrested for sedition and conducting illegal overseas activities preceded John and Annette home, creating the biggest media sensation since the 1975 sacking of Prime Minister Gough Whitlam. Throngs of journalists and television news crews besieged the airport perimeter and the feeder roads hoping for a glimpse of the traitorous spy or the alleged would-be assassin. They may as well have not bothered. The transfers from the RAAF jet to a heavily blacked out prison van and police vehicles with darkly tinted windows were carried out behind carefully erected screens and the AFP escort took great pains to ensure they also protected John and Annette from the prying camera lenses.

Although John McCarthy felt enormous relief that things had gone so well, he was anxious to have a private discussion with the AFP Commissioner. He knew he'd overstepped his authority and abused a rarely conferred privilege of his status as a special constable. To make matters worse he'd dragged a junior AFP member who was supposed to be on special leave into a private investigation and failed to trust the head of the country's foremost law enforcement body. How would he feel if he was in Stormy Knight's shoes? Would he be angry? Would he feel betrayed? Would he take out his ill feelings on the only person who couldn't fight back; Annette Thompson?

John was prepared to eat any amount of humble pie if it meant repairing his relationship with the commissioner and protecting the plucky young woman who'd been pivotal in both Nolan and Fleming's arrests.

As they drove out the gates of the RAAF base he reached for his mobile phone with the intention of trying to telephone the commissioner's office for an appointment but the iPhone vibrated in his hand before he could punch in the number.

'G'day Kiwi,' a voice drawled. 'Shit, for an old bastard you sure know how to stir up a bloody hornet's nest. What are you thinking of doing next, singlehandedly locking up all the bloody bikie gangs, or perhaps starting World War III?'

John couldn't tell from the commissioner's tone whether he was holding his anger in check and prepared himself for a barrage of abuse. 'Commissioner, I was just in the process of trying to telephone your office. I know I've got a lot of explaining to do and I would be very grateful if you would allow me the opportunity to apologise for abusing my authority and for not keeping you and your men up to date with what I was doing?'

'Your escort can take care of arrangements concerning former Sergeant Nolan and ex-Director General Fleming. Instruct your driver to bring you and Constable Thompson straight to police headquarters. I am anxious to hear what you've got to say.' The commissioner's voice was devoid of any emotion and he severed the connection before John could respond. He might just as well have been inquiring about the score in the third test of the Ashes cricket series which was currently underway in Perth.

Annette gave John an inquiring look. 'Was that the big boss?'

'Yeah, but don't worry, I'm not going to let you cop any flack because I dragged you into this.'

'You didn't *drag* me into anything. I volunteered remember? Besides, what's the worst they can do to me? If they sack me, I'll just come and work for you, or maybe I can get a job as a gardener at the Lodge if you won't take me on,' Annette joked.

'I might well be pulling weeds alongside you.' John laughed.

451

Philip Bacon had always known in the deepest recesses of his mind that his life of crime must eventually catch up with him. Like the skilled strategist and military tactician that he was he simply accepted the situation and rolled out his long mothballed contingency plans and prepared to adapt. There was no doubt that he was a survivor.

He'd half expected that Flipper Fleming would fail to silence Nolan. The man was no idiot and he'd not survived the Battle of Long Tan and the many crisis of his ASIO career and gone on to become its Director-General without superb political and tactical abilities but in Bacon's opinion he was intrinsically weak; if the lack of ruthlessness could be described as a weakness. He was also extremely conceited, a fault which created a tendency to underestimate others' intellectual abilities and life skills. This was evidenced by his failure to anticipate Richard Nolan's cunning by out-manoeuvring him and John McCarthy's dogged determination to unearth the truth behind the assassination attempt on his son and bring the perpetrators to justice.

No sooner had the news of events in Denpasar broken than the Boar flew into action. He knew every second was vital. The AFP would soon be knocking his door down with a warrant to arrest him and seize anything and everything remotely connected with the empire he built over the past forty or more years.

Although most of his assets were held in accounts spread between the Cayman Islands and various Swiss banks he accessed all his Australian bank accounts and electronically transferred every dollar overseas. Next, he contacted his sharebroker and against the man's protestations directed him to conduct a fire sale of his fifty-one percent holding in Shriver Pharmaceuticals. The company had suddenly become a major millstone. Whatever cash he could liquidate would be transferred to his Swiss bank account.

'It's none of your fucking business. And no, I don't need to give you a reason,' he told his shocked sharebroker. 'You'll pick up a nice commission in the process, so just shut your gob and do as you're told,' the Boar snarled as he slammed the phone into its cradle.

Next, Bacon opened his safe and removed wads of U.S. dollars, a small bag of extremely high quality diamonds and multiple forged passports covering nearly every First World country and a few less cooperative nations who treated requests to extradite wealthy fugitives with considerable disdain.

Grabbing an innocuous but extremely strong steel mesh reinforced overnight bag fitted with a special compartment that was impervious to being slashed and also to scanning devices; he stuffed it with his booty before moving to his desktop PC and laptop.

The contents of both computers were regularly copied and backed up to an overseas based company who specialised in providing discreet protection of electronic assets, so he had no hesitation in removing the hard discs from both machines and pounding them with a ball pein hammer until they were unrecognisable. As an additional safeguard he'd also copied his most important information to several flash drives which would be mailed to his various banks with instructions to hold them until he collected them personally or provided written authorisation for their retrieval by a nominated third party.

Although he felt inclined to retire and enjoy the proceeds of the last half a century Bacon was satisfied he could rebuild another criminal empire from any one of a number of countries if he chose to do so. Topping off the overnight bag with essential personal items including several changes of clothes and toiletries, he hurried to the basement, where his late model Mercedes waited, as fast as his corpulent form and flabby leg muscles allowed.

Not a sentimental man, the Boar felt little regret having to simply abandon the trappings of wealth and the privileges of his position as a Federal Senator. The wealth in his off-shore accounts when combined with easily-convertible diamonds would ensure a very comfortable retirement, as long as he kept ahead of his pursuers. He did feel anger though. He'd built his personal kingdom through hard work, considerable cunning and a penchant for covering the finest detail and he felt enormous pride in his achievements along with his equanimity and his apparent immunity from the efforts of the most determined criminal investigators. Now, it seemed he had thumbed his nose at the law once too many.

Thanks to Flipper, it's all going down the toilet!

He had no doubt others would eagerly step in to fill the vacuum once they learnt of his disappearance. They'd capitalise on the networks and supply chains he'd so carefully cultivated. It irked him and he hoped James Fleming would rot out the remainder of his life in the secure unit of a maximum security prison.

As he waddled breathlessly across the basement car park to his vehicle he was conscious that the building's security guard was watching him closely. The man would know something was amiss. Senator Philip Bacon simply did not run anywhere, if his current wobbling gait could be described as "running", let alone carry heavy baggage. There was usually some lackey at hand to attend to anything likely to bring sweat out on the powerbroker's brow, or he rang through and arranged for the security guard to carry his bags if he was embarking on one of his frequent jaunts to God knew where.

Forcing a smile which unbeknown to him was more of a grimace, the Boar slowed down his movements and tried to appear relaxed. 'Just late for a meeting, Frank,' he called. 'I forgot to check my diary.'

Depositing his bag on the rear seat of the Mercedes he called out, 'Do me a favour will you, Frank? If anyone comes looking for me, tell them I left last night. Oh, and wipe the memory on the CCTV cameras in case they check.' Opening his fat wallet he extracted a one hundred dollar note and pressed it into the guard's hand with a wink. 'Do it as soon as I drive out of the car park. Don't let me down will you?'

The implied menace in the last sentence left the guard with little doubt that he'd suffer grievously if he disobeyed. Like most in the senator's circle of influence he'd heard the rumours of people who'd suddenly disappeared or were mysteriously beaten by unknown assailants because they'd somehow incurred the senator's displeasure or interfered with his plans.

'Yes sir. You can depend on me Mr Bacon. I've never let you down. You've always looked after me and I appreciate everything you've done for me over the years,' he wheedled.

'And I'll look after you in the future as long as you keep your mouth shut. In fact, there'll be a nice fat bonus in your bank account towards your retirement, which I believe isn't too far away now, is it?'

'That's correct, sir. I've got six months until I can collect my superannuation.'

After Bacon drove out of the car park leaving a stench of blue tyre smoke in his wake, the guard breathed a sigh of relief. To be on the safe side he wiped the camera's digital memory, despite feeling certain that he'd never see the promised bonus or the curmudgeonly, elderly career-criminal-cum-politician again. He'd worked as the senator's security guard and factotum for twenty years and learnt from the outset to keep his suspicions and anything he saw or witnessed to himself, including the many visits from underworld figures, politicians from every spectrum, union heavyweights and various captains of industry.

The Boar was a major powerbroker in more ways than one but he was now clearly in some sort of serious trouble. Frank had never seen the man look so discombobulated.

In his sixties and unlikely to secure employment of any sort due to his own criminal past and advancing years, the guard debated his next move as he began collecting the various paraphernalia with which he'd adorned his security booth in an attempt to provide some pretence of personal comfort to an otherwise boring and unrewarding job. He debated whether to telephone his contacts in the criminal underclass who sometimes handled the senator's heavy lifting in the metaphorical sense. No doubt there'd be plenty who would be happy to pay for the knowledge Frank had acquired over the years if it enabled them to expand their own criminal empires. Some would be even happier at the prospect of seeking revenge on the senator, if indeed he was now at his weakest and then there would no doubt be a bevy of individuals who were waiting for payment for services rendered. The last group would be extremely angry if they thought Bacon was in the process of taking flight and likely to renege on payment.

In the end, Frank decided to telephone the Australian Federal Police, a strange decision for someone from his criminal background and years of association with a top politician who appeared to be coated with Teflon when it came to scandal, innuendo and rumour. However, although he had no love for law enforcement agencies and an almost total lack of civic responsibility, he sensed hero status and lucrative book deals lurked around the corner if he played his cards right.

Security Guard Frank was in the process of explaining to the AFP call centre operator who he was and the fact that he worked for Senator Philip Bacon, a long time suspect as one of the drug world's Mr Bigs when a phalanx of unmarked AFP vehicles pulled into the streets surrounding the Milsons Point Tower. He became aware of the unusual activity immediately thanks to the CCTV system his boss had had installed to provide coverage of the building's approaches. The images were relayed to a bank of monitors in Frank's security cubicle and to a large split-screen television in Bacon's apartment. While Frank had thought at the time his boss was being paranoid and the expensive technology unnecessary (*bloody over-the-top if you ask me)* he had often been grateful for its entertainment value, zooming in on many an unsuspecting young female, or witnessing the odd drug deal and the kerb crawlers importuning the area's prostitutes who miraculously appeared on nightfall.

'So, let me get this straight, you're Senator Bacon's personal security guard and you're calling to report that the senator is probably on his way to the airport because he thinks we're coming to arrest him. Why would we do that?' The female operator's voice was calm and lacked emotion but she failed to disguise the scepticism in her voice. Obviously not apprised of the raid underway, she had concluded that she was talking to just another of the many cranks who rang in each day with imaginative conspiracy theories and reports ranging from alien invasion to old busybodies who were convinced that a terrorist cell occupied the house next door.

'Don't worry, love,' Frank told her. 'Your mob has just arrived here now. I'll talk to the organ grinder not the monkey. It'll save having to repeat myself.'

Glancing at the wall clock, the guard noted that nearly twenty minutes had elapsed since Philip Bacon's departure at 6.00am. In the normal course of events his twelve hour shift would have finished at the same time Bacon had taken flight and automated access control systems would have timed-in, however this was clearly not an ordinary day.

Although the building's first tenants would begin arriving soon the AFP officers would be unable to gain access unless someone let them in or they waited until the building's day shift concierge took up his post in the foyer. The other alternative that they would force their way in did not occur to the guard. The strategic positioning of uniformed officers suggested they were content to wait until the building opened for business.

He was totally wrong in this assumption.

Unaware that their quarry had already left the building the AFP was not prepared to lose the element of surprise lest the wily senator begin destroying vital evidence.

'Fuck, the bastards are going to break the bloody door down,' Frank exclaimed, and raced to intercept the crew with the battering ram, bolt cutters and crowbars who were about to begin their assault on the glass doors.

Reaching the foyer just as two policemen lined up the heavy ram with the door's locks Frank shouted, 'Hey, don't do that. I'll unlock the doors.'

Clearly unable to conceal their disappointment at the loss of the satisfaction they gained from smashing in doors, the crew backed off and waited while Frank pushed the button which de-activated the door's locks and allowed the motor to retract the twin armour-plated glass doors. As the first of the policemen flooded through the gap, Frank identified himself and demanded to speak to whoever was leading the raiding party.

'First things first,' a deep bass voice thundered and began issuing orders to the heavily armed and Kevlar vested men brandishing a variety of electronic equipment and aluminium cases of forensic equipment.

Forced to wait, Frank surveyed the AFP commander noting the Inspector's pips adorning his uniformed shoulders and the gold braid around the peak of his cap. A name badge on his left breast proclaimed "A. Wilkins."

The fucker looks and sounds just like a young bloody Clint Eastwood.

After his men had sealed the building's escape points, a crew was dispatched to Bacon's apartment where they'd no doubt begin systematically working their way through every nook. Moving beyond the security guard's earshot, Wilkins spoke quickly and urgently to another FEDPOL officer whom Frank guessed was a detective sergeant or the equivalent. This man beckoned to two other AFP officers and they ran to one of the nearby unmarked police vehicles, slapped a magnetic blue light on its roof and sped off with the detective sergeant talking into the vehicle's two-way radio, no doubt alerting both state and federal officers to be on the lookout for a certain overweight, infamous political figure who'd been on just about every policeman's wish list for decades.

At last, Inspector Wilkins approached the security guard. It was clear from his first remarks that he'd already done his homework. 'Don't worry about introducing yourself. I know all about you. You're Francis Robin Briggs, born on New Year's Day 1949, convictions for burglary, aggravated assault and consorting with known felons. You've been Senator Bacon's dogsbody for the past twenty years, although you'd rather we assign you the more grandiose title of security officer. But that ain't gunna happen Franky boy. As far as we're concerned you've played a large part in allowing Philip Bacon to avoid his just desserts. But, thanks for ringing through and tipping us off about his sudden departure. Figure, you could turn the situation to your advantage somehow did you?'

Frank bristled. 'Fuck you. I was just doing my civic duty and providing notice of a fleeing felon, you great big streak of weasel piss. I've got a lot of really valuable stuff I could tell you about my former boss and his friends and what they get up to, but now you can stick it up your arse, because I'm telling you zilch.'

Wilkins smirked. 'Oh, I think you'll tell us everything we want to know, quite readily.'

'And why the hell would I do that?'

'Because although you're small fry in the scheme of things, you can be made to fit nicely into the category of an accessory to the many crimes of soon-to-be ex-Senator Bacon, drug lord, murderer, attempted murderer, treason, and God knows what else. So, unless you want to spend the rest of your miserable life in Long Bay you'll tell us everything we want to know.

'If you're a really good boy, we might let you retire to that fishing shack of yours down the South Coast.'

Frank's shoulders slumped as his imaginary balloon filled with dreams of fame and fortune suddenly exploded.

How the hell did he know about my fishing shack? These bastards will probably even stop me doing a deal for my story under the Proceeds of Crime legislation.

Philip Bacon's many security precautions included a police scanner in his Mercedes. The sudden burst of early morning coded radio traffic on the AFP band was too much of a coincidence. Thumbing the volume control on the Mercedes' steering wheel to increase the volume, he listened intently to the chatter as he drove. References to "the subject," a description of his vehicle right down to the registration plate, and the words "thought to be heading to Kingsford Smith Airport" confirmed his worst fears.

The metaphorical noose was tightening inexorably beneath his flabby jowls, ready to rope him in.

In a sudden fit of enraged panic, he understood his chances of fleeing the country had diminished to almost zero. Every cop, airport security guard and customs officer would be on the lookout. He was too well known, too infamous and he'd made too many enemies to expect anyone to provide refuge or help him with a workable disguise. This was one time when he couldn't rely on being able to bribe his way to freedom or offer sufficient inducement for anyone to become a party to his crimes.

He had become the quintessential pariah.

Stomping on the brake and almost causing a tour bus packed with Japanese tourists to ram into the rear of his vehicle the Boar cursed loudly as the sleek heavy coach swerved around the Mercedes with an angry blast of its horn.

Watching his rear vision mirror for a break in the traffic so he could execute a U-turn the senator yelled at his reflection, 'There's no way I'm going down because of bloody Flipper.'

Visions of protracted court trials, sleepless nights spent in grubby, cockroach-infested cell blocks, cameras shoved in his face at every turn and enraged citizenry thumping on the prison van as he was eventually driven away to spend the remainder of his days in the same prison as the disgraced ASIO Chief flashed through his mind.

I've had a good run. I guess it had to end sometime. I'm too old to spend my life on the run and there's no way I'm going to rot in prison.

Bacon smiled a savage mirthless smile. 'Let's go out with a bang Philip, old boy,' he declared.

As he swung the Mercedes wildly back in the opposite direction, an evil plan began forming in his hate-filled brain. He headed for the Hume Highway which would take him to Canberra.

+++++++++++++

Chapter Thirty

HMAS Kiama, Exmouth and Stanley rode at anchor in the baking sun waiting their turn to begin loading from the wharves situated both sides of the harbour at Finucane Island and South Hedland. Meanwhile, their escorting frigates, Warramunga, Parramatta and Toowoomba, sat outside the narrow winding entrance to the harbour to prevent undue congestion to the Pilbara's busiest seaport.

The pungent tang of salt blew across the water from the giant, glistening white hills of the nearby Dampier salt mines. With few landmarks or other points of interest in the moonscape-like terrain the salt mines and the sixty metre Leslie & Airey Rear Navigational Aids Tower at Mangrove Point had become tourist attractions in their own right. Not that there were any tourists in the town during January, the height of monsoon season when terrifying cyclones can sweep in at any time and daytime temperatures regularly soar to within fifty degrees Celsius.

Known by the indigenous Kariyarra and Nyamal people as Marapikurrinya, which translates to "place of good water", Port Hedland is one of those towns most people either fall in love with or detest in the strongest possible terms. Commander Turner of the frigate Warramunga was one of the latter. Despite the ship's air-conditioning systems running full bore, the blistering heat had brought out an uncomfortable heat rash all over his lean, muscled forty-five-year-old frame and he silently cursed the navy's admirals for sending him on what promised to be nothing more than a boring and protracted seagoing assignment.

At least we'll be escorting the Kiama to the beautiful Galapagos Islands; he mentally consoled himself as he idly watched a rusty antiquated coastal vessel crawl northward along the coast line. What's an ancient hulk like that doing in these waters? he wondered silently. The coastal cargo trade ceased years ago. Lowering his binoculars, he prepared to retreat to the cooler atmosphere of his personal cabin, concluding that the old vessel was probably now the privately owned toy of one of the Pilbara's many eccentric residents.

With a draught of nearly four metres and ninety-two metres in length, the vessel Commander Turner had been watching was in fact a former South African M.V. Assegai which had only recently been purchased by an anonymous consortium from the Seychelles at the bargain basement price of $400,000, which was little more than she was worth as scrap.

Although her pistons rattled and she leaked oil almost as fast as it could be replaced, the Assegai's ancient diesel engines worked well enough and the corroding hull had held together against the swells of the Indian Ocean as she'd journeyed to Port Hedland with a skeleton crew of low-paid Somali seamen who'd been told she was to collect a cargo of defunct rail wagons to be broken up for scrap.

Only the ship's captain and its new anonymous owners knew the vessel's true mission.

When she came abreast of the harbour entrance, the Assegai's helmsman spun the ship's wheel to direct its nose into the narrow confines of the channel, ignoring the repeated calls from the Port Hedland Marine Authority controller to "Stand to" outside the harbour until given clearance to enter the bustling port.

'What the hell's this idiot doing?' the operator yelled. 'Shit, we need to get a tug out there and stop him coming in. We've got bloody fully loaded super tankers just about to sail. That heap of crap can't come in here. It will cause mayhem. Apart from that Bio-Security need to check her before she even ties up.'

Frantically calling one of the Authority's tugs which were getting ready to assist a Chinese bulk carrier manoeuvre into the channel he alerted the crew to the threat posed by the Assegai.

'Stop the unknown vessel entering the harbour. She's refusing to answer and is posing a major threat to shipping,' the controller screamed.

'Roger, WILCO,' the tug's commander responded, throwing the throttles into reverse so he could break away from the towering steel leviathan. The tug's powerful diesels roared. The limpid green water boiled as its giant screws bit into the tropical sea raising clouds of stinking brown mud to the harbour surface. Slamming the throttles full ahead and using the side thrusters, the tug turned in its own length, its stern sank, and its bow rose creating an enormous bow wave as it gathered speed.

By this time the Assegai had already entered the harbour channel and it was obvious from its own bow wave that it had gathered speed in a race against the one vessel capable of foiling its skipper's plans. Reaching the dog-legged section of the harbour channel, the

Assegai put its engines into reverse thrust, effectively bringing the ancient hulk to a stop. Although the channel was one-hundred-and-eighty-three metres wide and forty-three metres deep at this its narrowest point, the bottom shelved steeply either side of the channel centre, meaning large ships had to stay within the middle of the waterway.

With its bow pointing toward the shoreline the Assegai's ninety-two metre hull effectively blocked ships of any size from entering or leaving the port.

'Thank Christ for that!' the harbour master who was watching from the tower exclaimed in relief. 'The silly bastard's woken up at last. Now, all we need to do is get the tug to push him back out until we sort out what he's playing at.'

Aboard the Assegai the captain ordered his crew into the lifeboats. Meanwhile the ship's engineer had busily opened all the vessel's sea cocks with the result that the engine room was soon immersed and the ship began sinking swiftly mid channel.

The tug's skipper hit his forehead with the palm of his hand and swore loudly as he realised the Assegai's skipper was deliberately scuppering his vessel to block the port. 'This is tantamount to terrorism,' he exclaimed. 'It will cost the country millions of dollars in lost revenue and take weeks before we can re-open the harbour.'

By the time the tug reached the waterlogged freighter, her stern was well below the waterline. There was clearly no chance of preventing her calamitous sinking and the tug's crew hove to and watched as the ancient ship's barnacle-encrusted bow rose out the

467

water. She paused for a few minutes as remaining pockets of air kept her afloat, then with an enormous sigh of escaping gases she slid beneath the surface and settled neatly upright in the glutinous harbour floor, her superstructure clearly visible just below the surface.

The Assegai's master and chief engineer who had joined the Somali crew in the ship's lifeboats waited patiently, their faces expressionless, for the tug to tether the vessels together and begin towing them back to the Post Hedland wharf where the local constabulary waited to unravel the motive behind mysterious sinking.

The resultant investigation would prove to be a protracted affair. None of the Somali crew spoke English and all were ignorant of the Assegai's true mission although once on the Australian mainland they wasted no time in capitalising on the situation by claiming refugee status. As for the ship's captain and engineer, both claimed they were on a legitimate mission to fill the ship with Port Hedland's scrapped mine machinery and old rail wagons and freight it to Bangladesh where both the cargo and the ship would be sold for scrap. Both claimed it was the crew, not them, who had sabotaged the ship.

'Why would we deliberately sink a valuable ship and create such trouble for everyone? I am a professional ship's master of many years' experience and excellent reputation and doing such a thing is a most grievous crime. Also, the ship's owners will be very unhappy and they will not pay us now.'

It seemed that the man had an answer for every line of questioning. When asked why he had ignored the harbour authority's order to stay outside the harbour until he received clearance to enter he claimed his radio had malfunctioned.

When advised there was no scrap awaiting collection, the Assegai's captain merely shrugged and claimed he was just following orders from the ship's owners whose names he could not recall.

'You perhaps find documents when you dive on the ship,' he suggested helpfully, with a knowing smirk. 'I am very sorry that your harbour is closed and ships can't get in or out but you have no justification for treating me like a terrorist and holding me prisoner. I will say no more. You speak to my solicitor now. Unless you are going to charge me with a crime I insist you send me home.' The skipper folded his arms and sat back in his chair. What was the worst they could do to him? If the worst came to the worst, a year or two in an Australian prison would seem like a holiday after a lifetime dodging pirates, managing mutinous crews and kowtowing to the often impossible demands of wealthy autocratic ship owners, especially when he knew a handsome nest egg was waiting for him when he returned to his native land.

Although everyone doubted they'd find anything of interest, navy divers soon penetrated the Assegai. They found the ship's safe open and empty. Although it was impossible to prove, all documentation had been obviously been destroyed and ditched at sea along with the ship's garbage. It was also obvious why the radio had malfunctioned. Someone had done a very effective job of irreparably damaging the circuit boards and wiring.

Meanwhile what to do about the Assegai presented a massive headache. Should they try and re-float her or blow her into manageable chunks? Whatever the decision, Port Hedland Harbour was effectively blocked and the governments of both Japan and China, who were severely disenchanted with the McCarthy government's Zero Carbon Energy Bill, were ropable. On home soil, a major furore was about to erupt over the loss of revenue and massive inconvenience to shipping. However the brouhaha over the hold up to iron ore exports had already begun to pale into insignificance. Operation CO2S had been leaked to the world's media, resulting in ridicule-laden headlines such as, "Ozzie PM Troppo Over Climate Change," and "Australia Uses Navy to Defend Sea Snails."

While the more conservative press attacked the Australian Government in a less sensational fashion, the underlining message to the world was that the nation was in the hands of incompetent, irresponsible Leftists who had scant regard for the sanctity of international treaties.

Shock jocks and talkback radio joined the fray, seriously questioning the fledgling and embattled government's competency to run the nation, citing the terrorist attacks, the assassination of Connor Bowker, the arrest of the head of ASIO, the sudden and mysterious resignation of Helen Knox, two assassination attempts on Matthew McCarthy and the latest manhunt for the allegedly corrupt Senator Bacon as proof that the country's entire political system was in chaos.

In a nation where cutting down tall poppies is almost a national sport it was grossly unfair. However, such is the power of the press that almost overnight Matthew McCarthy went from being proclaimed as the nation's darling to being cited as a dangerous megalomaniac.

Liberal Leader Brian Caldwell was literally rubbing his hands with glee and almost salivating at his rival's discomfort. Despite knowing most of what had transpired was beyond Matthew McCarthy and his ministers' control and had occurred due to the unfortunate simultaneous culmination of a sequence of events suddenly erupting like a volcano, he revelled in what had become for him, the perfect political storm.

Addressing the nation on the Australian Broadcasting Corporation's Four Corners programme, Caldwell dropped the biggest political bombshell since the 1974 sacking of the Whitlam Government by the then Governor General, Sir John Kerr.

'Matthew McCarthy must resign. Not only has he conspired to secretly breach an important international treaty designed to protect our fragile marine eco-systems, but he has wasted taxpayers' money by purchasing expensive bulk carriers to dump toxic material into the oceans.' Caldwell almost sneered as he delivered the next lines. 'He is misusing the country's navy by diverting its resources away from essential roles such as border protection on a hare-brained and unproved mission to preserve sea snails. Sea snails for God's sake! Have you ever heard anything so ridiculous?

'I have no hesitation in branding the Labor Government as criminally irresponsible in pressing ahead with this so-called Operation CO2S. Not only is it criminally irresponsible, it is demonstrating an arrogant disregard for the rights of other nations to harvest fish to feed their people secure in the knowledge that those fish aren't contaminated.

'McCarthy has made Australia the laughing stock of the rest of the world. He has failed to protect vital iron ore exports by allowing the sabotage of one of Australia's busiest harbours. He has seriously damaged international relationships with our greatest allies, Japan, India and China, and threatened the viability of Rio Tinto and BHP.

'I intend visiting the Governor General at the earliest possible opportunity and calling upon her to dissolve the House of Representatives as she is empowered to do under the Reserve Powers of Australia's Constitution. Should the Governor General not accede to my request the Liberal National Coalition will move to block supply in the next sitting of the Senate.'

In response, Matthew McCarthy called his Cabinet colleagues together for crisis talks. Seated around the table were the affable and newly-promoted Deputy Prime Minister and Treasurer John Hammond, Finance Minister Phoebe Swan, the Minister for Foreign Affairs Peter Banks, Attorney General James Phelan, Defence Minister Angus Cameron, Minister for Industry and Mining Nelson Hill, the Minister for Agriculture Peter Robotham and half a dozen other lower ranked but nonetheless important political figures.

The atmosphere in the cabinet room was understandably bleak. Knowing things would get much worse before they would get better; Matthew opened the meeting by laying his cards on the table.

'It seems we face a situation even worse than that faced by Gough Whitlam in 1974. I know we all claim publicly not to take any notice of opinion polls. We also know that's a huge fiction. Any career politician has his or her eye on the polls all the time, particularly during election time. Labor's ratings have plummeted to dangerously low levels and I acknowledge that I am the sole reason for the party's shaky political position. While I couldn't give a toss about my own political career, I am truly sorry for the way things have turned out.

'As it stands, if Caldwell is successful in his quest to bring on a general election, either through his bid to have the Governor General dissolve the House of Representatives or by blocking supply, we'll be slaughtered in a general election.

'Our back benchers are understandably worried and I am sure most of you must be questioning your own judgment in electing me prime minister, so I am offering my resignation.'

Looking around the room, the expression "stunned mullets" came to Matthew's mind. No one said anything and Matthew actually counted off thirty ticks of the old-fashioned railway station clock that adorned one wall.

Jack Hammond was the first to speak. 'Excuse my French, but Caldwell is full of fucking bullshit. Stand your ground Matthew. The current circumstances are unprecedented and there's no comparison to the events

473

of 1974. For starters, the GG is no one's puppet. She is a very astute woman with strong opinions as to what the world should be doing to combat the threat from climate change. She is also well apprised of the current crisis facing marine eco-systems.

'While in her role as governor general she is supposed to be totally impartial, I know for a fact that she cannot stand Brian Caldwell and will not be bullied by that pompous twit.

'I say again, stand your ground. Weather the storm. You will be vindicated and history will record you as one of Australia's most courageous leaders and a true statesman.' Hammond's head swivelled left and right as he stared into the faces of his colleagues, challenging anyone to dispute his opinion.

'Hear, hear,' they responded almost unanimously. Matthew couldn't help but notice that the sole exception was Phoebe Swan. Much to his embarrassment his eyes brimmed with tears at the almost unqualified support.

'Thank you for your vote of confidence. It means more than you realise and stiffens my resolve to carry on the fight,' he croaked emotionally. Clearing his throat he turned to stare pointedly at the finance minister. 'It pains me to have to say this but we have a traitor within our ranks. The scuttling of the Assegai could not have been planned and executed within such a very short time frame unless someone leaked Operation CO2S to this government's enemies and more particularly, to financially powerful enemies possessing unprecedented logistical and tactical expertise.

'There are plenty who oppose us but few who have the financial wherewithal and the logistical skills to find and purchase a ship the right size to effectively block the Port Hedland Harbour channel when sunk and then find a crew willing to sail her to Western Australia and sink it right about the time our three tankers were due to sail with their cargoes.'

McCarthy's penetrating blue eyes did not leave Phoebe Swan's face as he continued his allegations. Everyone's eyes were now on the finance minister whose face had turned scarlet as she squirmed in her seat.

'Do you have something you'd like to say, Phoebe? Now is the time to get it off your chest.' The prime minister sat drumming his fingers on the table as he waited expectantly for Swan to begin her denial.

Squaring her shoulders, the finance minister at last found her voice. It was filled with indignant rage. 'How dare you accuse me of such treachery in front of fellow Cabinet members,' she blustered. 'Why would you even single me out with such libellous allegations? I am one hundred percent loyal to the Labor Party and have always toed the party line since I joined the movement back in 1989.'

No lawyer, the prime minister nevertheless understood one of the basic tenets of cross examination; never ask a question of an opponent in front of witnesses unless you already know the answer.

'Because Ms Swan, I know your personal views on the Zero Carbon Energy Bill and climate change. I also know about your close, or should I say, intimate relationship with the treacherous former treasurer. While your private life and your sexual preferences are no business of mine, they became my business when you crossed the line and vowed to seek revenge for Helen Knox's forced retirement.

'Don't ask me how I know these things, just accept the fact that very little that goes on in this place passes my notice.

'I also have these.' The PM produced several large colour photographs. Their grainy but nonetheless distinguishable date and time stamped images depicted Phoebe Swan's recent meeting with the union boss, Keith Sutton. McCarthy flipped the photographs along the table for everyone to see.

'Don't try telling me you and Keith were just having a friendly ornithological visit that just happened to coincide with the same date we decided to launch Operation CO2S.'

Matthew's tone was scathing. 'Res ipsa loquitur, Ms Swan! Or, as I am sure your lawyer will tell you, the facts speak for themselves. Speaking of which, perhaps you had better consult a good queen's counsel, because I intend having the Federal Police investigate you and Keith Sutton the criminal act of sinking the Assegai and any other breaches of the Crimes Act that befit your outrageous conduct.'

In response Swan stood up abruptly, sending her chair sliding back against the panelled wall. As she stormed toward the door, Matthew thought, Her face looks like a slapped arse.

The finance minister grasped the handle and swung the heavy wooden door wide. Stopping midstride, she turned and confronted the room. 'Somebody had to stop your lunacy, McCarthy. You are singlehandedly ruining one of the world's most prosperous economies, and for what? Some bloody slimy, stinking sea snail that nobody but you and your whacko scientist friends care about. If sinking a bloody old rust bucket was necessary to stop you turning Australia into a Third World country, then I am proud of what I did.'

As Phoebe Swan took off at a stumbling run along the corridor, Attorney General James Phelan made as if to chase her. 'She's just admitted to conspiring to commit the criminal act of sabotage under the Crimes Act. That carries a penalty of fifteen years imprisonment. Coupled with the seven years for breaching official secrets she could technically go to prison for twenty-two years maximum. In fact, her behaviour may well fall within the definition of treason if she's found to have aided a foreign power.'

'Let her go for now,' Matthew responded calmly. 'Stormy Knight's men can round her and Helen Knox up when they're ready. Although I must confess I am worried that the loss of hers and Knox's votes makes our position rather tenuous if Caldwell calls for a vote of no confidence. However, I am more concerned about getting that bloody ship out of the channel so CO2S and shipping can proceed.'

Angus Cameron, who despite his Scottish name spoke with a true Aussie twang, offered his contribution. 'I've spoken to the navy's top salvage experts and also looked at what resources are available on the local front. I am conscious that we have to move quickly and simply cannot wait to bring in specialised salvage vessels, which is a pity because there are all sorts of tried and true technologies that would make short work of getting rid of the problem. However, if a cyclone were to strike while the harbour is blocked it could spell disaster for every ship trapped there.

'The Parramatta has already sent her divers down to assess the situation. They reckon cutting up the Assegai into manageable chunks is not an option. The water is too turbid to see more than a couple of centimetres and there's a colossal rip of approximately ten knots in the channel which limits their dive time to about thirty minutes twice a day at the turn of the tide.

'Coincidentally, the harbour is experiencing high astronomical tides of close to six metres at the moment which further exacerbates our predicament.'

'So what's the plan?' The prime minister struggled to control his impatience. *I wish bloody Cameron would just cut to the chase.*

Angus Cameron continued un-fazed by Matthew's testiness. 'Fortunately, we're dealing with relatively shallow water and unless there's a cyclone, wave heights in the harbour rarely get above two metres.

'The long range forecast looks good and if we get two weeks' clear weather the Parramatta's divers reckon they can re-float the Assegai.'

'And how do they propose doing that; by attaching huge drums or floats and filling them with air, or what?'

'No,' the defence minister responded. 'The divers have already closed the sea cocks and they've examined the hull and superstructure to assess how many apertures need to be sealed to make her airtight. They reckon they can weld up her hatch covers and put patches over anything else. They'll pump her out and fill her with enough compressed air to lift her off the mud. The local tugs can then haul her out to sea and either finish the job of re-floating her or let her sink somewhere out of harm's way.'

'If there's time and we're not hit by a cyclone I'd rather see them salvage her so the marine surveyors and the AFP can gather as much evidence as possible,' Matthew replied, although he couldn't suppress the niggling feeling that Murphy's Law would somehow play its part in the entire fiasco.

'Has she leaked any fuel oil or other contaminants?' this from the environment minister. 'We don't want added problems from the locals if the nearby mangroves and the fauna that shelter there are threatened.'

'No problems so far,' Cameron responded. 'Her tanks were almost empty and apart from the usual muck in the bilges which the harbour authorities have contained, there don't appear to be any environmental issues.'

'Thank God for small mercies,' Matthew sighed. 'Now all I've got to worry about is rabid journalists baying for my blood and foreign governments that want to censure Australia in the United Nations.'

+++++++++++++++++

Chapter Thirty-One

John McCarthy and Annette Thompson travelled to AFP headquarters with feelings of trepidation. On the way John telephoned Mary to reassure her that he was safely back on Australian soil and looking forward to getting home. They exchanged the usual endearments just as the AFP driver drew up outside the front entrance of the Federal Police Headquarters.

'Don't be too long darling,' Mary said. 'I've missed you and I want you home with me for a while at least. That damn job has turned out worse and more dangerous than I could ever have imagined.'

'It's all just about finished, sweetheart. You don't need to worry anymore.'

The next few hours would show just how wrong that statement was.

After the usual security checks, they made their way to the commissioner's office. To John's surprise they weren't made to sit and sweat like errant pupils waiting to be caned outside the headmaster's office. Stormy Knight's receptionist announced their arrival immediately and waved them into the head policeman's office with a smile.

John and Annette glanced at each other in surprise and pushed open the commissioner's door. Harold Knight was already on his feet and in the process of striding the half a dozen steps necessary to meet them halfway.

'Great to have you back safe and sound,' he announced warmly, extending his hand for them each to shake in turn. 'Don't worry about apologising for breaching protocols or keeping me out of the loop. I admit I was pretty damn annoyed to start with but I've had plenty of time to reflect on the difficult situation you were confronted with, John. I've decided I would probably have made the same decision under the circumstances.

'As for you, Constable Thompson, I don't quite know what to say. One part of me wants to give you a severe bollocking and another part of me wants to pat you on the back and compliment you for such amazing work.'

As Annette blushed and stammered for an appropriate response John interjected. 'I hope you'll go with the latter choice, Commissioner Knight. This young woman deserves most of the credit for the success of what was an extremely perilous and tiring piece of investigative work. Her imagination and ingenuity and sheer persistence put her in the category of one of the finest, most dedicated police officers I have ever encountered.

'On the other hand, I acted impulsively and had no business placing her in such danger. I could not have tracked Richard Nolan down without her help and I certainly couldn't have sprung him from Fleming's clutches without Constable Thompson's help.'

Knight smiled. 'Every policeman knows, when rash moves result in a successful conclusion one is declared a hero and the whole world sings one's praises. On the other hand, when departing from established procedures and protocols ends in disaster, everybody says you're a fool and the Establishment wants your guts for garters. Fortunately, your and Annette's actions resulted in the arrest of an attempted assassin and a man who has long been in the pocket of an extremely corrupt and evil politician.

'Unfortunately, said politician the not-so-honourable Senator Philip Bacon is still at large, although you'll be pleased to know we've already raided his home and located the listening device planted by Richard Nolan.' The commissioner waved them to a small lounge adjoining his office. 'But please sit down.

I'd like a blow by blow account of everything you and Annette have been up to.'

'It's the least we can do Harold.' John thought it was now safe to revert to first name basis. 'I just hope Nolan's recordings implicating Fleming and Bacon will be admissible. If the judge deems them to have been unlawfully obtained and throws them out we'll be forced to rely on the word of a disgraced former navy diver and self-confessed treasonist.'

'I don't think we'll have a problem. I just got word from our boys that Fleming has already agreed to a little plea bargaining in exchange for telling the whole story. He seemed enormously relieved that it was all over at last and he no longer has to lead a double life. We've also got the testimony of the ASIO agents he used to corroborate Nolan's claims.

'Flipper Fleming will still spend most of his life behind bars but he's a man who'll carve himself a useful niche within the prison walls and we might even let him write his memoirs, heavily redacted of course.

'It's just a matter of time before we catch up with Philip Bacon and I can't see even the best QC getting that evil bastard off the hook. Right now he's Australia's most wanted fugitive. As the old saying goes, he might be able to run, but he can't hide.'

'What about Richard Nolan, sir?' Annette wanted to know. 'I know he allowed himself to be used and he did try to murder John's father. I know that falls within the definition of treason because he's the prime minister, but I can't help feel some sympathy for him. The Director-General of ASIO threatened to have his family killed and then there's the matter of post-traumatic stress disorder after that horrible business during the First Gulf War. Even John agrees he should be cut some slack.'

Stormy Knight smiled. 'All of which he can use as mitigation when it comes to sentencing. We can't afford to have serving police officers running amok and trying to kill our prime ministers. The bloody country is close enough to anarchy as it is.

'Now, let's get on with how you and John tracked down Nolan and managed to get the Director-General of ASIO arrested in Bali.'

By the time John and Annette had related every aspect of their search for Richard Nolan and explained how they'd tracked him to Denpasar and rescued him from Fleming's clutches, the evening sky had darkened. John tried unsuccessfully to suppress a yawn as his body cried out for sleep. Seeing his distress, Stormy Knight stood up. 'I must apologise, John and Annette. I was so carried away by your account I forgot that you must both be near exhaustion. Let me arrange transport.'

John managed a grin. 'I guess I am getting a bit long in the tooth for such shenanigans. I hope when I wake up tomorrow Bacon's arrest will be front page news.'

John and Annette shared the same unmarked AFP vehicle which turned out to be the commissioner's personal car chauffeured by an armed officer of the Close Personal Protection Unit. John shook hands with the man and introduced Annette and then himself.

'It's okay, Mr McCarthy, I think every FEDPOL copper knows you two now,' he said, his handsome features breaking into a grin. 'You have become legends overnight. My name's Mike Patterson, by the way.'

John guessed correctly that the young officer would have been especially selected for his extraordinary driving skills, marksmanship and ability to acquit himself well under the worst possible scenarios. He couldn't help noticing that Annette was eyeing him with considerable interest and smiled inwardly.

'Take Constable Thompson home first, if you wouldn't mind,' he told Patterson. 'My old bones will hang together a bit longer yet.'

Twenty minutes later, the commissioner's Statesman Deville swung into John and Mary McCarthy's driveway. Mary, who'd obviously been watching out the front windows, came running down the path and threw herself into her husband's arms. 'Thank God you're home safe,' she blubbed, her tears staining his shirt front. 'I thought I was never going to see you again. Please tell me you won't do anything like that again.'

John hugged her, waving with one hand to Patterson as, clearly embarrassed, he backed the limo out into the quiet suburban street and accelerated away with a tiny farewell beep of the horn.

Like honeymooners John and Mary strolled arm in arm to the front door of their modest bungalow. Every light in the house was turned on and the garden brightly lit with floodlights that his wife had obviously had installed since he'd last been home. 'Geez Mary, are you trying to drain all the power from the national grid?' John joked.

'With everything that's been happening I didn't feel safe without you here. I swear I haven't slept more than a few hours each night. I would have asked Matt to come and stay with me instead of bunking down in that dreadful police barracks but the thought of having policeman wandering around the place all the time gave me the willies.'

'You could have asked Daniel to come and keep you company. You know our grandson dotes on you.'

Mary stopped walking and stood on tip toe to kiss him. 'In fact I did. Both Daniel and Sienna arrived today. They think you're pretty marvellous the way you singlehandedly tracked down and captured their father's would-be assassin, not to mention that slime bag, Flipper Fleming.'

'Not singlehandedly,' John reminded her. 'Annette Thompson's been like bloody Wonder Woman.'

'Surprise!' the McCarthy's grandchildren yelled in unison as they burst from the front door and threw themselves at their grandfather.

Tears welling in his eyes, John wrapped his long arms around them all. A huge lump seemed to block his throat and he didn't trust himself to speak for several seconds.

Thank you God for protecting them all while I wasn't here.

The two teenagers excitedly demanding to know about John's adventures, the foursome entered the house. John closed the heavy front door and ever conscious of their power bills, he turned off the outside floodlights.

Watching a block away from his car, Philip Bacon's upper lip curled in a sneer. He took another slug from the nearly empty whisky bottle and reached into the vehicle's glove compartment, withdrawing a holstered nine millimetre Browning pistol. He slid the well maintained firearm from its leather sheath and checked the magazine to make sure it had a full clip. Pulling back the slide to chamber a round he then flicked on the safety catch. Familiar with all sorts of ordnance, Bacon knew relying on the safety catch was a dangerous move but he was past caring. He donned the shoulder holster so the pistol sat more or less snugly in his armpit.

'Only dickheads put a loaded weapon in their waistband or pocket. Fastest way to get your dick blown off,' he told himself and began walking quietly but unsteadily due to his state of semi-intoxication toward the McCarthy house.

'Okay, Mr Bloody Super-Cop. Let's see how you handle what I have planned for you and your precious little family for fucking up my life,' the disgraced Vietnam veteran mumbled.

Although he was dead tired, John brushed aside any thought of going to bed in favour of spending quality time with Mary and his grandchildren. He knew he'd soon succumb to fatigue and just hoped he wouldn't fall asleep in the chair while they demanded the intricate details of his recent exploits.

'Okay you two, that's enough. Your granddad is exhausted and we need to let him go to bed. The story telling can wait until the morning,' Mary ordered as her husband struggled to keep his eyelids separated.

Dan nudged his sister and grinned as he looked pointedly at the clock. 'I suppose you're going to bed too Grandma. I guess you oldies need your beauty sleep.'

'Ew, don't be gross,' Sienna told her brother. At sixteen she couldn't imagine her parents let alone her grandies would still have sex. *They're so old. They must be like in their sixties.*

Mary laughed and whacked her grandson on his upper arm with a rolled up magazine. 'You cheeky little sod,' she scolded. 'You two make sure you lock up and turn the perimeter alarm on before you go to bed,' she said, and kissed them both.

John punched Dan on the shoulder lightly and kissed his granddaughter's forehead. 'Sorry kids, if I don't get some shut eye I'll be a wreck for the next week. I'll cook us a huge bacon and egg breakfast on the barbie in the morning.'

The two teenagers spent several minutes debating the merits of the programmes on Foxtel before deciding they'd challenge each other to a game of pool on their grandfather's recently acquired pool table. As they passed their grandparents' bedroom door Daniel pointed to the gap at the bottom of the door. There wasn't any light showing under the door. 'They wasted no time getting between the sheets,' he whispered.

'You've got a one track mind,' Sienna replied disgustedly. 'Listen, I can hear Granddad snoring.'

'I guess he would have been pretty exhausted after all he's been through, but the man's still a legend,' Daniel responded admiringly. 'Let's make sure we close the poolroom door so we don't wake them up.'

'It might be a good idea to take the phone off the hook too,' Sienna suggested. 'You can guarantee somebody will decide to phone if we don't.'

There was an extension phone in the pool room. Taking his sister's advice, Dan lifted the telephone handset from its cradle. Failing to notice the dial tone he held the receiver to his ear. 'That's strange. The phone's dead.'

'Maybe Grandma hasn't paid the Telstra bill and they've cut off the service,' Sienna joked.

'It's probably more like some hoon in his car has knocked down a power pole somewhere close. If it's still off in the morning, we'll let Grandma and Granddad know they need to get onto Telstra,' Dan decided, selecting a pool cue from the rack. 'Now, I bet I can beat you three games in a row.'

Situated at the rear of the house overlooking a kidney-shaped swimming pool, the McCarthy games room was fitted with sliding French doors that could be pulled back to connect the area to a spacious, covered outdoor entertainment area. With the inside lights blazing and the backyard in darkness neither teenager was aware of the stocky figure watching them through the glass.

Clutching the nine millimetre pistol in his right fist, the Boar reached out with his free hand and tried the brass door handle gently. He smiled in satisfaction as it gave way under his touch. Obviously someone had forgotten to lock the door.

Good. It saves me having to make any noise yet. I can have a little fun with these two kids before I start on poor old Granddad and Grandma.

The door slid almost silently on its runners as he opened a gap sufficiently large to accommodate his heavy paunch and sack of miscellaneous items he'd scavenged from the McCarthys' garden shed. Placing the sack just inside the door he stepped into the games room. Dan, who was in the process of sinking the last of four balls in a row, was the first to feel the sudden draught of cool night air. He lifted his eyes from the point of the cue toward the reason for the cold air.

'Fuck, who are you? What do you want?' he exclaimed in alarm as he focussed on what seemed like miniature cannon aimed in his direction.

Sienna, whose back had been toward the sliding door, swung around and squealed in terror.

'Shut the fuck up, both of you,' the Boar snarled. 'One more noise from either of you and your brains will be all over the room.'

Dan's gaze roamed quickly around the games room in search of a likely weapon to use against the repugnant-looking and obviously unfit intruder. He wondered why a man this age would be toting a gun and breaking into houses. Could he be an escapee from a mental institution?

Sienna, however, recognised their assailant immediately. As an aspiring politician she had made it her business to memorise the features and profiles of most serving political figures. 'Oh my God, you're Senator Philip Bacon,' she gasped. 'What do you want with us?'

'A shit load of revenge for your precious grandfather ruining everything I've built up over nearly half a century, but don't think you're going to waylay me with your stupid girlish prattle until you and your brother here work out a way to overpower me.' Waving the pistol in Dan's face he sneered, 'I saw you sizing up the situation. Compared with you I am a fuck-up physically but remember the bloke with the gun is always the boss.'

Daniel looked at the bulging sack lying on the carpeted floor. 'What's in there?'

'You're about to find out sonny boy.' The Boar went into a half squat and reached into the bag, his eyes never leaving Daniel and Sienna. He'd expected the two to be almost paralysed with fear and felt disappointed that they'd quickly regained their composure.

I'll have to do something about that or that big kid is going to try and be a hero.

'Lie down on your stomach, kid, and put your hands behind your back. Now!' he ordered when the young man failed to respond.

'What if I don't?' Dan asked. 'Are you going to add another murder to the list of crimes the Feds want you for? You won't get away with this you know.'

'Listen, smart arse, I'll only tell you this once. You might be brave enough to risk a bullet but it's not you I am going to shoot first, it's the little princess here. I am guessing you don't want to be responsible for her death or even worse, spending her life in a wheelchair when I blow her spine away, so do as you're told.'

Dan sank to his knees slowly and spreadeagled himself beside the pool table. His mind was racing. Once this man had him tied up Sienna and his grandparents were at his mercy.

Throwing a reel of strong twine at Sienna's feet, Philip Bacon snarled, 'Tie his wrists and feet together and make sure you do a good job because I'll be checking your handiwork.'

Sienna stooped and retrieved the ball of nylon twine. Tears coursed down her cheeks as she hogtied her brother. 'I'm so sorry, Dan,' she whispered. 'Should I just scream my lungs out and tell Grandma and Granddad to run for their lives?'

The Boar sniggered, his whisky-laden breath wafting over her. 'I heard that, Princess. You can do that if you like. In fact, knowing your grandfather he'll come bursting through that door to your rescue which will just speed things up from my perspective. Think about what it'll be like seeing them die before I put the final bullet in you. Now, lie down beside your brother while I tie you up. I'm pretty good with knots and can truss you up with one hand. Meanwhile Mr Browning here will be pointed at your pretty little head in case you get any ideas.'

Sienna's breath whooshed from her lungs as the Boar's full weight descended on her back via his knees. Looping the twine over her slim wrist he snared her other hand and brutally wrenched her arms together, causing her to gasp in pain.

'Don't worry about the loss of blood to your hands. Shortly, neither of you is going to be needing them anyway,' Bacon told them as finished securing the teenagers by tying them to the heavy slate bed pool table's legs. Stuffing both their mouths with rags he sealed their lips with gaffer tape and stood back breathing heavily to admire his handiwork.

'Okay, that should keep you two out of harm's way and stop you screaming the bloody neighbourhood down while I go to work on your granddad and grandma.'

Daniel and Sienna's eyes rolled wildly in their sockets and they writhed around on the floor as the true horror of the situation hit home. They'd both concluded the rogue senator was in a dangerously suicidal frame of mind. He clearly didn't care about the consequences to himself as long as he tortured his victims before he met his own demise.

Mary McCarthy woke suddenly from a deep sleep. She had no idea what had awakened her. John was snoring softly beside her and the house seemed quiet.

Too quiet.

Glancing at the digital bedside clock she noticed the time: 10.30pm. *Surely Dan and Sienna haven't gone to bed yet? I wonder if they set the perimeter alarm like I told them to?*

Reminding herself that teenagers have different priorities and may have forgotten, she decided to go and check. She slipped quietly from the bed, put on her dressing gown, and tiptoed into the hallway taking care not to disturb her sleep-deprived spouse. Sure enough the alarm panel by the front entrance had not yet been armed. 'Little buggers,' she muttered. 'They've gone to bed without setting the alarm. Don't they realise we're all targets since Matthew became prime minister?'

Mary was about to push the appropriate button, but something was wrong. A light showed one of the exterior doors had been left open. She checked the panel's index and was surprised to find that the games room door had not been closed. *Surely those kids aren't in the swimming pool this late?* Strange noises were emanating from behind the door to the games room that had nothing to do with teenagers swimming or playing pool. Puzzled, she opened the door, expecting to find Daniel and Sienna engrossed in one of their computer games that she could never get the hang of.

'Ah, Mrs McCarthy, what a pleasant surprise,' an unfamiliar voice said. 'Do come in and join the party.'

Mary took in the terrible scene that confronted her. Both her precious grandchildren were trussed up and gagged on the floor and she knew immediately who the paunchy man with the pig-like eyes was.

'How dare you come into my home, you evil man,' Mary spat. 'What do you think you're doing bringing a gun into my home and tying up my grandchildren? Untie them this instant and get out, because if my husband comes in here and sees what you've done he'll surely kill you.'

The Boar could not help but admire Mary McCarthy's fearlessness, but he swapped his grip on the pistol and savagely backhanded her across the face. 'Shut up bitch. Get down on the floor with your spoilt brats.'

Clutching the huge red welt left across one cheek by the gun's handle, Mary let her knees buckle and she toppled face down onto the carpet.

'Perfect,' Bacon smirked. Sitting astride the semi-conscious woman's shoulders he soon had her securely tied and gagged. The power he now wielded over his hapless victims had sexually aroused him; a state he had not enjoyed for years. Rubbing the unaccustomed bulge in his crotch he contemplated raping Mary McCarthy.

'You're a good looking sheila for someone who's a grandma,' he told her. ''I bet you keep old Johnny-boy pretty happy in the sack. Maybe I'll bring him in here and let him watch while you and I have a little fun.'

Mary, who had regained consciousness, could only glare at him in terrified disgust but instead of going to fetch her obviously still-sleeping husband the Boar upended the hessian sack he'd brought with him into the room.

A strange mixture of items fell from the bag and Mary's eyes focused on a five kilogram tub of chlorine powder John sometimes used to shock dose their swimming pool. There were also various bottles of chemicals and solvents including a small drum of hydrochloric acid that John mixed with water to clean the white gunk from the salt-water chlorinator's electrode that was essential for keeping their pool sparkling clean.

She realised with horror that the Boar was going to fashion the assortment of chemicals into a bomb.

Seeing her watching him in abject terror the Boar explained, 'I learnt a lot of useful skills from my days in the army and from running Shriver Pharmaceuticals. Did you know that one can construct a bomb from the most commonplace household products? Though bomb is not the correct terminology; improvised explosive device or IED is.

'The Taliban, Al Qaeda and other cash strapped terrorist organisations deploy them to great effect all the time and I thought you all might like to experience firsthand what a few kilos of this stuff can do. Of course I don't have a detonator, but even that's not a problem,' Bacon rambled on as he busied himself assembling his deadly device.

What does this evil price of work think he's going to achieve? Mary wondered, as her mind worked flat out for some way to prevent their deaths. *He is obviously so psychotic from his hatred that he doesn't care if he kills himself as well.*

Not knowing what else she could do, Mary began drumming her heels against the skirting board, hoping John would wake up and recognise the old SOS Morse code distress signal.

Meanwhile, John, who was in the middle of a dream about the beautiful waterways and mountain peaks of New Zealand's Fiordland, slowly regained consciousness as the urge to empty his bladder overrode his dream world. Sitting up quietly so as not to disturb Mary, whom he had not yet realised was no longer in bed, he stood up and staggered sleepily to the ensuite toilet. 'Bloody prostate,' he mumbled, glancing toward the other side of the queen-sized bed. That's odd, he thought. Mary must have gone to use the other dunny so she doesn't wake me up. At that point, John became aware of an odd drumming noise reverberating through the plasterboard walls. Just as quickly as the noise had begun it stopped and the house descended into silence once more. In his still befuddled state John assumed his grandchildren were horsing around in the games room. It wasn't until he'd just about emptied his bladder that his brain cells began operating to full capacity.

That sounded like someone tapping out S.O.S. It's too early for those kids to have hit the hay yet and the house is too quiet. Something's not right, he decided.

Unbeknown to John McCarthy, Philip Bacon had just knocked Mary unconscious with the butt of his pistol. 'Stupid bitch,' he growled. 'I better go and get bloody Granddad before he wakes up and does something silly.'

Returning to the bedroom, John was tempted to attribute the noise he'd heard to his overactive imagination and just roll back into bed.

What if Mary's had a fall? I better go and investigate.

Later John would be unable to say what made him open his bedside drawer and remove the old Police 357 Magnum revolver the Federal Police had provided as a concession to his role as a member of the prime minister's family and as head of security. He checked to ensure the weapon's chamber was full, slipped quietly into the hallway and came face to face with Australia's most wanted man who was also wielding a deadly weapon.

Both men raised their firearms simultaneously. Under the circumstances John would have had no hesitation shooting Bacon in his pig-like face but the crazed senator snarled, 'Don't do it, Sunshine.' Lifting his free hand he waved a small flick switch attached to a crude-looking device strapped to his belt.

'You shoot me and my thumb will no doubt convulse, setting off my little pride and joy here. Take it from me there's enough explosive material here to send your lovely wife and grandkids to kingdom come.'

John's hand didn't waver as he kept the revolver pointed squarely between Bacon's eyes. 'So, you've now turned into a suicide bomber as well as a drug pedlar, burglar and assassin. What happened? Did you discover you couldn't run away so your twisted mind decided to seek your revenge on me because your criminal empire has come crashing down?'

'Put the gun down, McCarthy,' the Boar ordered. 'This isn't a Mexican standoff. I've got the upper hand, because unlike you, I really don't care about dying. You, on the other hand have the lives of three other people to think about.'

John still refused to lower his magnum. He reasoned Bacon was intent on blowing them all up anyway. Maybe it would come down to him taking the slim chance or trying to shoot the Boar's left hand and disable it before he could flick the switch. In the meantime he would try to keep the man talking in the hope he could bring him to his senses.

Philip Bacon seemed to read John's mind however. 'I know you're a former police negotiator. You think you can build some sort of rapport with me and I'll change my mind or you'll distract me so you can get the upper hand. We're not playing that fucking game!' Bacon shouted. 'You hear me?'

'What have you done to Mary and the kids, Senator? At least have the decency to spare them. They aren't part of this. They're just innocent people caught up in events beyond their control.'

John lowered the revolver and threw it on a nearby armchair hoping the psychopath standing a few feet away could be persuaded to vent his anger verbally before he flicked the bomb's switch.

If I am going to die, I'd like some answers first.

He knew from many experiences as an unarmed frontline cop in New Zealand's police service where he'd found himself one on one with an angry, armed offender determined to kill that every moment he could wangle increased his chances of survival and he'd often advised rooky cops, "Always remember, your mouth and your brain are your best defensive weapons."

Now was his chance to prove it.

'Let's you and I go and sit down and talk this over, Senator. You need the chance to get all that pent up hatred and anger off your chest before you kill me. You need to make me understand what I've done to bring you to such a desperate state of mind before you kill me, or it's all rather pointless, isn't it?'

Bacon appeared to be considering John's proposition. 'I used to be one of the most powerful men in Australian politics. Nearly every prime minister since Harold Holt used to come to me for advice. I am a Vietnam Vet. I served my country and got spat on for my trouble by an ungrateful public when I should have received awards for meritorious service.

'After the war I worked bloody hard to create a major international pharmaceutical company supplying millions of dollars in medicines all over the world.

'I had it all, wealth, power, prestige, in fact I had the perfect life, until you came along and ruined everything.'

You also ruined thousands of people's lives, you piece of shit.

John knew he had to choose his words carefully lest the Boar return to his enraged state. 'There's no doubt you accomplished much of which you have a right to be proud, Senator, but what I don't understand is your relationship with the Director-General of ASIO and why the two of you wanted to kill my son.'

Spittle flew from Bacon's mouth as he shouted, 'Your son is a rabid lefty who is going to ruin Australia's economy with his whacko ideas about climate change. This blasted Zero Carbon Energy Bill he's ramming through parliament is sheer madness and his idea of a national anti-drug agency is a crock of shit that will drive the bikie gangs underground.

'I tried to reason with him and get him to see that he's just a bloody doomsday prophet suffering from tunnel vision but he refused flat out to even speak to me.

'All this shit about species extinction and the oceans rising is a load of bunkum.'

'What do you say about the allegations that have been around for years that you've been bringing illegal drugs into Australia and using the bikie gangs to distribute them?'

'So fucking what? People use drugs all the time. It's a fact of life. If they didn't buy them from me, there'd be a hundred other suppliers willing to meet the demand. At least the stuff I made was clean, not cooked up in some backyard shed with dubious ingredients. My stuff was the highest quality and I had to have a distribution network, so why not the bikies?'

McCarthy could hardly believe his ears. Like most criminals, Philip Bacon was able to justify his most heinous actions. 'How did you get the stuff through Customs?'

'Indonesian fishermen were only too happy to drop it off at prearranged points along the northern coast, but why the hell am I telling you all this? It won't do you any good.'

'I am just trying to understand, Senator. They say, confession is good for the soul and there's no point killing me unless you get me to see your point of view, remember?'

Although he had no evidence to support his theory, he suspected the recent attacks by JI had been financed at least in part by the profits from Philip Bacon's illicit drug empire but it was too dangerous at this point to make such a suggestion to the half-drunk crazed individual who was still menacing him with a gun and explosives. Better to keep to safer topics.

'I still don't understand why you had to resort to killing the prime minister. That's an act of treason.'

'Someone had to stop him. Sometimes it's the only way. I bet you didn't know that the fucking coal industry led by Mal Walker and your very own Helen Knox were the ones who knocked off Bowker. Walker was too gutless to try the same thing again with your son, so he came to me.'

Bacon smiled proudly. 'They all come to me to sort out their problems. That's why I've lasted so long in the filthy cut-throat world of politics and business.'

Jesus, I never realised there is so much corruption in Australia.

'What about James Fleming? How did you get him to do your bidding?'

'James Fleming is nothing but a weak, fucking poofter and a paedophile. I recognised that in him the first day I met him in Nam when I needed a lackey to run errands for me. He fitted the bill nicely although he gave me the shits and I tried to get him bumped off by reassigning him to the frontline. It didn't work. Somehow the jammy bastard managed to survive Long Tan. The Army thought he was a bloody hero and assigned him to their intelligence division. From then on it was all plain sailing for Flipper. He built himself a successful career in the intelligence world and I wasn't about to let someone who could keep me fed with inside information off the hook.'

'So it was your idea to get him to arrange Matthew's assassination?'

'Yeah, but I stuffed up badly there. I should have known he'd bugger it up but it all sounded pretty good. Your son is a mad keen diver. If anybody had the knowhow to make his death look like a diving accident it was that bloke Nolan. He is an underwater expert but the prick didn't have the bottle to do it himself, and asked Flipper to hire a couple of guys to do it. Turns out they were just brainless fuckups who panicked when their shots missed.'

John wanted to ask the thugs' names but thought it was pointless. Bacon probably didn't know and the Feds would eventually extract their names from Fleming.

'Senator, with all your money and influence, surely you could have fled the country or at least got your bikie mates to hide you until the heat was off. What went wrong?'

'I reckon that old fart of a security guard sold me out. That's the only explanation. I should have been in Venezuela or South America by now. I even promised to look after the bastard for the rest of his days if he let me get the head start I needed.

'You know, I've looked after that greedy prick for donkey's years. I gave him a steady job with good pay when no one else would employ him because of his criminal record, and that's how the bastard repays me. Fuck, you can't trust anyone these days.'

Despite the gravity of the situation John had to smile. 'There's no loyalty among thieves, eh?'

Bacon continued as if he hadn't heard John's remark. 'I was nearly at the airport when I heard on the scanner that the entire constabulary was looking for me.

'I knew a fat little bastard like me whose face is so well known would never get past the airport facial recognition systems. I reckon every cop and customs officer in the country knows me by sight. My escape route was blocked and the bikies wouldn't have any use for me once they knew I was up Shit Creek, so I concluded there was only one thing left to do and that was to inflict the maximum pain on the people who had wrecked my life.'

'So, by killing me, Mary, Dan and Sienna, you know Matthew will spend the rest of his life blaming himself, is that it?'

The Boar's patience was running thin. 'You've got it Sunshine. Now, the talking's over. It's time to finish what I came here for. Get in there.'

'One more thing before you kill me and my family; I want you to know that it's not only the illegal drugs you peddle that ruin so many lives. Some of your prescription poisons trap innocent people in a tragic cycle of addiction. But then again, I guess you worked that one out very early in the piece, didn't you?'

John's question was purely rhetorical and he continued his tirade because he too wanted to get something off his chest now that he was confronting the man responsible for his long battle against Bacon's methadone-based drug Septaphycine.

'If it wasn't for the people I love, I'd risk a bullet for the chance to rip your throat out for the suffering and the cycle of addiction you've caused with that muck Septaphycine that you peddle legally. It took me six weeks of hell to break free from my addiction to it.

'You've no idea how many times I've cursed you and your company. I've never hated anyone in my life but I detest you and all the evil bastards like you that have ruined the lives of so many people.'

'Think I give a shit about your hatred? Life's all about grabbing what you can while you can. It's all about survival of the fittest. We're all just animals. God is just a fairy-tale character invented by weak, gutless people too afraid to face reality. There's no afterlife and there's no hell.

'Console yourself with the thought that you'll soon be oblivious to anything and everything. Unfortunately for your son, he's going to endure a living hell for the next thirty or forty years knowing that you all died slow painful and horrible deaths because of his bullshit quest to save the world.

'That and watching you suffer before I blow us all away gives me great satisfaction in my last moments.'

The Boar motioned with his pistol toward the games room. John realised there was no longer any point trying to reason with this man who was evil personified. In the next few minutes he would have to take the risk of being shot or having his family blown up because they were all going to die anyway and there was no way he was going to allow Bacon to inflict further cruelty on those he loved.

With his arms raised, he walked slowly toward the open doorway where he could see Mary and his teenage grandchildren lying next to the pool table. Bacon followed, pressing the barrel of his pistol into the small of John's back.

As a former soldier the senator should have known better.

Dan and Sienna seemed unharmed although their wrists were swelling around the strong, thin nylon twine that cut into and immobilised their hands. Blood ran from a deep cut on Mary's scalp, staining her nightdress and gown crimson. She watched him enter the room, the whites of her eyes bloodshot and terror written all over her face.

John's already seething anger erupted in a volcanic rage at the sight of his beloved wife's injuries. Mustering all his strength so he became like a coiled spring, he spun on his right heel and chopped down savagely with his right arm, knocking the Boar's gun hand away.

Please God, don't let him flick that switch.

John's sudden, lightning-fast vicious chopping blow took the Boar unawares. Being right hand dominant, his brain naturally sent an instinctive message to his right hand first and he squeezed the Browning's trigger sending a single round harmlessly into the wall. In the split second before Bacon's alcohol-riddled brain could compute the situation and direct the required nerve impulse to his left hand to activate the flick switch, John followed through with a left-handed roundhouse punch to Bacon's head. The portly, aging and very unfit senator spun sideways and lost his grip on the bomb's activating mechanism.

As the Boar fell to the floor still clutching the pistol John thanked his maker that the fall hadn't knocked the switch to the on position and blown them all to smithereens.

Bacon fumbled for the switch but John's well-aimed kick to his left wrist shattered the many tiny bones, sending blinding pain shooting up the Boar's arm. Bacon screamed in agony but he wasn't done yet. With a roar of rage he brought the pistol to bear on the tall, infuriated figure looming over him. John dived headlong onto the Senator's prostate form in a desperate bid to knock the pistol away. Unfortunately, at such a close range Bacon could not miss.

The gun fired. Searing pain in John's right hip almost caused him to lose consciousness but he fought through the blinding waves of agony and nausea, his hands finding the Boar's throat. The gun fired again but this time the weight of John's body prevented the Boar from bringing the weapon to bear on his assailant.

With hands large enough to pick up a basketball singlehandedly, John often did not know his own strength and consequently he was infamous for his crushing handshakes. Now, he brought every ounce of pressure he could muster into a grip encircling the Boar's flabby throat. Squeezing until the other man's eyes bulged from their sockets, his heels drummed on the floor and his tongue protruded from his gurgling mouth, John had no thought for the lawyers who would later try to accuse him of murder. He'd never felt anything as satisfying in his life as literally squeezing the life from this evil man beneath him.

Die you bastard. It will save the country the cost of a trial and deprive bottom-dwelling lawyers from profiting from your defence.

At last the Boar went limp. In death he was transformed into an ineffectual fat old man with no capacity to hurt anyone.

John rolled off Bacon's inert form. Unable to stand because of the injury to his hip that was spouting geysers of blood, he clamped his free hand over the wound to stem the flow. Crawling first to Mary, he managed to free her hands and remove the gag from her mouth before he lost consciousness.

Mary's first action was to grab Dan's iPhone from his pocket. She dialled 000 and gasped, 'Please get an ambulance here as quickly as you can. My husband's been shot and he's bleeding to death.' After making sure the Triple 0 operator had the correct address, she maintained pressure to John's severed artery.

Turning her tear-stained face toward her still trussed grandchildren Mary sobbed, 'I am sorry my dears, I can't leave John to untie you until the ambulance gets here. I've got to keep pressure on his wound.' She was rewarded by understanding nods from both teenagers and a few moments later her keen hearing picked up the wail of fast approaching sirens.

'Don't die please, John. Please God, oh please God...' Mary wailed as she pressed firmly down on her husband's wound. Despite her ripping her gown off with one hand and bunching it into a pad, the blood continued to pour through her fingers, pooling on the carpeted floor in a huge crimson tide.

'Where the hell is that ambulance? He'll bleed out in a minute if they don't get here. Hurry up. Hurry up. Oh God please make them hurry,' she cried.

After what seemed like half an hour but was in reality only a few minutes, the wail of approaching sirens grew rapidly louder.

+++++++++++

Chapter Thirty-Two

Work on raising the Assegai commenced in earnest amid an unprecedented diplomatic storm. Nations angry at the holdup to their iron ore shipments and the vulnerability of their expensive super tankers locked in the cyclone-prone harbour demanded compensation from the Australian government. To add to the prime minister's woes, a string of countries lodged protests over Australia's plan to surreptitiously commence seeding international waters. Several nations even threatened to cut diplomatic ties and cease trading with Australia if it went ahead with what they termed "massive environmental vandalism that threatens already depleted pelagic fish stocks."

As expected, Brian Caldwell did his utmost to swing the Greens and Independents against the government, calling for a motion of no-confidence once parliament resumed. Caldwell even went so far as to lobby Greenpeace, Get Up and the Sea Shepherd, bombarding them with every argument he could muster from the vast array of research that opposed or cast doubt on the likelihood of McCarthy's ocean seeding programme succeeding.

Fortunately, the prime minister had already included these groups along with the Greens and the Independents in the loop, providing them with all the information at the disposal of the Woods Hole Institute and inviting their representatives to monitor Operation CO2S as soon as the Assegai was raised and moved out of harm's way.

Caldwell's request for an audience with the governor general was conveniently delayed when Her Majesty's Representative discovered an urgent need to attend to private family business matters necessitating a flight to London. As required by the Constitution, the most senior state governor automatically became the caretaker governor general during what was expected to be "a prolonged absence of an indeterminate period." The temporary incumbent refused to be drawn into the controversy, announcing, that 'matters of such a contentious nature should be addressed by the normal democratic process at the next sitting of the Australian parliament.'

The caretaker GG's announcement provided Labor with three months' grace.

While some of the independents refused to sanction Labor's plan they demonstrated surprising gumption by agreeing to sit on the fence. McCarthy and his colleagues guessed they hoped to claim a sizeable portion of the credit if the plan succeeded and if it failed they would join the throngs announcing, "We told you so." However, when McCarthy announced his promise to begin tackling the looming threat from the Great Pacific Garbage Dump at the conclusion of operation CO2S even Brian Caldwell offered unqualified support but he couldn't help adding the rider, 'Of course, Labor's stolen the idea from the Coalition.'

Amid all the brouhaha Matthew McCarthy took his Cabinet's advice to ride out the storm and await vindication. While he stiffened his resolve to steer the good ship Australia through treacherous waters filled with as yet unknown hazards and the most savage of political pirates there was one storm which neither Matthew nor his allies could hope to sail through unscathed.

Eight hundred kilometres off the Northwest Coast an intense tropical low gave every indication of building into a severe tropical cyclone. Weather satellites tracking the huge rotating cloud mass showed the system was sucking enormous quantities of moisture from the Indonesian archipelago.

Every coastal town between Darwin and Exmouth focussed on the system but Port Hedland residents treated the spectacle with more than their usual blasé indifference, watching anxiously for the development of a tell-tale eye; the harbinger of potential catastrophic destruction.

Knowing so much rode on the successful clearing of the harbour channel, commercial rivalries and dissension against the Australian government for its role in creating the crisis was put aside, at least for the moment. The masters and crews of every ship trapped by the sinking of the Assegai rallied behind the divers and sailors from the three navy frigates, keeping them well supplied with welding equipment, tools, compressors, and most importantly moral support.

Sealing the sunken ship proved far more difficult than first thought. Choppy waters, filthy conditions and treacherous currents took their toll on the few available divers possessing the requisite skills. Trying to weld with almost zero visibility and two metre swells running was nigh on impossible but the courageous divers lashed themselves to the sunken hulk and pushed on. One unfortunate diver suffered a debilitating gash to his torso when he accidently brushed against a rusted hatch cover made jagged by years of neglected corrosion temporarily halting the re-floating efforts. Fortunately, a former navy diver now employed as a FIFO worker stepped forward to fill the gap until a relief crew could be flown in from far away Sydney.

Meanwhile the weather bureau made the announcement everyone expected but dreaded. The whirling mass of cloud with wing-like tentacles spreading across the Australian continent from Broome to the Great Australian Bight had become Tropical Cyclone Carol, a strength three system that was still building ferocity. Now less than five hundred kilometres from the Broome coastline, she was moving in a south easterly direction and expected to strike land within the next forty-one hours.

The big question was, where exactly would she hit?

Although Carol was yet to vent her full fury, steep-sided waves that would have delighted surf-board riders rolled into the Port Hedland Harbour entrance, severely hampering the brave divers' efforts. Barges and tenders anchored in the channel to provide platforms for the salvage crews bobbed like corks. Taut as piano wires, their anchor cables emitted their own eerie tune as fifty kilometre per hour winds threatened to tear the anchor flukes from the thin layer of mud and crumbling limestone that comprised the channel's bottom.

Knowing the giant ships trapped against the wharves could be driven ashore by the full force of a category five cyclone, Gary Duscher, himself a former naval Chief Petty Officer turned harbour master, gambled on the navy divers succeeding in their mission to re-float the Assegai and ordered the masters of every ship to immediately prepare to leave the port and outrun Cyclone Carol.

Meanwhile, Pilbara residents, many of whom were veterans of previous catastrophic cyclones, plundered supermarket shelves, boarded up their windows and prepared themselves emotionally to ride out the storm. Some of the more foolhardy residents who consisted mainly of new arrivals and visitors who failed to understand the threat even bought up big on alcohol stocks with the intention of throwing cyclone parties against the sage advice of police and state emergency services. Unfortunately, it is impossible to legislate against stupidity but those who would be tasked with dealing with the consequences of irresponsible behaviour shook their heads angrily.

At last the welding operation was completed. Huge barge-mounted pumps began disgorging filthy, oil-slicked seawater from the Assegai while massive compressors forced air into the hull to hasten the process.

It was now too dangerous for divers to go anywhere near the Assegai. The powerful seas were throwing loose cables, busted rigging and all manner of deck-mounted machinery that had broken free about beneath the murky waters. It was almost if the ship was fighting back against the attempts to raise her from her watery grave and anyone foolhardy enough to venture near risked being killed or maimed.

Having previously attached steel cables to the Assegai, the Port Hedland Authority tug Hercules easily rode the swell, marking time until the Assegai's superstructure broke the surface. Her skipper, Malarchy "Spud" Murphy, a burly, red-headed Irishman with a stentorian voice, watched anxiously, along with the Hercules bosun and the exhausted navy divers, some even offering silent prayers that the rusted hulk would soon reveal its ugly, timeworn carcass once more.

The rolling swell threatened to rip the bilge and air hoses free from their anchor points on the Assegai's hull at any moment. If that happened, the entire operation would become a disastrous failure. Under the savage conditions there was no way of reattaching or repairing the hoses and whatever seawater that had been pumped out would be immediately replaced.

One of the Hercules deck crew suddenly shouted and pointed excitedly, 'Look, I can see her radio mast. She must be off the bottom now.'

All eyes followed the direction of the seaman's outstretched hand. 'Nah, it's just because the troughs between the waves are getting deeper,' the Spud responded cynically.

'No, he's right, look,' one of the navy divers yelled. 'Have a little faith for God's sake. I knew we could do it.'

Sure enough, millimetre by millimetre the Assegai began to break the choppy, windswept surface. Murphy's broad face split into a grin. 'The moment her deck is above the water, you fellas can board her, detach the air and pump hoses and close the valves to make sure she doesn't take on any more water.' Patting the Hercules throttle levers almost lovingly Murphy announced confidently, 'This big beast ain't called Hercules for nothing. As long as she's clear of the bottom, we will soon have her out of the shipping channel. It's a good job you blokes rigged her with explosive charges in case a cyclone such as this came in. You'll now be able to blow her to bits.

'I know the authorities wanted to examine her and gather evidence, but under the circumstances, she'd be too much of a hazard, so send her to Davey Jones' Locker.'

Boarding the waterlogged wreck from the pitching deck of the tug was out of the question so the navy's rigid inflatable dive boat powered across the intervening space, almost leaping clear of the water as it took each wave head on.

As the demolition crew drew closer, the RIB's helmsman powered down the twin Mercury outboard motors and skilfully approached the wallowing Assegai on its leeward side, allowing the two nimble, wet-suited divers to grab the Assegai's rail which was only a few feet above the ocean surface. Both men quickly scrambled onto the dead ship's wave-washed deck and set about closing off the valves as the sea surged around their legs.

Detaching the hoses, they jumped clear of the heavy, snake-like tubes that now whipped backwards and forwards like savage pythons intent on breaking their legs. Hanging onto the Assegai's guard rail, they waved frantically to the barge crews to haul the lethal hoses out of harm's way. Like giant moray eels anxious to return to their ocean home, the brass couplings splashed into the sea to be hauled back to the waiting barges which powered up their motors, weighed anchor and began plodding back to the relative safety of the harbour proper.

As soon as the Hercules' skipper was satisfied there was nothing to foul his tug's propellers, he eased the throttles forward, gradually increasing the strain on the massive, steel tow cables.

'Let's hope they don't snap,' he remarked to his crewman who had assembled in the tug's cabin as a precaution lest one of the heavy steel hawsers part company and come whistling back to decapitate them.

The muddy seawater at the Hercules' stern boiled furiously as her mighty bronze screws increased their revolutions, biting into the water, exerting colossal torque capable of moving the largest, fully-laden super tanker. Slowly, the tug and her ungainly submarine-like load made headway toward the open sea, closely followed by the navy RIB whose job it was to rescue the two divers from the doomed Assegai once the explosive charges were set.

Once clear of the harbour entrance, the Hercules changed course, taking her clear of the shipping lanes. Spud Murphy signalled to the two courageous men on the Assegai to set the timers while the RIB moved in to pick them up.

Maintaining the towlines until the Assegai disintegrated from the well-placed explosives was crucial in case something went wrong. If released too soon the stricken vessel could drift back into the shipping lanes once more, blocking ships from seeking the safety of open waters if the explosives failed to detonate.

Gradually letting out the towlines to increase the margin of safety against the shock wave when the timers reached zero, the Hercules maintained her readiness to resume the tow should it become necessary.

However, the navy men never doubted their capacity for destruction. Once aboard the RIB they wasted no time heading back toward the HMAS Parramatta, confident the Assegai would soon shudder and bulge grotesquely beneath the waterline as she was torn apart.

'Yahoo,' one of the divers yelled as three immense, simultaneous geysers of water erupted from the stricken vessel.

For a brief moment the old African freighter actually rose above the waves, displaying her barnacle-encrusted hull, which immediately split into three large chunks sinking quickly beneath the storm-tossed sea.

Murphy directed his deck crew to haul in the tow lines and the massive hydraulic winches soon wrenched the hawsers from the Assegai's remains. Turning the tug's broad bow toward the shore, Murphy rammed the Hercules' throttles full ahead. The giant tug raced at maximum knots with the following sea helping to propel her back to the harbour where the task of clearing all shipping was now absolutely crucial.

Being much smaller than the massive iron ore carriers waiting their chance to sail for India, Japan and China, the Kiama, Exmouth and Stanley were the first to clear the harbour where their escorts, Warramunga, Parramatta and Toowoomba took up their escorting positions. The six ships would initially travel due west in convoy until they outran Cyclone Carol, at which stage they would separate and head for their designated seeding zones.

By now Carol's eye was less than three hundred kilometres to the north. Having built to category four she was tipped to cross the West Australian coastline between Port Hedland and Karratha. While it was hoped the eye of the storm would miss major settlements, drenching rains and howling winds already enveloped most of the Pilbara region.

On receiving the news of the successful removal of the Assegai, Matthew McCarthy telephoned Spud Murphy and each of the navy divers who'd risked their lives, expressing his gratitude. As one familiar with the ocean's might and the hazardous nature of diving under such impossible conditions, he reckoned those involved deserved the highest praise, making a reminder in his diary to nominate them for appropriate awards on Australia Day.

Despite some famous internationally-renowned scientists stating they had been too alarmist concerning the effects of climate change, over the next few weeks it was obvious that the consequences of man's disrespect for the planet were in fact really beginning to bite as Lovelock and Gore had initially predicted. It was as if the planet had finally decided it would no longer put up with man's selfish and senseless destruction of the fragile, complex, interconnected and interdependent system known as the biosphere.

With no country being immune to what Lovelock had coined Gaia's revenge; Australia remained the only nation taking meaningful action.

The IPCC and the United Nations suddenly began adopting much stronger language in what were now almost daily pleas to world leaders to follow Australia's lead by aiming for zero carbon emissions, joining forces in announcing that immediate and concerted action was crucial to averting a worldwide calamity.

'Every nation must unite against the common foe of climate change,' they cried.

Unfortunately it seemed each country was too busy reacting to disasters such as famine, wild fires, drought, cyclones, the spread of vector-borne diseases, failing economies and a seemingly unstoppable flood of refugees to recognise and realise they must deal with the root cause of most of the world's problems.

As foretold by so many scientists decades earlier, Mother Earth had at last gone beyond the tipping point at which life could remain sustainable.

Water was the chief commodity in short supply. With the Himalayan glaciers which fed Asia's mighty rivers rapidly shrinking, upstream nations increasingly refused to share the life-giving liquid, constructing dams and selfishly diverting flows to maintain their precious crops and forcing downstream neighbours to resort to conflict, when they would have been better off joining forces to deal with the problem of a rapidly changing world climate.

Fed by spreading famine, rampant corruption and sectarian violence, the governments of African and Middle Eastern nations degenerated into further meltdown. As their financial systems crashed, anarchy became the norm in Egypt, Iraq, Lebanon, Syria, Palestine, Libya, Pakistan, Ethiopia, the Sudan,

Somalia, Rwanda and nearly every nation on the African continent.

Asia, Russia and the Orient weren't immune either. Sectarian violence, associated terrorism and anarchy had become a plague sweeping the world as entire populations rebelled against corrupt and inept leadership.

Inexplicably, as the chaos spread, warring factions still managed to find the money for weapons and ammunition, ignoring the plight of their own people who tried to flee to greener pastures that were becoming increasingly scarce.

'It seems the world will never come to its senses,' McCarthy told his family despairingly one night. 'Thank God we're an island nation but we're becoming increasingly besieged by the poor, unfortunate citizenry who are risking their lives to escape their suffering.

'Who can blame them for trying to reach our shores in such numbers? I fear it will only get worse unless powerful nations such as America and China show leadership.'

While the world seemed to be tumbling into a bottomless abyss, McCarthy's ocean seeding programme proceeded, but not without challenge.

Resentful and still smarting over Australia's successful action in the World Court to ban whaling in the Antarctic, Japan sent two warships to challenge the Kiama and its support frigate Warramunga's efforts to begin iron seeding.

Dogging both vessels at every turn the Japanese tried every strategy they could think of to hamper the Kiama and Warramunga's progress into Australia's

Antarctic Territorial Waters; an economic exclusion zone that extended two hundred nautical miles (or three-hundred and seventy kilometres) from Australia's Antarctic Territory. Unfortunately, only the United Kingdom, New Zealand, France and Norway recognised Australia's claim to the vast ice wasteland.

With Japan and other nations regarding the area where seeding was to commence as international waters, Australia had no legal recourse and was forced to play cat-and-mouse with the two Japanese frigates.

Finally, Commander Barry Hayes radioed his counterpart from HMAS Warramunga with the blunt, unambiguous message, 'If you continue to illegally block the course of my ship or the Australian Navy's Support Ship Kiama on the high seas, I will seek permission from my government to regard your actions as an act of war on the part of Japan and respond accordingly.'

A frantic message sent to the Australian Prime Minister describing Hayes' announcement resulted in immediate telephone call to his Japanese counterpart.

'Surely, your nation is not going to risk all out conflict because of Australia's attempts to take remedial action over declining phytoplankton?' McCarthy asked incredulously.

'Australia is endangering its own whale sanctuary by intending to dump iron ore into the Antarctic Ocean. It is also endangering precious fish stocks by this action. We demand that you stop.'

While McCarthy's blood boiled over the blatant hypocrisy of the Japanese who'd plundered Antarctic whale stocks under the guise of scientific research, he knew he must allow the other man to save face or the situation would result in shots being fired.

'You've made your point clear. I appreciate that Japan does not recognise Australia's territorial claims to Antarctic waters but it is illegal to impede the path of another nation's ships within its territorial waters or on the high seas. However, if there is any adverse outcome to fish stocks as a result of our iron seeding operation we will guarantee to pay your government compensation.

'Now, please ask your vessels to stand down because this operation will go ahead and I am sure neither of us wants the friendship between our nations to suffer, nor do we wish to see lives lost over this issue.'

McCarthy's tone left the Japanese Prime Minister in no doubt that he would order the Warramunga to take whatever action was necessary to ensure Operation CO2S went ahead.

'I will recall our Ambassador to Tokyo, to discuss the future of trade ties between our governments. In the meantime Japan will suspend all cooperation with Australia.'

Classic dummy spit. The little bastard will soon realise he needs us more than we need him.

'That is your prerogative, Prime Minister. When you have considered Japan's position I will be waiting to resume our discussion. In the meantime I wish you a good day, sir,' McCarthy responded tersely and hung up the phone.

Having had Japan's bluff called, the two Japanese frigates withdrew to a safe distance but continued shadowing the Kiama and Warramunga, which

521

immediately began distributing iron ore particles into the silicic acid-rich waters of Australia's Antarctic Territorial Waters.

Although the United Nations received strongly worded objections from Mexico, Peru, Chile, Ecuador and Argentina over iron seeding in international waters surrounding the Galapagos Islands, no nation was prepared to challenge Australia after Japan's capitulation.

As promised, Secretary-General Ban Ki Moon who was privately in favour of the operation delayed scheduling discussion by the UN assembly for nine months. By then the world would know if the expected phytoplankton blooms had occurred and whether they had any impact on atmospheric CO_2 levels, or if McCarthy and the Woods Hole Oceanographic Institute scientists' gamble had been a colossal mistake.

Miraculously, weather and sea conditions remained favourable in all three seeding zones, enabling the entire seventy-thousand tonnes of iron ore particles to be scattered across the ocean surface.

In the silicic depleted waters of the Sub Arctic Ocean where phytoplankton blooms were almost certain to fail, the Stanley's cargo had been enriched with silicic acid. As the Stanley steamed back and forth distributing its cargo, the iron sulphate was mixed rapidly by surface currents and ocean eddies into the upper ocean where it remained in suspension in the euphotic zone, that sunlit upper portion of the ocean that enables photosynthesis to occur.

The result staggered those aboard the Stanley and HMAS Parramatta. Within days a vast phytoplankton bloom became apparent as far the human eye could see. Satellite photographs clearly showed the tell-tale phosphorescent blue patch associated with the growth of diatoms, coccolithophores and other cyanobacteria, the microscopic marine creatures which form the basis of the marine food chain spreading for over a million square kilometres.

Krill converged on the bloom in vast numbers, closely followed by whales and pelagic fish species. Although these creatures gorged themselves to capacity on the millions of tonnes of biomass, this single bloom resulted in a marked decrease in atmospheric carbon dioxide levels.

The same story was repeated in the other iron fertilised areas and scientific observers estimated that nearly three gigatonnes of CO_2, which was almost the equivalent to a year of mankind's emissions, had been removed from the Earth's atmosphere.

In each instance, the blooms lasted between sixty and ninety days after seeding was discontinued, at which stage the carbonaceous shells of the dying phytoplankton and the white snow-like material from defecating sea creatures who had fed on the bloom, began sinking into the colder waters below the thermocline, eventually settling on the ocean floor where they would trap absorbed CO_2 for centuries.

While approximately twenty percent of the sinking bloom was demineralised, returning to the atmosphere as CO_2, there was no doubt as to the success of Operation CO2S.

World leaders, among them United States President Clement Turnbull, telephoned Matthew McCarthy offering their congratulations for the bold initiative.

'It's time for me to eat a large slice of humble pie,' the Panther told Matthew. 'When I failed to get support for tackling climate change at the Denmark conference, I threw in the towel on this issue. I knew I'd never get Congressional support for the types of measures you have planned for Australia.

'Our economy was in a mess and Americans have become tired of playing global policeman. I thought it better to focus on health reforms and internal matters but I still should have backed you.'

'I appreciate your apology,' Matthew replied. 'I too feel I owe you an apology. I was acting under extreme pressure after an attempt on my life and should never have taken out my anger on you; however, the success of Operation CO2S is only a temporary reprieve. Do not think it lets us all off the hook and we can continue business as usual. While iron fertilisation of the oceans has halted the greenhouse effect and has the capacity to revitalise the marine food chain, it will take some time for weather patterns to return to anywhere near normal. The problems associated with the unfettered use of non-renewable fuels, over-population and massive pollution of the environment remain. We have merely stepped back from the brink momentarily.

'Australia will now set another environmental bench mark by beginning the clean-up of the Great Pacific Garbage Dump, but unless all nations follow our example by addressing environmental issues, nothing will change.'

'I can at least pledge America's support on that particular issue, Matthew. I will make whatever resources we have at your disposal.

'I have also scheduled a presidential address on the state of the nation and the world. Prime Minister Cameron, Ban Ki Moon and the Chinese premier have agreed to add their voices in a worldwide plea for nations to come to their senses and follow Australia's lead. I just hope between us we carry sufficient weight to get the message across how close we came to a worldwide apocalypse.'

'It's a great start. Thank you, Clement,' Matthew replied over the lump which had suddenly developed in his throat.

+++++++++++++

Epilogue

John McCarthy's gunshot wound had shattered his hip joint, but Matthew hired the best orthopaedic surgeon he could find. A prosthetic joint was fitted successfully and although John's recovery took many weeks of painful physiotherapy he eventually walked again without a limp. He returned to his duties as the prime ministerial security advisor after promising Mary that in future he would leave the dangerous aspects of the job to much younger serving AFP officers.

As predicted, a number of publicity-seeking lawyers pressed for John to be charged with Philip Bacon's murder. An independently appointed judicial panel examined the available evidence and soon concluded that John McCarthy had no option but to take the senator's life. Had he not done so he would surely have passed out from blood loss, enabling Bacon to regain the upper hand and murder all four McCarthys.

Annette Thompson received an Australian Police Medal for gallantry. She passed her sergeant's exams with distinction and under the Federal Police merit based promotional system successfully applied for the position as Matthew McCarthy's chief personal protection officer, a position which carried the rank of Inspector.

The combination of Richard Nolan's verbal and taped evidence, James Fleming's confession and the statements made by Philip Bacon immediately prior to his death culminated in the arrests of Helen Knox and

Mal Walker; both being charged and convicted of treason for arranging the assassination of Connor Bowker. Knox was also convicted of inciting a riot, treachery and for being an accessory to Richard Nolan's crimes by assisting him to escape justice.

Mal Walker never revealed the identity of the man he'd paid to assassinate Prime Minister Connor Bowker.

Phoebe Swan and Keith Sutton were charged and convicted of sabotage and also for treachery for attempting to "overthrow by force or violence the established government of Australia."

All defendants received life sentences except for Richard Nolan who served five years as a result of his cooperation, the production of evidence crucial to the prosecution's case. The judge also took into consideration Nolan's post-traumatic stress disorder and made a point of absolving him of any guilt in relation to the unfortunate deaths of his fellow clearance divers saying, 'You were under imminent danger of losing your own life. Who has the right to censure you for what was nothing more than a simple error of judgment made in a split second. Given the same circumstances any one of us may well have made the same decision and I doubt that many people would have maintained the presence of mind to escape the devious trap set by the Iraqi Navy.'

Despite John McCarthy's efforts to have James Yeoman admit himself to a rehabilitation clinic where he would receive psychological counselling and treatment for his alcoholism, the former able seaman remained an embittered, dipsomaniac and recluse until his demise less than a year later.

Shortly after his aborted terror attacks, Nibras Als Arab also known as Amir Als Wawan, escaped to Indonesia where he proceeded to plot another attack on Australian soil. He was caught in the process of running a terrorist training camp by Indonesian Police who shot and killed Nibras and most of his recruits. Those who weren't killed eventually faced a firing squad.

While conflicts continued to rage in Africa and the Middle East, McCarthy and the newly formed and rapidly expanding coalition of environmentally proactive nations were confident changing weather patterns enabling the world to replenish its food bowl would help ease tensions.

America, China and India, the world's biggest polluters, agreed to speed up the development of green technologies, move away from fossil fuels and substantially reduce pollution and waste.

While some Islamic nations remained an ongoing threat to world stability there were promising signs of cooperation from Iran and almost unanimous agreement on the need to halt population growth through public education campaigns and the introduction of financial incentives for those who limited their families to two children.

Receiving official sanction from the UN, Australia continued its ocean fertilisation programme; each year managing to offset the world's CO2 emissions. Other nations joined forces in cleaning up the Great Pacific Garbage Dump, recycling most of the plastic harvested into an imaginative variety of useful, long-lasting products.

Finally, Matthew McCarthy was awarded the Nobel Peace Prize for "his courage in the face of adversity by taking the necessary action to save the planet from colossal species extinction, including the potential extinction of humanity."

++++++++++++++++++++++

Alan Greenhalgh

ACKNOWLEDGEMENTS

Thank you to the Royal Australian Navy Clearance Divers Association, especially CPOCD Maxwell CDT3 for his account of CDT3's involvement in the First Gulf War.

The Australian Vietnam Veterans Association, especially the brave Diggers of the Battle of Long Tan.

My good friend, former Western Australian Regional Commander of the Australian Protective Service, Brian Shoobert, for guiding me on matters concerning the Australian Federal Police.

My very loved and much appreciated wife and soul mate Chris, for enduring the hours of solitude that is part and parcel of my lifelong insatiable need and urge to write.

AUTHOR'S NOTE

No One Left to Clap follows on from my previous work "Climate Change; Your Life-raft to Prosperity and Survival" which sought through the "reverse psychology" of the hip pocket nerve to prod people into acting for the good of the planet. I felt by demonstrating the tremendous financial opportunities offered through investing in upcoming "green" technologies, more people could be coerced into sustainable living and would move away from the rampant consumerism that will be mankind's undoing if left unchecked.

Unfortunately, this turned out to be a hopelessly optimistic strategy for many reasons among which are our short-sightedness and our obsession with the acquisition of material goods which for many take precedence over everything, even the future of their children.

Although we profess to love our offspring, most of us would rather live in denial than face the looming apocalypse of irreversible climate change which demands immediate and courageous action if our loved ones are to have any sort of future.

We react well to natural disasters, rallying to help our fellow citizens, as in the case of Australia's worst natural disasters, such as catastrophic bushfires, devastating cyclones, heartbreaking floods and horrendous droughts, but notwithstanding our tremendous resourcefulness, empathy and compassion under tragic circumstances, it seems we are very inadequate in planning for and averting future tragedies.

We have a capacity not possessed by other species in our ability to look ahead, assess risks and imagine possible scenarios and make plans for the best outcomes, but in the case of climate change, it seems as if the task is beyond us, or too terrifying for us to fully comprehend. Perhaps, as individuals, we have been conditioned by the scope and pace of technological advances in our lifetime to believe that science will somehow rescue us. Perhaps too, we feel so powerless that we simply switch off to the terrible reality and hope it is all just a bad dream.

And then, there are many who simply refuse to acknowledge the inescapable evidence staring them in the face.

It's bad enough when ordinary people live in denial but when our top political and corporate leaders bury their heads in the sand all hope flies out the window.

At the moment, many of us are like frightened rabbits caught in the harsh glare of a hunter's spotlight. Paralysed with fear, we don't know what to do, and like the rabbit waiting for the impact of the fatal bullet, we remain motionless as we allow the ebb of time and the flow of events to determine our future.

There are still many who take the view that the current warming of the Earth is just part of a natural cycle and amazingly, some even refuse to believe that we humans have had any impact upon the climate. With so many so-called experts distorting the evidence, playing with statistical data and even raising counter theories that the planet may actually face a new mini ice-age brought about by sunspot activity, it's no wonder that ordinary people are confused. Some even proselytize that climate change is part of government conspiracy to force a new world order on us!

Perhaps the overwhelming weight of evidence put forward by the majority of the world's top scientists (many of whom are Nobel Prize winners) is based on flawed data. However, it seems inconceivable that so many highly educated, credible and esteemed individuals representing countries with divergent cultures, often with economies at opposite ends of the wealth spectrum and with competing trade interests would conspire to mislead us.

When experts with comparable credentials disagree on such a profoundly important subject, common-sense tells us we should side with the opinion expounded by the majority. And the majority now agree the planet faces wide-spread disaster, if we do not treat global warming and resultant climate change as a matter of the highest priority.

Even the most ardent denier of climate change must surely concede that we can no longer afford to be as blinkered and self-possessed as to believe humans can continue using the Earth's natural resources 125 percent faster than Mother Nature can replace them. Humanity must understand that it cannot continue drawing from the planet's natural bank account indefinitely. At some point our rapidly-diminishing natural resources must run out. What do we do then?

Having agreed that the Earth is in crisis, it matters not whether the cause of rising atmospheric temperatures is anthropogenic or natural; the consequences of continued heating of the planet will be the same; massive wide-spread human suffering and the death of entire populations who will simply be unable to adapt. Such a horrible predicament requires us to act with great urgency. Indeed, our response needs to be concerted and unified across the entire planet, much as we would expect it to be if we were somehow threatened by invasion from some inter-galactic entity hell-bent on wiping out this planet's human inhabitants.

As unbelievable as that scenario is, can you imagine how nations would unite as never before; pooling physical and financial resources, calling on every bit of ingenuity and accelerating the invention and introduction of new technologies, just to repel the common foe? Extraordinary measures would be implemented and readily accepted by entire civilian populations once they knew and understood that their very survival depended upon adopting a war footing.

Global warming, resultant climatic changes, acidification of the oceans, rising atmospheric carbon dioxide levels, unprecedented pollution of lakes, rivers, oceans and continents, species extinction, sea level rise, the spectre of massive famine and the spread of killer diseases and other horrors are no less of a threat, and demand an immediate global wide "call to arms."

Because human impact upon the planet has a built in delay, we do not know whether we have already left it too late to avoid truly apocalyptic consequences. Will the impacts already in the pipeline be too much for life to continue beyond the next generation? We don't know.

Climate science is a relatively new field with many

unknown factors. So-called experts continue to argue over the results of research simply because there is so much we do not fully understand about the complexity of the biosphere.

Meanwhile the situation continues to worsen.

One thing the majority of scientific experts do agree on is, we can no longer afford to sit around and wait to see what happens. We must act meaningfully now.

"We," means you, it means me, and everyone on the planet. It is not a problem for science or politicians alone. We are all affected and we must all do everything we can, regardless of whether we think our individual efforts will have any impact. If necessary, we must change the way we think, the way we live, work and play, but most of all, we must drastically reduce the size of our footprint on the planet and provide Nature with the chance to recover, even if that means being prepared to accept what may appear to be Draconian measures in the interest of our survival and the survival of our children.

Finally, I respect the right of every individual to disagree, to question, and to expound opinions and hypotheses contrary to those expressed in this book. I also respect the reader's right to hold the opinion that the book is based upon flawed research. However, the information contained within these pages has been compiled after consulting the most credible of scientific sources and is not mere speculation on the author's part.

If on the other hand, you know little about the climate change and this book frightens or shocks you I make no apology. In fact, I will have achieved my objective of jolting you from your complacency and ignorance with regard to the dire state of our poor besieged planet.

Most importantly, please do not force contrary views and opinions on those who are less well informed on the subject of climate change unless your evidence-based research can at least match that of two thousand of the world's top scientists (many of whom are Nobel Prize winners). To do so would be dangerously irresponsible.

If after having conducted comprehensive research you still disagree with the opinions on which this book is based, I applaud you for taking the time and the trouble to become well informed. Well done, you have expanded your mind and can at least debate the topic from an informed standpoint.

I sincerely hope I am the one who has been misled by the world's most esteemed scientists, the United Nations and the Intergovernmental Panel on Climate Change (IPCC).

If time proves them wrong (and I live long enough) I will rejoice in their ineptitude.

However, whether the science is flawed does not let the human race off the hook with regard to its stewardship of this precious, beautiful and fragile planet which we all continue to treat with abysmal disrespect. What sort of legacy are we leaving future generations?

All business leaders and governments who persist in denying the calls from the likes of such esteemed figures as United Nations Secretary General Ban Ki Moon not to delay acting meaningfully on climate change, be aware your children and your grandchildren (if they survive) may well hold you accountable for the demise of much of the life on this planet and the unspeakable suffering of billions unless you stop spending vast sums on disinformation campaigns, deliberately misleading the populace and muddying the waters for your own nefarious, profit-based, short-sighted motives.

Even worse are the politicians who during election campaigns, pledge to take meaningful action on climate change knowing that their apparent courageous stance would give them an edge over their rivals, only to retract or renege on those promises once in office. Make no mistake, you have betrayed your supporters. You have betrayed future generations and have destroyed the work of those who understand the need to live within the world's natural ability to replace the resources used by humanity and repair the damage we humans inflict upon the planet daily.

Election to high office carries the awesome responsibility of ensuring humanity has a better future by learning from history, by not repeating or perpetuating the mistakes of the past and working to eliminate greed and inequality. It also carries the responsibility of ensuring careful stewardship of the planet's resources so that all may share in a peaceful, decent standard of living.

Election to public office is not a right to exploit people or resources for one's own immediate gratification, and the many who view it thus are nothing more than cancerous parasites. Their actions are reprehensible and almost certainly guarantee massive and unnecessary suffering.

Those who lack the courage and moral fibre to

tackle the perpetrators of environmental terrorism and the exploitation of the planet's fragile ecosystems are complicit in its destruction. Their short-sightedness selfishness, greed and stupidity have pushed us inexorably closer to the abyss of total species extinction and the spectre of a Martian-like planet.

Would it be unreasonable to draw a parallel between the spineless, self-seeking behaviour of some of our current leaders and the atrocities, genocide and war crimes of history's monsters such as, Hitler, Stalin, Lenin, Pol Pot, Idi Amin, Slobodan Milosevic and a seemingly endless roll of monsters who persist to this day? I believe not for the consequences of such people governing nations will certainly be no less horrendous.

While such people may pat themselves on the back in the short term, the final result may well be that there is no one left to clap!

It is imperative that we win the battle against climate change.

Failure is not an option!

++++++++++++

SPEECH BY JOE MURPHY TO THE UNIONISTS

'Firstly folks, let me start by explaining just what this debate is all about today. The prime minister and his supporters will tell you that the Earth is warming dangerously. He will tell you that this warming is the consequence of us burning gas, coal and wood. He'll tell you that motor vehicle exhausts and coal-fired power stations create excess carbon dioxide gas. According to the prime minister and his scaremongers, this excess of carbon dioxide in the atmosphere traps heat against the Earth's surface causing dangerous warming of the planet.

'He will tell you that these warming trends will result in catastrophic climate change. He will tell you that the polar ice-caps and the Greenland ice sheet are melting dangerously quickly and that melting ice will result in rising sea levels. He will say the Earth will lose its ability to reflect heat back into space when the ice-caps have gone. He will tell you that storms will become more intense and that dangerous storms will happen with greater frequency and that droughts will become commonplace. He will assert that in the future we will not be able to control bushfires. He'll also tell you that tropical diseases will spread and that entire populations will be forced to relocate.

'That's just a few of the things he'll try and scare you with. He has an entire repertoire of disaster stories and predictions and if you listen to him and those of like mind, you will be convinced as to the end of the human race and all life on Earth unless the world follows the path he has mapped out for us.

'These statements are all lies. In fact, the entire global warming scenario is overblown and overstated and we need to stop this farce right now before it destroys our economy and our jobs. I intend to expose the prime minister as a fraudulent opportunist who stands to make millions from pushing his renewable energy bandwagon.

'Seventeen thousand, I'll repeat that number because it is significant, seventeen thousand scientists can't all be wrong. These seventeen thousand scientists all signed a petition stating that, quote "there is no convincing scientific evidence that carbon dioxide, methane, or other gases are causing, or will in the foreseeable future cause catastrophic heating of the Earth's atmosphere and disruption of the Earth's climate," unquote.

'Surveys of climatologists have also produced similar opinions.

'Satellite readings of temperatures in the Earth's lower atmosphere show no warming since readings began in 1984. These readings are accurate to within 0.01 degrees Celsius and are consistent with readings from weather balloons. Now, land based weather stations do show a warming trend but these weather stations are unreliable because they are not spread widely enough across the globe, they are often close to heat generated from urban development and the readings are subject to human error.

'Predictions of global warming are based upon computer modelling, not on historical data. Computer modelling is unreliable and those who use such modelling have been caught cheating by skewing the readings to suit the models.

'Those who support the arguments for global warming often quote figures from the United Nations Intergovernmental Panel on Climate Change (known as the IPCC). However, this is what that body says.' Murphy paused to let his words sink in. Donning his glasses he began reading from a sheaf of notes with which he'd armed himself. 'Again, I quote, "the Earth's atmosphere-ocean dynamics is chaotic and its evolution is sensitive to small perturbations in initial conditions. This sensitivity limits our ability to predict the detailed evolution of weather; inevitable errors in the starting conditions of weather forecast amplify through the forecast. As well as uncertainty in initial conditions, such predictions are also degraded by uncertainties in our ability to represent accurately the significant climate processes," unquote.

'Ladies and gentlemen, all that gobbledygook basically says that the even the IPCC and all its scientists simply don't know whether the Earth is warming up or not.

'If in fact the planet is getting warmer, a small amount of warming would actually be of great benefit to mankind. As an example, in 800 to 1200 AD, temperatures were actually higher than even the worst case scenario predicted by the IPCC. As you know, Greenland is so cold that today, it is one of the most inhospitable places on Earth, however during that period, the Vikings were able to settle Greenland because of the warmer temperatures.

541

'Further, the period from 5,000 to 3,000 BC which is referred to as, "the climate optimum" was even warmer, yet that was the period when mankind was able to build its civilisations.

'These are good reasons for believing that a warmer planet would actually have significant benefits for the health and welfare of our own much more advanced, and adaptable civilisation.

'Even if the world were to implement the types of reforms Prime Minister McCarthy advocates, it would take until the year 2100 for global temperatures to fall a miserly one degree.

'Now why is the world going to take any notice of what Australia does or says? Why should we let this prime minister introduce his extreme measures and policies at the expense of our jobs and Australia's economy, when this country produces less than two percent of the world's greenhouse gas emissions? Even if Australia were able to stop producing greenhouse gases immediately, it would make no significant difference to the world's climate.

'Now, I am not advocating that we do nothing about this so-called threat of global warming. However, the science is unproven. What we need to do is continue with research and continue developing technologies for reducing and sequestering greenhouse gases until the jury returns its verdict on climate change. We should take this route because it does not disrupt so many lives or carry the horrendous cost associated with Mr McCarthy's harebrained schemes. If, or when, the science is proven, we will then be ready to combat the problem, if there is indeed a problem at all.'

MATTHEW McCARTHY'S REPLY TO JOE MURPHY

'I recognise Joe Murphy's arguments as having come from a United States Government website established by the administration of former President George W. Bush.

'It is no wonder that so many people are confused on this vital issue. During his term in the oval office, Mr Bush and his government spent millions of dollars on a misinformation campaign designed to discredit the entire science of climate change and this particular website was just one of many strategies they used.

'Why did they do this? Well, they wanted to delay taking action, because the Bush family and its supporters have strong links to the oil industry. They were worried about the financial impact if the truth came out, and so, they resorted to censorship and distortion of the facts.

'During George W. Bush's reign, the National Oceanic and Atmospheric Administration actually blocked an internal report which concluded that global warming was caused by greenhouse gas emissions and that global warming may be contributing to the frequency and strength of hurricanes.

'Further to that, the White House downplayed reports that linked human activity and resultant increases in GHG to climate change. In fact, one prominent White House official and former oil industry advocate was actually caught-out watering down descriptions of climate change research that had been approved by government scientists.

'In my opinion, and that of top environmentalists such as Professor David Suzuki, the actions of the Bush administration border on criminality.

'I have no doubt that many of the seventeen thousand scientists that Mr Murphy says signed the report discrediting climate change did so because they were paid. Either that or they were influenced by colleagues who were paid off by the Bush administration and Big Business.

'It is a sad indictment on our society when individuals to whom we look for guidance become so greedy, materialistic and unethical that they are prepared to publish contra-opinion for monetary reward. Some would describe such people as scientific mercenaries with no moral or ethical compass, selling themselves to the highest bidder like common prostitutes. Whatever description you choose to use, there is no doubt that these men and women care little for the state of the world their children will inherit.

'To further back up the arguments on which he relied, Mr Murphy quoted from an actual report published by the IPCC. Unfortunately for Joe Murphy, that report is now superseded by the IPCC's 2013 report in which ninety-six-percent of scientists are now sure that climate change is real and that it is caused by man's activities. Those who signed the report were also unanimous in their calls for world leaders to take urgent and meaningful action to combat the problem.

'Back in 2007, seventeen thousand scientists may well have signed contrary opinions concerning climate change as Mr Murphy states, but I am of the opinion that quality beats quantity any day, so let's look at those who signed the IPCC's report. These men and women are recognised as being the world's top scientists. They do not have vested interests. They are not on somebody's payroll. In fact, many of the two thousand signatories are Nobel Prize winners in the field of science.

'If that doesn't make you sit up and take notice, I don't know what will.

'Earlier today Brian Caldwell spoke to you and he told you that climate change was a load of crap. He said miniscule changes in the Earth's atmospheric temperatures were not responsible for the increase in catastrophic bushfires and the severity of cyclones. While others may wish to bury their heads in the sand, Mr Caldwell has a responsibility as the alternative prime minister to ensure he does not deceive millions of Australians. Brian Caldwell is not a climate scientist, he has no scientific qualifications. He is not prepared to accept the indisputable evidence and he is living in denial.

'Joe Murphy also said to you that there has been no increase in the Earth's temperature since 1984. He stated that computer models are inaccurate and misleading and he says the modellers actually cheated. Now, I don't know whether those who used computer models cheated or not, but I do know that the statement that the Earth's temperature has not risen since 1984 is blatantly incorrect. So, let's look at the evidence.

'Global land and marine surface temperature records maintained since 1860 are proof that surface temperatures have risen consistently every year since 1980. Apart from 1997 and 1998, each year has been hotter than the previous year, and the current year is the hottest yet.

'Joe tries to downplay these records by saying the methods for recording temperatures are unreliable because weather stations are not spread widely enough across the globe, so let's look at other indicators, and there are many more indicators we can look at to prove that the Earth is heating up dangerously.

'NASA'S GISS direct-surface-temperature analysis show similar trends to those previously mentioned. Satellite data compiled over the past four decades records significant warming of the troposphere. That data also records a corresponding cooling of the stratosphere. These changes are evidence of increased atmospheric concentrations of greenhouse gases which any schoolboy can tell you cause global warming.

'In addition, records from sixty-three radio-sonde stations show consistent atmospheric warming trends since 1958. Add to that, borehole analysis, glacial melt observations, sea ice melt, sea level rise, proxy reconstructions, and permafrost melt, and you have incontrovertible proof that the Earth is undergoing a rapid and large warming trend.

'Our oceans are becoming increasingly acidic due to the increase in CO_2 levels and the Great Barrier Reef; one of the Seven Wonders of the World, is dying because of it. Fifty percent of the reef is already dead.

'I could bore you for hours with data resulting from countless creditable sources, but none of us really needs to look at statistics, graphs or the indubitable proof available in scientific records which have been kept over the centuries to know the Earth is heating up. We have all felt the increase in temperatures. Each summer, we break more records. Ask yourself, have you ever known there to be so many disastrous bushfires? Have you ever witnessed so many horrendous cyclones, tornadoes and floods? Do any of you remember icebergs floating in the seas around New Zealand in your lifetime?

'The situation has become so bad that authorities have had to introduce a new catastrophic rating for bushfire risk. It is no coincidence that local authorities now have to spend unprecedented sums on combating coastal erosion. In London, the Netherlands and elsewhere, flood barriers, dykes and seawalls are no longer adequate and have to be raised, or re-built, to meet the threat from rising sea levels.

'Strangely, some still refuse to believe that sea levels are actually rising but if you doubt that they are, go and speak to the peoples of Tuvalu, the Maldives Bangladesh, and those in the coastal areas of any nation that's not landlocked. They'll tell you how their homes and land are being inundated and their beaches eroded. You can also go online and look at the maps predicting how, worldwide, vast areas of coastal land will be inundated in the near future, displacing millions and destroying homes, infrastructure and productive farmland. The financial cost of this inundation is incalculable.

'Joe also inferred that the current warming trends are just part Earth's natural cycles, over which we have no control. Let me assure you, the current warming trends are not natural.

'Scientists tell us that approximately one hundred million years ago the Earth was in fact 5 to 15 degrees (C) warmer than it is today. However, that was before continental drift gradually re-arranged the Earth's major land masses. As the continents slowly drifted apart, the planet cooled steadily.

'I should add that during these times, the life forms living on this planet were also very different from what we see today because they had evolved to deal with the prevailing temperatures at that time.

'Ice core samples taken from the Arctic actually show that in the nine thousand years leading up to the beginning of the Industrial Revolution the Earth's temperature remained relatively stable. Since then, there has been a definite rise in temperatures over a relatively short period. Because this rise has coincided with increased greenhouse gas emissions and de-forestation, there can be little doubt that the progressive heating of the planet is due to man's activities. Nevertheless, the temperature increase has been most marked since the 1950s when consumerism became the Western World's new code for living. Factories that had geared up, or been created to churn out munitions and other stuff essential for the war effort were in danger of falling idle, throwing thousands out of work so they switched to pumping out products for the new "throw away" age that persists to this day.

'Joe was quite correct when he told you that there were periods during the planet's history when temperatures were significantly warmer than they are today. He said that the Vikings were able to settle

Greenland, and humans were able to begin building their civilisations during the two thousand years of the so-called climate optimum period, but what he forgot, or neglected to mention is, that during those warmer periods, the Earth's human population was only a fraction of what it is today, so fewer people were directly affected by the increase in temperatures.

'He also says that warmer temperatures will actually benefit the Earth's population. While that might be true for places such as Greenland, the majority of the planet's population will suffer enormously if we permit temperatures to continue rising. Entire populations will be displaced, and yes, there will be more damaging storms, uncontrollable bushfires and longer and more severe droughts. Vector borne diseases, such as malaria and encephalitis which until now have existed only in tropical climates will spread. Many of the very young, those in poor health and the aged will also perish from heatstroke. Major rivers, such as the Ganges, on which billions depend, could even dry up.

'Lastly, Joe Murphy says Australia should do nothing about reducing greenhouse gas emissions. He maintains that because we contribute less than two percent of the world's pollution it is justification for doing nothing. Well, per capita, Australia is the world's worst polluter. The two percent Joe cites does not take into account the pollution which results from the coal we sell to other nations. Using Joe's argument is similar to a drug dealer blaming his customers for the deaths and mayhem resulting from drugs. As a good global citizen, don't we have an obligation to the world to clean up our act? Shouldn't we be setting an example for other heavy polluting countries, such as the United States, China and India, in the hope that they will also jump on the bandwagon before it is too late?

'China and India's emerging industrial economies are now pumping seemingly endless volumes of harmful pollutant gases into the atmosphere. The Chinese continue to construct coal-fired power stations at a frightening rate. As both countries become richer, their people will expect and demand to have refrigerators, motor cars, air conditioners and all the things we in the West take for granted. While we have no right to refuse them a better standard of living, the planet cannot sustain the depletion of its resources and the pollution which will result from such unprecedented consumerism. Alternatives exist and the world must change over to those alternative technologies.

'The rate at which temperatures are escalating each year is sounding alarm bells among the world's top scientists. Any last vestige of the argument that global warming is merely a natural phenomenon has finally been dispelled by the latest evidence.

'Make no mistake, the world is standing on the edge of a precipice. The longer its populations delay acting, the greater the price we will all pay, not only in monetary terms but in terms of human suffering.

'The majority of Australians understood this when they elected this government and gave it the mandate to switch from a wasteful, unsustainable lifestyle to one that is sustainable. They knew and they understood that the alternative of doing nothing was no alternative at all.

'I acknowledge that change is frightening. I understand that you are worried about your jobs and your families but those fears are groundless. No one will suffer financially under Labor's plans to re-build this nation using sustainable technologies.

'Mr Caldwell also said that Australia cannot afford to lose the forty-seven-billion dollars that coal exports generate every year. In a moment, I will show you how we plan to replace that revenue source but for the moment I want you to think about these facts: coal-fired power stations provide fifty-five percent of our power needs; however they also contribute forty-two percent of Australia's greenhouse gas emissions and coal contributes a similar percentage of the world's total carbon emissions. Australia is becoming increasingly dependent upon revenue from coal exports, but the world will eventually be forced to stop burning coal and when that day comes, Australia will pay a much greater price than it will, if it takes action now.

'We obviously cannot close every coal-fired power station and stop coal exports overnight. However, we will race to replace those dirty polluting coal-fired power stations with power stations utilising renewable energy sources, such as hot-fractured-rock-geothermal, solar, wind and tidal power. Similarly, we will scale down coal exports as other income streams come on line and are able to replace the earnings from coal.

'We will also introduce a price of five dollars per tonne for coal and increase that by five dollars every year thereafter. That revenue will be used to fund carbon offset schemes and the development of renewable technologies.

So what are these income sources that will replace coal?

Number One: Under the government's Zero Carbon Energy Plan over-all stationary energy needs will be replaced over a ten year period with one hundred percent renewable energy sources, using current proven technologies and engineering. The ZCEP has been examined by a team of independent experts who have confirmed that the plan is fully realisable and fully costed. The ZCEP also addresses the common misperception that renewable energies cannot replace fossil fuels, either due to immaturity of the technology or due to cost concerns.

Number Two: Algal bio-diesel technology has advanced to the stage where this country can now replace the dirty, polluting, non-renewable diesel we pump out of the ground today with diesel produced from algae at competitive prices. While algal diesels still produce CO_2, the process removes a comparative quantity of CO_2 from the atmosphere, which means zero carbon emissions, unlike conventional diesel. Dried algal residues will then be used for cattle feed and fertiliser.

Bio-diesel plants will be established on non-productive land using previously useless saline water and effluent to grow the algae, meaning no loss of farming land, or need to use precious drinking water.

Number Three: Increasing food production will become increasingly important if the world is to feed its rapidly expanding populations and making existing land more productive is one of the keys. Australia is well placed to gain significant export earnings by becoming South East Asia's food bowl and we can do this by revitalising our currently undernourished soils with bio-char to boost crop production.

'If you aren't aware of it, bio-char is produced from the slow pyrolysis of organic waste materials. Slow pyrolysis involves heating biomass to very high temperatures without using oxygen to produce a substance very high in carbon which is an excellent fertiliser. Slow pyrolysis also removes and locks up CO_2, so we effectively kill three birds with one stone; reduce CO_2, reduce landfill and increase food production.

Number four: We will export our green technologies to a world hungry for non-polluting energy sources.

Number five: Australia will sell the carbon credits resulting from the production of bio-diesel and agrichar. Preliminary economic studies show that carbon credits alone will replace a significant proportion of the earnings lost by reducing and eventually eliminating coal exports.

'It is true that many of you will have to learn new skills but we will help you along the way. You will be adequately compensated if you have to undergo re-training. I understand too, that many of you do not want to move away from friends and family, so we will site these new sustainable technology industries in areas that will be most affected by the closure of mines and coal-fired power stations. You will not need to relocate unless you choose to do so.'

www.ingramcontent.com/pod-product-compliance
Lightning Source LLC
Chambersburg PA
CBHW030922020726
47498CB00001B/66